A WHISPER OF DEATH

A WHISPER OF DEATH

BOOK ONE OF THE NECROMANCER SAGA

PAUL BARRETT

Dedicated to Whitney Elizabeth Hunter. She believed in me when many didn't. Wish she could be here to see it.

Who was the man known as the Dark Savior? The numerous legends that have sprung up make the wheat of truth hard to separate from the chaff of hyperbole. I can tell you that, before the idea of Dark Savior ever came to be, he was a bitter and frightened young man.

-Excerpt from lecture by Corberin of Draymed, given at the University of Straph

E rick Darvaul sat in an uncomfortable iron chair on his manor's second-floor balcony, stared at the cliff, and watched his parents fall to their deaths. Their bodies splashed into the raging ocean, never to surface. He relived the event in his mind and did nothing to stop them, as helpless now as the night it happened.

A creature perched on the balustrade, clawed feet wrapped in between the spiked posts for support, barbed tail extended behind for balance. He did not look at the cliff. He stared at Erick, his creator, a pale, frightened man-child with a thin chest and skinny arms, dressed in the same dark shirt and pants he had worn since that fateful night a month ago. Erick's brown, curly hair flared around his soft face in a tangled mass. Blue eyes stared, seeing nothing but pain.

Created from Erick's blood, body, and soul, the homunculus knew his master's agony as if it were his own. At seventeen, Erick might be a man in years, but still a child in many ways; Blink feared for his master now more than ever.

"I know what you're thinking, Blink," Erick said, his voice soft.

"Perhaps you do. It's the same thing I've thought all these nights." Though they could share minds, Blink had not offered his concern to his master's scrutiny.

"You're afraid I'm going to follow them."

"I'm afraid they left you ill-prepared."

"For what?"

"For life without them."

Erick blanched. For a moment, his eyes locked with Blink's, then returned to staring at the cliff's edge. It would be barely visible to his master, even in this night's full moon. On past nights, Erick had viewed the bluff through Blink's eyes, using the familiar's heightened senses to better see where his parents had jumped. Tonight he seemed content with his limited vision.

"I'll survive," Erick said, but the words came out choked. "I'm glad you give a damn, because they didn't." A breeze blew, bringing the smell of salt from the ocean, eight hundred feet below. The ocean that swallowed Erick's parents.

Erick turned from the cliff and toward the town that nestled downhill of the manor. He frowned. "What's that?"

Blink shifted on the railing with his wings half spread in case the loose fencing gave way. Erick's father Darric had often talked of fixing it, but it would likely remain forever undone.

Pinpoints of light appeared from behind the town's outer buildings. Torches, Blink realized. Lots of torches.

"It's the villagers," Blink said. "What are they doing?"

Erick sat up and pushed away the hair that fell in front of his eyes. "They must know my parents are dead. They think the manor's empty, and they're going to destroy it and burn out the 'evil.' They've always hated us, and now they have their chance."

The town of Draymed feared his family. It had been a constant lesson from his parents, confirmed by Corby, the one villager who dared to speak to him.

"Do you think Corby told them?" Blink asked. "You wouldn't see him, so maybe he became concerned."

"I *couldn't* see him," Erick said. "It was too much, too many thoughts." Fear, despair, and hatred had warred through Erick, and he still didn't know which would come out on top. He didn't want his only friend caught in the storm. "He might be worried, but he wouldn't betray me to the whole town. Would he?"

Blink shook his head. "I don't know." He kept his voice soft as he asked, "What should we do?"

Erick ran a hand over his round face and rubbed his chin. "We hope the fence turns them away," he said, without conviction. Then he frowned. "If it doesn't, I'll let my undead show them they have every reason to fear us."

The cluster of torches bobbed toward the manor like a fiery glow-worm. Erick connected with Blink and studied them through his familiar's eyes. He recognized many of the villagers from Blink's nighttime forays and Corby's descriptions.

Reflected light showed him the five guardsmen who led the way, flanked by their commander, Brannon. They wore gleaming chain mail, partially hidden by tabards of brown with a diagonal green slash. Stout wooden shields bore a silver rose in the upper left and a redfish in the lower right.

Carn, the portly, balding mayor, wore a loose-fitting blue jerkin and gray breeches. He followed the soldiers, limping as quickly as his cane and game leg allowed.

A contingent of villagers followed. Men, women, and children trekked up the hill. All had full hands, wielding scythe, sickle, or hoe. The children carried torches, leaving their elders with hands free for bloodshed. Erick's previous bravado wavered under the impressive sight. He didn't have the power to stop such a mass. "It's the whole damn town," he muttered.

"You know, flying away is always an option," Blink said.

"To where?" Erick asked. "Some other place where we're hated.

3

No, I'd rather be killed defending my home than die among strangers." He looked at the cliff again, his mother's scream echoing in his head. "And it's better than the way they chose."

In the midst of the throng came Fathen, priest of the Sun God Caros, wearing the bright yellow robes of his office, an orange sunburst upon the breast. He towered a foot above his followers and carried no weapon or torch. His hair, the color of old oak, was braided and twined with gold cord. It trailed to his waist and gleamed under the flames. Light flared off his robe and played against his face, his cheeks and brow jagged as the island cliffs, eyes shadowed from the golden glow.

"Looks like the priest finally got his way," Erick said. Corby had often mentioned Fathen's vehement sermons about the evils of Necromancy.

"I can swoop down and kill him," Blink suggested. "Maybe the rest would lose their nerve." He flared his wings, ready to leap at his master's command.

Erick considered how the villagers would react to Blink's four-foot-tall form sweeping down on them, wings outstretched, clawed hands and feet swinging. His gray, gargoyle-like body would descend from the dark and send them fleeing, while he smashed into Fathen and ripped the priest apart with needle-sharp teeth. Erick smiled for the first time since his parents' deaths, but it didn't last. "It's too dangerous. You're fast, but a lucky swing could kill you."

The townspeople drew closer. A rush of sadness and anger radiated from Erick that almost swayed Blink off the balcony. He turned to find his master staring at the cliff.

"You were right," Erick said. "They said a day might come when we would have to defend against forces rising against us. But they never told me what to do if they weren't here. If I wasn't ready." His voice cracked. "I was supposed to leave them, not-" He turned, and Blink saw tears gathered in his eyes. "They could have at least given me a reason."

Blink put a clawed hand on his master's shoulder. "You still have me. I'm not going anywhere."

4

Erick swallowed, and Blink sensed a small portion of the anger drift away. "Yes, I have you, and I'm glad of that. If you hadn't been here, I may..." he swallowed.

"At least they taught me something useful before they abandoned me." Erick watched the approaching villagers. "I'll take as many as I can before they kill us."

The unpredictable ocean wind shifted, and the salt air grew tainted with burnt pitch. The smell reminded Erick of blood gone rank.

With his eyes fixed on the approaching torches, Erick pressed his middle finger against one of the balustrade's sharpened spikes. He winced at the sharp pain. Drops fell to the ground as he held his injured finger over the side. Erick spoke dark words in a low voice. "*Mahorela, aldone mucalz col cnila, abramge voh.*"

His pain was soon rewarded. "We wake, young master Erick," the *priquana*, the most common form of *quana*, said as they stirred in the open mausoleums behind the manor. Their quiet voices reached him, carried by blood and the power of his chant.

Blink leapt to the balcony floor. His loose gray breeches slipped. He tugged them up and tightened the drawstring.

Erick sensed his servants' uncertainty at being awakened. They continued to call. "We are coming to you. Is all well? Why is our sleep disturbed?"

The *priquanas'* voices echoed across the yard, funneled between the manor's wooden planks and the rows of herb trellises. Erick couldn't see them, but he sensed them shamble past the barn. The livestock, roused from sleep, added to the voices with nervous squeals, bleats, and clucks.

As the sound of the undead reached the mob, they stopped and cast uncertain glances toward Fathen. Where Erick heard words of anxious concern from his servants' mouths, the townspeople heard only wailing groans.

Good, they're afraid, Erick thought.

They aren't the only ones, Blink thought back.

Having second thoughts? Erick asked. The closeness of his *priquana* gave him courage. The dark energy of *Elonsha*, the power that infused his servants with an imitation of life, also protected them from the living. The villagers would have to go through them to get to him.

No, Blink answered, *but fear is healthy. Gives you an impetus to live.*

I want to live, but I'm not afraid of death. I know what comes after.

For you, yes. But are you sure my fate's the same?

Erick put his finger to his mouth, tasting the coppery blood as he considered Blink's question. When he died, Erick would go to the Heaven of Caros. But would Blink, who had been created from his master's essence? Daric's homunculus, Sniffer, had melted away minutes after Darric fell to his death. What had happened to Sniffer's soul? Did he have a soul? Questions Erick never thought to ask his father, and now it was too late.

But he wouldn't take the chance. He would live so Blink would live, and do whatever he must to survive. If that meant having his servants kill the villagers, so be it.

The undead came into view. The people of Draymed shrieked and muttered as they saw the glaze-eyed creatures, dressed in loose pants and shirts of unbleached cloth gray as their waxy skin. The villagers made a nervous retreat but stopped after several paces.

"What do you wish of us, Master Erick?" Javer asked. An army commander in life over a hundred years ago, he performed as overseer of the manor's *priquana*.

Wait.

The *priquana* stood and waited.

After their short retreat, the townspeople held their ground. Even at this distance, Erick heard them muttering, droning like the beehives in the manor's small groves.

Fathen strode forward until he stood beside mayor Carn and commander Brannon. They spoke, the priest occasionally pointing toward the house.

Erick wiped his finger on his trousers. *I don't like this. He's either building up their courage or telling them how to get past the* quana.

Or both, Blink offered.

Erick leaned over the railing and looked at the undead gathered beneath. He pointed toward the gate. "*Quana, zacare.*"

They lurched across the lawn. Fearful shouts bounced against the manor walls as people noticed the advancing bodies. Erick saw the *priquana* as if they still lived, with firm flesh and bright eyes. Only the silvery-black glow around them revealed their true nature. He had to concentrate to view them as the town did: shuffling beings of taut, withered skin, and milky, lifeless eyes that absorbed the flickering torchlight.

The mob withdrew further, but the guards held firm, their fear revealed in their nervous shifting.

Brannon gestured, and the guards moved closer. After a moment of hesitation, they seemed to decide the iron fence and closed gate gave them a measure of security. They edged even closer. When they stood within two sword lengths of the barred portal, they stopped, shields at the ready but weapons still in scabbards.

What are they doing? Erick asked.

It's a trap. They must have figured out a way to kill the quana. *They're trying to lure you into attacking.*

Impossible. They don't have quana *to fight with. Even if they found another Necromancer, he wouldn't help them.*

The *quana* continued their advance. With a task to perform, they had ceased their questioning; the only sound now was the whispery shuffle of shod feet over grass. As the creatures moved into the torch-light, the main body of the mob backed away. But the guards and town elders remained in stubborn immobility.

As Erick watched, the *quana* drew within twenty feet of the gate. The guards held their ground, swords undrawn. The villagers grew quiet, eyes alert with trepidation, hands tightened on axes and cudgels.

A few of the guards coughed and staggered, gagging on the *Elonsha*, a force so strong it permeated the physical world with a smell of rotten onions. Long accustomed to the odor, Erick allowed himself a tight smile at the soldiers' discomfiture.

The undead loomed within ten feet of the gate, yet the armed men displayed no signs of panic or defense. No soldier had put hand to weapon, and none of the villagers had run into the night.

Then, to Erick's amazement, the guards lowered their shields and parted, leaving the community's leaders exposed to the creatures.

It has to be a trap, Blink thought, claws scratching at the balcony floor.

"*Quana, alar!*" Erick shouted, halting them short of the gate. Faces under torchlight turned to search for him.

You may be right, Erick thought. *But if they've found some way to destroy the* quana*, why are they standing there? Shouldn't they be trying to push the gate open?*

How am I supposed to know? Blink asked.

Mayor Carn limped forward, supported by his thick cane. "Hello, the manor," he yelled, his voice as deep and impressive as his bulkiness. "Can you hear me?"

Quana, zacare.

The creatures advanced; the people reacted with screams and prayers to Caros. The guards scurried to protect Carn, bringing their shields to bear. Two drew weapons.

Erick smiled. The townspeople had no overarching strategy, but they didn't have much sense either. Why offer their leaders to him when they must know his creatures could kill them all? Or maybe they didn't. How much had the priest told them?

Maybe they're coming to surrender.

Puzzled by the villagers' behavior, Erick didn't offer a direct answer.

I don't get it either, Blink thought, reading his master's emotions. *You could always ask them.*

It would be easier to destroy them and be done with it. They have nothing I want.

Blink shrugged. Perhaps at one time, Erick's words had been true. But Corby's visits had opened Erick to the world at the bottom of the hill. The villagers did have something his master wanted: the companionship of living people.

The *quana* reached the gate. Their hands stretched through the dark iron bars. Erick tried to imagine being on the other side, watching as withered, bony arms reached out to grasp him. It must be terrifying. Erick hoped it was enough to make the intruders leave.

"*Quana, alar.*" The creatures stopped and dropped their arms to their sides. Living and dead stared at each other.

Carn used his cane to push aside the soldiers who blocked his way. He stepped to the fore and came almost within reach of the undead. Several people muttered fearful protests, but the mayor glared them into silence.

He yelled toward the balcony. "Kill me if you wish, and prove the people of Draymed righteous in their fear, but I wish to speak with the owner of this manor."

"Then speak," Erick yelled back. His voice sounded reedy in his ears compared to the mayor's stentorian tone.

Carn stared toward the second-floor balcony and squinted. "How old are you, boy?"

"Seventeen. I'm no boy, and you would do well to remember that if you want to survive this night."

Erick heard more mutterings but couldn't tell if they were fear or anger.

"Surely you are the owner's son," Carn yelled. "I would speak with the Necromancer Darric Darvaul."

"I am the owner's son. I'm also now the owner." Erick's voice choked despite his efforts to control it.

Carn hesitated and looked at Fathen, who shrugged. Carn turned to the manor. "Darric is dead?"

"You know that both my parents are gone. They leapt to their deaths a month ago, driven insane by isolation and hatred: hatred created and fed by your beloved priest. I guess you hoped I would go with them, but since I didn't, you've come to help the hell-spawn cleric finish the job."

Fathen stepped forward, his long stride putting him beside Carn in two steps. His sun-colored robes threw the mayor's drab shape into deeper shadow. "The law of the Temple makes it clear the Necromancers are sacrosanct," Fathen shouted, his voice more imposing than Carn's. "I have never preached hatred or violence toward the name of Darvaul. As for you, I was not aware of your existence."

"You're aware of it now," Erick said. "I am Erick Darvaul, son of Darric and Olena. And you lie, so-called priest. I know well that you

9

speak against my parents every chance you get. You forbid all in the town to approach the manor. You tell them we will absorb their souls and make them our thralls."

Surprise flared across the priest's angular face. He no doubt wondered how Erick came across such knowledge. "It is true I warn people away from this hill, but it was not my idea."

"Then whose was it?"

"Your father's. Twenty years ago, he demanded no one in the town approach the manor, on pain of death."

Erick's vision blurred; Blink recoiled from the pain within his master. "More lies! My father died because he longed for the town's friendship."

"If he desired the town's friendship, why did he not come to us?" Fathen asked.

"He knew it would be his death."

The priest shrugged. "It appears that was the outcome anyway."

Erick's eyes narrowed. The past month's pain and grief, ignited by Fathen's haughty comment, fused into rage. He didn't care about the rest of the town, but the priest had to die. "*Quana, quas alang de Caros!*"

"We obey," Javer said, and the others echoed the words, setting up a chorus of assent. They slammed against the gateway, forty undead smashing into the iron as one. The lock snapped. The gates flew outward. The edge caught a guard and knocked him to the ground.

Panic rippled through the crowd. The screaming villagers turned and fled. Several dropped their torches, where the dewy grass extinguished the flames.

The guards surrounded Carn and began a swift retreat, carrying the lame mayor. Fathen backed away, his face pale as he muttered prayers and threw useless gestures of protection toward the *quana*.

In the midst of the chaos, one person did not flee. A petite girl with long ebony hair walked *toward* the advancing creatures. A boy, taller but younger, his hair cut in the side-shaved manner of a scholar, tugged at her dark brown tunic. Erick recognized his friend Corby. Then the girl had to be his cousin, Elissia.

Elissia shrugged Corby away and put herself in the path of the oncoming *priquana*. She stared at Erick, ignoring the certain death ten feet away.

"Stop it!" she shouted, her commanding voice cutting above the crowd. "We didn't come to destroy you; we came to ask for your help."

2

I often wonder how different things might have been had I persuaded the leaders of Draymed to approach Erick differently. I have no doubt much sorrow would have been avoided in the short term, but it might have been at the loss of a dear friend, and ultimately the destruction of Krinnik.

-Excerpt from The Journey to Twr Krinnik *by Corberin of Draymed*

Stunned to see her in more than his imagination, Erick almost didn't react in time. The *quana* had hands outstretched, reaching for her throat, before he yelled, "*Quana, alar!*"

She never flinched.

Using Blink's superior night vision, he studied her, delighted at how much she matched Corby's description. She was Erick's age, and he could easily make out the mounds of her round breasts under her dark tunic. Her delicate but firm face offered a defiant stare, small nose wrinkled and lips pressed tight. Raven hair absorbed the torchlight, making her olive skin shine.

Something about her stance, fearless while those around her fled, struck deep inside Erick. Loneliness washed over him, a sense of how much he had lost with his parents' death. *She's even more beautiful than Corby said.*

Blink rolled his large eyes. *Yes, she is, but she's also stupid. She should have run.*

She's not stupid; she's brave.

Thin line.

Corby stood ten feet behind her, dressed in a rumpled brown tunic and pants, a haversack slung over one shoulder. Terror radiated through his pale, freckled face as he stood on the balls of his feet, ready to run.

The fleeing townspeople noticed the immobile *quana*. Their panicked run slowed to a stop, and they huddled a safe distance away. The guards took up protective stances around the mayor. The pounding surf echoed from far below.

Fascination with Elissia tempered Erick's anger. "My help? How can you have the nerve after what you've done to my family? To me?"

"*I* haven't done anything to you or your family," Elissia said. "I was told evil people lived here. It would be my life if I strayed too near."

"Lies told by the priest."

"They are not lies," Fathen shouted. He strode forward until he stood behind Elissia, towering over her. "You *are* evil."

"What evil have we done? We speak to the dead and comfort them. We answer their questions about the living. We—"

"You raise them from their graves and draw their souls from heaven," Fathen accused. "It is blasphemy!"

"The Gods gave their blessing to the Covenant," Erick said. "As you well know, *priest!*"

Elissia glared at Fathen over her shoulder. Her voice dropped but, still connected to Blink, Erick heard as if she stood beside him. "Are you trying to provoke him into killing us? Go back to where you were hiding and shut up."

Fathen returned her fierce gaze. "You can't speak to me like that!"

Her voice rose. "If you're going to use me as a shield and hurl insults, I'll speak to you any damn way I please. You're not helping, so stay quiet."

Gasps and mutters of astonishment rose from the crowd, while Erick's laughter rolled off the balcony.

Brannon stepped away from the mayor and walked toward Fathen.

He wore the same garb as his men, but a pin on his tabard, a cluster of three silver roses, marked him as a captain. "Elissia speaks the truth. We face a threat far greater than this boy, and we need his help. It's time to put aside your prejudice. His actions prove he is not entirely evil."

"How is that?" Fathen said. "He sent his creatures to attack us."

"Only after we mobbed him with torches in the middle of the night," Elissia said. She wrinkled her nose at the motionless *quana*. "They may stink, but we're still alive."

With a snort, Fathen said, "That proves only he didn't want to kill a beautiful girl. Perhaps he has other ideas for you."

Erick stepped back as a shock ran through his body. It was as if Fathen could read his thoughts, an unnerving idea.

Brannon drew his sword and placed it on the ground. He grabbed the priest by the arm. More gasps came from the crowd.

Carn thumped his cane. "Brannon, unhand him. You risk the wrath of Caros on all of us."

"I risk nothing worse than what has befallen us these past three nights. If the priest is true to his faith, he will do what he must, not what he wants."

As Brannon walked toward the gate, Fathen struggled to escape. Although he stood a foot taller than the commander, he could not wrestle away from the soldier's grasp. Brannon twisted Fathen's arm. The priest squawked in pain and ceased resisting.

"Let him go," a young man, standing in a cluster of yellow-robed men, shouted.

Brannon pushed past the *quana*, Fathen in front, until they stood at the threshold of the gate. "Erick Darvaul, I am Captain Brannon, commander of the Royal Guardians assigned to this outpost. I am a soldier sworn to the warrior goddess Sangara. As such, I have taken a vow to speak no falsehoods. To my knowledge, no villager knew of your parents' death. That is not why we stand before you. Fathen *has* spoken ill of your family. His motives for this are unknown to me. But in the ten years I've known him, he has never called for violence, only avoidance.

"The whole town has been taught that evil resides within the

14

manor and our lives would be forfeit if we approached. We are here now, and it is within your power to kill us and prove Fathen correct or to spare us and hear our request for aid. If you believe my words ill-spoken, then attack. I will not resist–"

Fathen tried to struggle away, but Brannon applied more pressure to the priest's arm, and he stopped with a grimace.

"Leave him alone!" the yellow-robed man shouted, stepping into the torchlight. A scar ran a ragged weal under his right eye to the center of his upper lip. The five similarly dressed men surged forward as if they would attack the commander.

"Sergeant, detain the acolytes," Brannon commanded. "They speak above their station."

The sergeant turned to face the quintet, hand on his sword. The acolytes stopped, but remained in a cluster, shoulders hunched and faces tight.

Brannon returned his attention to Erick. "As I said, I will not resist. But if you feel perhaps both you and the town have been living under a misunderstanding, then forestall your vengeance and listen to our plight."

Erick studied the people through Blink's eyes. He tried to read the intention behind their faces in the crowd, but he kept coming back to Elissia. A beautiful name for a beautiful girl. She stared at him, hands on hips, eyes defiant.

What do you think?

I've already told you. Blink thought. *She's very pretty.*

I mean about the town, Erick shot back in annoyance.

I don't know. If Brannon's telling the truth that means your father lied. Why would he do that?

Erick's whole world suddenly made no sense. His parents, his only source of human contact for seventeen years, were dead by their own hand. The townspeople--enemies full of hatred, according to his father--stood before him begging for his aid against something terrifying enough to drive them to seek him in the middle of the night.

An urge to do as Brannon suggested swept through Erick. He would kill the captain. Kill the whole town, save Elissia, who he would keep as payment for the loss of his parents, and Corby, for his bravery in approaching the terrifying manor on the hill.

That's the Elonsha, *not you,* Blink warned.

Erick nodded. *You're right. Thank you.*

Just doing my job, Blink thought.

Erick nodded. He was susceptible to his power's evil in his emotionally fragile condition, and it heartened him to have Blink stand vigil over him.

He stared at the crowd, tired of it all. He didn't hate these people. He couldn't hate people he didn't know. They reviled him out of fear because they had been told he *should* be feared. And they hadn't killed his parents, no matter how much Erick wanted to believe it. His parents had killed themselves, for reasons Erick couldn't fathom. He had spent a month trying to figure that puzzle out, with no success.

Blink made a wonderful companion, but with his parents gone, Erick longed for contact with living people. His conversations with Corby had brightened Erick's days before his parents had died and he had refused to see his new friend.

Erick didn't want to spend his life with his mother's books as his only connection to the world outside his walls, and the dead, ageless and unchanging, as his only companionship within. The townspeople needed him.

And, it surprised him to realize, he needed them.

Brannon stood fearlessly amidst forty undead, holding Fathen, whose eyes gleamed with terror even as his sallow face radiated hatred.

"*Quana, zacam!*" Erick shouted. Fathen flinched as the creatures moved, but this time they retreated.

When his undead stood twenty feet back, Erick halted them and shouted to Carn. "Come to the manor. I'll listen and help if I can."

A smile broke across Elissia's face and burned into Erick's heart.

Carn limped forward, steadying himself with his cane. A guard tried to stop him, but Carn whacked him with the knotted wooden pole and continued through the gate. Brannon followed behind the mayor, dragging Fathen along. The priest, pale and sweating, eyed the *quana* as the group moved toward the manor.

16

Erick sent Blink inside. The familiar soon returned with the bedroom lantern.

The trio had walked halfway across the yard when a cold shiver broke over Erick. The overwhelming stench of onions filled the air, and Blink reeled back.

A second later, a pale form leapt from the shadows and landed amidst the gathered villagers.

"Run," someone shouted.

It was a vampire. Erick's world tilted at the implications brought by the creature's appearance.

People scattered, screaming. The vampire looked up; its watery yellow eyes locked with Erick's. Even at the hundred-foot distance, Erick recognized his father's face.

3

The necromancers are, despite Fathen's assertions, exceedingly ordinary, in as far as I can see from my hidden perch. Those they work with no longer live, but once I moved past the feeling of disconcert such an observation brought, I found their routine of manor chores fascinating in its very banality. The family consists of a man, woman, and young man certainly no more than two years my senior, along with some winged creature with which I'm unfamiliar. Rather than conjuring demons from hell or screaming blasphemies to the sky, they occupied their day with farming, manor maintenance, and care of livestock. Hardly the frightening beasts the priest has made them out to be.
    -From the journal of Corberin of Draymed.

Erick stumbled backward and almost tripped over Blink. Malevolence radiated from the creature's soulless eyes and leering face. Loss ripped through Erick as he stared at the bald, pale-skinned thing his father had become. His teeth had sharpened, his hands elongated into claws. Tattered brown clothing, wet and glistening with algae, spoke of a watery grave. Blink let out a wail, and a sob caught in Erick's throat. He saw all undead as they appeared before death, but this ghoul was a mockery of his father, created from the deepest well of *Elonsha*. An aura of solid black surrounded it.

"How?" Erick asked in a choked whisper.

The vampire hissed, leapt at an old man hobbled by bad knees, and sliced open the elder's neck with sand-encrusted claws. Blood sprayed in an arc, splashing those who ran nearby. The villager stumbled a few steps before he collapsed. The vampire licked blood off its pale fingers and lunged for the next victim, a young girl who stood frozen and whimpering.

"Draw your weapons," Brannon yelled, rushing across the yard as he reached for a sword no longer at his side; it still rested outside the gate.

Guards dashed toward the monster. One of them placed himself between the girl and the beast. His sword thrust caught the vampire in the stomach, sliding through the mushy skin until it protruded from the creature's back with a pop.

The monster snarled, grabbed the soldier's neck, and twisted. Bones snapped. The body fell. The creature searched for the young girl, but the guard's bravery had given the mother time to grab her child and flee. The monster withdrew the blade and flung it away; the bloodless wound closed instantly.

The other guardsmen moved in. One slammed his sword into the creature's arm. Despite the severing fury of the blow, the blade bit shallow, the *Elonsha* absorbing the force. The vampire gave an irritated hiss. A backhand snapped the soldier's ribs and sent him sprawling. The guard screamed and clutched his injured chest.

Erick stood paralyzed; the appearance of his father in this form shattered coherent thought. He witnessed the carnage but could not will himself to move. Blink tugged at his pants.

Do SOMETHING!

Erick staggered back as his familiar's mental slap broke the paralysis. He turned and ran inside.

"Help us!" Elissia screamed.

"I'm going to," he said, knowing a valiant death would probably be his only accomplishment. He stopped and returned to the balcony with a curse. If Brannon and his men tried to fight, the vampire would kill them before Erick could prepare an offense. The soldiers had no weapons to deter this creature. The prayers

Fathen screamed as the vampire stalked them would hinder it even less.

"Brannon, get your men away," Erick shouted at the guard captain, who had reached the gate and retrieved his sword. Erick looked at his servants. "*Quana, zacare mahornila!*"

The undead lurched forward, advancing on the vampire as the soldiers withdrew. Brannon and another guard stooped to pick up their comrade with the broken ribs. The vampire snarled at the shambling undead.

Erick spotted Carn and Fathen, who stood in the yard. The villagers retreated down the hill, except Elissia. She ran toward the manor with Corby beside her.

"Get inside," Erick yelled. "I'll be right there."

He turned and ran through his parents' bedroom and down the hall, Blink on his heels. At the broad stairway, he descended the polished wooden steps two at a time while Blink flew ahead of him.

"Open the front door and let me know what's going on." He ran into a side hallway, flung open a small mahogany door, and moved as fast as he dared down the dark, narrow stone steps. He took them one at a time, putting his hands on either side against the cool brick wall.

At the bottom, he ran across the laboratory, the stone floor icy against his feet. Moonlight shone through a small window high in the wall. Erick knew the lab well, and he needed only that dim illumination to navigate around the numerous jar- and implement-filled tables.

Erick grabbed a rack of vials and pulled jars from the wall, thankful he knew the location of everything. *What's happening?*

The quana have surrounded the vampire, and he's trying to fight his way through, Blink told him. *They've got him pinned. All the villagers are running down the hill, and the soldiers are guarding the inside of the gate.*

The *quana* wouldn't keep the vampire trapped long. They were too slow and not aggressive enough to do more than minimal damage. With its quick reflexes and sharp claws, the creature would soon have the corpses at its feet, their power drained. If Erick survived, it would be at the cost of most of the manor's workers.

Erick hastened to assemble his philter. First, garlic to stun the creature. Its pungent smell made Erick's eyes water as he crushed two bulbs and dropped them into the vial. He grabbed a small tormentil root and chewed it into a paste. The root's bitter flavor filled his mouth, and he gagged as bile rose and soaked into the paste. He removed the sticky mashed herb and pushed it into the container. As he spit to clear his mouth, he sensed puzzlement from Blink. *What's happened?*

I'm not sure. The vampire is keeping the quana from hurting him, but he's not hurting them. He's trying to fight his way through. He's knocked some of them down, but he hasn't destroyed them.

It's father, Erick thought. Tears filled his eyes as he grabbed another vial and a dropper.

What do you mean?

Erick extracted ten drops of cayenne. *Dad created those quana. Even as a vampire, he doesn't want to destroy them.* As he added the liquid pepper to the mixture, Erick's soul wrenched. The thing with his father's face would have no such reservations about killing him.

Or would he? Erick wondered. Was there enough of his father left for Erick to reach? Could he free him from the vampire's embrace?

How did it happen? Blink asked.

Blink offered the most important question. How *had* his father become this abomination? *Elonsha,* no longer existed in high enough concentrations for such powerful creatures to spawn without aid. Even if another Necromancer lived on the island--and none did--they would never willingly create such a monstrosity.

Erick grabbed a bottle of lavender oil and moved to a cage set against the wall. Several rats occupied the wire prison. He opened the top, reached in for one of the dark, loathsome animals, and grabbed it by the back of the head to avoid its snapping teeth. Lifting it from the cage, he pried the animal's mouth open with the bottle. It hissed and flailed as Erick poured lavender down its throat.

It's almost through. Blink thought. *The quana are too slow.*

Where are the others? Erick desperately wanted to make the connection that would allow him to see through Blink's eyes but didn't dare take focus from his work.

Elissia and Corby are inside, next to me. Brannon and two soldiers are guarding Fathen, Carn, and the wounded man. They're still on the porch.

Get them inside.

I tried, but Fathen refuses. He threatened the others with holy condemnation if they came into this 'evil house.' Elissia dragged Corby in with her as soon as he said that.

Despite his fear, Erick smiled at her defiance. He shifted his grip, grabbed the rat by its tail, and ran back to the table. With a quick spin, Erick smashed the rodent's head onto the corner. It let out one sharp squeak and died.

He pried open the rat's cracked, paper-thin skull and flicked the broken pieces aside. With a crook of his finger, he scooped out the tiny brain and dropped it into the vial. He wiped the gore on his dark pants, grabbed two mint leaves with his other hand, and threw them in the vial to help hide the odor.

A surge of excitement emanated from Blink, followed immediately by disappointment. *One of the quana managed to knock the vampire down, but the vampire decapitated it.*

"Fuck," Erick screamed in frustration. He held his previously wounded thumb over the vial and gritted his teeth as he reopened the sealed puncture. Blood dripped into the vial. When the glass had filled, he pressed the injured finger to his leg and recited the incantation that would draw the *Elonsha* into the mixture. "*Mucalz col cnila pahmah, zodireda harga ae mucalz devonpho quana.*"

Elonsha whispered through Erick's being, filling him with a sense of power. It spoke to him of much more, but the agonizing questions about his father's fate gave him the ability to fight the temptation without Blink's aid. The concoction swirled as energy flowed into it; the liquid turned black and viscous.

It's broken through!

I'm coming. Erick slammed a cork into the vial, grabbed a small, square mirror, and ran up the narrow stairs. His shoulder struck the wall. He yelped as the rough stone tore his shirt and scraped his skin. When he reached the top, he shoved the glass container in one pocket and the mirror in the other.

Everyone huddled near the open doorway--Elissia and Corby

inside, the others on the porch--and Erick could almost see the fear that radiated off them as he dashed down the hallway.

"Move," he shouted. They scattered from the threshold.

Erick reached the porch and stopped. His knees weakened as he locked eyes with the vampire. It stood at the foot of the stairs, less than twenty feet away, and hissed in malicious agitation. Erick shuddered.

He looked at the others. Elissia and Corby had joined them on the wide wooden porch. They returned Erick's stare. The hope of survival kindled in their eyes, a faith that rested squarely on his actions. "All of you get inside."

"Be careful," Corby said. His voice broke, and he appeared on the verge of tears. Erick nodded, suddenly sorry that, distraught at his parents' death, he had refused to see his new friend for the past month, abandoning him with no explanation.

"Thank you," Erick said, hoping Corby inferred all the meaning in the statement: gratitude for his friendship, thankfulness for their time spent in conversation, and appreciation that Corby risked the town's wrath to visit him in secret. Erick wanted to say all that, but he had no time. And there might be no other chance.

Erick walked to the top of the stairs, hands in his pockets, the left one clutched so tightly around the vial he had to force himself to loosen his grip to avoid smashing the glass.

The *quana*, ten feet behind the vampire, shuffled toward the creature, continuing to obey their master's order to attack. One lay on the ground unmoving and headless.

The vampire, covered with scratches, glanced at the approaching undead. It hissed in outrage, turned, and charged up the stairs with bloodlust in its yellow eyes.

Erick pulled the mirror from his pocket and held it out. As soon as the vampire saw the reflective glass, it let out a pitiful, chilling shriek and retreated.

Emboldened, Erick moved down the steps. The vampire's gaze swiveled between Erick--hissing at the hated glass in the boy's hand--and the *quana* that closed in slowly but with a single-minded will.

Halfway down, Erick stopped. Though hampered by the mirror, the vampire remained far from harmless.

"Father?" Erick asked. "What happened?"

The creature glared at him.

"Are you there? How can I help you? What-"

The creature leapt over Erick's head. Drops of water, filled with the stench of rotten seaweed, fell from the beast and struck Erick's shirt. It grabbed Corby by the throat and sprang away, dragging the startled boy along, all before anyone could move.

With strangled cries, Corby fought the grip around his throat. The vampire hugged him to its breast and faced the advancing *quana*.

"*Quana, alar,*" Erick screamed, stopping the undead. In their attempts to destroy the vampire, they would have shredded the scholar.

"Corby," Elissia screamed as she ran down the steps. Erick grabbed her arm. "Let me go," she shouted, trying to shake his grasp.

"It'll tear him to pieces before you can help," Erick said. "And then it will go for you."

Elissia shrugged free of his grip but stayed on the steps.

With a triumphant hiss, the fiend turned its back on the motionless *quana*, Corby pinned against its chest. Corby, eyes wide and breath heavy, did not move.

"Let him go!" Erick yelled. The vampire snarled. Its hand tightened around Corby's throat, and he gasped as his pale face darkened.

"Stop!" Erick advanced a few steps. The creature retreated. It pointed in Erick's direction and placed its thumb and fingers apart as if it held something. It motioned violently toward the ground, and then spread the hand apart, showing it empty.

Erick dropped the mirror. The creature offered him an evil grin. Erick's heart stuttered, and he choked back a sob. Nothing of the father he loved existed in those heartless yellow eyes. His father was dead, a victim of his own weakness, and this creature no more than a parasite that used an honorable man's death to its advantage. Erick resolved to destroy this fiend and put his father to rest.

Its pitiless gaze still on Erick, the vampire lifted a foot and ground it into the dirt. Erick followed the mimed instruction, using his heel to avoid cutting his bare foot on the shattered silver glass.

"Let him go," Erick said, his throat tight. "It's me you want, isn't it?"

The creature nodded; its fangs gleamed with saliva as it grinned even wider.

"Then free him. Take me, but leave these people alone."

The creature hissed, puffed out its chest, and shook Corby, who yelped, voice high and terrified.

"Okay!" Erick raised his hands in a placating gesture. "Stop!"

The vampire held up one crooked finger and motioned Erick forward.

Trying to ignore the dread building in his heart, Erick looked at Elissia, then at Carn. "All of you get inside the manor. If things go wrong, you'll be safe there until morning."

"What are you doing?" Fathen asked. "That demon will kill you. If you die, we all die."

"If I don't let it take me, it will kill Corby."

"Better him than everyone."

. Elissia moved again, this time toward the cleric, and Erick put out a restraining hand.

"Quit grabbing me," she said, stepping back.

Erick stared at Fathen with undisguised contempt. "Once it kills him, then what? Do you think it will go away, never to bother you again? I have a chance of stopping it. Or I can leave now and let it kill you all."

Fathen glared back but offered nothing. Erick nodded. "Not so willing when it's you being sacrificed, are you?"

The vampire gave an impatient hiss.

Erick turned back to the creature. "Release the scholar." Elissia started in surprise, no doubt wondering how he knew such a thing.

The vampire laughed, a harsh whispering sound that raised bumps on Erick's arms. It lifted Corby into the air and slapped the back of his head with an open palm. Corby's eyes closed, his head lolled forward in unconsciousness. With an almost casual flip, the vampire sent him flying toward the group.

"Blink!" Erick yelled, but the familiar had already launched into the air. Despite his child-sized stature, Blink had the strength of a large, well-muscled adult; he caught Corby in midair and flew him into the manor.

"Corby is safe inside," Carn said. "Run for the house and hide until morning."

Having seen the creature's speed, Erick didn't consider the suggestion an option. "You came to me for help. Trust that I know what I'm doing."

Carn nodded, his face grim. "Strength of Caros go with you."

Do you *know what you're doing?* Blink thought as Erick squared his narrow shoulders and walked toward the waiting creature.

I'm doing the only thing I can. His entire being wanted to run, but such an act would be futile. Even if he reached the safety of the manor and prepared a better attack, the monster would be free to rampage until the sun rose or all of Draymed lay dead. Erick had to confront the vampire now, while he still had courage. *Caros, lend me your strength to send this creature to its end,* Erick prayed.

When he reached the bottom of the stairs, the vampire motioned him to stop. Erick obeyed. The creature leaned forward. Its nose twitched with a repulsive snuffling sound. Erick stood rigid, not daring to move. The vampire was using its keen sense of smell to search for anything amiss. Erick closed his eyes and prayed to Denech, the God of Luck, that he had sufficiently concealed his hastily prepared mixture, and that the blood on his abraded shoulder would help.

The sniffing stopped. Erick heard a shuffling sound; a waft of fetid, salt-tinged air passed him. He opened his eyes and almost screamed. The fiend's grotesque face stood inches from his own. Erick backed away but two strong claws, damp and cold as an old cellar, gripped his shoulders and held him.

Here was his best chance. He grabbed the vial and started to pull it from his pocket.

The vampire's fangs plunged into his neck.

Pain, sharp but brief, was quickly replaced by a warm tingling feeling. Every nerve in Erick's body came alive. He shuddered and moaned as pleasure, more potent than he had ever experienced in his life, coursed through his veins.

Relax, his father's voice, harsh yet persuasive, said in his mind. *Release yourself to me, and you need no longer be alone and hated. Your mother is waiting for us. Join me, and you will be feared and respected. You will know the peace and freedom true power brings. And we will again be a family.*

Erick's worries disappeared as the tingling pleasure continued. The truth in his father's words comforted him, and he yearned to see his mother again. He had been so alone since their death. What reason did he have to continue living? Ready to give himself to the realm beyond, he prepared to surrender to the angel at his throat.

His head lolled back, and he glimpsed the others through clouded vision. They had not moved into the manor. Corby lay in the hallway, but the rest stood on the porch and stared at another figure thrashing on the wooden floor.

Distant, agonizing screams reached Erick's ears, and a voice cried out in his mind. *Erick, help. It hurts.*

It was Blink. Erick's mind cleared as his familiar's screaming and writhing shattered the mental haze like a mallet through glass. Fathen was right: if Erick surrendered, a horrid fate would befall Draymed. Erick's death would render Blink catatonic, unable to help the others, and eventually kill him. Defenseless, the town--Corby and Elissia-- would be easy prey.

Through his weakening vision, Erick perceived the monster's promises as the lies they were. This creature had no power but the power to kill and feed, no freedom but the freedom of damnation. The same fate lay in wait for him if he gave in to the beast's dominion.

His father's voice spoke again, this time in its usual timbre. The voice Erick knew and loved. "Release me," it said.

Erick clutched the vial and drew it from his pocket. With the last of his strength, he smashed it against the creature's bald head.

The vampire yanked back. Its fangs ripped from Erick's neck. Warm wetness coursed down his throat and a dull drumbeat throbbed in his head.

27

Smoke poured from the vampire's head. Its skin sizzled, burned by the garlic. The garlic Erick had carefully hidden with the mint leaves.

"*Quana, zacare.*" Erick tried to scream, but his weakened state allowed only a croak, barely above a whisper.

It was enough.

As it whirled in agony, the sputtering and hissing vampire did not see the *priquana* move toward it, their dormant feeding instincts revived by the fluid's contents: bile, brains, blood, and the dark power of *Elonsha*.

Though still not quick, the *priquana* attacked with renewed aggressiveness, their strikes fierce and deadly to the wounded vampire. The fiend clawed and bit at its attackers, but the number of *priquana* soon overwhelmed it. The creature howled in impotent fury as the mass of undead flesh bore it to the ground.

As Erick fell, his vision fading, he quickly recited the Litany of Release.

"*Toltorg deteloc de mahorela desa gizirom qaas. Caros, bilorax oi gah moad todriax.*"

A chill wind whipped through the common, but Erick couldn't even work up the strength to shiver, too frail to be tempted by the *Elonsha* that passed through him. The vampire shrieked in searing agony as its lifeless soul ripped from its corpse. Darkness, blacker than the surrounding night, enveloped the body for the briefest moment, and then scattered in all directions, growing diffuse as the energy dissipated. The remnants of the tortured soul faded, and the body stilled. The *priquana* continued feasting.

"Thank you," a ragged voice whispered.

Erick smiled through a choking cry. The soul, be it his father's or that of some other damned being, had been released, free of its tortured existence. He had almost won. He only had to stop the *priquana* before they devoured the entire body, so he could examine it to determine how the vampire came to exist. Two words would render them immobile. "*Quana, a-*"

Darkness took him.

~

He wasn't alone. Another presence moved nearby, drifting around him, a malevolent entity that sought the destruction of all he knew. But the dark kept him safe; in the unconscious netherworld, the Master could threaten, but not harm.

"You did well," it whispered with the breath of damned souls. "But I know where you are. Soon I will know where all of you are. You think yourself safe, but I grow stronger, and sanctuary is an illusion. You are hunted. Prepare yourself, Necromancer. I will come and destroy your world."

Erick refused to respond, and the Master laughed with a sound of open graves. "You are right to be afraid. Enjoy your time of peace; it shall be gone much sooner than you would like."

The presence faded, leaving Erick alone in the dark with no memory but terror.

4

_____

The Necromancer's familiar, known as a homunculus, is, much like all things done by these foul sorcerers, an abomination. It is formed from a mixture of the Necromancer's blood and semen infused with healing herbs. The Necromancer's hellspawn-inspired powers further blaspheme this debased mixture. In contempt for all that is sacred to holy Krinnik, the creature spawns from this vile tincture and rises to do whatever its master desires, a base servant in thrall to a contemptible master.

-Excerpt from *On the Evil Ones* by Howrena, Master Herbalist of Kalador

Erick, *are you in there?*

The voice reached toward him through the darkness. Its familiar sound promised a way out of the interminable void surrounding him. But he held back. The lonely, frightening darkness still felt safer than the intrusive voice.

Erick, answer me.

The hold of the darkness loosened, and memory grew stronger. An outline formed, something with wings and claws. A demon, come to take him to the Lower Hells? Erick retreated into the dark.

Erick, please wake up.

More details. Gray skin, a large, almost comical nose. Sharp-toothed grin. Not a demon, but someone he knew before the void took him.

Erick, you have to come back now.

The darkness lightened to a dull twilight. Details sharpened. Recognition came. He had to answer. He groaned as he tried to open his eyes, heavy as bricks.

"He's coming around," the voice--Blink's voice--said.

"Thank Caros." A quiet, feminine voice.

"He'll be wanting water, I'd bet," a third voice, soft but male, said. "I'll go get him some."

Erick heard footsteps, leather on wood, leave the room. He opened his eyes to find Blink and Elissia staring at him from opposite sides of his bed. Murky light filtered through the shears that covered his bedroom windows, a lantern glowed on his nightstand, and a clean linen sheet covered him to his waist.

He closed his eyes as a stabbing pain shot through his head. "How..." He started to speak, but he sounded like a dying frog. Prickly heat ran through his throat as he swallowed.

"Don't try to talk," Elissia said. "Corby's gone to get you some water. I wanted to say thank you," Elissia said.

For what?

"He wants to know for what?" Blink said.

"How did...oh, that's right, your mind connection."

How does she know about that? Erick asked.

We've had lots of time to talk.

Erick opened his eyes. Elissia smiled at him and took his hand. The warmth of her touch sent a thrill through his spine. She wore gray pants and a blue tunic that matched her eyes. The top clung to her chest, offering Erick a view he could enjoy waking to every day. She appeared even more beautiful than the last time he saw her.

"I want to thank you for saving my cousin from the vampire."

Did I? Erick thought, offering a bemused smile.

Don't you remember?

Erick shook his head but stopped as pain racked through it. Everything seemed hazy and unreal, someone else's nightmare. But the ache in his head and throat told him it all happened. He tried to push past the fog in his mind and remember.

A voice inside his mind chuckled, a mocking sound from his unconscious dreams. *Remember it all*, the laugh said, and like the sun, the sound burned away the mist of his muddled visions. The night returned to Erick in terrifying lucidity. He'd fought a vampire. A vampire that had threatened Corby. A vampire that had once been his father.

The horror must have shown on his face. Elissia's thin brows furrowed in concern. "What's wrong?"

"I'm-" he tried to talk but shook his head in frustration.

Corby walked through the doorway, carrying a glazed earthenware mug in one hand and brass pitcher in the other. As always, it surprised Erick how much younger than his fifteen years the scholar looked. His slender face, tight cheeks, and bee-stung lips gave him a feminine appearance. He had nutmeg brown hair, shaved close to the scalp everywhere except the crown, where it hung like a patch of weeds growing from a close-cropped lawn. Dark, bushy eyebrows stuck out against his fair, freckled skin, thick as the hair on his head. He wore a brown supertunic, cinched at the waist by a black leather girdle. A strap over his shoulder held a leather haversack against his side, and a small ruby pierced the top of his left ear.

"This is my cousin Corby, but I understand you two already know each other," Elissia said, an accusation in her tone.

Erick reached out an aching arm to accept the proffered mug of water. *She knows about his visits?*

Like I said, we've had time to talk.

He drank the water, which cooled his throat but hurt to swallow. When he finished, he said, "I'm so sorry." His voice came out barely above a whisper.

Corby and Elissia exchanged confused glances. "Sorry about what?" Elissia asked.

How could he even begin to tell them? They would hate him for it. He considered saying nothing, taking the coward's way out. But that had been his father and mother, leaping to their deaths. Erick refused to accept that path.

Blink put a claw on Erick's covered leg. *All you can do is tell them and hope they forgive you.*

Erick nodded. "My..." he coughed to clear his throat, which still burned with dryness. "My father was the vampire."

Corby didn't seem particularly surprised, but Elissia's face bunched in confusion. Erick could almost see her working her way through what he said and knew the exact moment the full force of his statement hit her. The shocked O of her mouth and widening of those almond-shaped blue eyes were a sight he would never forget.

"Your father? Eight people dead. Frazen dead. Because of him?"

"But-" Erick started to explain, to make her understand, but another bolt of pain hit him. He closed his eyes, trying to will it away. He heard Elissia walking toward the door.

"Elissia, please wait," Erick said, but the tightness of his throat made his plea so soft he doubted she heard him.

Blink, stop her, he thought, opening his eyes in time to see her disappear through the doorway.

Let her go and give her time to accept it. If I stop her now, it won't do any good.

As he heard the downstairs door slam, Erick said, "I've made a horrible mistake."

Corby still stood there, holding the pitcher. He raised his dark eyebrows and said, "I suspected as much, but I didn't tell Elissia, because I feared that would be her reaction. Frazen, her only friend in this benighted village, was the second killed."

"I didn't know that."

"How could you?" Corby asked. "That's why she came that night, to ask for your help, like the rest of the town."

Erick wanted to scream. Both for the loss of life inflicted by his father, or whatever remained of his father, and for the chance of friendship ruined by his blurted admission.

What were you going to say?" Corby asked.

"What?"

"You were going to say something before Elissia left. What?"

"That the vampire wasn't my father."

"Then why did you say it was?"

"It came out wrong. I'm still not thinking straight."

Corby scratched at his head, and Erick caught a scent of the sandalwood oil the scholar always slicked in his hair. "But it looked like him, obvious deformities aside. Was it or wasn't it?"

At one time, Erick would have found Corby's dispassion odd, but since they had come to know each other, he knew the boy kept his emotions under tight rein. Inside, Corby might be feeling as sad and outraged as Elissia, but he wouldn't show it.

"He was my father," Erick said, "or at least it was my father's body. But the change to a vampire destroys the mind, or at least the part that knows right from wrong, that experiences love and compassion. My father may have been in there somewhere." Erick paused, pushing back the sorrow that wanted to close his throat. His father had been in there, unreachable, and Erick had done the only thing he could to free him. He had to believe that. "But the will of *Elonsha* gave him only the need to kill and feed."

"He seemed to recognize you." Corby poured more water in the cup for Erick. "And he knew enough about compassion to recognize your friendship with me and use it against you. Also, thank you for saving my life."

"It's my fault you were in danger in the first place."

Corby shook his head. "That's the part I *don't* understand. How is what your father did your fault?"

Erick laid his head back on the pillow. His entire body moaned in pain. "I should have known something was wrong. I should have been able to stop them from killing themselves."

"You expect too much of yourself. That's one thing you and Elissia have in common," Corby said. He pursed his full lips. "Was your parents' death the reason you didn't want to talk to me this past month?"

Erick nodded. "I wouldn't have been good company. I had to try and work out what happened."

"I could have helped."

"Perhaps, but it doesn't matter now. I'm sorry."

"Don't be. I understand."

Something in Corby's tone told Erick his friend accepted his reasoning but didn't agree. He had heard a similar attitude in his parents anytime he explained why he needed to break away from them someday and live his own life, outside the confines of the manor. He realized he could now, and no one would stop him. But he didn't know anymore if he wanted to.

The sound of water pouring into his cup brought Erick back, and he realized he had drained the vessel a second time without realizing it.

"Can suicide create vampires?" Corby asked.

"Not that I've ever heard."

"So even if you stopped your father from killing himself, you might not have stopped him from becoming a vampire." Corby frowned and ran a hand through his top fringe and wiped the hand against his tunic, just below the girdle. "Did you know he was a vampire?"

"No."

"Do you know how he became one?"

"I have ideas."

"Such as?"

Erick hesitated, then realized he wanted to talk. *Needed* to talk. He had been so used to only his parents understanding; it just now occurred to him that others might be able to listen and help him. "There are three ways. One is that he performed a special ritual that would change him. Why he would do that, I have no idea. But much as it hurts, I hope that's what happened."

"Why?"

"Because another way is that a Necromancer created him, but there are no others on this island. That leaves only the possibility that Eligos turned him, which would mean the *Inconnu* have returned." Despite the warmth of the blankets, Erick had to suppress a chill.

"Fathen preaches that the *Inconnu* no longer exist. That they never existed, except as boogies the Necromancers used to justify their existence."

"Fathen is an idiot."

"Not a point I'm inclined to argue," Corby said. "Do any of those methods involve you helping?"

"No."

Corby shrugged. "Then I can't see how it was your fault."

Erick stared at Corby. Put in such plain words, the scholar's logic made great sense. The facts didn't make Erick feel any less guilty, but it gave him hope that Elissia would eventually reach the same conclusion, and forgive him. "I know I've said it before, but you're smart."

"Well, I am a scholar." Corby offered a broad smile. As always, black spots dotted his small teeth, from his habit of tapping a quill against them.

"Could you tell Elissia?"

"That I'm a scholar? She already knows."

"No, that it's not my fault."

"Oh, she knows it too. Or at least she'll figure it out once she calms down. Aunt Beatru might be more of a problem, though."

"Who?"

"My mother's sister. Elissia lives with her, although she considers it more like being imprisoned." He frowned. "That's one thing she and I have in common." After a moment, he shook his head and turned to Erick with a start, as if he had been caught telling a secret. "What do you do now, about the vampire?

Did I stop the priquana in time? Erick asked Blink.

No, Blink answered. *They only left the bones, which dissolved as soon as the sun hit them.*

Erick shrugged. The motion made his shoulder hurt. "There's nothing I can do since I don't know how he was created. My chance at finding evidence disappeared when the *priquana* consumed the body."

Corby's question worried Erick. It made him aware that he had no idea what to do if the Master of Shadows had broken his exile to menace the world again. His father had taught him how to combat the ancient evil, but not how to recognize it.

It's ancient evil, Blink thought. *Something tells me it won't be too difficult to spot.*

Corby set the pitcher down on the nightstand. "'No sense inviting trouble to your doorstep; it comes freely enough of its own accord,'" he said, quoting an old Zakerin expression. "I'm sure you can handle whatever happens."

Erick wished such confidence was justified.

"I should apologize also," Corby added.

"For what?"

"I should have warned you about the town somehow. Should have been brave enough to come up even if I did think you were angry at me."

"It's okay, and I'm sorry you thought I was angry. But why did the whole town come, and in the middle of the night?"

"Fathen had assured them you would be out working your foul magic in the dark of night." Corby shrugged. "I couldn't tell them any different."

"No, you couldn't." Erick smiled. "Guess we're back to Fathen being an idiot."

Corby offered his stain-toothed smile. "Guess so. I imagine you're hungry. I'll leave you to get dressed and get something to eat. I suggest you talk to Elissia when you feel better. I'll tell her to expect you." He turned to walk out.

"Which house is hers?" Erick asked.

Corby turned back. "Small house near the temple. Ask for Oren and anyone can point you to it."

"Thanks. And Corby?"

Corby smiled and waited, the question on his slender, boyish face.

"Thanks for taking care of Blink and me."

Corby's cheeks reddened. "You saved my life. It was the least I could do."

After Corby left, Erick pushed aside the dark yellow cover. "Why don't I have any clothes on?" he asked.

"You usually sleep naked," Blink answered. "Although unconscious is a better word for what you've been the past three days."

Erick lifted into a sitting position, and a wave of dizziness ran through his head. When it passed, he said. "I've been out for three days?"

"Almost four. It's late afternoon."

"That would explain why I was so thirsty."

"I was out for a day and a half," Blink said. "Elissia told me that Corby's mother Hara stitched and bandaged your neck, and Brannon put you in bed. Corby and Elissia cared for us while I was out, and then I kept you clean, and Elissia fed you soup she made herself."

"She did? That was kind of her. I wonder if she regrets it now." His face flushed. "Did she see me naked?"

"Corby helped me change the sheets when necessary, but you were naked when I woke up, so she may have."

Erick's face burned as he considered the possibility. His mind gladly provided him with enjoyable scenarios. Had she tended to him? Helped bathe him while Blink lay unconscious? Touched him in forbidden places? A surge went through him and made him light-headed.

"I see you're feeling better," Blink said with a goofy grin.

Erick followed Blink's gaze and grinned back. "Just thinking about—"

"I know what you were thinking about," Blink said. "It's what you think about the majority of your waking hours. You have a filthy mind."

"I think of it as a good imagination," Erick said. He swung his legs over the side of the bed and sat fully upright. His muscles protested, and another wave of dizziness made him grab the iron bars of his headboard. "At least we won."

"Does it bother you?" Blink asked.

"Father killed himself," Erick said, voice tight. "I only killed the thing he had become. I only which I would have known about it sooner. And that I could have saved him."

"It was a close thing," Blink said. "Next time, I'd rather you hit the vampire with the potion *before* he bites you."

"Next time, I'll try not to get bitten at all." Erick touched his neck for the first time since he awoke and sucked in a sharp breath at the intense pain. A thick cloth bandage encircled his throat, holding pads of cotton fabric against the bite marks. His hand brushed across soft, fuzzy stubble on his cheek.

"Do you think Corby was right? Will Elissia think it wasn't my fault?"

Blink didn't speak for a moment. He didn't have to read Erick's thoughts. The need for acceptance suffused his master's eyes and face.

Anger flashed through the familiar at what Erick's parents had put their son through. How could they have kept him so isolated? How could they have left him like they did?

He put a taloned hand on Erick's knee. "I don't know people any better than you do, but Elissia and I talked. I told her what a caring person you are. She said what you did for Corby was the bravest thing she had ever seen, and she wished half the people in her life had your courage. She stayed here day and night, against her aunt's wishes, and made sure we were both cared for. She and Corby were the only ones in town to do that. It was their way of repaying what you did." Blink paused and looked into his master's eyes. "What do you think?"

"I guess if anyone would give me a chance, she would."

"That's what I think too." Blink removed his hand and offered another wide grin. "But just in case she's rousted the town, and they're heading up here with torches and pitchforks, maybe you should get up."

Erick chuckled, even though it hurt. Blink always made him feel better, and talking with Corby had given him hope.

He searched for his clothing and found nothing on the wooden floor, save the brown, woven throw rug that had been buried under his clothes since his mother's death.

Seeing the rug brought back a memory and broke something inside Erick. His smile disappeared as he sank to the bed. Tears flowed as the hammer of the past crushed his heart.

The one chore his mother kept for herself was laundry. Everything else she left to the manor's undead servants, but the laborious duty of scrubbing and rinsing clothing and bed linens belonged to her. She would take the dirty garments to the copper washbasin that sat beside the well as she whistled an old sailor's tune, while young Erick tagged at her heels.

"Are you okay?" Blink asked, alarmed by Erick's sudden change. "Do you need something?"

"I need Mom back," Erick said as he opened his mind to let Blink share the memory.

As a child, Erick helped—or tried to help—with the laundry, pulling the heavy linens from the basket until they draped over his head. He would stumble blindly toward the lines until his mother grabbed him, laughing her soft laugh. By the time everything had been hung, Erick stood soaking wet, and several clothes needed rewashing to remove the stains of grass and pollen. His mother would threaten to pin him up next to his shirts, chasing him across the yard as he squealed in delight and ran into his father's arms.

As he grew older, the fun disappeared and he quit assisting, but his mother never lost her enthusiasm for the chore, despite the monotony and difficulty.

"It clears my mind," she said once in answer to Erick's questioning her pleasure at the tedious task. "When I'm cleaning, I don't have to think about anything but the task at hand, and that's nice sometimes."

Erick hadn't understood the answer then but had appreciated the sentiment in the past month. He sometimes wished he could douse his dark thoughts like water on a fire.

He wiped at his eyes, wondering yet again why his parents took their lives. The months before their fatal leap ran through his mind; as always, nothing alarming presented itself. Both Darric and Olena behaved as they ever had. His mother tended the gardens and instructed Erick in his studies, both of them spending four hours a day in the manor's extensive library. His father passed his time working with the *quana* on the many physical chores around the estate: feeding livestock, splitting wood, and keeping the manse itself patched and presentable.

His mother insisted their home remain at the height of respectability, both inside and out. It was a request neither Erick nor Darric understood, but Darric accepted it with good humor and Erick with unreserved grace, as he did the many etiquette lessons his mother gave him.

When he was not engaged with the manor, Darric spent time teaching Erick the art of Necromancy, filling Erick's mind with herbs, formulae, and rituals. Once the lessons were done, Erick would be sent away, while Darric remained late into the night.

Erick's eyes dried as the process of searching his memory for clues overrode his emotions. It was a fruitless exercise, but he hoped it might someday provide an answer. "Where are my clothes?" he asked Blink.

"Elissia and Karin washed them and put them away."

"What? She worked with the *quana*?"

"She did," Blink said. "They bothered her at first, but she got used to them."

Erick considered this, amazed again at Elissia. He understood her appreciation at him keeping Corby alive, but she seemed to be doing more than necessary. Erick only knew about people from his parents and his mother's books, and more recently from Corby, but Elissia seemed unique. And beautiful. He wanted her to be a friend, like Corby. And he had already stumbled. "Maybe I should have just stayed quiet."

"No," Blink said. "You did the right thing, tough as it was."

"We'll see." Erick stood slowly and walked to the dresser. His legs wobbled, and the soles of his feet prickled as if they had pins stuck in them. He pulled a gray linen tunic, brown pants, and undergarments from the dresser and began to dress. As he pulled the tunic over his head, further dimming the room's already soft light, something flickered in the back of his mind, a sense of unease at a dream he couldn't remember but knew he should.

He came back into the light, but the discomfort remained. "Bad things are going to happen."

"Like what?"

"I don't know, I just feel it." If he could remember the dream, he knew it would tell him everything, but it remained elusive.

He tried to shake his dismal thoughts and decided standing in a gloomy bedroom that smelled of medicinal herbs and the almost oppressive cleanliness of fresh-washed sheets didn't help. He turned up the lantern to brighten the room. "I think you're right. I need some strength. Would you make breakfast? I'm starving."

"Right away." Blink leapt into the air, flapped his wings, and disappeared through the doorway.

Erick smiled, thinking about the connection he shared with Blink, a bond that had saved his sanity in the days following his parents' death. A homunculus, created from Erick's blood, semen, and soul,

Blink was closer to his heart than any friend--or even a brother-- could ever be.

Darric, aided by his familiar Sniffer, had performed the familiar binding ritual shortly before Erick's thirteenth birthday, speaking the words and slicing the boy's wrist over the cauldron, while Erick loosed his seed into the metal pot.

After the bleeding, they bound Erick's wrist, and he went abed for three days while his mother fed him herbal concoctions to rebuild his strength. On the fourth day, he went to see the half-formed lump of gray flesh. For the next three days, he watched for hours as his progeny took shape, each day its body more complete than the previous.

On the tenth day, the four-foot tall, oyster-colored body was formed: leathery wings, a squat torso with stubby arms, thin tapering fingers, short, powerful legs; and a long, thick tail that bulged near the end, terminating in a wickedly pointed tip. The oblong head had a wide, sharp-toothed mouth, sizeable rounded nose, bat-like ears, and almond-shaped eyes. Some might have considered his familiar ugly, but to Erick it was beautiful. Every lesson in his life was death and *Elonsha*, but this, a gift of the Covenant, was the one thing of life and creation Necromancers could do. He cherished it.

That night, they performed the final ritual. As Erick lay beside his creature, Darric spoke words that seared into his mind, not with pain, but with love. The love of friends, couples, and family. His father spoke of bonds beyond love, bonds of devotion lasting through and past death.

When his father finished, Erick felt a tug in his guts, as though something escaped. His body tingled from scalp to toes, and his mind's eye felt a stirring beside him as his creation came to life. He heard its first thought in his mind, a thought of adoration and ever- lasting devotion to the one who gave it life.

Its eyes opened, and Erick saw the ceiling from two angles, each slightly displaced from the other. The double vision startled him, and Erick closed his eyes to clear his sight. But even with his eyes shut, he still saw the ceiling. Then the angle shifted, and Erick saw himself lying on the table. He turned his head and opened his eyes, staring at the creature that stared at him. It was like a view into two angled mirrors—he and his creation reflected across eternity. Then the creature blinked, and the connection disappeared, but returned whenever Erick wished it.

Erick immediately named the homunculus Blink.

But as close as they were, Blink was only one being, and at times he and Erick were *too* close. Erick wanted to meet people that didn't know everything about him. He wanted to share stories and divulge secrets and make discoveries. That's why he had struck up the friendship with Corby when he found the scholar lurking outside the manor fence. Why he wanted to befriend Elissia. And why he hoped he hadn't lost her permanently.

5

The Necromancers brought horrors into the world which had never been seen. Caros willing, we will never see them again. Although I do not warm to the idea of letting one of their kind reside in our kingdom, we will do what the will of the Gods and the Temple of Caros demand. But if they must live here, thank Caros they wish to live on the [Keystone] island. At least there, any harm they cause in future may be contained.

-Letter from Queen Alana of Zakerin to the Caros Prelate of Kalador

Elissia paced through the manor's large garden. She wanted to rip out the late summer hyacinths that grew over the trellises of the gazebo. She longed to take a hammer and smash the decorative stone bench that sat in the middle of the enclosure. The desire to shred the herbs and crops raged in her.

She wanted to do all that so she would not do the same things to Erick. He deserved to be beaten for the horror he had brought into the world.

But *had* he brought it into the world? That question had stopped her from attacking him in his room. He was a Necromancer. He brought people back from the dead. A power useful for nothing but evil, to hear the priest tell it. Still, Erick had not hesitated to destroy the vampire. Had risked his life to save Corby and the whole town. Why would he destroy something he had created? Was it some ploy, forming a monster to attack and then coming in as the savior, thereby getting in the town's graces?

Elissia stopped pacing and plopped onto the stone bench. That was the kind of plot her father would come up with, destroying what he loved for some nebulous gain that most would consider unimportant. But after spending time talking to Blink, Elissia couldn't fathom Erick being that manipulative.

And Erick had said it was his father. She hadn't coaxed it out of him or learned it secondhand. He had come right out and stated it, and apologized for it. What could the ulterior motive be in that? Try as she might, she couldn't figure it out. Her father said everyone had motives, reasons that had self-preservation as top priority. Either Erick wasn't adept at preserving himself, or he was far smarter than her and had already thought several moves ahead.

She stewed about it for several minutes, teetering between anger and indecision, when movement caught her eye. Blink waddled into the other end of the herb garden, almost a hundred feet away. He flinched when he spotted her. Instead of coming over, he dashed back into the manor.

She waited, wondering if Erick would come out to talk to her or send Blink to chase her away. Or he might send Corby to take her home since her cousin no doubt stood inside apologizing for her abrupt departure.

She eventually heard a shuffle of feet across the ground behind the lattice that enclosed the bench on three sides.

The large blooms of the hyacinth blocked her view, but the shadow playing across the flowers was too large and upright to be Blink and didn't have the shy hesitance of Corby. It had to be Erick.

He came around the trellis, and she hurled a question at him. "Did you make your father a vampire?"

He stopped moving and took a step back, shock in his round face. "What?"

She didn't give him time to think. "No what, just yes or no."

He frowned. "No. Not only no, but by the Festering Hells, no."

"Okay," she said. Daughter of a master liar, Elissia had learned early to perceive deception. Erick either spoke the truth or was the best actor she had ever seen.

"Why would you ever think I'd do something like that?"

He had been truthful with her, so he deserved the same respect. "As a way to put the town in your debt and force them to accept you."

Disbelief showed in the cock of his head and the lowered eyebrows, and she didn't blame him. It sounded even weaker spoken than it had in the silence of her thoughts.

"That's asinine. Why would I give up someone I loved for a town I cared nothing about? And damn near die in the process."

Because my father would. She almost said it out loud, but that would lead to questions she wouldn't answer. "You wouldn't, and it was a stupid idea. But I have those occasionally."

Erick nodded and smiled. "I wanted to try and explain more, but you ran out too fast.. I probably could have found a better way to tell you, but I'm inexperienced at this."

"You're doing fine," Elissia told him. From the way his face and eyes lit up, she might have told him he had been made a king. "You want to explain now?"

The brightness left his expression. "Is it enough right now to know that I didn't do it? That I'm so sorry about your friend? It's too nice an evening to talk about such things."

Elissia nodded, only now noticing how wan he appeared in the day's dying light. She needed to remember he had been out for almost four days, and no doubt his shock and grief at his father's return equaled hers.

But he was right. The evening was too pleasant to wallow in grief. She had said her goodbyes to Frazen. The young girl's cares were as gone as she was. Elissia could do nothing for her, so she had to care for herself now, just as she always had.

She sat on the bench and waved her hand toward the carefully tended herb garden, a collage of plants and vines laid in orderly rows that stretched over two acres, near as she could tell. "I've been in Draymed three years, and I still haven't gotten used to so much green."

Beyond the garden lay some wooden buildings, one obviously a barn and another a windmill. Near those lay fields of hay and vegetables, which the undead servants tended like any other farmers. If she approached them, that illusion would disappear. The sight of their withered flesh unnerved her, but she could grow accustomed to it. She could never see them as normal, but she didn't consider them abominations, no matter what Fathen said.

She turned back to Erick and caught him blushing as he drew his eyes up from her shirt. She smiled to herself. Boys had regarded her that way for several years now, but none with the charming innocence revealed in Erick's red cheeks or swiftly averted eyes. "It's very prosperous land. How much of it do you own?"

"It goes that way to the cliff." Erick pointed past the trellis toward the fields, ripe with wheat and corn. "About three hundred acres, I guess."

Elissia barely kept herself from whistling. Though small for holdings on the mainland, Erick's parcel made him the largest landowner in Draymed, and possibly the whole island. He probably didn't realize his wealth. To obtain such a tract, one had to be nobility or, at the least, have connections to the aristocracy. Was Erick a baron? It gave Elissia great pleasure to think he might be lord over the village and not even know it.

But his ties to the land complicated things. After what she witnessed four nights ago, and what she learned from Corby and Blink about Erick's powers, a plan had formed in her mind. In Erick lay the means for her to return home, and right an injustice done to her. She had suffered for three years, and that was more than enough.

To accomplish her retribution, she would have to convince Erick of many things, the first being to leave Draymed. If he knew the importance of what he owned, and she had no reason to think he didn't, he might not have any desire to go.

Another factor she had to consider. It wouldn't take the other girls long to learn of his wealth and be clamoring for his attention. She had little fear they would win, with their dull looks and simple country charm, but they presented a distraction. One of them might snag Erick through sheer persistence, or trap him with fatherhood.

She needed to hook him before they did, an easy task. He was obviously infatuated with her. She could take him back into his house and-

Stop it, she scolded herself. *Not everything has to be about personal gain, no matter what the old bastard says.* She could win Erick without resorting to spreading herself open. She would sooner convince that insufferable acolyte Keven to spirit her away than lasso Erick with her legs.

And if she couldn't persuade Erick, so what? In ten months, she would reach her majority and could leave Draymed without fear of being hunted down and brought back, like the two previous times. She had refused to become a whore back home, why consider it an option now? Erick was a sweet, naïve boy, but still a boy, despite his seventeen years. It would be easy to take him by removing her clothes and bedding him. But that would lead him to believe something that wasn't true. To accept as a given an emotion she hadn't even considered.

Men equated sex with possession. If they bedded you, they owned you. If you were lucky, they might grow to love you. But boys like Erick thought sex *was* love. Elissia could use that to her advantage, but she shared her mother's belief; love had to come first, sex later. Such an attitude caused her no lack of grief at home. But she never wavered, though it had cost her dearly. To trap Erick with her body would betray her beliefs. She wasn't willing to do that, not even for a chance at early freedom.

She would let Erick decide between her and the other girls who came hunting for him. She would win him, but she would do it fair, a straight-up clash, her personality and attractiveness against all the Zakerin girls and whatever wiles they thought they possessed. *A fair fight without resorting to sex. Wouldn't that make the old prick grind his teeth?* Elissia thought with savage glee.

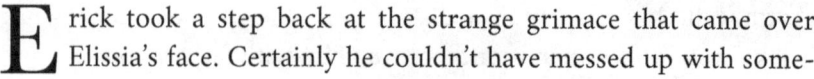

Erick took a step back at the strange grimace that came over Elissia's face. Certainly he couldn't have messed up with something as simple as telling her how much land he owned.

Maybe she had remembered why she sat out here looking at the land, instead of sitting inside talking about the manor. He didn't want to discuss his father, but it might be best to plunge ahead before her anger returned.

With dread akin to his encounter with the monster, he said, "I didn't make my father into a vampire, but he...he may have done it to himself. Unfortunately, I have no way of knowing now. It wasn't my fault, but I still feel responsible, so I want to apologize. I wish I could have stopped him before he killed anybody."

"I do too," she said, and Erick caught the slightest hitch in her voice. "But you didn't know, and once you did, you stopped him. You could have told us all to go to the Hells that night. I know people who would have, for far less reason."

He sat on the edge of the bench, as far away as possible, though he wanted nothing more than to move closer. A breeze rattled the vines and blew Elissia's black hair into her face. She shook her head and brushed the stray locks aside. A tingle ran through Erick at her lithe movements. Why did she affect him this way? He tried to think of something to say, but couldn't.

She tugged at a strand of hair and cocked an eyebrow, which gave her a mischievous appearance. "Corby said you asked a lot of questions about me. Why?"

"Because I wanted to know about you. Corby talked about your generous spirit."

Elissia laughed. "There are others who would offer a different opinion, but I am good to Corby. He's like my—" She stopped and frowned. "He's my only real friend in town, and I'm his. But I guess you are now, too."

Erick didn't know if she meant he was Corby's friend, or hers. He desperately hoped she meant both.

"So, did Corby answer all your questions?"

"All the ones I asked him," Erick said.

"I'm here now, so you can ask me whatever you didn't ask him."

Erick shifted on the bench. He couldn't ask what he really wanted to know. He had learned enough from his parents to understand that some questions were off limits, especially with someone you just met. "I don't really have any questions right now."

Elissia smiled, and Erick suspected she didn't believe him. "Okay."

They sat for a time in silence, Erick enjoying Elissia's presence. He found it different than his experiences with Corby, when they sat at the fence and talked. Different, and profoundly, inexplicably better. Erick had learned about the physical nature of the relationship between men and women, and he knew his parents loved each other. But he found that an abstract notion. No one had ever explained the intangible joy of just being in the presence of a female. Erick had never been so giddy, and he had no idea why.

"How come you never came into town?" Elissia asked.

It took Erick a moment to register she had spoken, lost as he had been in enjoying her closeness. "I was forbidden."

"Why?"

Erick shrugged. "Same reason you were. If I went down there, I would have been killed. That's what my father said. Blink flew in at night sometimes and looked at things for me. It was the closest I dared."

She studied him with an unreadable expression that nonetheless made Erick feel she considered his worthiness. He must have passed whatever test she put him through, because she smiled. "Well, now that your father can't keep you locked away and fill your head with nonsense, maybe you'll see how wrong he was."

Shocked by such an unexpected statement, it took Erick a moment to reply. "You never knew my father. Don't talk about him like that."

"I didn't know *him*, but I know listening to a father isn't always the best course." Elissia's voice rang with bitterness.

The resentment in her statement stopped Erick's angry retort. What had her father done to her to make her so mad? It didn't matter. Her problems gave her no right to talk about his family as if she knew them.

"My father was a great man and a wonderful teacher." His tender throat wanted to close up as a wash of grief tried to intrude, but he pushed it aside. He stood and turned away.

Cloth rustled as she stood up. "I'm sure your father was all those things, but the other night it sounded like someone was lying, and I know it wasn't Brannon."

He turned to her. The setting sun ignited her hair like a burning coal. She was beautiful, but her spiteful mind dampened Erick's interest. "I know it wasn't my father."

"Do you really? His vow to Sangara aside, Brannon has no reason to lie. Are you so certain your father *didn't* have a reason?"

"Yes!" Erick's voice wavered as tears threatened.

"Really?" Elissia asked. "He became a vampire without you knowing it. What else did he do you weren't aware of? Parents keep secrets. They'll tell you one thing and mean another. They'll expect you to be something you're not and try to make you do things you don't want to do."

"Your parents, maybe, but not mine."

"Oh, that's right, I forgot that you were free to come and go as you pleased. I forgot that you weren't cooped up in a creepy house with corpses, or that your parents were so happy that they didn't throw themselves off a cliff. And of course, you knew your father would come back as a monster and kill eight people."

Erick wanted to hate her for rubbing his parents' suicide in his face, but something in her voice wouldn't let him. Where Fathen's tone had pushed him over the edge, Elissia's filled him with confusion. She didn't seem angry so much as...sad.

"Maybe you should leave," Erick said, afraid that if she stayed any longer and said any more, he *would* end up hating her.

"Maybe I should," Elissia agreed. "But you need to be your own person, not your father's. He's not who you think he was. They never are."

"And he's not who *you* think he was, either," Erick said.

"Maybe," Elissia said, eyes downcast. She shook her head and walked away from the garden.

Erick watched her go, wondering if he had seen the last of her.

～

A s she stepped outside the manor gate, Elissia finally released her anger. She kicked at the ground, jumped around, shouted, and shook her fists.

"Have you lost your mind?" a soft voice asked.

She turned to her left to find Corby sitting, back against the iron fence, quill in hand, a piece of parchment laid against the haversack in his lap. Lines of black dotted his thin lips from where he had rested the pen against them. In her anger, she hadn't noticed him as she stormed from the manor house.

"I'm furious," Elissia said.

"That much is obvious." Corby put the quill down. "Why?" He put the lid on his jar of ink.

"Erick is naïve beyond belief. Can't he understand what his parents did to him? They ruined his childhood, keeping him locked up with dead things."

"Did you tell him that?" Corby set his haversack aside and pulled his knees up to his chest.

"Sort of."

"And I'm sure you did it in that understanding tone of voice you use so well?"

"Yes," Elissia answered, softening her voice.

"And you're surprised that he took offense?"

"No," Elissia said, letting her shoulders slump.

"So, what are you really mad about?"

Elissia sighed and flopped down beside Corby, who laid his head on his knees and stared at her.

"I'm mad that Franzen is dead. I'm mad that you almost died. I'm mad that I'm still stuck here."

"And," Corby prompted when she stopped for a moment, her face tight.

"I'm mad at myself for being such a bitch. Poor Erick wakes up after three days unconscious, the first thing he does is take the blame for something he couldn't control, and I tell him his dead parents were imposters who spent their lives lying to him." She let out a growl of frustration and tore up handfuls of grass.

"Want to talk about it?"

"Not really."

Corby nodded, unfolded himself, placed the haversack and parchment on his lap, and continued writing.

That was why Elissia loved her cousin so much. Unlike her aunts, especially the childless Beatru, Corby knew just what to ask, when to listen, and when to keep his mouth shut. She had heard others their age complain about his snobbishness and how much he showed off his superior knowledge, but she suspected jealousy brewed at least half of that poison. Corby was the smartest person she knew, aside from his father, and he wasn't afraid to use his intelligence.

Elissia knew she had lashed out at Erick as payback for his revelation about his father. She had lost her only friend to the monster that ravaged Draymed. She had almost lost Corby, and the part of her most like her father blamed Erick and wanted retaliation. So she had used the tactics her father used every day against his enemies. She told Erick not to be like his parents in the same manner her father employed. And only after she left did she realize what she had done.

Anger had been her father's gift to her, one she could never return. It disgusted Elissia that she had fallen so quickly into his mode of thinking, his use of words and innuendo to get his way. Even three years and an ocean apart, he influenced her in ways unexpected and disconcerting.

"Can we ever escape our parents?" Elissia asked.

Corby stopped writing and put the pen to his lips. After a moment, he took it away, leaving another thin line. "Probably not. All we can do is hope to take what they give us, improve on the good parts, and leave the bad ones behind."

Elissia nodded. "Erick's father was hiding something from him. Nobody spends that much time alone in a basement for a noble purpose."

"Did you tell him you had been up there spying on them?"

"I almost did, but then we got into the argument, so he can wait."

"Oh, the famous Elissia silent treatment." He went back to writing. "What I can't believe is that you didn't tell *me* until yesterday."

"At least I just looked around. You talked to him. And for almost a year." She gave her cousin a light slap on the arm. "And you told me nothing."

"I love you, cousin, but some things I want to keep to myself as long as I can. Now that the whole town knows about him, I'll lose him."

"You won't lose him. He'll still be your friend."

"Yes, but he won't be just *my* friend. He'll find others, people he likes more, and then he'll abandon me."

Elissia sighed. Although Corby spoke with no emotion, like a teacher stating facts, his placid demeanor hid great turbulence. His soft-spoken intelligence and unwillingness to stand up for himself made him an easy target for the other boys in the village. In Erick, he had found someone who appreciated him.

"Cousin," she said. "Erick risked his life to save you from a vampire. Do you really think he's going to leave you behind?"

Corby continued to write. After a moment, he stopped, "Perhaps not."

Elissia smiled, and Corby offered a small, tentative grin.

"Do you like him?" Corby asked.

The question came out casually, but Elissia suspected it was fraught with meaning. She picked up one of the ripped blades of grass, long and thick, and began tearing it into thin strips. "I don't know him well enough yet to say. He's not like any other boy I've met, that's for certain."

She remembered his ivory skin, which blushed so quickly, and the curly brown hair that hung to his shoulders. His eyes, the pale blue of sapphires, gave her a warm sensation she had never thought to feel with anyone. They made her feel, oddly enough, safe. "He's more interesting than anybody else around here. Except for you," she added when Corby pouted.

"No, he's much more interesting than I am. All I can do is remember things. He can raise dead people. Do you think he might teach me how, or at least let me watch sometime?"

Elissia shrugged and let the grass fall from her hand. "Maybe. Did you know he owns three hundred acres?"

Corby whistled. "There's a perfect reason to like him right there."

With an indelicate snort, Elissia said, "Maybe for you, but I could give a piss about land. If I can keep the other harpies from sinking their claws into him and convince him there's more to life than Keystone Island, I can get him to go with me to Kalador."

"Are you still harboring that fantasy?"

"It's not a fantasy," Elissia said, hands balling into fists. "I reach my majority in less than a year, and I can go, Beatru be damned. But Erick is legal now. If I can convince him to leave, he can take me with him. The sooner I'm away from here, the better."

"And you really think you can swoop in and oust your father? Overthrow him and take your 'rightful' place as leader of your people?"

"With Erick's help and his undead, yes, I do." Elissia face heated up, and she forced herself to calm down. "But it's more than that. I miss Marcus. Every day. You can't know what that's like."

"No, I can't," Corby said. He ran a hand through his hair. "And what about me? I'm a year younger than you, so I'm to stay behind? Left here alone, without your protection?"

Elissia pursed her lips. "I didn't think about that."

"You never do. When it comes down to it, you only think about yourself. I wouldn't expect any less." Corby spoke without rancor, but guilt assailed Elissia anyway. Selfishness. Yet another facet her father passed on to her.

"Don't worry," she said, putting an arm around Corby's shoulder. "You're smart, and I'm sneaky. We'll figure out something."

~

Erick closed the kitchen door and slumped into a dark wooden chair beside the dining table. "Elissia won't be joining us for breakfast."

"I gathered that," Blink said, setting a plate of scrambled eggs and bacon in front of Erick.

"She shouldn't have spoken about Father like that."

"Agreed."

Erick picked up his iron fork and stabbed at the eggs. "Who does she think she is? She knows nothing about me, nothing about my family, and she feels like she can say anything she wants to me. Damn her." He stuffed eggs into his mouth.

"You like her, don't you?"

"I've liked her ever since Corby first described her, but that's not the point. What good is her beauty if she's also spiteful and rude?"

"I think what you're most afraid of is that she may be right."

Erick stopped eating as Blink expressed the thing Erick couldn't. Elissia had no right to put doubts in his mind, planting them like evil seeds, even as he stood there protesting his father's innocence. "Is she? Did Dad lie to me?"

Balancing on a three-legged stool, Blink placed the dirty iron skillet in the sink and poured water from a bucket onto it, causing it to sizzle and smoke. "I don't know, but like I said the other night, why would he?"

"I don't know either," Erick said. "I don't *think* he would, but she's convinced Brannon wouldn't."

Blink sat the bucket on the counter, jumped off the stool, and trundled to the table. "There's always the possibility Fathen is lying to *everybody*."

Erick gaped at Blink. "I never thought of that."

"That's because most of your brains squirted out of you when you created me, and I got them."

"Yeah, but at least I kept all the beauty for myself."

"Oh, that hurts."

Erick gave a faint smile. "It makes sense. Fathen tells the towns-people my father demanded they stay away or he would do something wicked to them, and he tells Father the family is not welcome in Draymed or they'll be killed. Maybe he hoped the isolation would chase us away. It must have driven him mad when we didn't leave. I wonder if Elissia even considered that."

Blink sat in the chair beside Erick. "Why do you think they stayed?"

"You know how stubborn Father could be. If he were working the manor, he wouldn't stop until he finished, and Mom would have to drag him to supper. The last few months she complained that he stayed in the lab too late every night. Besides, this was home. Mom often said, 'better the evil you know than the one you don't.'"

"Still, it must have been a lousy way to grow up." Although he and Erick were close and often shared thoughts, Erick never offered much about his past, before Blink's creation four years ago. Blink didn't know if shame or lack of interest kept his master reticent. Out of love, he didn't seek out the memories entwined in Erick's thoughts.

"It wasn't that bad," Erick said. "I had Mom and her books, and my studies, and the two *priquana* children to play with. I don't think I missed much not being around people. If they're all like Elissia, I didn't miss anything."

Blink grinned. "Perhaps, but you haven't stopped thinking about her since you came back through the door."

Erick glared at the homunculus. "Haven't stopped thinking about how rude she is."

"More like how pretty she is. Planning on making a few homunculi tonight?" Blink asked with a wink.

"You're disgusting," Erick said with a glare that quickly turned into a shy smile as he stared at the table to avoid eye contact.

"But I'm right," Blink said.

Erick shifted in his chair and placed his elbows on the table. "The possibility that Fathen lied is a good theory, especially since it would give me a reason to have the *quana* beat him half to death. My parents never talked much about the past, but I know they lived here before Fathen showed up. We need to find some others who lived in Draymed before Fathen and see if they know anything that could help us."

"How are we going to do that?" Blink asked.

Erick grinned. "We're going to go down to town tomorrow, like normal people, and ask."

6

"I find the Gods to be of little use, but I do feel the hand of Denech may have been involved with my meeting Erick. As for the rest, we managed that on our own."
 - Elissia of Kalador, speaking to Corberin of Draymed

The next morning, Erick stood with Blink outside the manor as a warm breeze blew across the grass. He wore a white linen shirt and green breeches, both clean thanks to Elissia. He had bathed and applied a tincture of oakmoss, strong and earthy, from his father's shelf. He hoped he hadn't put on too much.

He stared down at Draymed, a large square of about fifty wooden houses. A few stone buildings occupied the center, the temple to Caros the largest. Another twenty or so wooden buildings stood scattered outside the perimeter. Farm and pastureland bordered three sides, and the ocean held the town's eastern edge. Two piers extended into the water. Small fishing vessels tied to the closest dock bobbed in the gentle swell. A dirt road, barely a cart's width, headed northwest, and a footpath led southwest toward the jungle, two hours away.

"I'm not going," Erick said. Despite his easy assertion last night, the thought of walking into the village alone terrified him.

"Yes, you are," Blink said. They had decided he should stay behind since several of the townspeople had not seen him up close. They didn't want to frighten anyone unnecessarily. "I'll be here and can be there almost as quick as you call. Do you really want Fathen to go unpunished if he's guilty of lying? Think about how different your life could have been."

Erick gave a gentle scratch at the cotton batting tickling his neck. He had changed the bandage soon after waking, wincing at the wounds left by the vampire, large and ugly despite the expert stitching by Hara, the midwife. He swallowed, his throat still hot and dry. "If you put it that way, I guess I have no choice."

"You don't if you want to learn anything about Fathen. And you can't yell an apology to Elissia from here." Blink grinned. "Well, you can, but I doubt she'll hear you."

Erick smiled. "Wish me luck of Denech."

"I always do," Blink said.

Erick reached the bottom of the hill and walked down the town's main road, through a cluster of small homes on either side, all plain brown wood but clean. Many had summer flowers in troughs beneath oilskin windows, and several of the doors had the emblem of Caros burned in the center and painted yellow. A large dog covered in shaggy black fur lay on a mat and watched, tail wagging and tongue lolling, as Erick passed.

This time of day, most of the villagers tended to farm duties or other work, so he encountered no one until he spotted

three women scrubbing clothes in a basin and talking. They wore plain brown dresses, and Erick guessed them near his mother's age. Sweat gathered on their brows from the work and the warm day.

As he drew closer, Erick caught the spring smell of hyacinth from the basin. It again reminded Erick of his mother, and the memory brought a sharp stab of pain and anger at his parents. As Necromancers, the evil that allowed their abilities also kept them from the Heaven of Caros. Unless they could prove to Alakaneth, Shepherd of the Dead, that their benevolence outweighed the taint of their birthright, he would judge them wanting.

By killing themselves, Erick's parents sealed their fate. Their souls writhed in the Abyss, bereft of any spiritual link to the world they left. Erick lived as the only proof his parents ever existed.

He stopped in the middle of the road as heartache overwhelmed him. They had left him, truly left him, with no chance they would ever be reunited, and he still didn't know why.

He pushed aside the grief with anger. He'd cried enough. They left him, perhaps because they no longer loved him, maybe because they saw no hope in continuing isolated from the town. Perhaps...any number of reasons unfathomable to Erick. Whatever their motives, Erick refused to let it crush him. They hadn't considered him in their decision, why should he consider them?

Be strong, Blink said. *Stronger than they were.*

I am stronger than they were, Erick thought back. He straightened himself and walked toward the women, who had stopped their washing and stared at him. His face grew hot. *Great way to make an impression, staggering in the street*, he thought.

"Excuse me, ladies," he said, bowing as his mother had taught him. "Might you tell me where I could find Oren's house?"

The ladies smiled; one put a hand to her mouth as if suppressing a giggle. The tallest of them said, "You looking for Oren or Oren's handful?"

Erick didn't understand the question, so he decided to be more direct. "I'm looking for Elissia."

The woman holding up her hand wiped at her mouth. "Didn't take her long, did it?"

The tallest nodded and frowned. "Go down the road just past the temple. That's the big stone building there. Turn right. Oren's is the fourth on the left."

"Is that where Elissia lives?"

"She lives with that scholar's brat, and a fine pair they make. But her head rests in Oren's home."

Erick wondered if he had roamed into a foreign land. The tall woman's tone made it obvious she cared nothing for Elissia.

"Thank you," Erick said.

"Youngster," the woman who hadn't spoken said. "Thank you for what you did."

The gratitude surprised Erick. He nodded. "Sorry I didn't do something sooner."

"Be careful of the girl," the tall woman said.

Puzzled at the statement, Erick moved toward the temple of Caros. A flat-roofed building of square stone blocks painted bright yellow; it stood out like a beacon of the God it represented. Easily twice as large as any other building, it had a set of ten stairs, twenty feet wide, that lead up to a portico and double doors plated in bright gold.

As Erick walked past, the doors opened, and five acolytes walked out, dressed in yellow homespun robes. Erick recognized them from the other night, especially the vocal one with the large facial scar. He led the pack, talking and gesturing with his hands as they strolled down the stairs. Erick continued walking.

"Hey, corpse boy," a voice called. The same voice that had told Brannon to leave Fathen alone.

Erick turned to see the five acolytes approach him. Varying heights and sizes, they had a typical Zakerin appearance, with dark brown hair and tan skin. The one with the scar was the tallest and widest. The ragged blemish ran from his eye to his lip and gave him a sinister countenance, aided by the scowl he wore as he stared at Erick.

The boys, all near Erick's age, surrounded him. They wore thin silver chains on their necks and wrists, denoting their servitude to the sun god. Erick knew Fathen wore similar emblems, made of gold to signify his priestly status.

The scarred boy glanced around to make sure no one stood near, while the others crossed their arms and tried to appear imposing. The street was empty except for the three women, who kept their attention on their washing.

Apparently satisfied the laundresses wouldn't interfere, the tall boy poked his finger in Erick's chest. "I want you to stay away from Elissia. She's mine. You understand, corpse boy?"

Erick blinked in surprise. He had expected to hear a rant about the evils of Necromancy, not a warning from a jealous suitor.

It surprised him more when he experienced his own twinge of jealousy. He had no hold on Elissia, and no right to be envious of this scarred acolyte. "It was her idea to take care of me, not mine, so you can take that up with her."

Erick tried to step past the large acolyte, but he shoved Erick back hard enough to knock him into one of his cronies.

"Stay away from her," the boy growled. "You want to chum with that fey bookworm cousin of hers, fine, but I care for Elissia, and I care what happens to her. She deserves a man steeped in the Sun, not the corruption of Night. I won't have you debasing her."

That sounded more like the argument Erick expected. "What if I refuse?"

"Your presence is an offense to all that is holy. A word from me and half the town would be here to strap you down with rocks and drag you into the ocean. You should leave now and stay away." He grinned, cracked his knuckles, and balled his hands into fists.

Erick thrilled at the prospect of danger. The threat of imminent violence made his heart beat faster. Unlike the outright fear his encounter with the vampire engendered, this was a nervous rush he had never experienced. He found it strangely enjoyable.

Do you need me? Blink asked.

Remind me again why I saved the town.

Because there are also people like Elissia and Corby who live here.

Right. I think I'm okay, but if I start screaming, come quick. Erick looked at the bigger boy. "So now you want me to stay away completely? What's your name?"

"Keven."

"Keven, do you know what I do up there in the manor?"

"Yeah. You play with dead people."

"Probably has sex with them," one of the acolytes said, and the others snickered. Erick didn't hide his revulsion at the idea. It surprised him acolytes of Caros would have those dirty thoughts, but he didn't put it beyond Fathen's ken to spread such rumors.

Erick appraised Keven and then stared into his brown eyes.

"You're big, but you're not very bright." His gaze took in the others. "None of you. I've been kept away from town for seventeen years. I'm not going to stay away anymore. And if I wish to speak to Elissia, walk with her, or maybe even kiss her, that will be her choice. Not yours."

Keven's face grew redder as Erick spoke. He stepped forward and raised his fists.

"Do you plan to kill me?" Erick asked.

The question made Keven pause. For a moment his scarred face grew uncertain, and his hands lowered. "Killing is a sin. We won't sink to your level of depravity." He raised his fists again. "But I'm going to beat the hell out of you. I will protect Elissia's honor."

"I've never killed anyone. Beside the point." Erick stepped up and put his face inches from Keven's fists. "Listen well. If you hit me, you're going to have to kill me. Those 'corpses' as you call them, do whatever I tell them. So, I want you to understand something."

Erick leaned in closer and lowered his voice. "If you ever put a hand on me again, I will have them hunt you down and beat you until you're near death. If you or any of your gutless sycophants tell anyone in town I just threatened you; I will have them find you and rip off your arms. And if I end up dead and even *think* you're responsible, *I will come back* and tear your throat out with my teeth. Now, do *you* understand *me?*"

With each sentence, the disciples' faces turned paler. A couple of them appeared on the verge of fainting. Despite the fright in his face, Keven held his ground. "We have the protection of Caros, and your foul magic can't touch us."

Erick laughed. "What kind of horse dung has Fathen been feeding you? The Necromancers' powers are sanctified by the Gods. There are six Necromancers left, and there can only be six at a time. Caros can make you by the thousands. So, who do you think he's going to protect if it comes down to it?"

"Caros will protect us, because we are blessed, whereas you are a necessary evil that the Gods were coerced into accepting."

Erick couldn't fault Keven's bravery, even as he marveled at his idiocy.

Back to that thin line again, Blink thought.

"Let's put that to the test," Erick said. "I'll summon an undead now, and we'll see how long the five of you last."

That got through to the large boy. His face drained of color. "You can do that?"

"Of course," Erick said. He moved his hand in an intricate and useless gesture. "You've seen my power in action. So I'll use mine, you use yours, and we'll see who comes out still alive." He pointed at the ground. "Rise, my pets."

The air chose that moment to stir into a slight breeze, sending a cloud of dust dancing down the street. Erick could only imagine what Keven and the other acolytes thought they witnessed as they turned and fled up the temple steps. Their robes flapped behind them, the thin material as flimsy as their faith.

"I'm glad we've been able to reach an understanding," Erick shouted after them.

Rise, my pets? Blink thought.

I figured it needed to be dramatic, Erick thought back.

Could you really come back from the dead?

Of course not. Erick remembered his father and his mood soured. *Well, not in any way I'd want to.*

Was it a good idea to threaten them? Blink asked.

I don't care. They can ignore me, but I'll be damned if I'll let them push me around.

Erick continued walking, turning right at the temple as instructed.

This road narrowed down from the main road, large enough for little more than an oversized cart. The temple dominated the right side and wooden houses the left. A few gulls tottered in the street, picking tidbits off the ground.

As he walked toward Elissia's house, Erick pondered his encounter with Keven. It amused him to realize Keven viewed him as a rival for Elissia's affections. He was certainly interested in Elissia, but what did he have to offer her? He was a Necromancer, shunned, a social outcast, with no friends but the non-living, whereas Keven was an acolyte of Caros, well-respected and assured of position in the town.

Elissia cared for him only as a return favor for his rescue of Corby.

Now that he had healed she would return to her life, being, at most, a newfound friend. Keven had nothing to fear from him.

That's no way to think, Blink thought. *He should fear you. If you're interested in Elissia, fight for her.*

Maybe, Erick thought back. *Let's see if she still even wants to see me. Then I'll think about the rest.* If Elissia no longer wanted to speak to him, perhaps he could find a way to meet other girls in the village, although he suspected they would be hard-pressed to match Elissia's courage or beauty. Corby had never talked about anyone but Elissia, but Erick assumed others existed.

He counted four houses and found Elissia's. It resembled the houses around it, with the sunburst symbol of Caros burned and painted into the door. A sturdy, large-bellied woman stood outside the doorway. She shook a dark blue rug. The rug gave a sharp cracking sound as dirt puffed from it in a small cloud. A red kerchief held back her graying hair like a streak of blood splashed on ashes. A momentary shudder ran through Erick, and he touched the bandage on his neck.

"Hello," he said. She stopped cleaning and stared at him. "Is this where Elissia lives?"

"Yes," the woman said, voice deep and throaty.

"You must be her aunt. I'm Erick. Thank you for letting Elissia care for me."

"Don't thank me," the woman growled, giving him a baleful stare over her large bosom. "I would have let you die--and good riddance. But Elissia had other ideas, and she has my husband wrapped around her manipulative little finger. Thank her."

Taken aback by the woman's spite, Erick didn't know how to respond.

"Who are you talking to?" Elissia asked from inside the house. She walked up next to her aunt and saw Erick. "Oh, it's you." She stared at him.

This whole outing had become a disaster. He fought down a momentary urge to flee back to the manor. "I upset you yesterday. I wanted to apologize."

"I'm fine."

"That's right, she's fine," Beatru told him. "So you can go about your business and leave her better off."

"I can handle this, Aunt Beatru," Elissia said.

Beatru gave him a last glare and went inside the house. Elissia stepped out and closed the door. "Don't let her bother you. She doesn't trust you. But she doesn't trust me either, so I wouldn't put too much weight on her opinion."

Erick nodded. "I'm sorry about yesterday. I think you may have been right, but I didn't want to hear it."

Elissia stared up at the sky. "I'd like...well, I want to apologize too. What I said about your father was unfair." She paused, and then looked at him. "But I still think it wasn't necessarily *wrong*."

"I think it is wrong. Blink and I talked about it. Fathen has been lying to everybody."

I wouldn't say that with so much conviction, Blink thought. *We only suspect it.*

Elissia's lips pursed and brows bunched, creating a delicate dimple just above the bridge of her nose. After a moment, those dark brows rose. "I'd keep that to myself if I were you, but you may be right. Fathen has always struck me as a duplicitous son of a bitch, and I know a thing or two about those." Her eyes narrowed. "You want to find out, don't you?"

"Yes."

"Be careful who you talk to and how you ask questions. From the gossip I've picked up, a lot of the town seems willing to accept you, or at least doesn't care. But Fathen still has several people convinced you need to be chased out, my aunt not the least of them."

"That's another reason I wanted to talk to you. I was hoping you and Corby could help me since you know people better than I do. I wouldn't even know where to start."

Her lips pursed again; an expression Erick found incredibly attractive. After a moment, she shrugged. "We're not that well-liked in town either, so that makes it a challenge. But Caros knows there's little of that in this backwater. I'll talk to Corby. We'll come up to your manor and figure out a plan. Wait for us there."

"Thank you," Erick said. "Oh, I won't interfere with you and

Keven, if that's what you want."

"What are you talking about?"

"Keven told me you're his. That's fine; I won't interfere. Not that I could have anyway." He stared at the ground. He wanted to interfere. He wanted to prove himself better than Keven, but he had no idea how.

"He is handsome," Elissia said. "That scar gives him a roguish demeanor. And his father owns a large portion of land. But it's not like we're betrothed. Occasionally a girl wants more than land and looks."

Erick turned from his study of the dirt to find Elissia's white teeth gleaming against her olive skin.

"I'm not his. Not yet." She reached out and hugged him.

Stunned, Erick didn't move. Her breasts pressed against his chest and his breath caught in his throat. She smelled of cinnamon and cloves, and her hair tickled his chin. He thought he might fly apart from the sensations bounding through his body.

Far too soon for Erick, she pulled back. He knew from the heat in his face that he must resemble a cherry, and he was thankful he had worn loose-fitting breeches.

"You smell very nice. I'll talk to you later." She gave him a wink and walked back into the house. Erick turned and headed toward the edge of town, mind whirling as the hug gamboled through his body.

E lissia stood at the door and listened to Erick walk away. He had already fallen for her harder than she could have hoped. As soon as she saw his downcast pout, it came clear to her. She had no interest in Keven, a complete horse's ass so far up Fathen's backside she wondered he could breathe. But letting Erick think such interest existed worked to her benefit. She could hint that the best way to garner her attention was to remove her from Keven's influence. Keven had too many ties to Draymed to leave it, but if Erick accompanied her to her home on the mainland, they could get to know each other better.

She wouldn't promise anything, but she would be grateful to her escort. *Very* grateful. Erick's mind would gladly fill in the implication. At that point, getting him to leave would be as easy as teaching fish to swim. She could return to Marcus sooner than she ever hoped and start plotting revenge on her father. It was a great plan.

And the exact type of thing her father would do. She mentally snarled at herself. Could she sink to the depth of using a boy's naivety to scheme her way out of town? Could she promise something she wouldn't deliver to escape this backwoods village?

She knew the answer and hated herself for it.

"Best you avoid that boy," Beatru said, and Elissia sensed the woman's disapproving stare bore into her back. "There may be some good hidden in him, but he's tainted, and the evil will take him someday, just like it did his parents."

Happy for someone to lash against, Elissia whirled on Beatru. "Leave me alone. If I want to hear Fathen's lies echoed in my ears, I'll buy a parrot."

Elissia ignored her aunt's gasp and stormed across the main room. She pushed aside the thin, brown curtain that hid her bedroom. Metal rings rattled against the rod as she flung the flimsy material across the opening, wishing it were a proper door she could slam. She had a proper door when she lived in the warrens back home.

As Elissia sat herself down on her thin, hard bed, the curtain slid open, and Beatru filled the doorway. "You ungrateful witch. You'll not talk to me like that anymore. I've put up with your impertinence long enough. You'll learn proper ways if I have to beat them into you. I'll be damned if you'll end up like-"

Elissia ground her fists into the homespun blanket. "Like what? Like Father? At least he's done something with his life."

Beatru snorted. "Yes, we should all be proud of what he's become. I thank Caros I got your uncle away in time."

"Got away?" Elissia asked with a bitter laugh. "Dragged away was more like it. He should have married my mother; they're both alike, docile as titmice in temple."

"Your uncle isn't docile, only respectful, something you know nothing about. You could learn from him."

"Learn what? How to be meek, a pushover, a-"

Beatru took two steps forward. Elissia brought up her arms to ward off a blow, but Beatru said quietly, "A person who cared enough to take in a young girl when no one else wanted her."

Elissia brought her hands down and stared at her aunt's jowly face. She wanted to offer a cutting retort, but couldn't. Beatru was right. Elissia slumped back against the wall.

Her aunt sidled over to the wooden chair in Elissia's room. As she settled her weight on it, it groaned like a creature seeking escape from misery. "I've no wish to fight with you. I tell you only what I feel. I know this boy fascinates you because he is different from the others, but what can he offer you?"

A way out of here, Elissia thought. "Something better than this. You wouldn't understand."

"Of course, because I was never a young girl." Despite Beatru's gentle tone, the sting of the words pierced Elissia. "Yes, he has land and a fine manor. Perhaps he has wealth too. So what? The only thing he will offer you, in the end, is misery. And these are my words, not the priest's. I feel it in my heart. He deals with death, and it surrounds him like a stench. Stay away from him."

"And if I don't?"

Beatru shrugged, and the chair groaned. "I can hardly stop you, but he's not welcome here."

Beatru stood and left. Elissia slumped farther down on the bed, exhausted. Was her aunt right? Would Erick bring death to the town? Hadn't his family already? If so, then the sooner Elissia convinced him to leave, the better. Then both she and Beatru would get their wish.

But what if she overestimated her ability to convince Erick? He was tied to the land, after all, she realized with mounting despair. Maybe even more than most. He had three hundred acres, had lived here all his life, and had watched his parents die here. What if, no matter how much he cared for her, he wouldn't leave his home?

"Please, Denech," she said, offering a rare prayer to the God of Destiny. "Help me persuade Erick. Help me change my fate." She had to convince him somehow. Staying much longer on this island was going to kill her.

69

7

"I saw the sky turn blood red; the mighty mountain laid low.
When the Ten faced the Three, the world shook
With each astounding blow.
I saw boulders fly like birds, and dust to make the land disappear
When the Ten faced the Three, Twr Krinnik fell
And the world was freed of fear.
-Tarin Flos, Poet, "When the Ten Faced the Three"

E rick ran toward the manor, filled with exuberance he hadn't
experienced since before his parents' death. Elissia seemed to
honestly like him. The aftermath of her hug still tingled, and
warmth that had nothing to do with the mid-morning sun ran
through him.

Halfway up the hill, he slowed his pace as weakness stole over him.
His breath came ragged, and heaviness filled his limbs. His neck
throbbed and he cursed his stupidity. He didn't have the best stamina
uninjured. What made him think he could run a half-mile uphill four
days after being drained by a vampire?

Do you need any help? Blink asked.

No, I'm okay, Erick thought as he walked up the hill, pulling in huge breaths. *It will just take me a moment.*

He reached the fence to find Blink sitting there with a pewter cup filled with milk. Erick drank it down in long swallows.

"You know," Erick said, after he caught his breath, "there may only be two people in the town worth saving, but I'm glad we saved them."

"I'm sure there are others." Blink scratched his large ear with a talon. "You just haven't had a chance to meet them."

Erick nodded. It didn't matter. Corby and Elissia were two friends he never expected to have, and for now he needed nothing more. Especially with the hope that Elissia might become more than a friend.

"As soon as you're done swooning, there's still a manor to run," Blink said. "And we're down four *quana*."

"The vampire took out four?"

Blink nodded, and Erick sighed. He would have to replace them. The manor used just enough workers to run smoothly. Being down four would soon result in tasks undone and upkeep problems.

"You might want to make some *vohquana*, too," Blink said. "In case the vampire was just the start."

That sent a shiver through Erick. "What I need to do is look through the tomes and see if there's a chapter on what to do if the *Inconnu* return." He could only assume his father would have instructed him eventually, but now he would have to figure it out himself.

"Don't be too hard on him about that," Blink said. "Really, after a thousand years, how remote were the chances?"

"Maybe not remote enough," Erick said. His inability to examine the vampire gave him nothing to prove or disprove the Inconnu presence. The lack of certainty put him in a constant state of unease. "One problem at a time."

If more undead were to come, he would need fighters that could protect him. *Vohquana* were the warrior class of *quana*, faster and able to wield weapons, but they took longer to create and required considerable amounts of blood and herbs.

"I'll make some fighters. Do we at least have any gobbets left from the fight?"

"No," Blink answered, as Erick feared. "They were too deteriorated by the time I woke up and found them."

The day that had started out so promising turned bleak. Not having full corpses, since they kept no family graveyard, Erick would need to unbind another *quana* and use strips of its flesh as the primer for the new creations. That would put them down five for a few days. "I think we may have to learn how to milk cows," Erick said.

"I'll do that if you shovel the manure," Blink said with a grin.

Erick smiled back. "Let's go see if I have enough ingredients or if I need to harvest some more."

They entered the laboratory from the outside, opening the angled cellar doors and walking down a short flight of stone steps into the chilly basement.

He had not cleaned up the clutter left from the hasty vampire preparations. The dead rat still lay on the table, the bloated body the only sign- of decay in the basement's cool air. "Blink, will you get rid of the rat?"

"Certainly." Blink waddled to the table, grabbed the creature by the tail, and flew out of the laboratory.

Erick cleaned up the table and gathered the herbs that would serve as the binding and growing agents for three *vohquana* and two *priquana*. He set the plants on the worktable, dividing them according to their function and place in the ritual: To his left a vial of dark green comfrey root oil and a two-inch twig of brown gravelroot--elements for the growth of bone and cartilage.

Beside them sat shards of willow bark and a pot of fine black cohosh powder, herbs to excite the slabs of cold muscle extracted from the donor body. These would grow into shapeless forms and transfigure into the body and appearance of whatever souls offered themselves from the Heaven of Caros during the binding ritual.

In the middle lay the elements to stimulate the flow of blood: the gray-brown bark of the prickly ash and a handful of dried hawthorn berries, red as the life fluid they created.

On his right, Erick placed the jar of bitter chamomile and the chopped root bark of the black haw vine. They would supply the *quana* their nervous system, giving them the power to react to their surroundings and obey Erick's commands.

Last on the table came the herbs that would give his new creations flesh: deep yellow, dried marigold petals that still held their pungent smell, and two handfuls of kelp, removed from their vat of salt water. To the side, Erick placed two additional ingredients: three thin stalks of damiana and a pot of powdered yellow ginseng. These would give the *vohquana* the strength and stamina of warriors.

"At least that worked out," Erick said as Blink flew back into the lab. "I have all the herbs."

Erick wandered toward the rack where his father kept thirty vials of blood stored. He did a quick calculation; the *vohquana* required seven pints each and the *priquana* three, leaving him six full pints. With no other family member to give a weekly donation, Erick would need half a year to refill the supply, assuming no other losses. The day kept getting worse.

He reached the wooden rack and froze. "Blink, where's all the blood?"

Blink trundled next to Erick. Except for two containers on the bottom shelf, all the vials on the stand were empty. "I don't know. Do you think the vampire was down here before you fought him?" Blink asked.

"I... guess," Erick said, "but why would it drink old blood when it could get fresh?"

Blink shrugged as he examined the area. "Look." He extended a taloned finger.

A small puddle of dried blood lay spattered on the gray flagstones; Erick spotted two drops several inches away. Moving along the floor revealed several more drops, as if someone walked away bleeding.

Or carrying a dripping vial, Erick thought.

The flecks led him across the lab until they stopped with three splatters on a section of stone wall between an herb cabinet and bookshelf. Chewing on his index finger, Erick studied the area to see if the drops led in some other direction, but they ended against the wall. He knelt and touched the spots. They flaked away as he scratched at them, leaving brown residue on his fingers. Erick stared at the wall, and a chill washed through him. "You don't think?"

"Couldn't be," Blink answered as he jumped onto a side table. "Your father would have told you...wouldn't he?"

"Four days ago, I would have said yes. Now, I don't know." He placed his hands against the bare section of wall, feeling for any way to move the stone. Only now did the peculiarity of having this area of wall naked strike him. Shelves, cases, or equipment covered the rest of the walls from top to bottom, but he never thought to question why nothing occupied this space; it had been that way ever since his father allowed him down here.

No obvious method to move the seemingly solid granite revealed itself, and Erick wondered if he sought to create something from nothing. He thought about the adventure stories his mother gave him to read; some of them had secret doors. He tried to remember the ways to access such portals. Most involved a lever or mechanical device, usually concealed by an innocent-looking piece of equipment, like a candlestick. But Erick had cleaned the lab often enough to know it contained nothing more mechanical than an herb grinder.

Did the wall itself hold a trigger? He studied the gray stone, staring as he willed the secret to reveal itself. The wall gave nothing, as solid in appearance here as elsewhere.

Except.

Closer study revealed a line of mortar darker than the rest, as if freshly applied and not yet dry. He stepped back to get a better perspective. A rectangular outline composed of the mismatched cement resolved itself. The subtle difference could easily be missed under casual inspection.

Erick frowned as an unexpected sadness hit him. "Looks like father did have another secret." He returned to the wall. Despite the discoloration, Erick knew the mortar could not have remained wet so long.

He touched it to be sure and, to his surprise, his finger pressed easily into the material. It wasn't mortar, but an imitation. He scraped at the fake cement with his finger. It peeled away and dropped to the floor with a wet plop. Erick stood on tiptoes to reach the top, and within two minutes he exposed the thin outline of a doorframe.

Erick's heart thumped as he stood back. A secret door existed in the lab, a dismaying revelation. What other things had his parents hidden from him?

He pressed against the center of the newly revealed portal. It did not swing open but gave a soft click. Erick removed his hand, and the wall made an almost imperceptible outward movement.

A surge of dread went through him. Considering his father's fate, he feared nothing good lay beyond this wall. He contemplated turning away and letting his father take this last mystery to his grave, but he couldn't.

Erick moved to the right edge of the false wall, which extended just beyond the stone lip, allowing the barest grip. He took hold with his fingertips and pulled outward; the revealed door swung open.

The stench of decay struck him. He had long ago grown accustomed to the onion-like scent of *Elonsha*, but this was entirely different. This was the corruption of the poorly sealed coffin, the reek of a sun-bloated animal whose body has ruptured from within. Erick gagged, and his knees nearly buckled; Blink almost fell off his perch. He flailed his wings, sending two glass beakers crashing to the floor.

"Holy Caros, what is that?" Blink asked.

"I don't know." Erick ran to the other side of the room, near the open doors, where he drew in warm, fresh air, though it hurt his throat to do so. Even this refuge didn't last long as the fetid smell drifted across the chamber.

Time and proximity eventually allowed him to endure the noxious odor, and he moved toward the open door, curiosity overcoming his revulsion.

Erick stood in the doorway and found splashes of dried blood against walls and floor, a slab of decayed flesh and bone on a table, and a large book atop a wooden podium. Another shiver of foreboding ran through him. Whatever occurred in this room had nothing in common with the Necromancy he had learned.

"Blink," he said in a shaky voice. "Light a lantern and bring it over here."

Using a flint and spark plate—no easy task with his taloned hands —Blink lit one of the metal and glass lights and hopped to the entryway. As the yellow light drew near and more of the room revealed itself, Erick's fear grew. The blood was not random splatter, but ancient glyphs drawn in intricate patterns around the podium. Erick recognized but could not read them.

The slab of desiccated flesh had been a man, wrists slit and heart removed from his split-open chest. A long sacrificial knife, its triangular blade dark with rust-colored blood, lay beside the dead man's head, a head stripped of both flesh and eyes.

Blink gasped at the ritualistic carnage. "What happened?"

"I don't know," Erick whispered, wiping sweat from his clammy forehead. Whose mutilated body lay on the slab? And why?

On the pedestal, the tome lay open, the spidery writing visible but unreadable from Erick's position. As he stared at the book and watched its shadow play in the flickering lantern light, an irresistible curiosity to see the inscriptions on its pages came over him. The tome spoke to him, its voice a seductive whisper. *Come to me*, it murmured. *Learn my secrets.*

Erick stepped forward and leaned over to read the book. The letters and language were an old form of *Lonsh*, the language of the *Inconnu*. Erick could translate few of the words, but as he stared at the symbols, comprehension came to him in a voice soft and raspy as dry leaves blown across tile. It told him what he must do to bring forth Eligos, the Master of Shadows, and give him life.

I will give you the power to do all you wish, the book said, the letters growing faint as dark mist covered his eyes. He stood above Draymed. The people fled in terror as he sent forth wave after wave of undead to crush the town and destroy all within, revenge on those who isolated him so long.

The fog grew darker, and this time he sat upon a throne of gold, dressed in bright raiment of silk and fur, a crown of glimmering platinum upon his head. Below him, the people of Draymed cowered and begged for mercy. He laughed at their pleas and sent them into the fields and shops to toil for his amusement and wealth. At his feet sat the beautiful Elissia.

His empire spread. With the power the book offered, his reign extended to the whole of Keystone Island. In every village, from Spire in the north to Jungledeep in the south, people abased themselves before him, bowing to his every whim as they offered anything he wished.

I don't want this, Erick screamed in a tiny voice.

But you do, the voice insisted. The cloud of darkness blew away, sending a chill through Erick's soul. The voice knew the truth.

As a Necromancer, Erick faced the seduction of *Elonsha* every time he created a *gateloah,* an undead creature. Even when his gifts remained unused, the whispery voice spoke to him, ever in the back of his mind, seeking to corrupt him. But those entreaties were like drops of water compared to the torrent of power that poured from this book.

The ritual to return the Master revealed itself, an incantation so easy a child could do it: a handful of herbs, a few runes and glyphs drawn in blood, and a human sacrifice.

You will be all you desire before the night is old. Read further.

BLINK, PLEASE! Erick's mind shouted even as his hand turned the page.

Your pet cannot help you.

Erick screamed again, pushing with all his will to break through the barrier imposed by the voice.

❧

B link watched, aware that this room oozed with evil, as Erick stared at the book with frightening intensity and his lips moved in feverish silence. A spiteful force radiated from the tome, and Blink's head spun at the *Elonsha* pouring through the chamber. His master could be reading nothing benevolent within the grimoire's pages.

Even worse, Erick's *thoughts* were unreachable. When Blink tried to link with his master, he encountered something he had never experienced. In his mind's eye, he saw a wall of black stone, unfathomably large. Spikes dripping with green ichor protruded from its ebony surface. Terrified those barbs would impale him, Blink withdrew and watched, frightened to touch Erick lest he damage him.

His paralysis broke when Erick's voice slipped through the barricade. It was barely a murmur--*blink please*--but it set Blink in action. He launched himself into the air, grabbed Erick by the shoulders, and pulled him from the room, back into the sunlit laboratory.

When Blink released him, Erick whirled around with clenched hands. Blink withdrew a few feet.

"How dare you, you little bastard!" Rage suffused Erick's round face, eyes wide and cheeks flush. He advanced, raising his fists.

"*Erick, stop!*" Blink screamed verbally and mentally, his barbed tail poised to strike, ready to render his master unconscious.

Erick froze. The sound and thought of his familiar smashed through the black cloud created by the book's enchantment. He swayed, fists unclenching as he lowered his arms to steady himself against a table. Darkness drifted away, and he stood in the dim confines of the laboratory, Blink hovering with tail up. The wind from his familiar's wings blew across his face, drying the sweat that had formed.

Erick slid to the floor and looked at Blink through the black specks that danced before his eyes. "I'm so sorry." He sucked in a deep breath. "We need to burn that book."

Blink didn't hesitate. Destroying the written word went against everything Erick had been taught, but they both knew some words shouldn't be kept. Blink grabbed the lantern in the entryway and flew above the book.

It whispered to him, offering him the power to be his creature and rule others, but such words held no influence. His love for Erick defeated any such promises. Blink dropped the lantern. The lamp's fragile glass shield shattered, spreading flame and oil onto the thin, dry pages. The book caught immediately; the fire leapt high, singeing Blink before he could fly away.

"Thank you," Erick choked out, his back to the room and eyes squeezed tight. Tears ran as he listened to the book's dying screams, mixed with threats of his destruction for defying the Master of Shadows' wishes.

You will burn, the book promised. *All you know will be as smoke.*

~

S oon nothing remained of the book but ashes, which drifted in the air and floated to the floor. "Close the door," Erick said in a thin voice. "We'll clean it up later."

"What happened?" Blink asked as he pushed the stone wall shut. "I lost you."

Erick shuffled toward the staircase leading into the manor. "The book tried to trap me and make me do its will."

"What did it want?"

Erick stopped at the foot of the stairs and collapsed on the bottom step. "The book was a copy of *Teloc Sapah,* the Dark Words. It details the direst rituals available to Necromancers: Lich creation, Spectre summoning, all the rites that require human sacrifice. The *Inconnu* wrote all the copies, and each book contains *Elonsha* directly from their blood. The books are so dangerous that Necromancers destroy any they find on sight. If the book is opened, the released *Elonsha* can force a Necromancer to do the bidding of its author. You saved us both, as well as the people in Draymed. Thank you."

"Of course," Blink said in a soft voice.

While Erick waited for his strength to return, Blink closed the outer doors, plunging the room into dimness. The smell of burnt paper filled the lab. Erick stood and mounted the stairs, his pace ponderous as his thoughts. Questions without answers racked his brain.

Do you think he summoned the vampire? Blink asked, tuning in on Erick's thoughts as he followed him up the stairs.

"No," Erick responded wearily. "Vampire creation doesn't require human sacrifice. I'm certain now he *was* the vampire. Whatever he tried to conjure turned against him or went wrong, and it cursed him somehow."

"That's one good thing," Blink said. "If he was the vampire, at least that means the *Inconnu* haven't returned."

Erick stopped at the top of the stairs as a chill ran over him. "The book wanted me to summon Eligos. What if it did the same thing to father?"

~

E rick did little the rest of the day, and the *quana* remained unmade. His encounter with the ancient tome and the implications surrounding its discovery were too oppressive for him even to consider performing a Ritual, and he had no blood for it anyway. He spent time in the garden culling herbs but stopped when he realized he'd harvested several unusable plants.

The day dragged by. Questions circled in Erick's mind until they lost meaning or reason. Beneath it all churned growing anger at his father, who dared not only to keep an illicit and dangerous book but also to tamper with forces so abhorrent that his kindred Necromancers decreed them anathema.

He tried to sort out his feelings as he bathed and prepared for bed. He stared at himself in the mirror and ran his hand over the red welts, crisscrossed with thick black thread, left by the vampire--his father. They were his forever, a lifelong reminder of how close he had come to being damned, with no chance to appeal to Alakanath, no possibility of redemption.

He didn't bother to bandage them again.

New fury raged in him as he considered the betrayal of his trust. Fathers cared. Fathers were kind and helpful. They weren't liars and murderers and sneaks. The most confusing thing was that his father appeared to be *all* of these things.

As he crawled into bed, grief and shame replaced the anger, and he wept. He should have noticed a change in his father, no matter how subtle. He should have found the secret door and burned the tome sooner. Guilt pounded against him until fatigue overtook him and he drifted into a disjointed dream, full of scattered images and muted sound.

Faces came at him, swirling in from all angles. Elissia and Corby stood on one side, staring at him. Beatru and Commander Brannon stood on the other, their eyes filled with tears. Men in dark clothing, faces hidden by black cloth, searched for him, ready to kill him on sight.

A smoky cloud passed his vision, and he saw other faces. A brown-haired man with a bland countenance glared at him with undisguised hatred. Corby stood beside a dark-haired boy, unknown to Erick, but with a familiar face. Behind them, a fleet of ships sailed on calm water, Erick standing at the bow.

These images flew through Erick's sleeping mind in rapid order, connected by no string of reason. The ships disappeared as a flat-topped mountain--bigger than the whole world, it seemed—rose up and crushed them. At the foot of the mountain, armies of undead clashed, Erick commanding one, a figure in black leading the other. Erick found himself high off the ground. He leaped, and pain shot through his legs.

A symbol appeared before him, etched in thick lines. Even in a dream, he knew he should recognize it, but its significance eluded him. Eight circles in a line, pierced by a dull gray arrow. He stood under the symbol. Although it floated in the air with no solidity, it crushed upon him like a bag of stones. He tried to flee, but the symbol followed him, ever above him.

His flight found him standing before his manor. The weight disappeared as the symbols scattered, blown away like smoke. A presence on his chest revealed the same symbol resting below his neck, a golden amulet held by a thick leather cord. A thin glow suffused the gold, and the warmth of the talisman against his skin no longer crushed but comforted Erick. As he reached to touch the medallion, a flicker of orange caught his attention. He looked up to see his home engulfed in flame; stricken with terror, his dream self screamed.

Erick, wake up! Blink screeched in his mind. *There are armed intruders in the manor.*

8

The Eligoi *existed solely for the chance to sacrifice themselves for the greater glory of the* Inconnu. *They gave all to join, forsaking family, friends, and any life they had known. They trained without ceasing and killed without remorse. It is said they drank the blood of babies to give them strength and harden their hearts, but that is only rumor and, as the order dissolved shortly after the death of Eligos, impossible to confirm.*

-Timone Narvis, Scholar of Kal-Adar *On the Inconnu and their Followers*

Erick snapped awake in his room to the dim yellow light of the lantern on his oak nightstand and Blink missing from his roost. He closed his eyes and connected with Blink, who perched on the right newel post at the bottom of the stairway. Erick viewed the world in the bright hues of his familiar's night vision, a world of sharpened edges and deeper shadows. A figure slipped inside the open front doors. The mystery being closed the door and joined two others already inside, so quietly that even Blink's sensitive hearing picked up nothing. Black clothing cloaked their bodies and faces, exactly as Erick dreamed.

You need to hide, Blink told Erick.

What are you going to do? Erick rolled out of bed.

Hope they pass me by, and then try to poison them.

Erick wanted Blink to attack now, but it would put him at three against one. Nerve-racking as it was to Erick for Blink to wait, the familiar stood a better chance with surprise.

The trio communicated with hand gestures and flowed up the stairs without a glance at Blink, who sat immobile on the post.

Erick dropped the connection and tried to think of a hiding place; he dismissed under the bed or in the wardrobe as too obvious. He glanced at the window. If he could get to the *priquana*, he could rouse them and keep the intruders at bay while Blink sedated them with his envenomed tail.

Halfway to the window, a chill ran across his naked body. He reached to the floor, grabbed his brown breeches, and slipped them over his legs.

No sooner had he pulled the drawstring than the door swung open and two figures stole inside.

The intruders froze and stared at Erick across the moonlit room. They were little more than inky splotches, their eyes bare glints through black hoods.

They recovered quickly and spread to either side of the room. Erick backed toward the window. He would never be able to open it in time to flee. *Hurry up, Blink.*

The third figure stepped into the doorway. Each man drew a long knife. The slim blades gleamed.

Erick ran toward the nightstand, grabbed the lamp, and turned up the wick.

The figure in the doorway motioned with his hand. As the two men at his side moved to flank Erick, the man fell forward. His knife clattered across the floor. Blink hovered in the doorway, tail extended.

The others threw their daggers at Blink. Erick flung the lamp at the shadow to his left. A twinge of pain in Erick's thigh told him Blink had been hit.

Erick's target flung his arm up in a sweeping arc and deflected the lantern. It slammed against the wall and shattered. Oil splashed and caught fire.

Blink--knife protruding from his leg--closed the distance and lashed out with his tail. The barb sank into the assassin's throat.

Erick turned as the last intruder drew another dagger and threw it. Erick flung himself forward across his bed, straightening his arms as he flew toward the man. The knife sailed overhead. His fists struck the invader's stomach. Although not a hard hit, it pushed the man back and gave Blink the opportunity to strike.

But the attacker was prepared. He grabbed Blink's tail and twisted. Blink hissed in irritation.

He *wasn't* prepared when Blink pulled the knife out of his thigh and stabbed the man in the arm. This wrenched out the first sound any of the intruders had uttered--a shriek of agony. The scream was as short-lived as the man. He shuddered and fell to the floor. The growing firelight revealed a dull blue paste clinging to the blade. Erick shook with relief that the knife had struck Blink and not him; he lacked his familiar's immunity to poison.

Fire engulfed half the room, latching on to the drapes and wooden floor. The stifling heat forced Erick to breathe in gasps, making his throat raw. Sparks danced through the room like deadly fireflies. As the flames reached him, the second assailant caught fire. The stench of burning hair and flesh filled the air.

Erick and Blink rushed toward the door. *Pick him up,* Erick thought as he jumped over the prone form lying in the doorway.

Why? Blink asked even as he lifted the dark figure by the arms.

He can tell us why they attacked. Erick raced downstairs while Blink flew, dragging the assailant behind him. When Erick hit the foyer, he sucked in deep breaths of the colder air. Tears filled his eyes from the pain.

Before Blink could land, Erick rasped, "Take him outside and meet me in the lab." He couldn't save the manor, but he wanted to rescue what he could of his books and equipment.

While Blink struggled toward the front door, Erick ran down the hallway, pushed open the cellar door, and bounded down the stairs into the lab.

Dizziness hit him as he reached the bottom. He put a hand against the wall to keep from falling and forced the vertigo away. Once he got outside, he could collapse, but he had to stay strong now.

He couldn't save everything, so he had to rescue what could not be easily replaced. The tomes of Rituals were the most obvious. He grabbed a sack and tossed books into it, heedless of how they landed.

The sound of flames crackled through the door as Blink opened it and flew down the stairs, followed by a gust of hot air. After a glance at Erick, Blink found another sack and began stashing books.

His bag full, Erick ran to the outside doors and pushed them open. With a muscle-straining heave, he ran up the three stone steps and tossed the heavy sack into the yard.

The clouds glowed the color of weathered copper. Flames engulfed the manor's upper floor. Hungry orange tongues tore at the wood like a dog with a bone. Sparks drifted high and landed on the herb garden; the heat turned the greenery to withered char.

An explosive pop sounded from above, followed by the crash of a collapsing roof section. Erick ran down the stairs as Blink came up with a filled sack.

"That's all of them," Blink said. "We should go."

"Okay. I need one more thing." He rushed into the lab and seized a large wooden box by its leather strap. He wanted to take so much more, but another loud crash and a wave of heat dissuaded him. With the exception of the box's contents, nothing else in the lab warranted risking his life.

He ran back out to find Blink on the ground, panting heavily and holding a claw to his wounded leg. Erick knelt beside him. "We need to get away from the house. Can you fly?"

"Of course. It hit my leg, not my wing."

"Then grab a sack."

Blink stood and picked up one of the book-filled bags. Erick snagged the other and ran across the yard, passing their unconscious attacker where Blink had dropped him. Erick didn't stop until he reached the other side of the gate.

He dropped the box and sack and collapsed. His vision dimmed, his ears rang. Blink flew back and returned moments later, dragging the black-clothed man. "I still think we should have let him burn," Blink said, his voice muted by the bells in Erick's head.

"You don't look well," the familiar continued. "Let me help you."

Blink put his clawed hand on Erick's shoulder, and a surge of energy went through Erick. The faintness and ringing disappeared, and his vision cleared. He looked at Blink. The familiar's grey sheen had lightened, and his pale blue eyes had lost some luster. He had given vital energy to Erick at his own expense.

"Thank you," Erick said.

"My pleasure," Blink answered, his words slow and slurred.

The sound of pigs squealing in terror reached Erick. The barn had caught fire in several places. Too late, he realized he could have saved them. In his selfish terror, he had forgotten about the animals.

You would have passed out before you got halfway to them, Blink thought as he flopped onto his back. Erick wasn't convinced, despite the weakness that even now made his hands shake.

The lowing of the cows joined the pigs' squeals and soon turned into painful bellows. Erick wanted to cover his ears but didn't. He listened as the animals' deaths accused him.

Townspeople hurried up the hill. A few of the villagers tried to question Erick. Mesmerized with shock and disbelief, he had no answers for them, so they soon gave up.

Hands landed on his shoulders and Erick tensed until he turned to find Elissia behind him, Corby beside her. Nobody spoke. Erick tried to take comfort in their presence but found none.

Erick watched, knees to chest and arms wrapped around his legs in helpless frustration, as the manor burned to the ground, his home reduced to scattered bonfires in less than an hour. Here and there, blackened boards pointed toward the clouds, edges and ends pulsing red as they released wisps of smoke into the air. His nose and lungs felt clogged with ash and his face sticky with tear-tracked soot. At some point, his stitched neck had torn and started bleeding. Trails of blood gone cold clung to him.

He stared at the skeleton of his house, feeling as burned away as the smoldering timbers. He had no concept of what to do next.

A stern face appeared in front of him, blocking his view of the destruction. Numb, it took Erick a moment to recognize Brannon, and longer to realize the captain addressed him.

"What?" Erick asked, pulling himself out of his daze.

"Is that man responsible for this?" Brannon pointed at the prone, dark-clad figure.

"No, I'm responsible," Erick said. The admission caused new tears to flow. At Brannon's puzzled stare, Erick wiped at his gritty eyes. "He and two others were trying to kill me. I threw a lantern at one of them and missed. Blink took care of the others."

"That man tried to kill you?"

"Yes."

Brannon signaled for two guards to step forward. They approached as Brannon pointed to the figure. "Put him in a cell. We'll deal with this later."

The guards grabbed the unconscious man and carried him away.

Blink sat nearby. At some point a bandage had been applied to the familiar's wound, stopping the trickle of blood. *How are you?*

It could be worse, Blink thought back.

Erick turned to Elissia and the others. Concern shone in Elissia's soft face, while Corby stood near, expression stoic but hands shaking. Two friends. He had no home, but Blink was right. It could be worse.

"Are you okay?" Elissia asked.

"Not really." Reluctantly, he slid his shoulders from beneath her warm hands and stood. His head swam from the sudden movement. The air, no longer warmed by the fire, rippled goosebumps across his chest.

Like that first night, a lifetime ago, most of the town had shown up and stood gathered near. Sympathy and concern marked most faces, but Erick remembered Elissia's warning that not everyone in Draymed approved of his presence.

Fathen stood to one side, his thoughts unreadable, his five saffron-robed acolytes, including Keven, beside him. Did the priest have enough hate in him to hire assassins?

Too drained to worry about it, Erick spoke to the townspeople. "I'm tired, and I'd like to sleep now. Could you all leave, please?"

People stared at him. Expressions turned to puzzlement, but no one moved. Unsure what they wanted, Erick said, "I don't think the house is going to burn much more, so there's no reason to stay."

Some of the people lowered their heads and began to walk back down the hill. Carn stepped forward, his voice loud. "We are not here to gloat in your misery, young Darvaul. We only wish to help you."

"Thank you," Erick said, his voice bitter. "But you're too late."

Fathen took two long strides until he stood by the mayor. "Perhaps we are. And on behalf of the town, I apologize. A house is only a creation of wood, easily rebuilt. Crops can be replanted and animals fostered. Consider this a chance to start anew. Your father and I disagreed in the past, and that has led to a bitter life for you, and left us a poorer town for not knowing you. It is time for us to start again, as friends."

Fathen's voice sounded firm and believable, but his eyes betrayed him, darting from Erick's face to the book sacks that lay at his feet. Smugness in Keven's scarred face showed his pleasure at the turn of events.

Sudden conviction came upon Erick that Fathen had been responsible for this night. As a priest in a powerful religion, he certainly had enough money and resources to hire killers.

"I want nothing from you," Erick said. "I never needed anything from you before, and I sure as hell don't now. Leave and no longer disgrace this hill with your presence." Erick waved an arm at the acolytes, ignoring Fathen's surprise. "And take your minions with you."

Several people gasped in shock, but fewer than Erick expected. Elissia lifted her hand to hide a smile, and Erick took heart from that. "To the rest of you, thank you for your concern. We can be friends tomorrow. Right now, I want to stay by my home one last night, so please go away and let me sleep." He turned to Brannon.

"Do you wish a guard to remain?" the commander asked.

Erick shook his head and waved his hand in a direction toward the sleeping *priquana*. "I have my own guard."

"As you wish." Brannon turned to the crowd. "Time to go home, citizens. There is work tomorrow, and the hour is late."

His loud voice spurred the townspeople to action, and they filed down the hill. A few offered Erick muttered expressions of concern, which Erick barely had the strength to acknowledge. Fathen and his flock offered him dark stares, but Erick ignored them.

Erick turned to Elissia to find her in whispered conversation with Corby. After a moment, he ran toward town. Elissia returned to Erick.

"What's going on?" Erick asked.

"Someone just tried to kill you. You don't think you can stay here alone, do you?"

"Come along, Elissia," Beatru said, standing beside her husband.

"I'm staying here," Elissia said.

"No, you're not," Beatru said. "I'll not allow it."

"And how is that?" Elissia clenched her fists.

Beatru and her niece glared at each other across the yard, Elissia's fists at her side, Beatru's meaty arms across her ample chest. Neither moved, but Erick feared Beatru might charge across the yard and snatch her much smaller niece.

Elissia's uncle, a bulky man with graying hair and several missing teeth, leaned in and whispered to his wife. Her face hardened.

"Suit yourself," she snapped, although Erick couldn't tell if she addressed Elissia or her husband. Beatru turned and walked away, but not before offering Erick a glare that wished him ill.

"You don't have to stay," Erick told Elissia.

"Yes, I do," she said.

Erick, drained of emotion, stared at the remains of his house. Elissia sat on one side and Blink on the other, offering wordless comfort. The night wind blew, and Erick shivered. Elissia put an arm around him. After a moment's resistance, he laid his head on her shoulder. The close contact intoxicated him. Her clean smell, like fresh flowers, settled against him, relief from the stink of char and ash. Her hand rubbing his arm sent jolts of sensation through him. Hesitant, he leaned in and kissed her. She returned the kiss; her breath tasted like cinnamon, and the kiss went from his mouth to toes, hitting every nerve on the way. He shuddered. He pressed his mouth harder against her. Overcome by loss and desire, and almost before he realized it, he used his weight to push her back to the ground. She went down, and he rolled himself on top and pressed against her, his head faint and body alight as he wished her chest was as bare as his.

Elissia moved beneath him. A moment of pain broke through his fired nerves, and suddenly he lay on his back, air rushing from his lungs and his head thudding against the ground. Blink rustled his wings in agitation but made no move to attack Elissia, who sat beside Erick, shaking her head. "Not now. Not like this."

He sucked in a lungful of air. What had she done? He had to outweigh her by twenty pounds at least. Was she that strong? "I thought you wanted to," he croaked out.

"No, *you* want to. And only because you're upset and think it will make you feel better. It might, for a bit, but then what? You're not ready."

Not ready? Did she think of him as some little boy who couldn't finish? "Maybe *you're* not ready," he retorted, fighting the thudding pain in his head, neck, and groin.

"I'm not. Not yet. Maybe not ever."

What did she mean by that? He sat up and rubbed the back of his head. "It's all too confusing." He lifted his knees and put his head against them so she wouldn't see his tears.

elcome to life, Elissia thought, hiding her confusion with W silence. His hunched shoulders told her he was crying, although he tried to suppress it. A pang of sympathy hit her that he thought he had to hide his misery, given such circumstances. She still couldn't fathom why he cared what she thought, why he cared what any of them thought. She looked at Blink, who only stared at his master.

She rested her arm across his shoulders. He tensed, but then relaxed and seemed to almost fold in on himself. She shook her head. He had no experience with people and reacted only on instinct. When confronted with compassion, he had responded with the same impulse that afflicted most boys. Erick wasn't the first amorous man-child she had fended off, or even the most dangerous, but he was the first that made her hesitate.

She flushed at the memory of his body atop her, his eagerness. There was an innocence to his lust, so unlike the frantic attempts of the boys at home. There they viewed her as a prize, something to win to get to her father. Her chastity had become a challenge in a place where such virtue held scant value. Erick hadn't been raised that way; he only reacted to what he thought she had offered.

Beatru might think her niece wanton, and done her best to spread the idea to the whole town, but Elissia saw no point to sex without the love that was supposed to exist behind it. She knew what a loveless relationship had done to her mother and had vowed not to let it happen to her. Another reason to return home and change things.

And another reason to not let feelings complicate matters. She liked Erick a great deal but, strange and exotic as he seemed at first, he was not much different than the other boys, just more naïve.

She mourned Erick's loss of his home, but now he had no reason to stay here. He could help her by acting as her majority holder, allowing her to travel legally and return home. While they traveled, she could work on getting him to help with removing her father from power.

Her plea to Denech crossed her mind, her request that her fate be changed. Had this horrible event been because of her hasty prayer?

Of course not, she chided herself at her foolishness. The gods never answered prayers, certainly not the prayers of one who seldom talked to them. If they did, she would still be at home, with Marcus at her side, and her father would be living out of a gutter.

She sighed, rested her head on his shoulder and listened to his muffled sobs. A soft smile touched her lips. Now perhaps she could use the promise of what he wanted to get him to leave with her.

As soon as the thought formed, she frowned and banished it, disturbed it had so easily popped into her head again. That was her father's way, the way she'd left behind. She wanted to go home, to return to Marcus, but she wouldn't become her father to do it. She sighed.

"You're right," she said. "It's very confusing."

~

Sometime later, a noise attracted Erick's attention. He raised his head and wiped at his eyes. Elissia removed her arm from his shoulder and stood. The cool air touched his bare back, and he shivered as he watched Corby trudge up the hill. He wore a dark blue tunic and brown pants and lugged two large patchwork quilts. Balanced on the quilts were a sword and a staff of dark, polished wood, each end capped with an iron ball.

"I'm back," Corby said as he set his load on the ground.

"What are you doing?" Erick asked.

"I brought blankets and weapons. I'm going to stay and help protect you, in case there's another attack. Can't promise how competent I'll be, but I'll try."

"I don't need you to stay here. I've got the *priquana* to protect me."

"Maybe," Corby said, running a hand through his hair, which Erick noticed was not oiled and stuck up more than usual. "But they seem too slow to be useful in a fight. You saved my life, so how do you think we'd feel if we stayed at home and something happened to you?"

Erick knew they were friends, but they didn't realize the risk. If they did, their resolve might change. "I-"

"Don't bother," Elissia said. "We're not going anywhere, so just accept it."

A lump rose in Erick's throat. "Thank you," he said in a choked voice. "It could be dangerous."

"Possibly," Elissia agreed. "But at least it will be exciting."

"If we were smart, we'd go inside," Corby said. "But if you want to spend a last night by your destroyed house for vague sentimental reasons, who are we to stop you?"

As Elissia gave Corby a death stare, Erick said, "I don't think we'd be any safer in town. For all I know, Fathen hired these men to kill me."

Elissia turned her glare on Erick. "That's crazy. Fathen dislikes you, but he doesn't hate you enough to have you assassinated."

"How do you know?"

"I can tell. Trust me. I've known people with a reason to kill, and your simple existence isn't enough. If it were, he would have hired someone long ago to murder your whole family."

Erick frowned. Assuming Elissia was right, where had the killers came from and who sent them? Did it have anything to do with his father and the *Teloc Sapah*? He sighed. More unanswered questions. He didn't know how many mysteries he could take.

Corby held out a short sword. "Here, put this on."

"I don't know how to use that."

Corby's dark eyebrows rose, but his hand didn't move. "It's simple. Stick the pointed end into anything you want to hurt. Take it. I brought these also. They belong to my older brother since mine would be too small."

He rummaged between the blankets with his free hand and pulled out a blue tunic with a pair of soft, brown leather shoes folded inside. "He would kill me if he knew I took them, but he's on night watch."

Erick took the clothing and sword, surprised at how much the weapon weighed. He slipped into the shirt; it fit poorly, being too broad in the shoulders and chest and too long at the waist, but it would have to do until he found a way to get better. The shoes came closer but chafed at his heels. "Thank you."

"You're welcome," Corby said.

Erick buckled the sword around his waist. He cinched the belt tight to help draw in the shirt, and the sword rested awkwardly on his hip. He would never actually use it, but to say so would probably start an argument, and he wanted to avoid that. He also wondered where Corby got it, being a scholar, but decided not to ask. Probably something else he stole from his brother.

"I assumed you didn't need one," Corby said to Elissia, pointing at Erick's sword.

Elissia shook her head. "Way too unwieldy. I prefer these." She reached into her boots and produced two daggers with tapered blades and flat handles made of shiny steel that gleamed under the moonlight.

A sudden image of a knife glinting in his bedroom hit Erick, and he shivered. "Where did you get those?" he asked, unnerved. He half expected to see more deadly shadows moving toward him.

"They were a gift from Marcus."

Who's Marcus? Erick almost asked, but decided he didn't want to know. Probably a suitor, someone she cared about a great deal. It explained why she had rebuffed him earlier. Too tired to feel jealous, he also suspected he didn't have the right. Did he expect she would just be waiting for him, unloved, ready to swoon over the mysterious Necromancer when he emerged?

He stared at the pile of smoldering embers that had been his house. He had lost much, but not everything. He and Blink were still alive, and he was no longer alone. Elissia might never be more than a friend, but he could accept that.

His sadness drifted away, replaced by a vague fear about the future. Elissia's words returned to him; neither he nor Draymed were safe as long as he remained here. Someone in the town had sent assassins. Or worse, the assassins were connected to the *Inconnu* and his father's tampering with the *Teloc Sapah*.

What were you trying to do, Father? Erick thought, staring toward the ocean.

"Why don't you get some rest?" Elissia asked. "We'll watch tonight."

"I should wake the *priquana* and bring them here, to help in case something happens."

"Can you keep them at a distance?" Corby asked as he picked up the iron-shod staff. "I suspect that mine and Elissia's sensibilities are more delicate than yours."

"What?"

Elissia smiled. "He means they stink, but you're probably used to it and don't notice."

"You're right; I don't. I'll keep them close by. That way, if something happens, I can call them to help." He opened his rescued herb box and grabbed one of the five dark iron needles lined against a wall of the case, held by tiny loops tacked to the wood.

He stepped away from the others, pricked his ring finger, and recited the incantation that woke his servants. When they drew within thirty feet, he shouted out, "*Quana, alar.*" The creatures dutifully stopped and waited.

"Do you have to do that every morning?" Elissia asked when Erick returned to the group, sucking on his finger.

Erick pulled his finger from his mouth. "No. They sleep like we do, although 'sleep' isn't the right word. I only have to use the ritual if I must wake them before their time."

"Why?"

"The *Elonsha* fades over time and has to replenish. When they're dormant, their souls return to the Heaven of Caros."

Elissia shook her head. "It's a strange thing."

"You don't know the half of it," Corby said. "I'll tell you about it while Erick sleeps."

"It's going to get cold. We should go see if any of the outbuildings are still standing," Erick said through a yawn even as his legs folded and he sat on the ground. Blink sidled beside him.

"We'll be fine here." Corby grabbed one of the quilts and wrapped it around Erick and Blink.

"Thank-" Erick fell into sleep before he could finish the sentence.

Erick started awake in the darkness. Thin fog covered the ground, glistening blue from the moonlight.

The quilt lay damp on the ground. Erick had curled in on himself, hands wrapped around his knees, sword pommel jammed into his side. Blink snored gently, his face barely visible above his enfolding wings.

Elissia and Corby lay on either side of Erick and Blink, Elissia wrapped in a dark green cloak, Corby covered by the other patchwork quilt.

Moving slowly to not disturb the others, Erick stretched to work out the stiffness of sleeping on the ground. His arms and shoulders ached, and he struggled not to groan. His side throbbed where the sword hilt had dug in, and a fatigue headache pounded against him; his eyes felt like orbs of salt.

The remains of the house and stables stood out stark, embers still smoldering, leaving blackened, gray-tipped stubs of wood and piles of cinders that drifted in the wind. The herb trellises had turned black and withered. The garden had become a landscape of ash. The outbuildings survived untouched, but they and the harvested fields were all that remained of Erick's home. The *quana* stood, patiently awaiting the commands of their master.

Staring at the remnants, he tried to dredge up a sensation other than the blank emptiness that engulfed him, but nothing came. Even the brief optimism of last night had gone. In the midst of his companions, loneliness bore down on him.

Carefully, he moved one of Blink's wings aside and lifted the bandage to check on the wound to the homunculus's thigh.

Only a thin scab revealed where the knife slashed Blink's leathery flesh. During the night Blink had unconsciously siphoned back the energy he had given Erick to speed the wound's healing. Now Erick knew why he felt so tired.

He stood and walked toward the remains of the house, tiptoeing through the debris. Prized possessions had turned into blobs molded in black and gray.

The floor had caved in over the lab, filling the basement with shattered glass, broken furniture and burnt flooring. The herb cabinets lay crushed, their fragile contents burned away and scattered.

He reached what had been the kitchen, and a glint amidst the char caught his eye. He picked up the glimmering item. Though tarnished with soot, it had survived the fire. His mother's gold necklace, a treasured heirloom she'd always worn. How had it endured without melting?

He wound the chain around his fingers and stared at the amulet. Created by the mountain craftsmen of Makern, far to the north, it showed eight interlocking circles pierced through the center by a thin, golden arrow: the symbol of Denech, the Gods' Seer and Deliverer of Fate. A fragment of the previous night's dream--this symbol crushing him with dreadful weight--flashed through Erick's mind.

As the talisman brought to mind his mother, now truly gone from the world, a dark emotion built within him: anger.

He stared down the hill at the little town. Fury from a deep corner of his soul welled up and filled him. The town was responsible for *all* of this. When he and Draymed ignored one another, Erick had been happy, and the village remained content in its blissful ignorance.

But then he became entwined with the town, and it brought him nothing but trouble and grief. He killed the vampire plaguing *them*, not him, and it nearly cost his life. His interference in *their* problem attracted the attention of something darker. Now it was *his* problem, while Draymed went about its business unconcerned. His house, his possessions, his parents, all gone. All he knew no longer existed, shattered beyond hope of resurrection. But the town remained, uncaring about the strange Necromancer, perhaps even a little pleased that the forlorn house, the product of so many nightmares, had been destroyed.

As he pondered the thought, his anger grew. Grim ideas swirled in his mind. They feared him; maybe he should give them a reason. What had his power gotten him? Years of study and practice for what? To lose it all while apathetic automatons continued their lives unhindered?

He looked at the necklace again and thought of his mother. She was worth any ten of the townspeople; maybe it was time to teach them that lesson.

Something stirred at the corner of his eye, and he turned. Elissia stretched, yawning as her raven hair lay across her face. She was the worst. She had started it, insisting he kill the vampire, demanding he interfere. He would teach her the price to be paid for involving him. He stepped toward her--

And his rage vanished like mist in a strong wind. Elissia had nothing to do with his decision. The town was not to blame; they only asked for his help, he was the one who agreed, because that's what he had been trained to do. He stopped, unsure what had incited such unreasoning rage and hatred.

A noise of footsteps through grass and harsh breathing drew his attention. It came from down the hill. Fear flashed through Erick as he turned, expecting more assassins.

Instead, Fathen and his five acolytes trudged up the hill. They had shed their usual priestly garb for dark brown clothing, although

Fathen still carried his staff of office. All the acolytes wore daggers, except Keven, who had a large mace slung over his broad shoulder.

The fear didn't leave Erick. He hadn't dismissed the idea of Fathen's involvement in the arrival of the assassins. His appearance at this time, dressed for concealment, boded nothing good.

"What are you doing here?" Erick said, pleased to see them all start in surprise. They had no doubt expected to catch him still sleeping. "I told you to leave and never return."

Fathen stopped ten feet away and rested against his staff. He appeared no worse for the walk up the hill, but his acolytes sucked in deep breaths.

Blink, wake up, Erick thought, even as he said to Fathen "What do you want?"

"I want to talk," Fathen said. "Now, without the rest of the town around, to see if we can resolve our differences."

"Do you always need five armed men to talk? Or perhaps you came up here to try and finish what your assassins couldn't."

Erick didn't know people well, but the shock on Fathen's craggy face appeared unfeigned.

"Ill-stated," the priest said, "but perhaps not unwarranted. I had nothing to do with the people who attacked you."

Elissia and Corby stirred behind him. Fathen glanced in their direction. A murderous frown crossed Keven's scarred face when he spotted Elissia.

"Just like you had nothing to do with turning the town against me."

"No, I had everything to do with that," Fathen admitted. "But as I told you, your father threatened the town with death, and that is why we stayed away."

"But why?" Erick asked. "Why would he do that?"

Fathen shrugged. "We argued. The particulars don't matter, but it ended with your father taking something that belonged to me and threatening to kill any who approached the manor. Now that he is dead, I thought perhaps you could return my property, and we can let the past be the past."

Elissia and Corby stepped up next to Erick. Tension roiled off Elissia, and the rage hadn't left Keven's face.

"And what exactly did my father take?"

"A book. Nothing important, but it has value to me."

Erick's hand tingled. He still gripped his mother's amulet. Without having to ask, Erick knew what book his father had taken. Hoping he was wrong, Erick asked, "What did this book look like?"

"It had a black cover crossed with five strips of leather. The ink was dark brown and fading."

Erick closed his eyes as anger trembled through him. "Those strips weren't leather; they were human flesh. And the ink was blood. It was the *Teloc Sapah*, a book so evil that it should be in possession of no one. What vile circumstances brought it to your possession?"

Fathen straightened himself, a glint of anger in his dark eyes. "That's irrelevant. What is relevant is that your father took something that did not belong to him."

"You should not have possessed in the first place."

Fathen strode forward, his acolytes following. The sound of metal rang as Elissia drew her daggers and Corby stepped up, staff held at the ready.

Fathen stopped, surprise on his craggy face. "Who was he to make that decision? The book belonged to me. He took it and *struck* me, and then threatened me with death. He should have burned on a pyre at the hands of the Paladins right then, and would have if..." Fathen stopped and took several deep breaths. Erick studied him, certain the priest almost let something slip.

When he had regained control, Fathen glared at Elissia. "You dare to draw weapons on me?"

"I'm just admiring how sharp these are," Elissia said. "Keep things civil, and no one will have to find out just how sharp."

Keven stepped forward, the mace still on his shoulder, but Fathen held up a hand to stop him. "Your hostility is unwarranted," he told Erick. "We have not threatened you. I apologize for my outburst. As I said, the past is the past. Caros teaches us to forgive, and so I shall. I take it my book is in one of your bags. Return it to my possession, and we shall consider this matter over."

"I can't do that," Erick said. "As soon as I saw the book, I burned it."

Fathen's face went blank, as if unable to grasp what Erick told him.

Then, he turned deep red and glared at Erick. "You devil-born bastard spawn," he thundered. "You had no right to destroy what was not yours." The acolytes drew their weapons.

"As a Necromancer, I had the duty to destroy such a foul book."

"I should kill you now and send you to the Festering Demons where you belong."

The mace came off Keven's shoulder, and he smiled. Blink leapt into the air. Elissia jumped in front of Erick, daggers at the ready. Erick prepared to call the *quana* to his defense, wishing he had kept them close.

A chill wind, tinged with the smell of rotten onions, swept across the group, stirring up ash. From behind Erick, a deep voice spoke. "Do that, priest, and I shall kill *you.*"

Erick wheeled around and found himself face to face with his dead father.

9

"It was the child that did it. I could accept the death of soldiers, of knights, even of camp followers who were unlucky enough to be near when we attacked. But when I saw one of my vohquana *tear into the chest of a frightened squire, a boy of no more than ten, I knew then I must turn away from the path I had chosen. The child's screams will haunt me until I die."*

-Necromancer Fallon Thage, on his betrayal of the *Inconnu*

Shimmering translucency surrounded Erick's father, who appeared as Erick remembered, a sharp-cheeked, friendly face with short brown hair, not the twisted balding shape of the vampire. He wore a blue tunic and brown pants, almost an imitation of his son, but his colors were pale and faded. Water clung to him and fell to the ground in drops that made no sound and left no mark. Erick's vision wavered as happiness and anger warred within him. But above all that were questions.

A commotion behind him made Erick look over his shoulder. Four of the acolytes fled down the hill, leaving Fathen and Keven standing alone. Keven had gone pale, his scar red against his wan face, but he kept a tight grip on his mace. Fathen's wide eyes stood out even in their deep recesses. Elissia trembled at Erick's side, daggers wavering in her unsteady hands. Only Corby seemed unfazed by the shade's appearance. His brown eyes gleamed with curiosity.

"Begone from this place, demon," Fathen commanded, but the waver in his deep voice robbed him of any authority.

"Not likely," Darric's ghost said. "This is my home. You are the one who must leave." He floated toward Fathen, silent, his feet unmoving.

Keven's nerve broke. He grabbed Fathen's shoulder. "We should go." The contact breached protocol, but the cleric didn't seem inclined to point it out.

Fathen held his ground. "My god protects me."

Darric stopped. "Your god does no such thing." The ghost reached out a hand and slapped it at Fathen's head. The immaterial form passed right through Fathen, insubstantial as wind.

Fathen's eyes grew wider and face paler, two things Erick didn't think possible. He staggered back as if the slap had been a physical blow. Keven let out a cry and steadied his mentor.

"Lies," Fathen said, his voice caught between outrage and a sob.

Darric shrugged. "Perhaps. But if you don't want to find out for certain, leave. No one threatens my son, especially not you."

Fathen appeared ready to say more, but Keven tugged at the priest and spoke into his ear. The priest listened, then nodded and, with a baleful scowl at all of them, turned and strode down the hill, his back straight.

They watched until Fathen and his acolyte were near the bottom. Then Erick turned to his father.

A scream of rage from his right startled Erick. He whirled to see Elissia charging, fists raised. He flinched back, but she ran past him and swung at Darric. She passed through his insubstantial form and stumbled in surprise, but kept her footing.

"What are you doing?" Erick shouted as Elissia spun around, disgust on her flushed face, her chest heaving.

"He killed my friend. He killed all the others in town. He deserves to die." She coughed, and her throat worked as if she gagged. Erick knew the strange onion smell of *Elonsha* had hit her when she passed through the ghost.

"I'm already dead, and much worse," Darric said.

Elissia coughed again. "Then perhaps you got what you deserve," she said in a flat voice. She pushed black hair from her face and sat on the ground, shoulders slumped. She didn't cry, but Erick could almost physically feel her pain. He wheeled on his father and tried to fight down his anger.

"You have a lot to answer for," Erick said. "Why did you and Mom jump off the cliff and leave me alone? Why did you lie to me about the town? What were you doing with the *Teloc Sapah*? And how, in the name of Holy Caros, did you become a vampire?" Tears of indignant rage formed, but Erick fought them back. He'd grown tired of weeping. He wiped at his eyes.

"I understand your anger, son, but I did everything for you."

"For me?" Erick asked through a bitter laugh. "How did keeping me isolated from the town do any good? How did killing yourself help me? And why should I believe you're going to be any more honest dead than you were alive?"

Darric frowned. His insubstantial form grew more solid as it took on a darker hue. A chill wind carrying the scent of onions swept across the hilltop. Erick shivered at the swirling *Elonsha* as Darric spoke. "If you knew anything at all, you wouldn't ask such questions. I kept us from Draymed—and Draymed from us—because of the man who just left this hilltop. Fathen hates us, in case his threats didn't make that clear to you."

"Why? The Necromancers have the favor of the Gods. Why would a priest of Caros hate us?" Erick's teeth chattered from fear and cold as his father stared at him, grim and threatening. Ash whipped and clung to Erick's loose shirt, stirred by the unnatural wind. His father's dark eyes drifted past him, and Erick followed the gaze. Elissia sat rooted to the ground, her bravery replaced with wide-eyed fear. Corby crouched behind his cousin, a hand on her shoulder.

The wind stopped, the aura dissipated, and Darric returned to his former pale color. "I apologize, son. I am not myself anymore. You are right to be upset." He turned to Corby and Elissia. "Don't be afraid; I won't harm you."

"He can't harm you," Erick said. "Not physically, anyway."

"But he hurt Fathen," Corby said.

"No," Darric said. "I showed Fathen what I would like to do to him. I revealed how much I want to hurt him for the pain he has caused. That he accepted it as what I *could* do is his ignorance."

"So, you did lie to him," Corby said with a smile.

Darric's glowing face returned the smile. "Yes, I did." He turned back to Erick. "Look down, where you were standing when you had such vicious thoughts about your friends."

Erick saw a fragment of paper no bigger than his hand–its edges jagged and marked with the curled blackness of fire–covered in illegible writing. Erick knelt to examine it.

"Don't touch it," Darric warned.

Erick recognized the page as a fragment of the *Teloc Sapah*, a splinter of parchment that somehow escaped both fires. Though faint, the dark hue of *elonsha* still swirled around the scrap. The malevolence of this sliver birthed his evil thoughts about the town and his friends. Erick shuttered at the power before him. "Fathen hates us because we owned that book."

"Yes and no," Darric said. "He hates us because I discovered he had the book and I threatened to kill him if he didn't hand it over immediately."

Erick looked at the ghost. "I don't understand."

"I should start from the beginning."

"Please."

"No need to get snarky, son." Darric snapped.

"Ever since our family came to the island about a hundred years ago, our relationship with Draymed was never a warm one. But they understood us as a 'necessary evil' and left us alone.

"Three years before you were born, Fathen arrived in Draymed. I don't know why the Temple of Caros sent him here since they had never before showed any interest in the town or us. I saw his arrival as an omen, a chance to improve our standing with Draymed and be seen as people instead of Necromancers."

Erick nodded. He could understand that.

"After all," Darric continued, "a priest of Caros would have knowledge of the Covenant and could help his followers understand they did not need to fear us.

"A few weeks after Fathen's arrival, I visited him. He was brusque when I spoke to him. I think perhaps he had been sent here against his will, but I don't know for certain.

"Despite his anger, he agreed to speak with the congregation and explain about us, so that we might have more respect among the townspeople. He invited me into his study to discuss it further. That was when I saw the book."

"The *Teloc Sapah?*" Erick asked in disbelief.

Darric nodded, a barely perceptible motion in his translucent state. "How he came upon it, I don't know, but it sat there on a podium, open as if he were reading it, although he couldn't have known the language. As soon as I saw it, I demanded he hand it over. I explained its evil will and told him I must destroy it. He refused, and we argued. In the end, I struck him and seized the book. I told him the book belonged to the Necromancers, and if anyone approached the manor, they would be set upon by *quana*. I left with the book while Fathen lay on the floor holding his jaw.

"When I returned home, I told your mother that the priest was completely irrational and threatened us with death if we went to town. My words were so adamant she never had any reason to disbelieve me. She ran to her room and wept, but soon accepted it, as she knew she must."

Corby cleared his throat, catching Darric's attention. His soft voice had a slight waver as he spoke. "You told Fathen the book had to be destroyed, and then you told him it belonged to the Necromancers. Which was the truth?"

Darric gave a grim smile. "Both. At least, so I thought at the time. Although I had learned about the book's strength, I didn't truly *understand*. There is a vast difference, young scholar, between knowing about a thing and experiencing it.

"The minute I touched the book, it tried to claim my mind. My thoughts grew twisted. The book told me secrets of great power, demanding I keep it for myself and not destroy it. But it didn't belong to me; I belonged to it."

"How can a book have that sort of power?" Elissia asked.

"All books have power," Erick said, reciting one of his mother's favorite mantras. "The power to teach, to amuse, to terrify, to make us think. The power of the *Teloc Sapah* is just more," Erick shrugged, "...powerful."

"That's a dangerous understatement," Darric said. "The book is all power, filled with words and *Elonsha* directly from the black souls of the *Inconnu*."

The morning darkened for a moment. Elissia and Corby glanced at the sky, but Erick kept eyes on his father.

"How come it didn't affect Fathen?" Corby asked.

"It only works on Necromancers," Erick explained.

"Not exactly true," Darric said. "It affects other people, but slowly, and only if they're in close proximity or trying to decipher the book. Since Necromancers are the only ones in constant contact with *Elonsha*, we are more susceptible to the book's corrupting influence. After I left with the book, I had Sniffer spy on the town."

"Sniffer?" Elissia asked with a faint smile.

"My familiar," Darric answered, and his father's smoky eyes brimmed with sadness. "A name given by a child to one he loved. Sniffer listened to Fathen's sermon as he told the town we were to be avoided on the threat of death. No one was to approach the manor, lest the evil Necromancers take their souls. So we became isolated, no longer even able to bring our surplus food to the docks to sell. That's why so much of our land went unused."

"Why didn't you tell me any of this before?" Erick asked.

Darric's misty form swirled in agitation. "Haven't you been listening? The book wouldn't let me. There were days—even months—when I could forget its existence, but it always festered at the back of my mind. It constantly tempted me with hints of power, visions of glory. There were occasions when I almost told you or your mother, but the words stuck in my throat. Or worse, I would tell lies. I went to destroy it any number of times but always failed in the end, stopped by the book's will to survive. I held out for twenty years. But, as you already know, the book finally won."

Erick nodded. "I saw the ritual. What did you summon?"

"I summoned the one thing I would have given anything in the world to avoid. I summoned the soul of the Master of Shadows."

Blink gasped as darkness covered Erick's vision and a whispery voice from a barely remembered dream echoed through his head. *I will come for you and destroy your world and everything in it.* His father had done the thing Erick feared and released Eligos into the world. An ancient evil unleashed by a person he loved and respected. Black motes swam before his eyes. The world tilted, and he collapsed.

Blink, Corby, and Elissia ran to his side; Erick barely noticed Elissia's gentle hand on his shoulder. "Are you okay?"

The words came to him as if she spoke through mud-filled cotton. Erick's entire will centered on his father's ghost. He jumped up and pushed back the dizziness that tugged at him. "You bastard! How could you do that? What about Mom? What about me? What about the *Covenant?*"

Darric's face twisted in anguish. He stepped forward with his hands held out. "Do you think any of that mattered? The book had me under its will. All it cared was that I bring forth its master. I fought it. The Gods know I fought it, but I didn't have the strength."

"I escaped the book and burned it without a second thought. Are you telling me I'm stronger than you were?"

"The Ritual drained much of the book's power, so it was weaker when you found it. I had the will to save you, so please don't be too angry."

At Erick's perplexed frown, Darric continued. "At the Ritual's end, Eligos entered my body. He commanded I kill you and your mother, the first of the Necromancers we slay together. But I fought him; and this time, I won."

Understanding threatened to crush Erick. He stared at the ground. "You killed yourself to save me?"

"Yes," Darric answered as he moved closer. Misery roiled off his father's ghost. "The Master could have demanded I kill anyone else, and I wouldn't have been able to resist. But his first order was your death. I would never let that happen. Your mother didn't understand what I was doing. In trying to stop me from jumping, she perished with me."

Erick let the tears fall, ashamed of his misunderstanding. His anger drained away. "How did you become the vampire?" he asked, voice tight.

"The Master's 'gift' for my disobedience. My self-death didn't drive him out as I hoped. It opened my soul even further to him, giving him more power over me. He ritualized me into a vampire, but I was still trapped within my body and could see everything."

"But vampire creation requires a human sacrifice," Erick said.

Darric's mouth pressed in a grim line. "I wish your mother hadn't fallen with me."

Erick sat down, unsure how much more he could take. His stomach twisted. "So mom is—"

"No." Darric knelt beside his son. "Her blood is what Eligos needed, but her selflessness freed her soul of his power. She is well beyond his reach."

"At least that's something," Erick said. His vision blurred and he found it difficult to breathe.

"Eligos wanted me to watch you suffer and die, and become a *gate-loah* under his control. But you surprised him. My soul screamed in joy when you destroyed my body."

Darric looked at Elissia. "For the death of your friend and all the others in the town, I'm truly sorry." He turned to Corby. "I must also apologize to you, for the vampire's attack. I discovered your visits a few months ago but didn't stop them. It pleased me Erick had at least one friend outside the manor, though it pained me that I couldn't allow him more. The vampire used that knowledge against Erick, but I imagine you already figured that out."

"We did," Corby said. He ran a hand over his hair. "At this point, logic would suggest that since Eligos was the vampire Erick killed, then Eligos is now dead, but instinct tells me such malignance is not so easily destroyed."

Darric nodded. "You have good instincts."

Corby smiled.

"Eligos did not die, but the loss severely weakened him. It will take him time to regain strength and find a host. Even now he calls to his followers, and the dark energy of *Elonsha* builds in the world again. The *Eligoi* who attacked last night were an answer to his summons."

"Those were *Eligoi*?" Erick asked. At his father's answering nod, Erick trembled. The *Eligoi* was a name of darkness from his earliest childhood. Fanatic assassins loyal to Eligos, they existed only to kill in his name. Blink's nocturnal wandering was all that had saved them from death. "What am I going to do?" he choked out.

"You have to go to Broken Mountain," Darric answered.

"Broken Mountain?" Erick knew the name well, its history drilled into him.

"What's Broken Mountain?" Elissia asked.

Before Erick could answer, Corby spoke up. "Once known as *Ter Krinnik*, the Summit of the Earth, Broken Mountain's treacherous peaks and cliffs witnessed the final battle between the Inconnu and the Ten Necromancers. The ensuing destruction shattered the mountain, scattering tremendous slabs of stone and reducing the peak to a fraction of its former height. The Necromancers won the day, destroying the Inconnu and sending them forever from Krinnik."

Elissia stared at Corby, her mouth open. Corby said, "Why does my wealth of knowledge always surprise you?"

"That's very concise, but Master Katlish's account is not totally accurate," Darric said.

"How's that?"

Darric gestured to Erick, who continued. "Only Bolfri and Saburoc were killed. Eligos, being the most powerful, could only be banished. According to the Covenant, if Eligos returns, the surviving Necromancers are to gather at Broken Mountain, where the souls of the four who died will show them how to again trap the Master of Shadows."

"Wouldn't it have made more sense to write it down in a tome?" Elissia said.

"Tomes can be lost," Erick said, "or fall into the hands of our enemy, and give them a chance to plan against us. And we have to gather somewhere since a Necromancer alone can't defeat Eligos. The site of the Master's banishment makes the most sense."

Darric smiled. "Exactly. Because of my sins, Alakanath has suspended judgment on me until Eligos is removed from the world. Until then, I am a spirit, tied to this location. After, I will be judged."

"I fear I will be judged wanting," the ghost told his son, "but there is still hope for you. You must help trap the Master. It will not be an easy journey. As Eligos grows in power, so too will his followers. They will be on the move, seeking you and the others. Your only defense is to stay ahead of them and reach Broken Mountain."

"Is that all?" Erick asked in a bitter voice.

Darric did not react to his son's tone. "No." He pointed at the sacks of books. "I know you made a great effort to save those, but you need to leave them behind as soon as possible. You rely on them too much, which is my fault for letting you use them for so long. Start using the mnemonic procedures I taught you to learn the rituals and formulae. At some point your life may depend on remembering the proper Ritual at the right time; besides, you won't have the books much longer."

"Why not?"

"You need to destroy them before you reach the mainland."

Erick didn't have to ask why. The tomes could not fall into the hands of Eligos's followers. With the Master free again, he could begin training new Necromancers to his cause. Without the rituals, they would be crippled, giving Erick and the others more time. He forced a smile. "Then I guess I'll have to study them on the ship and learn quickly."

"Farewell, son. Help banish Eligos and free my soul. Whether I go to Caros or the Demons, I will accept my fate. I'm sorry for more than I can ever tell you. But I believe in you. Take what we have taught you and use your will and strength to do what I couldn't."

"I miss you, dad. I miss mom."

"I know, but know that at least your mother waits for you in the Heaven of Caros. If you succeed, perhaps Alakanath will show mercy, and I too will be there when the day comes that you join us. Luck of Denech, son."

The barest pink light of dawn appeared on the horizon. Darric faded away.

Erick wiped his face. He looked at the ruins of his home, and then glanced at his mother's necklace, still in his hand. Wearing Denech's symbol was supposed to bring luck. Perhaps it was a good omen the necklace survived the all-consuming fire, a divine sign.

Or maybe it's just a nice way to remember your parents, our home, and all the other things we've lost, Blink thought to Erick.

Maybe. Erick slipped the talisman over his head. He turned away from the house and found Elissia and Corby engaged in whispered conversation.

"Blink, grab one of the sacks." Erick picked up the other heavy bag. "Thank you for being my friends," he said to Elissia and Corby. "I wish I could have stayed longer, to get to know you better. I..." he stopped, terrified at the prospect of leaving. The manor was the only home he had known. He had to go before he lost his nerve. He forced himself to continue. "I'll probably never be back, so goodbye."

He started to walk away, but Elissia blocked his progress. She had a crooked smile on her oval face, and Corby stared anywhere but at Erick. "You can't get away that easily," she said. "We're going with you."

10

I'm often asked if, given a chance to do things again, would I still have traveled with the Dark Savior? I find such musings an exercise in futility since I will never have the chance, but the answer is always yes. I lost much, but had I stayed behind, my life would have been so much the poorer for my timidity.

-Excerpt from a lecture by Corberin of Draymed, given at the University of Straph

T hings had worked out flawlessly for Elissia. After being here for three long years, trapped, Erick now had a way for her to return home. She had learned early in life to take advantage of an opportunity when it presented itself.

Erick stared at her and Corby with an expression of shock so earnest that she almost laughed.

"What are you talking about?" Erick asked.

"We're going with you," Elissia repeated.

"No, you're not. Broken Mountain is a long way away, and you can't travel that far."

"Are *you* aware of how far it is?" Corby asked. "Or how to get there?"

"Not really," Erick admitted. "But I can..."

"First, you have to go to Keyport, which is a day's walk. Then you have to find a ship to Kalador and take at least a five-day journey across the World's Circle Ocean to the mainland; then you go northwest up the Routh Krinnik about sixty leagues. On foot, since I doubt you can no longer afford a horse."

"Thank you. Now I know the way."

Corby shook his head. "I'm trying to show you I can be helpful. We're your friends."

"And that's why I *don't* want you to go with me," Erick said.

Elissia smiled. Erick thought he was protecting them from danger, but he had no idea how little he knew. "You're going to Kalador?"

"I guess I have to since that's what Corby said."

This time, Elissia did laugh. "Then I most certainly have to go with you. I couldn't live with myself if I let you march blindly into that wyvern's nest without some protection."

Erick frowned. "I can protect myself. And I have Blink."

Elissia walked up to Erick and took his soft hand in hers. "Kalador is a completely different world. As soon as you step off the ship, the Procurers will steal you blind, and then the Royal Force will 'recruit' you as a soldier or sailor, depending on which they need at the time. That's assuming some rich noble doesn't spot you and take a liking to your beautiful blue eyes and curly brown hair. As for Blink, the only way he'd be welcomed is stuffed and mounted."

"Is it really that bad?" Erick asked

"I'm downplaying it to keep from scaring you," she answered.

Corby spoke up. "And if the things we can see on the mainland are half as intriguing as what I saw here, I'll learn enough to earn my journeyman's diamond." He pointed to the apprentice's ruby in his ear.

"What about your aunt and uncle?" Erick asked her.

"What about them?"

He turned to Corby. "And your parents?"

The apprentice scholar shuffled his feet and ran a hand over his hair. He started to speak, stopped, turned to Elissia.

Although Corby had never shared the reason, Elissia knew the friction between her cousin and his parents rivaled that of hers with her Aunt Beatru. He had almost shouted with joy when she whispered that she wanted him to come along. In many ways, he wanted to escape more than she did, but he didn't have her experience with defying authority. "What his parents don't know won't hurt them," she told Erick.

Erick's round face scrunched in indecision, so she pressed on. "We don't have time to argue. We're going, and that's all that matters. The town will be stirring soon. There's no telling what Fathen and Keven might be planning. We need to move before he rouses anyone against you, if he hasn't already." Hating herself even as she did it, she moved closer, rubbed her hand against his upper arm, and said, "Now let's go before it's too late."

~

Arrows of delight shot through Erick at Elissia's touch, but he tried to ignore them. He had no idea how he would get to Broken Mountain, but he didn't want it to be through endangering his friends. Dire enough he had *Eligoi* assassins coming after *him*; he didn't want to see Elissia and Corby under their knives.

Who's to say they're any safer here if the Eligoi *come searching for you after you've left,* Blink thought. *Maybe you should let them come along. We'll be safer in a group than going it alone. I imagine Elissia knows what she's doing. She's full of surprises.*

Yes, she is, Erick agreed, remembering how easily she threw him off last night, and the knives she had pulled seemingly from nowhere. He sighed, realizing he had little choice. "Okay. What do we do?"

Elissia smiled and let go of his arm. Erick immediately missed the contact.

"We need to get you past town and waiting out of sight," Elissia said, "then Corby and I will gather supplies as quickly as we can and meet you."

"Do we have time for that?" Corby asked.

"We'll have to make time. We can't get far without money. I'll be fine as long as I can get in and out before Beatru wakes up. And your parents sleep late. What rotation is Cary on?"

"Night," Corby said, "so he'll have just gone to bed."

"Then let's move."

"I have one thing I need to do," Erick said.

"Be quick," Elissia said as she frowned at the horizon.

Erick walked to the *priquana* near the outbuilding. Here stood the last ties to his old life, and deep reluctance to say goodbye made him pause. Others thought them abominations, perversions of nature, but to Erick, they had been his family and only friends for seventeen years. He couldn't take them with him, but to let them go admitted his life here had disappeared beyond recovery.

"Thank you," he said through a tight throat. "I release you from your service. Return now to the Heaven of Caros, to remain there through eternity. *Addo zonreng bliar Krinnik.*"

"*Ge zonren.*" The *priquana* spoke as one and collapsed. Erick watched their silver-tinted souls soar skyward, while the dark *Elonsha* spread across the soot-covered ground and dissipated. The bodies, no longer held by the balancing powers, turned to dust.

Turning his back on everything the hill of his home represented, Erick walked toward the others. His throat still clenched, he said, "Okay, let's go."

～

Corby and Elissia led, followed by Erick, a sack over his shoulder. Blink flew above, the other bundle of books held in his stout talons.

They moved as quickly and quietly as they could in the still air, Erick having trouble dealing with the sword that hung from his belt. It kept banging into his knee, so he had to use his hand to hold it still.

They skirted the edge of town farthest from the water. Lantern light glowed in a few glazed windows. At any moment, he expected someone to dash around the corner of a building and challenge them. Stress rolled through him as the temple of Caros came into view, taller and set above the other buildings, but all remained quiet. Fathen and his acolytes didn't burst through the walls brandishing swords and screaming accusations.

"It almost too quiet, isn't it?" Corby said, his voice shocking Erick with its seeming volume.

"Yes," Erick whispered.

"It's always like this just before dawn," Elissia told them. "The spice harvesters have already left, and the farmers are in the fields, so they won't bother us."

The trio returned to the dirt road, stopping beside two eight-foot high pillars that straddled the path. Painted yellow and weathered from the salt air, they marked the border of Draymed.

"Go down the road until you pass over the first hill and can't see the town anymore. Corby and I will meet you soon."

"You sure I shouldn't go with you?" Erick asked.

Elissia shook her head. "I can move faster and quieter without you."

"Be careful."

Elissia winked at him, and a thrill ran through his body. He still didn't like the idea of his friends in danger, but he had to accept his excitement at having them with him.

Erick walked down the road, glancing back to see Elissia and Corby strolling into town. They split up, and it only then occurred to Erick that he had no idea which house belonged to Corby.

He glanced up the hill at the smoking skeleton of his home. His whole life gone in less than a night. He wondered how different it might have been if-

No sense even dwelling on it, Blink thought to him. *It can't be different. But you have the chance to make it what you want it to be.*

Not really, Erick thought back. *Father's dead, and I have to fix his problems. I have to suffer because of his mistakes.*

Stop it! You have to do what you were born to do, nothing more. If it hadn't been you, it might have been your son. Or his son. Your father did the best he could. Forgive him and move on.

I'll move on, Erick thought, *but it may be a long time before I can forgive him.*

As he walked, the town disappeared behind the rolling hills that surrounded it, but his home remained in full view. He sat down in the clipped grass, stared at his shattered life, and waited.

~

The sun had begun to rise, the day growing warm, before Elissia and Corby came into view. Elissia wore a light green, bloused tunic, loose-fitting brown pants, and a well-worn pair of walking boots. Erick couldn't help but notice how well the outfit went with her dark skin and black hair. A black carrying sack hung over one shoulder.

Corby walked beside her, eating a pear. He had a large pack strapped to his back, and a large leather satchel slung on one hip. A dark rawhide belt girded his waist, covered with half-round bulbous protrusions set in a line. From the top of each of these chambers extended a thick metal pin, topped with a globe of tawny tree rubber. At his side, in a long leather sheath, rested a smooth wooden blow-pipe, and he still had his iron-tipped wooden staff.

Underneath the equipment, he wore a brown tunic and pants and brown walking boots. A green, wide-brimmed traveling hat covered his partially shaved head. He made Erick think of a walking tree, and he smiled.

"I was starting to worry," Erick said when they reached him.

Elissia shrugged. "You have to move slowly when you want to be quiet, and we have a small house. The hardest part was finding where my aunt hid the money."

"You stole your aunt's money?"

"No, I stole my money. My father sends them a monthly stipend. Beatru didn't think I knew about it and tried to convince me my upkeep came from their pocket, but I'm not an idiot." She pulled a small pouch from a front pocket in her pants and shook it, making a soft jingling sound. "It's not much, but we'll have to make do. I've got something for you."

She slipped the pouch back into her pocket,

"removed the sack from her shoulder, reached in, and pulled out a smaller burlap bag. Erick could smell it before he opened it. Herbs of various types filled the bag, creating a strange potpourri.

"I have no idea if any of them are useful," Elissia said, "but Corby and I grabbed what we could. It will have to do until you can get what you need in a town."

"Thank you," Erick said. They had managed to grab a surprising number of useful plants, and Erick suspected Corby had been the driving force behind the effort. "Although I have no idea why I would need them before we get off the island."

Elissia shrugged. "Never hurts to be prepared. We better go."

As they started walking, Erick asked Corby, "Is someone going to come after us? Won't your parents worry when they find you missing?"

Corby didn't answer immediately, and Erick sensed the scholar's discomfort.

"Father might be upset he's lost his apprentice," Corby finally said. "But beyond that-" He shrugged.

"I would worry more about my aunt or Fathen raising the hells," Elissia told Erick. "If it were just you, they wouldn't care. But Corby and I are breaking the law, traveling under our majority. They expect that of me, but they're going to think we've either kidnapped Corby or that you've ensorcelled us in some way to follow you."

"I can't do that," Erick said.

"Do you think my aunt cares about that? And let's not forget Fathen threatened to kill you."

"What do we do?" Erick said as he imagined the entire town storming down on them, just like the night they marched up the hill. Except this time, they'd be after his blood.

"We move as fast as we can and stay ahead of them. Have Blink keep an eye behind us for any pursuit. If it comes to the worst, I'll fight to wound and then run. I've been dragged back twice; I'm not going to let it happen again."

It bothered him to hear Elissia talk about hurting people. What sort of life had she endured that she could speak so cavalierly about fighting? Although Corby had told Erick much about Elissia, he had never talked about her past, always deflecting such questions as some-thing Erick would have to ask her.

"You've run away before?" Erick asked.

Elissia nodded. "Poor planning on my part. I was naïve to think

Beatru would let me go. She has some strange moral imperative to see me 'raised in a proper Zakerin fashion.' Both times, I got a strap across my ass and a tongue lashing. This time I think I might see the inside of the guardhouse, so I'm not going to give her a chance."

"If we can leave the island," Corby said, "we'll be safe from pursuit by the guards. Their jurisdiction doesn't extend beyond that, or so my brother told me."

"Then I hope we can catch a boat today," Erick said.

"Put that out of your mind," Elissia said. "The tides run out in the morning this time of year, so the ships would have already left. We'll be spending the night in Keyport."

A perfect chance for Brannon and the Royal Guardians to catch them, Erick realized.

Quit worrying about what hasn't happened yet, Blink thought. *I'll keep an eye out. We'll be fine.*

They crested the hill and prepared to go down the other side. Erick took a last look at the charred ruins of the manor, forlorn in the early morning light. A shiver went through him, a sense of foreboding that he would never see this place again.

His stomach rumbling with hunger and knotted by fear, Erick turned away from his home and his past and walked down the road to his uncertain future.

11

Quana, or zombies as most know them, come in three varieties. Priquana, which means first undying, are the simplest of the creatures, capable of menial work and everyday tasks. Vohquana, which means warrior undying, are, as the name implies, creatures intended for fighting. Vohquana comprised the bulk of the Inconnu armies, but they are far from the only creatures in the Necromancer's Art, as this tome will explain further.

-Excerpt from *On the Necromancer's Art*, by Corberin of Draymed

Damn, Blink thought to Erick, *I forgot how much Corby likes to blabber.*

Erick smiled. Corby had talked almost nonstop since they left Draymed over two hours ago, pausing only to catch his breath or let the others answer the occasional question he posed. Even now he patiently explained to Elissia how the city of Kal Adan, situated on the southwestern edge of Zakerin, held superiority over her sister city, Kalador.

Elissia bore it with fine humor, occasionally rolling her eyes at her cousin's pedantic tone. Erick found the younger boy's chatter enjoyable and informative. Their talks when Corby visited the manor revolved around either Draymed or Erick's life as a Necromancer. It surprised Erick to discover how much Corby knew about the world outside their small town.

The young scholar also displayed an engaging, odd wit, and entertained them all with stories and jokes.

After an especially humorous jest, Erick said, "You're quite entertaining. You should consider becoming a bard."

Corby blushed. "I've thought about it. But if I get in front of more than five people, I become shy and clam up."

"Five people?" Elissia said with a rueful grin. "More like anyone other than me. This is the most I've ever heard you talk."

Corby blushed even harder. He moved to run his hand across his hair but stopped when he hit the wide-brimmed hat. "I just feel comfortable around the three of you." He reached into the sack at his side and pulled out three apples, offering each of his companions one.

Erick walked and munched on the fruit, overcome with giddy delight. His book sack and herb box weighed him down. The bandage around his neck itched. His curly hair, drenched with sweat, clung to his ears and forehead, and his shirt stuck to his damp skin. The sword scabbard banged against his calf and made it difficult to walk. The loose shoes given to him by Corby chafed, and he would have blisters before sundown. His stomach rumbled, the fruit doing little to sate his hunger.

Despite it all, he had no desire to complain. He walked on the road, traveling to places he hadn't formed in his imagination or read about in books. Even the prospect of guards starting out from Draymed to track them down for what amounted to kidnapping didn't dampen his enthusiasm. He had lost a great deal, but Blink had been right. Once he fixed what his father had ruined, he had a chance at his own life. In the bright, hot day, such a prospect seemed easily in reach.

They crested another hill and a plateau extended before them. Covered with high green grasses and dotted with bright red and purple flowers, it terminated against the Keys, which stretched as far as Erick could see.

"Hardly worthy of being called mountains," Corby said, spotting the range. "You know the tallest one, up near Spire, is barely over a thousand feet." Corby launched into a discussion of the range.

Erick only half-listened to Corby's lecture, instead pondering his best method of reaching Broken Mountain would entail, and beyond that, how he and the other Necromancers would defeat Eligos. He found it difficult to imagine and again wished his father had taught him more about combatting the Master of Shadows. He wondered how much of his father's lack of tutelage had been the influence of the *Teloc Sapah*. Had the book never come into their lives, would he be better versed in combat with the *Inconnu*? Had the book not existed, would he have ever needed the knowledge? The questions circling each other like vultures picking as his brain were enough to give him a headache.

"Well, can I?" Corby asked.

"What?" Erick had lost all thread of the conversation.

"I asked if maybe I could read some of your books sometime."

Bewildered, Erick stared at Corby. How had they gone from mountains to his books?

"No," he answered quickly.

"Why not?"

"Because they're none of your business."

Corby dropped back, and the smile disappeared from his round face. "Of course." He quickened his pace.

Erick still felt confounded. In all their talks, Corby had never asked to see his books. Had thinking about the *Teloc Sapah* somehow put the thought in Corby's mind? Did the book have that ability?

No, Blink said. *Elissia commented that the books looked heavy and Corby said he would like to read them sometime. Nothing more sinister than that.*

Oh, Erick thought. Elissia frowned at him, and Corby walked quietly—a first—with his gaze fixed straight ahead. Erick, who couldn't remember pouting past the age of seven, thought fourteen was a bit old for such behavior. But he had acted poorly.

"Corby, I'm sorry, but my books are only readable by Necromancers."

Corby slowed down until Erick and Elissia caught up. "Why?"

"We're the only ones who can read the language. Part of the Covenant with Caros was that the remaining Necromancers would never teach others the Art because they might be tempted to use it for the wrong reasons."

"I can understand that," Corby said. "You should have said so in the first place."

"Sorry, you caught me thinking about something else."

"Have you ever been tempted to use it for your own purposes?"

"No," Erick answered with great sincerity if not total honesty. It tempted him every time he used it, always whispering how he could do so much more, but his father had taught him well the dangers of such thinking—lessons Darric would have done well to heed. And Blink always stood ready to pull him back from dark thoughts if resistance became too difficult.

"I'm glad to hear that," Corby said as he removed his hat and fanned his face. "To be honest, your power frightens me."

"It frightened a whole town, so don't feel bad."

"Did I ever tell you about..."

Corby launched into another anecdote, but Erick didn't pay much attention. Corby's question had brought another disturbing thought in a day full of them. What if the other Necromancers didn't have the same qualms about their abilities as he did?

An hour later the grassland gave way to more farms; these covered primarily with potatoes and turnips. Harvesting had begun, and groups of field hands worked at pulling up the tubers. Some waved to the quartet, while others ignored them.

Soon after passing the fields, the group entered Roadfork Village with the noon sun beating down. Blink landed beside them as Corby explained the village had been so named because of its position at the juncture of the eastern arm of Keystone Road and the southern road to Jungledeep.

The hamlet offered a half-dozen well-kept, brown wooden buildings, all geared toward travelers. The group decided to eat a midday meal at the tavern that served as the village's center point.

"My father and I ate there once on a trip to Keyport, so I can vouch for the food," Corby said. "Not that it would matter since it's the only place in the village that serves food, so it's either eat there or go hungry."

"Do we have time to stop and eat?" Erick asked, mindful of possible pursuit.

"We need to eat," Elissia said, "so we have to take the chance. Plus, I think we all need some water. At least I know I do. We might want to get you some better fitting clothes too, and pick up some water skins." She turned to Blink. "You should wait somewhere out of sight."

"Why?" Erick and Blink asked in unison.

Elissia pushed a hank of black hair from her face. "Trust me; you won't be welcome in town."

"If he's not welcome, then I'm not. Either he comes in, or we go around." Erick said.

"You need to eat."

"You can bring something to me."

"But-"

"I have an idea," Corby said.

He removed his hat and ran a hand across his hair. It surprised Erick the scholar hadn't rubbed it to the roots. "Blink can pass for a gargoyle."

"That's the stupidest-"

Corby held up a hand, and Elissia stopped. "I imagine no one here has seen a gargoyle, as they are not indigenous to this island, and I'm certain no one has seen a homunculus. But gargoyles are known as friendly, even out here, and are considered lucky. Their skin is greener than Blink's, but again, I don't expect anyone will know the difference."

Elissia didn't look happy, but she turned to Erick. "Are you sure?"

Erick nodded.

"Okay, but don't be surprised if we get asked to leave."

Erick discounted Elissia's pessimism, but as soon as the quartet stepped into the tavern, the amiable chatter of the noonday diners died like a rain-doused fire. Several men with the plain clothing and weathered features of farmers stood and left their unfinished meals, their eyes avoiding Erick and the others.

The overweight proprietor frowned at the departing men, but his round eyes grew wide as his waist when he spotted Erick and his companions.

A trio of men in one corner muttered amongst themselves as they studied the group. Another patron, dressed in the rugged leather and homespun cloth of a road traveler, slid past them with a sidelong glance and exited. The half-dozen or so who remained seemed stuck between a desire to leave and abject terror. They all stared at Erick, and it seemed as if the tavern itself held its breath.

"Have none of you ever seen—" Corby started.

"Don't bother," Elissia said. "Now you see why he needs to wait outside?" she asked Erick.

Erick spoke so everyone could hear him. "No, I don't. He has as much right to be here as anyone."

"Maybe, but is it worth dying to prove a point?" Elissia whispered as she nodded toward the three men in the corner.

Erick didn't know what seasoned fighters looked like, but the trio certainly matched his imagination of such people. All were well-muscled, and each bore some manner of scars. One had a jagged weal that ran across his face from forehead to chin, similar to Keven's but much worse. Erick shuddered to think how the man survived such a blow. Large two-handed swords sat against the wall behind them, within easy reach. "Maybe we should all leave," he said.

"I'll go," Blink said, and several people gaped at hearing Blink's voice. Either because he actually spoke or because it came out a smooth, rich voice that belied the homunculus's appearance, Erick didn't know. "I won't stay where I'm not wanted."

I'm sorry, Erick thought.

Don't be, Blink thought back. *At least you tried.*

Blink waddled out the door, and the tension lessened, although the warriors still eyed them. The others returned to their meals. The proprietor, sweating from either nervousness or his obesity, took their order and served them quickly, as if he wanted them gone as soon as possible.

Erick studied the tavern's patrons. The warriors aside, these villagers were interchangeable with the citizens of Draymed. The same brown hair, the same drab farmer's outfit of sack pants, long-sleeved bleached linen shirt, and mud-coated boots. They offered occasional glances at the new group, eyes full of fearful curiosity.

When they finished eating the dull fare of goat's cheese and boiled chicken, they left the tavern to find Blink missing.

Where are you? Erick thought.

Relax. I'm on the outside of town in a small valley.

Erick connected through Blink's eyes and figured out his familiar's location. It surprised him to find Blink in the air.

"He's this way," Erick said as he started to walk. The others followed.

The sound of laughter and clapping greeted them before they reached Blink. They found him fifty feet past the town's last building, in a small dip in the road. He hovered twenty feet in the air, holding a young boy in his claws. On the ground, five other children provided the joyous sound they'd heard, while the lad in the air screamed, "Higher, higher."

"Melteth's tits," Elissia swore. "Blink, what in the name of the Festering Hells are you doing? Get down here."

Blink glanced at Erick, and Erick nodded. Blink flew down and settled the child gently on the ground before landing beside Erick.

"What are you thinking?" Elissia repeated. "If the townspeople saw..."

"Calm down, 'lissi," Blink snarled back, baring his pointed teeth. "The children asked for rides, and I said yes. They don't have the same problem with me as others do."

"You idiot. What if you dropped or hurt one of them? What if someone spotted you?"

"What if they had? Am I supposed to spend this entire trip skulking and hiding?"

"Maybe."

"Like hell."

"We should leave," Erick said. He had never seen Blink this irritable, and he found the familiar's anger toward Elissia disconcerting.

"Fine," Blink snapped. He rolled his eyes at the children. "The 'grown-ups' are making me leave."

The children groaned in disappointment and watched as the group walked down the road in awkward silence.

What is wrong with you? Erick snarled mentally.

I'm pissed, Blink spat back. *We're wandering homeless toward scary unknown places and most likely getting killed for the trouble.*

This is hard for me too. You think I wanted the manor to burn down and be forced to leave behind everything I know? It is scary, but being mad about it isn't going to make it any better. Weren't you the one who said I had to do this?

Yes, but that doesn't make it any easier for me.

Why didn't you bring this up sooner?

Because I thought I could handle it. But I don't know if I can. It's too much too fast. And if I can't even enjoy what fun there may be on this 'adventure,' what's the point?

Blink sounded ready to cry. Erick had never seen his familiar so upset. *Please, Blink. I'm going to need you to help me through this.*

Blink didn't offer anything back for several seconds. *I'll think about it. Just leave my mind now.*

The homunculus broke off the connection, and they crept through a break in the mountains known as Passgate Gap. Even the loquacious Corby remained silent. The peaks of the Keys, covered with mahogany and roble trees that scattered the sun through their large branches, loomed on either side as they walked through the gap. The dimmed light did nothing to improve the oppressive atmosphere.

Erick strained his neck as he tried to see the tops of the hills. He had often seen these tors, barely visible from his manor, but never considered how tall they were. From this vantage point, Corby's assertion that they weren't mountains did nothing to convince Erick. He wished he could offer some comfort to Blink, some way to convince him it would all be okay. But he couldn't, not honestly, and that scared him as much as Blink's uncharacteristic behavior.

E lissia wanted to boot Blink in his squat gray ass. She also wanted to kick herself for not expecting him to do something so stupid. She watched Erick's back as he walked, head up, staring at the mountains, no doubt mad at her for being mean to his familiar. They were both so naïve. It gave Erick a frustrating charm, but he and Blink needed to lose it quickly. Guilelessness was inconvenient at best and could turn deadly. Her father had pounded that lesson into her since age seven; it was one of the few she still accepted.

Erick could be taught, and no doubt the unfriendly reception in the tavern opened his eyes. Blink posed another problem. Impulsive as a toddler, he couldn't be trusted to stay hidden, and it wasn't fair to expect it of him on such a long journey. But he needed to remain out of sight if he wanted to stay alive. Elissia had to convince them of the situation's seriousness, a difficult thing if Blink believed she fought against him. She considered the options as they walked.

But the tense silence and dark, brooding faces kept her unable to focus. After an hour, she tired of the sullen mood and halted on the road. "All right, everybody stop."

The others paused, and she saw their surprise. With nothing planned, she went on instinct. "Blink, I spoke rashly because you startled me. I didn't mean to spoil your fun, and I'm certainly not trying to be anybody's boss, but the world is a much harsher place than you think it is. If one of those warriors had left and seen you with that boy in the air, no amount of explaining would have kept them from killing you, or us."

"But they *didn't* see me," Blink retorted.

Elissia forced herself to not shout at him. "They didn't there, but what about the next town?" She looked from Blink to Erick. "I thought living in Draymed would have at least taught you that people are frightened by what they don't know or understand. Blink, you will be the first homunculus anybody has ever seen. You are going to scare everybody. You need to be unobtrusive. Otherwise, someone will kill you."

"Not without a fight, they won't."

"Maybe not, but how is dead with a fight any better than dead without one? And it's not just you. The rest of us could end up dead, too, because we would do everything to protect you. Do you want that?"

"No," Blink said, raking the ground with his claws.

"Good, because not only do *I* not want to die, I also don't want you to die. I like you, you miserable toad."

After a moment, Blink smiled; his needle-sharp teeth made Elissia shiver, and she knew him. How were they ever going to get him through towns without confrontations?

"I'll try to behave," he said grudgingly.

"Be careful. And if you're not sure, ask. I'm not an expert, but I have traveled outside of Draymed, and so has Corby. That's worth something." She offered Blink the expression she knew worked on most of the young men: head lowered, her eyes, lids half closed, peering through the strands of black hair that hung over her face. Making her voice the height of self-mockery, she said, "Forgive me?"

Blink grinned again. "How can I deny a face like that?" He looked over at Erick, still smiling. Elissia followed his gaze and found Erick blushing.

"I still think he could pass as a gargoyle," Corby said.

"Maybe," Elissia conceded. "Once we get off the island, into a bigger city. But for now, let's keep him hidden. Deal?"

They all nodded, Blink the slowest to respond. She nodded back. "Let's walk. We're wasting time."

The Keys gave way to a small band of foothills and then rolling grassland. The lighter, adventurous mood returned to the travelers. Corby continued telling stories and jokes, and once even burst into a tavern song.

The grass eventually turned into farmland. Stalks of corn taller than Erick surrounded them on both sides of the road. Birds flittered through the vegetation, ignoring scarecrows staked high above the plants.

With everyone in better humor and the sun descending, casting a beautiful orange light across the corn, Erick almost forgot about the possibility of pursuit. It slammed back to him as the sound of hooves overtook Corby's singing.

"Someone's coming," he said.

"Shit," Elissia said. "We should have had Blink watching from the air."

"We need to hide."

Elissia looked back the way they had come. "Too late."

Erick turned and spotted two horses in clear view. He stopped since running was useless and hiding no longer an option. Fear buzzed through him.

The horses drew close to reveal two soldiers from Draymed Erick recognized from the night that changed his life. They wore the blue and gold tabards of the royal guard, and Erick caught the glimmer of chainmail beneath. Sweat beaded their foreheads, the part not covered by their leather caps. They wore similar clothing, so Erick could barely tell them apart, except that one had a crooked nose.

The one with the nose spoke in an authoritative voice. "Erick Darvaul, Elissia Torin, and Corberin Scolis of Draymed, I am here on the orders of Brannon, Captain of the Royal Garrison of Draymed. You are to surrender your arms and return with us."

"Not a chance in hell," Elissia said.

Before anyone could react further, the corn shook like a wind storm had descended upon it as a group of armed men leapt from the vegetation and surrounded them.

1 2

The Necromancers are anathema to all we stand for. They take the gifts of Krinnink, Talan, and Caros and pervert them for the foulness they call magic. Herbs meant to preserve life are mixed with blood to create mockeries of life. Grasses intended to heal are debased to bind unwilling souls to corrupted flesh. The oath of all healers must be to offer no succor to Necromancers. Though we are sworn not to harm, nowhere is it written that we must aid. Those who practice the Foul Arts are to be left to die.

-Balana Noreth, Prime Chirurgeon of the Holy Order of Healers

Ten swordsmen sprang from the corn on either side of the roadway and scrambled to block any retreat.

Blink leapt into the air, tail arched over his back, and hovered above Erick. The wind rustled Erick's hair. The guardsmen drew their swords. Erick backed up, expecting to be ridden down, but the two men turned to face the new arrivals.

Elissia whipped a dagger from her boot. She shrugged off her pack. Her nimble arms slipped under the straps until the bundle fell away. Corby readied his blowpipe and placed himself between Erick and the ambushers, pipe in one hand, iron-tipped staff in the other.

He also slipped his pack, although dealing with the blowpipe and staff made it much less graceful.

The men carried broadswords and wore loose-fitting leather jerkins covered with crisscrossed strips of metal rings. Half of the men had splintered wooden shields. Two wore dented metal pot helms. Erick recognized one of them as the road-worn man from the tavern who had left after the farmers.

A burly man with tremendous arms, greased brown hair, and a missing left ear stepped forward. "Put your packs back on. We want the curly-haired one and the animal. The rest of you may go."

"Animal?" Blink bristled from above.

Elissia rose to her full height, still half a foot shorter than the smallest bandit. "You'd do best to let us pass unmolested if you wish to see the sunrise tomorrow."

Erick goggled, astonished at her defiant attitude.

The crooked nosed guard spoke up. "You are interfering with the business of Queen Alekita's Royal Guard. Be on your way."

The bandit chuckled, revealing a mouthful of stained teeth, two of them capped with silver. "There's always someone who wants to be disagreeable." He pointed at Corby with his sword. "How about you, young one? I'm not fond of killing children or men of learning, but you wouldn't be my first of either."

"He's my friend, and I'll protect him," Corby answered. He held up the blowpipe. "You'll be the first to die."

The leader sighed. "I hate having to do extra work." He waved a hand.

The bandits attacked, rushing forward with swords raised.

The assailants had taken no more than two steps when Elissia let her dagger fly. Corby blew into his pipe, sending the dart sailing toward the leader.

Elissia's knife slammed into an unprotected throat. The bandit went down gurgling. No sooner had the dagger left her hand than another appeared. She backed away, aiming for her next target.

Corby's dart hit low. It sank into the leader's leather armor but failed to penetrate the cured hide.

The crooked nosed soldier charged forward, while the other

remained frozen. With an awkward tug, Erick pulled his sword from its sheath, head and heart pounding.

He retreated from three men, waving his sword at them in full, slow arcs. Noise and movement surrounded him, forms hard to distinguish in the long-shadowed light of the low sun. Cries of pain and the whinny of horses reached his ears.

Blink flew toward the attackers. He barely avoided a nasty slice across his leg as one leapt and made a quick upward slash. Blink flapped his wings, lifting higher into the air.

Keep them busy, Blink thought to Erick.

Do I have a choice? Erick thought back.

The attackers spread and surrounded him on three sides. He retreated as they advanced. Trying to watch all three at once, he was focused on the man at his left when the one on his right attacked.

DROP! Blink screamed in his head. Erick collapsed. The sword passed over with a terrifying whistle. *Roll back.*

Erick rolled, losing his weapon. Three swords thudded into the dirt around him.

Run.

Erick jumped to his feet and fled through the high corn as fast as he could.

～

E rick disappeared into the grass, pursued by three bandits. Elissia couldn't do anything for him. He had Blink to help him. She found Corby in more immediate danger. As promised, he had taken the leader out first. His second poisoned dart had pierced the man's cheek and put him down, screaming in agony. Before Corby could reload, another attacker slammed him to the ground, his sword cutting a deep notch in Corby's staff. Elissia ran in behind the man and delivered three rapid stabs to his kidney, punching the sharp blade through the leather armor.

Roaring, the man staggered forward and whirled to face her. He swung his sword in a wide, wild arc as dark blood gushed from his back. Surprised at his resilience, Elissia tried to retreat. The flat of the blade caught her across her upper arm. Pain, instant and staggering, flashed across her arm. The blow's force sent her skidding several feet on the dirt road. She fell. On instinct, she dropped her dagger and cradled her injured arm. The pain dimmed her vision.

"Elissia," Corby screamed from far away.

The bandit stood over her, ready to kill her. She had given her life to save Corby. Her last thought, as the sword descended, was how disappointed her father would be that she had turned out so noble.

But the blow didn't land. The bandit's forearm fell to the ground, sword thudding across the dirt. Blood sprayed from the stump left by the Royal Guardsman's sword and spattered Elissia. She rolled away with a grunt of disgust and wiped at her face. The man wheeled on the mounted soldier with a disbelieving stare. The cavalryman drove his weapon through the bandit's chest. His face went vacant and his eyes glazed. He fell to the ground with a watery sigh.

"Look out," Elissia shouted as another bandit ran toward the guardsman. Too late. The bandit launched himself into the air. He slammed full body into the soldier, unseating him from his horse. They crashed to the ground. The horse fled with a terrified whinny. Elissia rolled away to avoid being trampled. She shielded her eyes from the dust thrown by the animal's hooves.

When she uncovered them, she found the soldier with blood gushing from his mouth. The bandit yanked a sword free from the man's chest and turned toward her, a leer on his ugly face.

"Leave her alone," Corby screamed as he charged the bandit. Holding his staff like a spear, he smashed the rounded butt into the man's face. His nose crunched and scarlet blood spattered. The man fell back. Corby followed and slammed the staff against the man's head.

Corby struck the bandit repeatedly, the staff sounding the crack of bone and splitting of skin. Madness filled Corby's brown eyes, a blood rage Elissia had never seen. It frightened her so much she had to force herself to rush her cousin and push him away. He wheeled on her, and she feared he might swing.

"Corby, he's dead. You got him."

"What?" Corby said. He looked down at the bandit. The man's

head had become an amorphous blob of red, white and gray. Blood and bits of soft gray tissue covered the end of Corby's staff. The fear on her cousin's face tore into Elissia's heart.

He ran over to the corn and vomited.

~

E rick forged his way through the corn. Green blades and yellow silk whipped at his face. A twinge of guilt at leaving the others pulled his conscience. But he could do nothing for them other than die. Footsteps and grunting came up behind him; he didn't dare look back. *At least I won't see the blow that kills me.*

After a few seconds, he caught a stumbling thump among the footfalls. *One down,* Blink told him. *Keep running.*

Erick's breath grew short. He hadn't run this far or fast for years. The corn nicked his hands with shallow, painful cuts. He didn't know how much longer he could keep going. *Hurry up.*

No sooner had he thought it than another bandit dropped.

Two down, Blink thought.

The remaining man's footsteps ran frighteningly close. Erick tried to push harder but had reached his limit. His breath came in ragged gasps. He wouldn't last much longer. He was going to be caught, despite Blink's efforts.

DROP! Blink yelled again, but too late. A sting slashed across Erick's back. He cried out at the pain. He fell, flipped once, and landed on his back. An ear of corn landed beside his head, the crushed kernels sweet in his nose. Dazed, Erick saw his attacker looming, dimly outlined in the twilight. The man raised his sword.

Desperate, Erick scuttled on his back. Three stinging cuts ran across his palm. Blood welled from the lacerations. Thankful the corn had done the work for him, Erick reached out and grabbed the bandit's leg.

At the contact, the man's *nanta,* the life force of his soul, slammed into Erick. Though tinged with the taint of unnecessary violence, it was still healthy and vibrant. Drawing on the power of *Elonsha,* Erick tugged at the *nanta* and drew it to himself. He didn't have to pull hard; the *nanta* almost forced itself into him.

The man stiffened. The blade fell from his hands. Erick barely noticed the steel as it hit the ground beside him. Energy coursed through him as he drew out the man's vital essence. The man collapsed and lurched sideways into the corn, crushing several stalks. Erick continued to absorb his life. Unlike the rotten onion scent of *Elonsha*, the *nanta* had the rich aroma of freshly baked bread. Erick could feast upon such energy for days and never grow tired of the vigor flowing through him. He could—

Erick, stop it, Blink's voice shouted into his brain. *You'll kill him. Stop.*

I can't, Erick thought back. *I don't want to.*

Something heavy slammed into Erick. The smell of bread disappeared, but the vibrancy remained, tingling through his scalp and tickling the ends of his fingers. It slowly dissipated and Blink loomed over him with a wide-mouthed frown.

"What were you doing?" the homunculus asked.

"Protecting myself," Erick said.

"But you almost killed him."

The unconscious man's unnaturally pale blue skin and shallow breathing slammed Erick with the enormity of what he had almost done. A whispering laugh echoed through his head. He shivered. The Necromancer's Covenant forbade him from killing by his hand. To do so risked leaving him too open to *Elonsha's* corrupting influence. Killing the man by physical means would have been damning enough. To do so in the way he almost did, by absorbing the *nanta*, would have almost certainly destroyed his soul.

"Thank you," Erick said, in a shaky voice. His father had told him to use the soul drain only as a last resort, and only if certain he could control it. Had he not used it, he would be dead. But had Blink not stopped him—

"It's why I'm here," Blink said. "But you have to be more careful."

"I know," Erick said. "Father never told me how good it felt. It's better than—well, I can't describe it. But I never want to use it again." He tried to shield the lie from Blink but didn't know if he succeeded.

As he stood up, Erick looked at his hand. The lacerations had disappeared. He probed for the scratches on his face only to find them not there. "How is my back?" he asked, turning it to Blink.

"Completely healed," Blink said.

Erick also had no fatigue from his run. "How are the others?"

Erick connected as Blink lifted into the air. Elissia ran in their direction. One soldier stood by his horse, but they saw no sign of Corby or the other soldier.

Blink waved at Elissia and yelled, "We'll be right there." Elissia returned the wave and turned toward the road.

Erick disconnected from Blink. "Where's Corby?" he asked, expecting the worst.

"I can't see him. Let's get back."

Erick studied the man he had drained. Some of his color had returned, but he still looked sick. "Do you think he'll be okay?"

"As long as he doesn't die, does it matter?"

"What about the two you hit? How long will they be out?"

"At least until morning. I gave them a heavy dose."

Erick moved toward his companions, wiping corn silk from his shirt as Blink took to the air.

He emerged from the corn to find Elissia waiting for him. The soldier without the crooked nose stood by his horse, pale and unmoving. Corby stood beside the corn, bent over, hands on knees and mouth open. Relief filled Erick at the sight of the still-living young scholar. "Is he okay?" he asked Elissia.

"I don't think so," Elissia said. "It's his first time."

"First time?"

"He's never killed anybody before."

"Neither have you, but you're not sick," Erick said.

Elissia gave him a strange look, seemed about to say something, and then shook her head. "Are *you* okay?"

"Yes. Blink protected me. I'm sorry I ran."

"You had no choice," Elissia said. "It was three to one. You wouldn't have survived."

Erick found her assessment harsh, even if true. "You're hurt," he said, pointing at the splotches of blood on her face and blue top.

"It's not mine." She wiped at her face.

Bodies littered the road. Blood soaked into the dirt, turning it muddy brown. Erick winced at the bandit with the missing arm and smashed head and frowned when he spotted the crooked-nosed soldier with his chest pierced. "What happened?"

"I'll tell you later," Elissia said. She turned to the surviving soldier. "There's four of us and one of you. We don't want to fight you, and it looks like you don't want to fight anybody. So what are you going to do?"

Erick considered Elissia's words and noticed the sweat on the soldier's pale face. His weapon rested in his holder, and he had no blood on his armor. He'd done nothing during the fight.

The soldier removed his helmet, revealing short brown hair, and wiped at his face. At that moment, he appeared younger than any of them, scared and alone. "I need to take Geran back."

"Leave him," Erick said.

"What?" the soldier asked.

"What?" Elissia repeated.

"Does he have a family?"

The soldier nodded.

"Then tell them Geran fought bravely, and he will continue to serve as a true soldier, working for me."

"What are you doing?" Elissia asked out of the side of her mouth.

"What I know how to do," Erick whispered back. "Trust me."

She nodded, although uncertainty marked her face. "You can also tell Beatru or Fathen or whoever sent you not to bother sending anyone else," she told the soldier "We'll be off the island before they can find us. The mainland is vast, and I'm skilled at hiding. They lost. Accept it."

The soldier nodded again, misery clear on his face. He donned his leather helmet, mounted his horse, spurred it into a gallop, and left them behind.

Elissia turned her attention to Erick.

"We need protection," Erick said. "You're both good in a fight, but I'm not. Blink can only do so much. I need someone else. *We* need someone else."

"But he's dead," Elissia said.

Erick cocked his head at her, and Corby, still leaning over at the side of the road, spoke up. "He's a Necromancer. Dead isn't an obstacle."

Her almond eyes widened, and her mouth formed its cute O of shock. "You're going to make him a zombie?"

"No, I'm going to call him to service from the Heaven of Caros, if Alakaneth has deemed him worthy to go there."

Elissia narrowed her eyes and stared at him. He waited for her reaction. Finally, she said, "It makes sense. Things certainly would have gone worse if he hadn't been here." She shrugged her arm, winced, and looked around at the other bodies. "Why not raise them all?"

Erick shook his head. "Lots of reasons, not least being I don't have enough supplies. But we wouldn't want the bandits. Having died so recently, they'd retain enough of their memories to know why they died, and I would have difficulty controlling them."

"That would be bad," Corby said, and Erick thought the scholar went even paler.

"We need to keep moving," Elissia said. "How long will it take?"

"Not long."

She nodded and walked toward the middle of the road. Erick pulled out the bag of herbs she had given him and sorted them, hoping his friends had grabbed the plants he needed.

He found a piece of willow bark, thankful someone in Elissia or Corby's family enjoyed willow tea, and placed it beside the dead soldier. A movement caught his eyes. Corby sat on the road, a blank expression on his face. Elissia removed a coin pouch from the belt of one of the dead men and emptied four small bronze coins from it.

"You're taking their money?"

She looked up, black hair hanging over half her face. "They won't need it anymore."

It didn't seem proper, but Erick couldn't say why. She was right; they wouldn't need it anymore. He supposed it was only fair, a payment for their attempt to kill him and his friends. Still, something bothered him. *Is it wrong?*

Disrespectful, maybe, Blink answered. *But I don't think they deserve respect. And considering how she probably feels about what you're getting ready to do, I wouldn't push it.*

Erick noticed Elissia watching him, almost as if waiting for a rebuke. He shrugged. "I guess you're right."

Her eyes blinked twice, and her mouth opened slightly. After a moment, she nodded and went back to her work. "Are the other three dead?"

"Yes, Blink killed them," Erick blurted. He didn't like lying but feared if he told the truth, the men soon *would* be dead. More blood he didn't want on his hands. Stealing from bodies he could tolerate, but he couldn't accept killing unconscious men. He didn't know if giving permission to kill on his behalf violated the Covenant, but he wouldn't take the chance.

He stared at Elissia, unsure what to think of this dagger-throwing, body-looting killer who knelt nonchalantly beside a cooling corpse and examined a rolled parchment she had removed from it. Her actions spoke of an unpleasant past, but he imagined accepting such circumstances were about to become a huge part of his life.

Elissia removed the leather tie from the tan scroll and unrolled it. "Blink, get the pouches from the other bodies and any daggers if they have them."

Blink looked at Erick.

Go ahead.

Blink took off.

"I should check your arm," Corby told Elissia.

"It's fine," Elissia said, even as she flexed the arm in a circle and grimaced. "Just bruised and tender. At least it's not my weapon arm."

"What happened?" Erick asked.

"I got hit with the flat," Elissia answered. She didn't even glance up from her reading, as if such events happened every week.

Erick returned to his work of summoning Geran back. Newly dead, Geran returned easily, requiring only the willow bark, a drop of blood, and a short incantation. He was a *sohquana*, the highest form of *quana*. Created from a fresh corpse, the *sohquana* had some reasoning powers and autonomy, but they gained nothing beyond the abilities they had in life.

Corby inspected the corpse with his scholar's interest. "We'll have to hide the hole in his chest."

"There are some other things we'll have to do," Erick said. "*Elonsha* will give him the illusion of life for a few weeks. After that, other things will begin to happen that we'll have to hide."

"What things?"

"You don't want to know."

"I'm a scholar."

Pleading danced in Corby's wide brown eyes, a need to have his mind occupied. Corby had killed a man. Not just killed, based on what Erick saw, but brutalized. In some way Erick couldn't understand, Corby wanted Erick to help him. "There's going to be deterioration," he said. "We'll have to mask the smell and disguise the decay. Or, more likely, release him from the binding and try to find another means of protection."

Elissia walked over to Geran, who now stood motionless, his eyes unfocused. "Is he okay with this? Is he even aware of what's happening?"

"He is aware that he has been returned from the Heaven of Caros to aid a Necromancer, as required by the Covenant. In a few moments, he will be able to understand all of us, but he can only communicate with me."

Elissia nodded, but Erick thought a slight shiver ran over her body. She held up the unrolled scroll she had been reading. "I'm not sure we want you to go into Keyport."

"Why not?" Erick and Corby asked in unison.

"Tell me if this person sounds familiar." She read from the parchment. "'Target is a Zakerin boy between fifteen and eighteen years of age, five and three-quarters feet in height, with a slight build. Hair is brown, shoulder length and loosely curled; eyes are pale blue; skin is fair, with no known scars or markings. Might be accompanied by a stunted, gargoyle-like animal, three to three-and-a-half feet tall, with a large nose, protruding brow, clawed hands and feet, a tail ending in a stinger, and pale blue eyes.'"

Erick gulped as Elissia continued to read. "'Targets are to be killed on sight and heads or bodies brought to Kalador base.'" She held the scroll out for Erick to take.

"Animal," Blink fumed as he rejoined them carrying three daggers and one small leather pouch. "There's that word again. I'm not an animal; I'm a familiar. There's a big difference. And I'm four feet. That's not stunted."

Elissia offered the scroll to Erick. The symbol at the bottom almost made him drop the parchment. Three rings, a large circle flanked by two smaller ones, with a vertical line piercing the largest. "The mark of the *Eligoi*," Erick said.

"The what?" Elissia asked.

"Assassins loyal to the *Inconnu*," Erick told her. "*Eligoi* are what attacked the manor."

"These men weren't trained assassins," Elissia said. "All things considered, they weren't even great bandits. If they had been, we wouldn't be having this conversation. They must have been a backup plan."

"Could a bounty have been placed on Erick and Blink?" Corby asked.

Elissia shook her head. "A bounty would mention a reward. These men were specifically hired. The leader said something about a contract." She pointed at one of the bodies. "Anybody recognize this one?"

"He's from the tavern at Roadfork," Erick said.

Elissia nodded. "Bounty or not, I'd bet others are searching for you. Keyport isn't safe. We got lucky this time, but we can't count on that."

"But we have to go to Keyport to get a ship."

"I know, so we're going to have to disguise you." She studied Erick for a moment. Reaching out, she ran her fingers through his hair. The electrifying sensation surged down his spine straight to his groin. Mercifully, she only did it twice before backing up. "That's what we'll have to do," she said. "I'm going to town to get supplies."

"To town? But you just said it wasn't safe."

"It's not safe for you. I'll be fine. And I'll be back quick as I can."

"I don't like it," Erick said. "One of us should go with you."

"I can move faster by myself. There's nothing to worry about. They're not looking for me."

Erick already knew winning an argument with Elissia, once she made up her mind, was harder than catching a fly. "Can I at least let Blink keep an eye on you, in case anything happens?"

She seemed about to refuse, then smiled at Blink. "That's a good idea. It should be dark enough by the time we reach town for you to hide easily."

"Will shops even be open?" Corby asked.

"The ones I need will be," she said. "You two should clear the bodies off the road and then hide."

Elissia turned and walked toward town, while Blink took to the air ten feet above her.

Erick and Corby began working, taking the bodies a few feet into the corn. The death didn't bother Erick, but he could tell by Corby's shallow breathing and complexion, wan even in the golden light of the setting sun, that the corpses were almost more than the scholar could handle.

"Are you okay?" Erick asked.

Corby nodded and swallowed. "I'll deal with it. I have to."

Erick nodded. He knew if Corby wanted to say more, he wouldn't hesitate to speak.

A few minutes later, the rotten onion scent filled Erick's nose, and a brief flash of yellow flew from the sky and struck Geran. The soldier straightened up and said, "I am here to serve."

Corby almost dropped the feet of the body they were moving. "That's unnerving."

"Sorry," Erick said. He knew Corby only heard a deep groan or growl.

They had soon cleared the bodies and settled in the grass on the opposite side of the road to wait for Elissia.

"Have you ever killed anybody?" Corby asked.

Erick shook his head. "I can't." He paused. "Well, I can, but it would be dangerous for me to do so."

"But Blink can?"

143

"He can if necessary, but he shouldn't when at all possible."

"I don't understand why he can and you can't, when, from the way you've explained it, he's a part of you."

Erick shrugged. "It was a bargain made by gods, dealing with a power of evil difficult to comprehend. I don't understand all of it either."

They were quiet for a moment, when Erick asked, "What's it like? Killing someone."

Corby didn't speak immediately, and Erick thought maybe his friend wasn't going to answer. "I honestly don't remember much of what happened. I saw him about to attack Elissia, and then everything went black. When I came back, I had done-" He waved his hand in the vague direction where they had left the smashed bandit, "that. It's..." he paused and shook his head. "I don't want to talk about it right now."

Erick nodded. Remembering what his mother did for him when he was upset, he put his arm around Corby's shoulders. The scholar tensed for a moment then relaxed and laid his head against Erick. They sat in silence, Erick unsure what he could do to help Corby, as the sun disappeared.

Elissia returned an hour later, as the last light disappeared from the sky. Corby had fallen asleep against Erick's shoulder. She had a strange expression as she emptied the bag she carried, revealing clothing, scissors, and a shearing razor. Corby awoke at the noise, then jumped up and moved away as if Erick had caught fire.

"You okay?" Erick asked.

Corby nodded, walked over to Geran, and studied the undead soldier.

Nonplussed, Erick turned back to Elissia. "What are those for?" he asked, even though he already knew.

"We can't do anything about your height or the color of your eyes, which leaves your hair as your most distinguishing feature. At least they don't know about the gash in your neck, so that's to our advantage too." She reached back in and pulled out a dirt brown robe with long, flared sleeves. "We can disguise you as an acolyte to Krinnik. They shave their heads upon acceptance into the order."

"I don't know anything about Krinnik's doctrine," Erick said.

"Acolytes aren't expected to know much, and I'm sure Corby could give you enough tidbits about their dogma to let you pass."

Erick sighed. So many changes, and now another one. It was a small thing, but his mother had been the only one who ever cut his hair. It seemed to Erick that letting someone else cut it insulted her, a way of saying he no longer cared about her.

I think she would understand, Blink thought. *To save your life, you do what you have to do.*

Erick considered a moment. *You're right.* "Okay," he said. "I guess we all have to get used to changes from now on, don't we?"

That we do, Elissia thought as she glanced at Corby, who studied Geran like a fisherman might examine his latest catch. The change in her cousin today had frightened her, and she hoped it wasn't permanent. The viciousness Corby unleashed on the mercenary went beyond anything she had ever witnessed. Corby had always been the stoic one, the solid one. She was counting on that during this journey. For any number of reasons, she didn't even want to consider the prospect that he might come unhinged,.

"I'm afraid so," she said. She laid the brown houppelande on the ground and pointed at one of the roadside boulders. "Let's get our hair cut so we can go to town."

"Our hair?"

"Yes, I'm going to trim mine, too. Not as drastically as yours, of course, but it's gotten too long for running around and fighting thugs. As my wretched father says, 'Shortest is safest.' Come on."

As Erick took a seat, Blink reached into the bag, pulled out a hooded cloak, and put it on.

"What's that for?" Erick asked.

"It's my disguise."

"If he has to walk with us instead of flying," Elissia said, "he can keep this wrapped around him, and he'll look like a young child. It's not great, but it's better than nothing." She held up the scissors, tilted Erick's head forward, and set to work. She noticed him wince during the first few clips. "Stay still."

"Sorry," he answered, voice tight. Elissia wished she could feel as deeply about her parents as Erick did about his. Different lives. Erick had parents who had cared for him, something Elissia could only dream about. She pushed the self-pity back into its bottomless pit and concentrated on changing his appearance.

~

An hour later, four travelers walked into the lamp-lit streets of Keyport, their passage seen by few. Those who noticed them paid little heed to the unremarkable group. It was merely a young acolyte to the earth god Krinnik, a soldier, a scholar's apprentice, and a young girl, either sister or concubine to one of the others.

Had they paid more attention, they might have glanced up to see the winged creature that followed the quartet, flitting from rooftop to rooftop, a wadded cape and bulky sack in its talons. But people were either heading home or to the alehouse, and neither destination lay in the sky. They kept their eyes forward and their minds on their own concerns. The travelers made it to an inn—*The Eel's Gills*—unscathed.

13

Harken all who would love Caros. The Father of All resides in his house in heaven, watchful over his children. The strength of Caros shall be your strength. The wisdom of Caros shall be your wisdom. The words of Caros shall be your word. Attend then, to the passages within, so that they may fill you for all your life.

-Opening of *Testament of Caros: The Tome of the Father and Mother*

Unable to sleep, Fathen walked through Draymed, past the homes of the slumbering villagers. He had changed into a plain yellow cotton robe, bereft of any ornamentation save crimson cuffs. A breeze blew through the hamlet, carrying lingering smells of baked fish and warm bread. Fireflies gleamed and a dog barked in the distance. It was the sort of summer night Fathen would enjoy if he could escape his sullen thoughts.

His dark mood had begun as soon as he spoke with Erick and learned the fate of *his* book, burned by the Caros-cursed boy. To make matters worse, Erick's father had returned as a ghost, a perversion of Caros's will. Shame burned in Fathen that the spectral figure had frightened him away. He asked forgiveness for his cowardice. As usual, he received no answer.

He brooded through the day, roaming aimlessly, much as he did at this late hour. He remembered nodding absently at the townspeople he passed, his practiced blank face concealing his contempt for Draymed 's inhabitants. A face he had worn ever since Perius Oerus exiled him to the island twenty years ago as punishment for his vision, a vision the timid elders of the Temple didn't share.

Caros ruled the other gods. Why then, Fathen reasoned, did the Temple of Caros not reign as sovereign lord over the other faiths? It had been so in the past when clergymen with courage and strength kept the minor temples in their place. But the leaders grew complacent, and, bit by tiny bit, the other faiths slipped from beneath the Temple of Strength, growing in power, challenging the might of Caros's priests. It happened so subtly few noticed it and grew so prevalent no one questioned it.

Faith is faith, the elders told him. Except for the unrepentant Melteth and the insane Vadali, it didn't matter which power people revered as long as they worshipped. So what if Talan's Luminary had more power in Starrasen? Who cared that few thought of Caros in the northern mountain ranges of Amelan, where the clerics of Krinnik held sway, placing the sun god as a pawn to the earth god's will?

The idea of other gods venerated above Caros offended Fathen to his core. He had grown up steeped in the belief. Faith had been drilled into him by a father who reinforced his dogma with a backhand, and a stern-willed mother who punished less than total devotion by withholding food and love. Fathen entered the priesthood as soon as possible and never left, his life devoted to the only True Temple.

Unable to suppress his anger at the sublimation of his deity, Fathen espoused his views to any who listened. Some agreed, but few admitted it openly. Those who opposed him did not hesitate to share their condemnation.

When words no longer worked, he grew militant and preached that all faithful followers of Caros must take up arms and fight to reclaim their god's just position. If the other faiths would not capitulate peacefully, then forceful subjugation became a necessity.

Within two weeks of his first such speech, Fathen found himself on a boat, exiled to Draymed, where his combative leanings would go unfulfilled.

Fathen's nocturnal wandering brought him to the guardhouse. He stared at the lamplight shining beneath the door. The prisoner who'd burned Erick's manor and tried to kill the Necromancer rested inside. As the aggrieved, Erick had the right to name the prisoner's punishment. But when Brannon had sought Erick out, the captain had discovered him missing.

In due order, it came to light that Elissia and Corby had also left. Good riddance to them all, Fathen thought, but Beatru had been outraged. She had demanded Brannon send guards after them, certain Erick had enthralled her niece and the scholar, and they now traveled as his slaves. Fathen knew Erick's powers didn't work in such a manner but did nothing to dissuade the incensed woman. With any luck, the two guards would bring him back in irons. Better yet, maybe Erick would resist, and they would kill him.

If the man inside the guardhouse had succeeded, Fathen would be in bed, slumbering soundly, feeling avenged for Darric's insult. The Necromancer had dared to lay hands on a priest of Caros, an affront that should not stand. But bereft of the Temple's support, and knowing the futility of any attempt to persuade the apathetic town, which had let the immoral family reside unmolested for years, Fathen could do nothing but let the offense fester in his heart.

As he stood outside the door, he wondered why someone would seek to kill Erick now.

Ask, a voice whispered. Fathen whirled around. The bright moonlight allowed for few shadows, but Fathen peered into those and found nothing. Draymed lay silent except for the muffled crash of the waves and the chirruping insects that sang through the night.

He opened the guardhouse door and walked inside. The guard on duty—Bereman—glanced up from his whittling on a piece of oak and nodded. He wore a long-sleeved brown shirt and gray pants but had not bothered with armor or weapons. His thin gray hair reflected silver in the lantern light. Old and withered, Bereman had retired his commission half a decade ago, but the recent death of one Royal Guardian and injury of another left the unit short-handed. Brannon had re-commissioned the aging soldier for light duty until replacements arrived from Kalador. Bereman was not talkative, which suited Fathen. He grabbed one of the chairs and dragged it in front of the cell. The unnamed man sat awake on the bed.

"Has he slept?" Fathen asked.

"Not a wink," Bereman answered, eyebrows twitching as he squinted to better see the priest in the dim light. "Nor eaten. Only took a sip of water this evening and then spit it out."

Fathen lowered his lanky body into the chair and studied the prisoner. Nothing at all imposing about the man. Light bronze skin, black hair, muddy brown eyes. He could easily have been any one of the thousands of Zakerin farmers and spicers that inhabited the island. He had an instantly forgettable face. That trait alone made him an ideal assassin. His clothing, all black cloth, was the only thing that marked him different. Black was the color of Melteth, the Night God, worn only by thieves and apostates. Zakerin law declared such clothing illegal except for a strip of silk or dyed cotton worn about the neck for those in mourning.

"Why did you try to kill the Necromancer?" Fathen asked.

"I am Eligoi. I serve the will of Eligos." The prisoner answered in a flat voice

Fathen started at the man's pronouncement. The *Eligoi* were a cabal of mythical assassin-priests loyal to the Master of Shadows. The man lied. Indeed Eligos once existed, and maybe the *Eligoi* had been real, but that had been over a thousand years ago. Eligos was not a god. Even if he somehow survived the betrayal of the Necromancers, he would still be long dead.

"Are you a cultist?" Fathen asked. Perhaps the prisoner belonged to a secret order, worshipping a forgotten master, much as covens existed that prayed to the Festering Demons, and sects that revered Alaisanatha, she who fled from Heaven. The Paladins of Caros hunted such factions, so it stood to reason groups existed that sought to put the Necromancers to death. It was the only reason to explain why three assassins—a rare breed found only in the larger cities—would travel five days across the ocean to attack a seventeen-year-old boy.

"I am *Eligoi*. I serve the will of Eligos,"

"Eligos is a thousand years dead. How can you serve him?"

"I am Eligoi. I serve the will of Eligos."

Fathen continued for five minutes, trying different questions but getting the same response. Frustrated, he decided on a more direct method. Turning to Bereman, he said, "You must be hungry. Go get something to eat."

"I'm not supposed to leave the prisoner alone."

"He won't be alone; I'll be here. Now leave us be."

"But Brannon said-"

"Brannon is not here. Depart," Fathen demanded.

Bereman hesitated, then turned and hobbled out, closing the door quietly. With the exception of that willful child Elissia, and Brannon, who split his spiritual loyalties between Caros and Sangara, the people of Draymed behaved as a true flock.

Fathen lowered his head, resting it in his palms. His black hair, unbraided, hung almost to the floor. He hoped the prisoner understood the significance of the guard's departure. "Why did you try to kill the boy?"

"I am Eligoi. I serve the will of Eligos."

"Eligos is dead," Fathen snapped

The guardhouse turned cold. Fathen shivered as the chill blew through his thin yellow robe. For the briefest moment, his breath fogged before him, but no sooner had the frigid air appeared than it left. His heart thudded. The tiny room had changed. All the lanterns still burned, but darkness crowded the chamber, the air oppressive. Claustrophobia pushed in on him. If the prisoner noticed any change, he gave no sign.

Not dead, a voice whispered, and Fathen whirled in the chair, a shout lodged in his tightened throat.

He noticed the darkness beside one of the beds. A deeper shadow that pulsed and danced in the corner, murkier and more solid than the flickering lanterns should allow. Fathen stood.

Stay, priest.

The voice whispered in his head with such force that Fathen stumbled back to his seat, all thoughts of approaching the shadow gone.

"What...what are you?" he asked, his voice little more than a raspy croak.

I am a fragment of He That is Served, and I want the Necromancer dead for the same reasons you do.

Fathen's eyes narrowed as he tried to discern a form in the shadow, a person hiding behind some evil-inspired cloak of night. But the pulsating mass held no shape, and to gaze at it more than a few seconds made Fathen's head throb. Some inner voice begged him to depart and speak no more to this formless shade, but curiosity rooted him. Curiosity and not a little fear at what the shadow might do if he tried to leave. "I don't want him dead."

You lie, the whisper stated. *This very day you spoke a wish to kill him.*

"I spoke out of anger."

You spoke the truth of your heart, without fear, as you once did. Why do you wish the boy dead?

"I don't," Fathen said.

Why were you angry?

"If you know about this afternoon, then you know why I was angry."

The shadow, though still pulsing and shapeless, grew taller. *Do not be smug, cleric. You have no right. Tell me why you were angry.*

Fathen shuffled in his chair, chagrined rather than angered by the reprimand. "He destroyed something that belonged to me."

What?

"A book."

The Teloc Sapah? *The Dark Words?*

"Yes," Fathen answered.

That is a book of great and terrible might, with the energy to conquer a continent. How did it come to be in the hands of a lowly cleric of Caros?

Fathen bristled at the insult. He prepared to claim the book as an inheritance, but the belief that this strange entity knew the truth stopped him. "I took it."

Stole it? From whom?

"From the Temple. It angered me to be sent to this island, so I decided to take something they held dear. They tried to study the book to learn how to defeat its creator, should he return. A waste, since the book's author was long dead and would never return." Fathen wondered if his rigid belief in Eligos's death had been misplaced. "The scholars had scant success in deciphering the book, but I decided they would study it no longer."

He should stop, but now that he had started, something inside him broke, like a dam holding back a lake of putrescent water. It spewed forth, pouring over the gates of his tainted soul and spilling from his mouth.

"They kept in the archives, under lock and key, with a constant guard, but I did not care. I wanted to make the Temple pay for their weakness.

"Getting the key from the archives master was as simple as walking. He was an old monk, half-deaf, who slept like the dead."

Fathen shivered at his choice of words and then continued. "I snuck into his chamber and retrieved the key from his dresser. The door guard was not so easy. I had to catch him by surprise and subdue him. I took the book, returned the key, and boarded the ship the next morning, the book hidden deep in my trunk."

Relief came to Fathen, and he only now realized how much he had wanted to tell the story. He had no one in town with whom he could have shared this, not even his faithful acolytes. But this blot of shadow, this shapeless darkness, would not judge his actions.

Subdue? An interesting word choice. There was a hint of wicked humor in the whispered voice.

"What do you mean?" Fathen asked.

You have been honest with me, but to know true power, you must be honest with yourself. Did you subdue *the guard?*

"Yes," Fathen answered, hesitant.

His thoughts returned to that night, memory blurred with the distance of time. He approached the guard, a youth of no more than eighteen, flush with the excitement of his first position of responsibility. Fathen stood before this youngster—the face of a child dressed in the steel and leather of a warrior—and held the archive key aloft, professing an errand for the archive keeper. The guard, following his orders, would not allow him passage, stating only the archive master and those accompanied by him were allowed after sundown, and only then by special dispensation from the bishop.

Fathen tried pleading, begging, and cajoling, but the young guard took his duty seriously. Fathen grew insistent; the guard remained obstinate. Angry and frightened of rousing others, Fathen drew his heavy-hilted dagger. He would knock this child senseless with a well-aimed blow to his unprotected temple.

He delivered a precise, unexpected blow, but what should have been the rounded pommel had become the pointed blade. Instead of a solid thud, a sickening pop sounded as the dirk pierced the skin, a grating hiss as metal slid between bone, and a hollow rush as the soldier exhaled a dying breath. The splash of warm blood struck Fathen's hand as he pulled the knife away, stunned and dismayed. He had not wanted this to happen. This-

"-was an accident!" Fathen said, his mind returning to the present. "It was an accident. I only meant to knock him unconscious."

An accident? You wanted to kill that boy. He made you angry, and you wanted to kill him like you want to kill Erick. Isn't that the truth?

"No."

Look deeper.

"It's not true."

Look deeper. The darkness lunged from its corner and surrounded Fathen. It swirled about him. Its shadowy bulk blocked the lantern light and blinded him to the room.

In removing the distraction of light, the darkness showed Fathen his genuine self. Stripped of rationalization, bereft of false memory, and shorn of all pretenses, the truth lay bare before Fathen, the reality he had denied to preserve the illusion of his sanctity. The revelation staggered him, and he slumped over.

The shadow returned to its corner. *Tell me the truth. Tell yourself the truth.*

"I... I wanted to kill him," Fathen said, his voice choked.

Why?

"He made me angry," Fathen agreed. "The soldier disobeyed my wishes. He countermanded a direct command from a senior priest. He needed reprimanding. To disobey the righteous is death, so says the Tome of the Father and Mother."

And the Necromancer has made you angry?

"Yes."

He has insulted you, burned your book, and turned others in the town against you.

"Yes," Fathen said, his voice hard.

The Necromancer needs to be reprimanded, doesn't he? To defy the righteous is death.

"He deserves punishment." Fathen frowned. "But he has left town, and I don't know where he's going."

I know his destination. I will help you find and punish him if that is your wish.

"It is. But what aid can you be? You're nothing but a shadow and a voice in my head."

The whisper took on a menacing tone. *Have you not learned the shadow is always stronger than the light? As soon as your blade pierced that boy's brain, you fell under the shadow. You are denied the light. You have preached the words of your dying god for twenty years, but what have you done? Have you saved anybody?*

Fathen tried to speak in his defense, but the relentless voice went on.

Have you ever offered comfort to your fellow believers, or counseled them with words of wisdom? No. You give them rote passages from an ancient book that has lost all meaning to you, and you fill them with blandishments you barely remember. Do you know why?

"Why?" Fathen asked, voice trembling, face flush.

Because your faith abandoned you, and when you killed the youth, your dying god abandoned you.

"That's not true," Fathen shrieked. "I am still beloved of Caros, and he guides my heart."

That is the truth you wish. Here is the truth you know. Once again, the cloud leapt toward him, surrounding his head and body.

He witnessed clearly—as if it happened now and not twenty years ago—his arrival on the island. Bitter and filled with gnawing guilt at his theft of the book, he had no sooner stepped into his new chapel than the townspeople assaulted him with their petty complaints about the lack of rain, or the scarcity of eggs in their henhouses. Their provincial grievances aggravated him, but he struggled to fit in and accept this congregation as his own. He failed and soon found himself dreading every encounter with the people, knowing he would need all his composure to not scream in their faces.

Then Darric visited him, and things turned worse.

Seeking vengeance against both the theft and the violence to his person, Fathen worked to rally the town against the family on the hill. He told them the Necromancers were foul spawn of the dark god Melteth, servants of demons, and the will of Caros demanded they be destroyed. He railed and pleaded and threatened, but could do nothing to overcome the lethargy of the townspeople. As a last plea, he told them of Darric's threats against the village, but he sorely miscalculated the depth of fear hidden beneath the tranquil surface. Rather than being angered, the villagers grew terrified. They vowed to go nowhere near the manor. Livid but powerless, Fathen hid his anger beneath a placid grin that soon became his fortress, walling off his rage.

Fearful of being interrogated about the theft of the book, he waited six long months before sending word to the Temple in Kalador. Without offering a reason, he asked for permission and a cadre of paladins to rid the island of the death mages.

In the guardhouse, blinded by the darkness that showed him light, Fathen shook with rage as he remembered the responding letter, signed by Perius Oerus, the Prelate of Zakerin himself. A long-winded missive, full of details outlining Fathen's responsibilities, it boiled down to one sentence which had burned into the cleric's brain. "The family of Necromancers is sacrosanct to all ten gods, as you should well know, and you are to avert hostility away from them."

Fathen shredded the letter but obeyed the edicts, his loyalty to Caros still outweighing his hatred of the Temple and Darric. He swallowed his bitterness and hostility and slowly learned to ignore the house on the hill.

As the years passed, his rage faded, replaced by a dull, pervasive resentment toward life and those around him. His sermons turned lifeless, becoming—as the voice said—a bland recitation of words that had lost all meaning. His plans for the subjugation of the other doctrines lay dormant, almost forgotten.

But the dreams began to return, brought to the fore by the swirling miasma. The Temple had sent no communication in over a decade. They had forgotten him, abandoned him. Even Caros had deserted him. There had been a time when the sun god spoke to his heart, Fathen seemed to remember, but it had not happened for untold years.

"It's all true," Fathen agreed in a strangled voice, sick at the loss of his salvation and the waste of his life. Twenty years bereft of a god, and he hadn't known it.

Your dying god has forsaken you, but there is another who will claim you. It is time to deliver your forestalled vengeance. Darric is dead, but his son still lives. I will help you find him.

"What must I do?"

In this form, I can do nothing. I require a talba, *a container for my essence.*

"Again, what must I do?"

"Kill me."

Fathen nearly fell from his chair. Speaking to the formless shadow, the priest had forgotten the prisoner. "What?"

"Kill me," the prisoner repeated, standing at the bars. "I have failed my master. He will take my body for his *talba,* but I must die for him to do so."

"I can't kill you."

Your spirit is already damned. There is no hope. There is only revenge. Without me, you will not have it. Perform this deed, and I will help you find the Necromancer. You will leave this island behind forever.

"But I can't just kill him."

You will also destroy the Temple that wronged you. Together we will crush it, and you will rise as the leader of a new Order, a cult more potent than any your dying god ever conceived.

The words struck like music on Fathen's soul. He envisioned himself filled with passion before a congregation, a gathering that flocked to hear his words sound out with fervor, a feeling he had almost forgotten. He would lead, and they would follow. Fathen, leader of the Order of–

"Eligos?" Fathen said to the shadow.

Yes, the shadow answered. *I am returned, brought to life by the energy of your book. I offer you power and worship that Caros would never give you. We will crush his followers—those who spit upon you—and bring up a new religion, and you will be there in the beginning. You will become my Eloa Ecrin, my High Priest. All you need do is kill the one who has requested it. As you have killed before. To kill is to kill. It is the same in calm as in anger.*

The prisoner stood with his arms spread, his chest pressed against the bars. "I am ready. I give my will the grace of Eligos. Although you kill me, I will still serve my master."

Fathen hesitated. If he were truly damned, the killing would not matter. But what if his soul were cleansed, his sin forgiven by his loyal service, however perfunctory?

You must decide soon. If the guard returns, I will depart, and I will ensure you remain on this island until you rot.

That decided it. Fathen had no wish to remain chained to this forsaken village any longer. The thought of power after so many years of subjection burned through him and ignited his fervor. The man offered himself as a willing sacrifice. Didn't true belief always demand sacrifice?

Moving quickly, to complete the deed before he could consider it, he grabbed a dirk from the rack on the wall and stepped to the jail cell.

"No, you must strangle me. The body cannot have a mortal wound."

"Choke?" Fathen asked. "I can't—"

The man reached through the cell bars and slapped Fathen. "Be a man and not a cur. Prove you have the courage to do more than run from ghosts."

Enraged at the man's audacity, Fathen grabbed him around the throat and squeezed. The man gasped, his eyes going wide, but he did nothing to stop Fathen.

Fathen closed his eyes, not wanting to see the man die. But every wheeze and failed attempt to draw breath drummed on his ears and vibrated through his hands. It took longer than Fathen would have imagined. Tears stung his eyes as he squeezed harder, feeling the spasms of the man's throat.

At the last, the man's hands went to Fathen's arms, too weak to have any effect. They slipped away, and the man grew heavy. Fathen let go, stepped back, and opened his eyes.

The man slid down the door until half his body lay on the floor and half pressed against the bars. Death glazed his open eyes.

A deep scream bounced through Fathen's mind, a paralyzing sound of agony. Gone in a moment, it left him dizzy, stunned at the realization at what had been lost to him forever. He had sealed his fate, and he would never know the peace of the Heaven of Caros. But if Eligos could live a thousand years, then he could too. Perhaps he could live forever, and never know the torments of hell.

Fathen sensed rather than saw the shadow moving. He turned to face the body. The shape slithered across the floor like a blot of the blackest ink. It slid over the corpse until it covered the body. Then it sluiced into the body, like liquid absorbed by a towel, until none remained. His breath shallow, Fathen moved closer to the motionless body.

The corpse blinked; Fathen fainted.

14

Light has gone, where has it gone?
Grace has gone, where has it gone?
Darkness abides, now my only friend.
Blessings cursed, now my only fate.
-The Apostate's Lament, Unknown

Fathen regained consciousness on the floor. Sharp pain in his right elbow told him he had landed on his arm. The prisoner stood in the cell with no evidence of his recent death.

Fathen sat up, weak, nauseous, light-headed. "What happened?"

"I have taken over this body, and it is now my *talba*," the man said, voice soft but less whispery than the shadow. "Release me, so we can depart before others arrive. With luck, we will reach the Necromancer before he leaves Keyport."

As Fathen stared at the unimpressive face of the man he had just killed, but who now stood alive as a newborn babe, his stomach roiled in anguish at his irrevocable decision.

He pushed the dread aside. He must be content with his choice. He had served Caros for twenty years, and what did he have? Nothing. Perhaps Eligos could serve him better.

Fathen used the cell bars to pull himself to his feet. The dizziness dissipated as he walked across the room and snagged the key off a nail tacked into the wall.

The key turned in the lock. The door swung open without a sound. The prisoner stepped out.

Fathen tensed, expecting an attack now that Eligos no longer needed him. Instead, the man said, "Thank you, *Eloa Ecrin*."

Pleased, Fathen nodded. "Master."

"Not master yet," the reborn man said with a cold smile. He walked to a cabinet against the wall, opened it, and fished out five daggers. Thick bands of shiny wax sealed three of the dirks inside their black scabbards.

"What do I call you, if not master? Eligos?"

"I am not truly Eligos yet, and that name would bring undue attention. Call me by the name that belonged to this meat. Andras."

"Not Eligos yet? I don't understand."

"I will explain when there is time." He walked to the small rack of weapons. After a glance over the armaments, he grabbed one of the standard swords issued by the Royal Armory in Kalador, three feet long, formed from steel smelted by Court blacksmiths.

After a few experimental swings, Andras frowned. "Children forged this toy, but it must do until I find something suitable." He sheathed the weapon and held it out to Fathen.

Fathen looked at the scabbard. "I haven't wielded a sword in over fifteen years."

"The skill returns quickly, and you will have use of this before we are finished."

Fathen took the sheath from Andras and drew the sword. It felt right, as if a missing part of him had returned. He swung it, recalling his training under the captain of the Temple Guard, a bald man whose name Fathen had long forgotten. His awkward strokes were not as clumsy as he had feared. Fathen sheathed the weapon and buckled the belt around his waist.

"Can we leave town unnoticed?" Andras asked.

"At this late hour? Easily."

"Do you have any coin?"

"Some," Fathen said. "I never had much need for it here." After the briefest hesitation, he added, "There are items in the fane we can sell in Keyport. They're mine as much as anybody's." *Just as the book was yours?* A voice asked in his mind.

"Retrieve them. I will meet you beyond the posts. Give me your sword, so you don't arouse suspicion, should you be spotted." Andras' voice took on a menacing tone. "Do not betray my confidence, or your death will come quickly—and with great pain."

Surprised as much as frightened by the unexpected threat, Fathen said, "I have damned myself beyond hope of redemption to see my desires come to pass. Why should I betray you?"

Andras's muddy brown eyes revealed a sinister spark that had not been there before his death. As those eyes appraised Fathen, a cold wind passed through him, and he caught a scent of rotting onions. He shuddered but never turned away from the assassin's gaze.

"You are right," Andras said at last. "You have no reason to betray me, but neither did the Necromancers."

Fathen broke off the stare and turned to the door. "We'd best leave before Bereman returns."

As if summoned by the words, the older guard opened the door and walked through, followed by Brannon. Engaged in conversation, they strolled five feet into the building before they saw a stunned Fathen and a free, armed prisoner.

Fathen stood immobile as Brannon reached for his sword. Before it cleared the sheath, a *whisk* sound flashed past Fathen's ear, followed by another. Both men dropped to the floor, Bereman with a dagger in his chest and Brannon with one protruding from his unprotected throat.

Fathen ran to the fallen soldiers. Bereman's eyes glazed over as blood darkened his brown shirt. Brannon struggled, his breathing wet and gurgling. He tried to grip the dagger in his neck, but his hands held no strength. His dimming eyes beseeched Fathen. "Run for help," he managed through the blood foaming in his mouth.

Fathen placed his hand on the guard captain's forehead. "May Alakanath see you safely to the heaven of Caro-"

Light flashed before Fathen's eyes. Searing agony ripped through his head. He fell, hands clasped to his temples. His tongue had grown too large. He gasped for air, swallowing to clear his gummed throat.

Andras bent down and offered his hand, which Fathen grasped like a floundering swimmer reaching for a thrown rope. As soon as their palms touched, Fathen's vision cleared and his throat opened. He sucked in air as his body convulsed.

Andras gave him a grim smile. "Those gods are no longer yours to hear your prayers. You may wish to refrain from saying their names in reverence."

With a sharp tug, Andras helped the priest stand. Fathen remained rooted as he waited for his wobbly legs and quaking body to still.

Brannon struggled to move. Andras went to him and knelt. He looked into the captain's eyes, grabbed the knife, and twisted. With a last spray of blood, Brannon lay still. The reborn man yanked the dagger out and wiped the blood on the captain's blue tabard. Stepping past the motionless Fathen, he retrieved the other knife from Bereman and cleaned it. "Are you fit to travel?"

The shakes were disappearing. Fathen offered an unsteady nod.

"Dim as our chances are, we will try for Keyport before the weekly ships to Kalador sail."

Andras walked toward the exit, and Fathen followed. His first step almost sent him to the floor, but his strength returned by the time he reached the door. He stood at the threshold and glanced at the two bodies. He knew the proper emotions: despair, sadness, and pity toward the victims, people he had known. But rather than those, he felt vindicated for Brannon's actions on the night they went to Erick's manor, and a sense of elation that he was leaving this accursed town. A scrap of regret tried to intrude into his happiness, remorse for the unnecessary death of Bereman. The emotion turned to anger as he realized Bereman now ascended to the Heaven of Caros, a place forever barred to Fathen. He turned away and found Andras watching him with a satisfied smile.

As they left the guardhouse, Andras spoke in his grave, whispery voice. "Welcome to the shadows."

∼

F athen easily slipped into the fane and gathered the few valuable items of silver and gold, taking great pains to avert his eyes from the tapestry of the sun, the house of Caros, which hung above the pulpit. He feared it might burn him as if he stood before the actual God and not a woven representation. His plunder tucked in a burlap sack, he left the temple without a backward glance.

They passed the twin white posts marking Draymed's border. Fathen wondered what the town would make of the deaths and his disappearance, but realized he didn't care. He no longer tended the sheep of Draymed.

He looked at Andras, the man who died from strangulation and now walked as if he never experienced the cold hand of death, and shuddered. "How did you rise from the dead?"

Andras glanced at him. "If you mean this body, it did not rise from the dead. It is a *talba*, a container that holds my fragmented spirit, as a wineskin holds liquid. If I were to leave, it would drop like the rotting meat it is."

"What about the soul?"

"Andras's soul. It is no more. I absorbed it for its energy to bind to the *talba*."

Fathen tried, but couldn't comprehend the idea of a soul no longer existing. Before thinking about it could drive him mad, he pushed it away. "What did you mean when you said you were not yet Eligos?"

"Enough questions. I am weary, and we must use our concentration for walking."

"Answer this last, and I will ask no more tonight."

The dangerous flash appeared in Andras's eyes. Fathen feared he had pushed too hard, but Andras turned his attention to the road.

"The *Teloc Sapah* is a book of great power," Andras said. "The *balitum Eligos*, the ritual of summoning the Necromancer Darric performed, was intended to bring forth a portion of my essence to guide the summoner. No doubt that is all the Necromancer wished. A fraction of my being to question, to learn from, maybe to torture with the knowledge of my imprisonment.

"When the Necromancers betrayed me, they sealed my spirit in the

Aesir, a realm where nothing penetrated. Even my solitary thoughts were muddled, scattered by the emptiness that surrounded me. Occasionally I would hear the briefest voice, a fragment of ritual that tried to find me, but never enough for me to grasp.

"But this time was different. The pull of the ritual came through, faint but clear. A tendril of *Elonsha* wormed its way past the numbness, and I grabbed hold and sped down the thin strand. The Necromancer may have wished guidance or power, but I saw a chance of escape. Knowing the power fed to the ritual would not be enough to allow me to slip my prison, I used what little I had to consume the Necromancer's mind. The moment I arrived I sensed the *Elonsha* surrounding Erick and I commanded the father sacrifice his son. This would give me the power I needed and more.

Andras's voice grew grim. "I did not count on the father's resistance to my will. In the weakness forced on me by the ritual, I could not crush him. He refused to forfeit the boy and ended his own life. I revived him as a vampire, and the boy destroyed the creature. I underestimated them both. It will not happen again. The father is dead; the son will soon follow."

"So if Erick is killed, you will be freed of your prison?" Fathen asked.

"Yes. The power that runs through him is such that I will be freed and have excess *Elonsha* to revive my brothers from their state of death. I have sent my thought out to the *Ecrin* who still serve the Fist. They seek the other Necromancers to destroy or seduce to my cause. But Erick shall be sacrificed to my glory and complete what his father started. Now you understand why I want the child destroyed."

Fathen nodded grimly. "It will be a pleasure to cut his throat for you myself."

∾

They traveled through the night, pressing for Keyport. Despite the torturous stride Andras set, the sky began to lighten with no sign of the town. Instead of slowing, Andras walked faster. Fathen moaned as he tried to keep pace.

Shortly before the sun broke over the horizon, Andras stopped in the middle of the road, so abruptly the priest almost ran into him. Andras stared at the road. Fathen followed his gaze.

"What do you see?"

"Blood," Andras answered, pointing at dark splotches on the packed dirt. He followed the stains and signs of struggle and found the dead men laid out in the rows of corn.

"Bandits?" Fathen asked.

Andras shook his head. "Mercenaries. Hired to capture Erick. We-" He stopped, body tensing, hand moving to his sword.

"What-"

Andras hissed Fathen to silence. "Listen," he whispered.

Fathen strained but heard only insects buzzing and the scattered chirps of early birds.

Andras sprang further into the field, his sword out. Fathen fumbled to draw his weapon and follow while trying to avoid corn stalk blades striking his face. He soon lost ground to Andras's rapid stride, and the man disappeared in the green.

But he hadn't gone far. Fathen found him standing beside three men dressed similarly to the bodies near the road. Unlike the others, these men still lived. One lay unconscious and the others sat beside him. They groaned softly, holding their heads.

"What happened to them?"

Pointing to the welt on the neck of one of the seated men, Andras said, "The death mage's bastard child was busy."

"You mean that talking animal he calls Blink."

Andras nodded. "His familiar. A creature created from his essence as a protector. They are bonded for life. One of the precious gifts I gave the Necromancers before they betrayed me." He looked closer at the pale skin of the unconscious man, and a smile came to his plain face. "We almost had him. Perhaps next time."

"What do you mean?"

Andras shook his head. "Not important right now." He pulled a knife from his belt. "Take their swords and lay them over there."

Puzzled, Fathen did as instructed while Andras kicked the two conscious men to a more alert state.

"Stop!" one of them yelled, half-heartedly blocking Andras's foot. "Take what you want and leave us be."

The other stared at Andras with alert eyes, his lethargy gone. His pale skin, black hair, jet colored eyes, and bulky frame marked him as hailing from the far western land of Starrasen.

"You have failed," Andras told them. "The Fist is displeased."

"There was more than the contract said," the talkative one, obviously Zakerin, told them. "There were two soldiers, a girlchild, another boy, and the gargoyle."

"The soldiers were members of the Royal Guard sent to bring back the others," Fathen told Andras. "The girl was Elissia, a troublesome child who's smitten with Erick. I suspect the other was Corberin, a scholar who is Elissia's cousin and follows her like a toddling child."

Andras looked back at the man, who dusted himself off, trying to regain a modicum of professional pride. "There were ten of you and only six of them, three of them children, one of them a *female*. Explain."

"They fought like fury. That gargoyle struck like a demon of death. I did my best, but I was overcome." The man pulled himself up and grew bold. "I was hired for an ambush, not a fight. I demand to be paid for risking my life."

"Demand?" Andras snarled. He turned to the quiet one, whose dark eyes fixated on him. "What of you?"

The man shrugged. "I failed. In pursuit of the boy, I failed to consider my surroundings and my other enemies. I was struck from behind —and so disgraced." The man bowed his head. "My life is forfeit. The Fist do as it please."

Andras offered his cold smile. Fathen found the strange grin unsettling on such a plain face.

"Do you wish for a chance to kill the thing that cheated you of your honorable combat?" Andras asked.

"My honor is gone. It cannot be regained."

"Look at me," Andras said. The Starran raised his head. Andras locked eyes with him. Fathen unconsciously stepped back as he sensed a thin aura of power flowing from Andras toward the kneeling bandit.

"Your honor in this world is gone," Andras said, the strange, whispery quality of his voice thickening. "But in the world that is to come, your honor can be regained, as a servant of the Fist. To your people you are dead. To Eligos you are but newly born, your honor intact, if you wish it to be. All you need do is pledge your life in fealty to the *Inconnu*. Renounce your confining blood ties to Sangara and revel in the freedom of Eligos. You shall have honor beyond your dreams."

"Renounce Sangara?" the man asked in a trembling voice, eyes fearful.

"She has renounced you. Did she not allow you to be cravenly struck from behind? She cared more for the life of your victim, a *Necromancer*, than she did for you. It was she who abandoned you." The man still appeared uncertain and frightened. "You fear her retribution?"

The man nodded.

Andras laughed, a sound that made Fathen shiver. "There will be no retribution. Eligos is far stronger than your bitch goddess. He will protect you."

The other bandit swiveled from comrade to stranger with a bewildered expression. "Wh—"

"Be silent!" Andras commanded, his eyes again flashing. "Your time to speak is past."

The pale-skinned man made his decision. Bowing his head, he said, "I will accept the honor of Eligos. What must I do?"

Some deep part of Fathen's brain screamed for him to stop this, to keep this man from following him into damnation, but he ignored it. He might have forsaken Caros, but resentment toward the other gods still lived in him. If an adherent of Sangara could be turned away from worship of the War Goddess, Fathen would let it happen.

"What is your name?" Andras asked.

"Talva."

Andras again offered his bone-chilling grin. He held the dagger out to the potential convert. "Talva, your Zakerin companions have displeased the Fist. Kill them both."

Talva acted without hesitation. Before the other man could protest, the Starran grabbed the poniard, spun it so the point faced his companion, and slammed it into the surprised man's chest. A bone cracked as the knife broke a rib on its way to the man's heart. His eyes grew wide. They pleaded with Talva as he removed the knife and thrust it in a second time. The mercenary sighed and slumped to the ground.

As the man gurgled his last breath, Talva pulled out the bloody knife and scuttled the few feet to the other, still unconscious bandit.

Fathen turned away in dismay and disgust, but his ears reported the whispering of the knife as it sliced across the throat of the supine man. It had to be his imagination, but Fathen swore he could hear the blood as it poured out of the body and soaked into the ground.

An icy, onion-scented wind blew across the field, rippling the grass. A distressed scream made Fathen turn around.

Talva writhed on the ground beside his gory work. Although he screamed, he wore a smile of ecstasy. Andras stood motionless, but he appeared taller, more powerful. The air around both figures darkened. A strange surge of pride rolled through Fathen. The warrior of Sangara no longer existed; he was now one with them.

After a few seconds, the wind stopped, Talva lay motionless, and the darkness subsided. Talva still smiled. Fathen noticed the Starran bore four red, puckered scars on his cheek, two small circles and a slash below encompassed by an irregular line. It bore a vague resemblance to a skull. The priest reached up to his face but discovered no similar mutilations.

Andras walked to the convert and looked down at him. "Rise, Talva. You have proven worthy to be called disciple, so stand as one, with honor." Andras picked up Talva's sword and handed it to the smiling man. "Take your sword as a warrior of the *Inconnu*. From this day forth until you kill the winged creature named Blink, who has stolen your honor, you will be known as NalTalva, Talva the Vengeful." He held out the sword. "Do you accept this title?"

"I accept." The newly named NalTalva took the sword and sheathed it.

"For now, we will part company. But I have a task for you, to prove both your loyalty and your proficiency. When you have completed this task, come to *Twr Krinnik*, which is now called Broken Mountain. Do you know the village of Draymed?"

NalTalva nodded. Fathen winced, sensing what was about to happen.

"Go to this village, kill as many of the inhabitants as you can in any way you see fit, and burn it to the ground. Now."

"Wait," Fathen said as the Sterran turned to leave. "Why?"

"Because they hid a family of Necromancers for unknown generations, so they are enemies to the *Inconnu* and shall be punished."

"As you say." Though outwardly he shrugged, Fathen found the idea of Draymed's destruction harder to accept than he expected. But he could do nothing to stop it, and to try would only invite disaster on himself. "There is one I would ask you to spare if you can," he told the waiting killer. He reached behind his neck, undid the clasp of a gold chain, and pulled the amulet from beneath his shirt.

Disgust, and a flicker of fear, passed in Andras's eyes as the circle and eight rays symbol of Caros came forth, dangling in Fathen's hand. Fathen removed the two gold chains on his wrists and gathered them with the necklace. He held it all out to NalTalva.

"Take these and show them to Keven. You can recognize him by the scar that runs from his eye to his mouth. Show him this; tell him I now follow a better path. I would like him to continue as my strong arm. If he agrees, return him to us. If he doesn't," Fathen hesitated and had to force the words past his throat. "Kill him."

NalTalva glanced at the chains before he turned his narrow black eyes to Andras. With a frown on his unlined face, Andras nodded.

NalTalva returned the nod, took the chains, and sprinted toward the road.

"Thank you," Fathen said.

Andras said nothing as he returned to the road. Fathen followed. Perhaps the momentary rest tricked his mind, but now that he no longer wore the servitude chains of Caros, his steps came easier and his fatigue lessened.

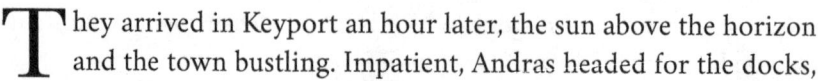

They arrived in Keyport an hour later, the sun above the horizon and the town bustling. Impatient, Andras headed for the docks, almost running. Fathen had a faint hope that despite the delay with the bandits, they would catch the ships still languishing in port—hopes that were dashed as they reached the empty berth and saw the five galleons heading out, already at least a half-mile away. Erick had escaped.

"What now?" Fathen asked, disappointment and anger turning him surly. "Will you sink the ship or give us the power to walk across water?"

Andras turned to the tall man. Speaking in a flat, toneless voice, he said, "If you are to be my *Eloa Eclin*, you must learn that I do not take blasphemy or insult as willingly as your old deity. Your dying god is distant and aloof. I am here in front of you, and there will be consequences should you question me in such a manner again. Do you understand me?"

Fathen nodded, shaken more by the evilly emotionless voice than the threat. "My apologies. Fatigue made me speak out of turn."

Andras gave a curt nod, indicating neither acceptance nor rejection of Fathen's regrets. "There are other ships that leave port, so we will seek passage on those. If none is available, we will wait out the week until the next cargo vessels leave. Do not fear that the Necromancer has eluded us. We are not the only ones seeking him."

15

The Mother says those you would love, love without reservation. But those you would hate, take care you consider the import. Hatred is easy but taints she who hates more than she who is hated. To hate is to place a dagger in your soul.

-Testament of Calea: The Tome of the Father and Mother

Erick stood on the deck of the galleon *Anakara* and watched the craft plow through the water. The three travelers stood at the bow with their undead guardian, while Blink nestled in the crow's nest, away for the moment from prying eyes. The salty air filled Erick's nostrils and excitement pounded through his body.

The sun on the horizon cast an orange glow on the water as he watched the receding Keystone Island. Wonder at the experience of traveling quickly overtook the pangs of loss.

The crisp breeze blew cool and strange across his hairless head. He ran a hand over it, finally over the nasty shock the tavern room mirror had given him last night as he saw what Elissia's scissors had wrought.

He wore the clothing Elissia had somehow acquired for him, a gray three-quarter sleeve tunic, brown pants, a thin white sash with the globe and hammer symbol of Krinnik embroidered on the ends in red stitching, calf-high leather boots, and thick gray socks. He knew he could easily pass as a junior acolyte of Krinnik, as long as no one asked any questions concerning dogma. But sailors tended toward the worship of Talan, so he believed himself safe in that regard.

The ship's rocking, as it sliced through the water sending forth sprays of foam, almost hypnotized him. Gulls followed the boat with raucous cries and swooped so close Erick could have touched them.

Elissia turned to him and asked, "How do you feel?"

"Wonderful," Erick replied. "Still sore, but better than I have in a long time."

"You don't feel nauseous?"

"Should I?"

Elissia pointed toward the side of the ship. Corby bent over the rail. He wore brown twill pants, a cream-colored shirt, and a blue waist-length doublet, sans buttons. Only his scuffed shoes and wide-brimmed scholar's hat remained from his old wardrobe. Corby held the green hat in one hand.

"What's wrong with him?"

A passing sailor overheard and replied loudly. "Land dwellers. They're all well and good until you get 'em on a ship, then their stomachs show 'em why they'll never be navy men."

Laughter rolled among the mariners within earshot, but Erick still didn't understand.

"He's seasick," Elissia explained. "The motion of the water makes some people ill. Your stomach feels fine?"

Erick nodded. "Will he be okay?"

"It should pass in a few hours. Come on, let's go see our cabins and put our gear away." She walked over to Corby. "We'll be down below if you feel like joining us."

The three cabins, though small, turned out to be comfortable, with soft beds, plush coverings, and copper washbasins. "These cost a lot, didn't they?" Erick asked.

"Almost everything we had," Elissia said. "But it's worth it. Ship travel is miserable enough without trying to sleep below decks, surrounded by sailors. I'd be too much of a distraction for them."

It took Erick a moment. "They wouldn't touch you!"

"No, they wouldn't," Elissia agreed. "But it would get annoying having to stab a few before they got the hint."

"You could have gotten just two rooms and saved some of the money for town."

"I didn't think it would be appropriate for us to share a room alone yet," Elissia told him with a wicked grin.

"That's not what I meant," Erick said. At the thought of being alone with her, his passion stirred. Thankful for the loose clothing, he nonetheless turned aside to expose less of his front to Elissia. "Corby and I could have shared a room."

Elissia shook her head. "That wouldn't be wise."

"Why?"

She hesitated and then shook her head again. "You've never slept with someone next to you, have you?"

"No," Erick answered.

"If you're not used to it, you wouldn't get much sleep. There'll be plenty of time for us all to share sleeping space, so enjoy your time alone."

"I've had plenty of time alone. I don't know that it's that enjoyable."

Elissia offered a small smile. "You'll be surprised how quickly people become annoying. Let's go to the galley and see if they have anything for Corby's stomach."

~

As Elissia predicted, Corby recovered by midday.

"Now, if I can avoid eating anything for the next five days and we don't have any rough seas or foul weather," Corby said, "I'll be as right as a quill pen in an ink bottle." He glanced at Erick, who leaned against the railing beside Elissia with the aplomb of a lifelong sailor. "Why didn't you get sick?" he asked with a touch of petulance in his voice. "Everybody gets seasick on a first voyage."

"He's right," Elissia confirmed. "I was *extremely* ill my first time, even more so than him."

Erick shrugged. "I guess I have a naturally strong stomach."

"Considering your line of work," Corby said, "that makes sense."

"Shh," Elissia said. "As far as anyone on this ship knows, his line of work is being an acolyte of Krinnik. Make sure it stays that way."

Corby squared his shoulders. "I know how to keep a story straight. But how long before someone notices Geran isn't exactly right?"

Erick had been pondering that question. As long as they kept the chest wound hidden, the soldier would pass as alive for several weeks. But all living beings felt uneasy around the undead, even if they didn't know the source of the discomfort. If the sailors tried to speak to the soldier, the ruse would slip even faster. Erick had left Geran in the cabin until he could decide what to do.

Corby's pale face gave him the answer. "Geran? You mean the soldier who's deathly afraid of water and is going to be seasick this entire voyage?"

Elissia and Corby both smiled. "Good idea," Elissia said, and Erick dared to hope things might turn out well.

Then she looked at Corby, and her smile disappeared. "You want to talk about what happened yesterday."

Corby frowned and tugged at his hair. "I'm not even cognizant of exactly what transpired."

"It's called a blood rage. It-"

"I've read about them," Corby said. "But I thought such a thing was only endemic to the Hucaran Horsemen."

"No," Elissia said. "They're known for it because they've learned to harness and direct it to great effect, but it can happen to anyone in combat."

The frown didn't leave Corby's face. "I think. No, I hope, it was just the shock of seeing you in danger, and that it doesn't happen again. I don't want to kill anymore."

"I hope you don't have to," Elissia said. "However," she told Erick, "*you* need to learn to protect yourself."

"What? That's why I have Blink. And Geran will help."

"Unless we're outnumbered, and they're both busy elsewhere. We lucked out yesterday. We can't count on that every time. You've got to fight."

"I can't kill."

"I don't like to kill either, but—"

"You don't understand." Erick stared out over the water. "I can't kill. If I do, the taint on my soul opens me too wide to the influence of *Elonsha*. I could become like my father, or worse."

"I don't understand," Elissia said, her almond eyes echoing her confusion.

"*Elonsha's* nature is malevolent energy," Erick said. "The gods shield me from the ambient power, and Blink shields me when the power is active, which is every time I use it. If I kill someone with my own hands, the stain it leaves is a way in for the *Elonsha* that can't be countered."

"But what if it's to protect yourself, or to save a loved one? Surely the Gods know the difference."

"The Gods do, and that is tallied when a person goes before Alakanath to be shepherded, but *Elonsha* doesn't care. All it seeks is the weakness; all it knows is the evil of the act itself."

"So Elonsha is stronger than the gods?" Corby asked, and Erick caught both the disbelief and underlying fear in the scholar's voice.

"More primal, possibly older, and certainly quicker to react. The gods are removed from Krinnik and act according to their own needs. *Elonsha* is here and active, and will grow stronger, now that Eligos has returned." Another twinge of anger at his father hit Erick, but he let it go. He no longer had use for such emotions.

Elissia sighed and looked at the deck. "I don't understand, but I'll take your word for it. We have a problem. You won't kill, but you have to protect yourself. Geran and Blink can't be everywhere. If you somehow get cut off from us, then-" A smile crossed her face. "Sometimes I'm too clever for my own good."

"What are you talking about?"

She reached down and pulled a dagger from her boot. "I'll teach you how to use these. Not as useful as a sword, but better than nothing. I'll show you how to aim for the legs, and how to hamstring, which will cripple your opponent with little chance of killing them. What do you think?"

Erick considered it. Blink made a fine protector, but he was not invincible. Geran might eventually have to be released, and Erick didn't know when circumstances would allow him to summon another *gateloah*. If Elissia could teach him to defend himself without having to kill, he would be a fool to pass up the chance. It also meant time spent with her. "I think you are very clever," Erick said. "I'll do it."

"Great," Elissia said. "We'll start tomorrow. Another chapter for Corby's book."

"His what?" Erick said.

The scholar blushed and appeared ready to leap over the side to hide his embarrassment. "It was supposed to be a secret."

Elissia smiled and waved a dismissive hand at Corby. "He's writing a book about his journeys with you. Right now, he's calling it 'The Quest for Broken Mountain.' Congratulations, you have your own historian."

Erick offered a small smile, then stared at the dagger in Elissia's hand as the full weight of what he had to accomplish bore down on him. Once he reached Broken Mountain, the other Necromancers would be there to share the burden, but with assassins and hired bandits hunting him every step of the way, even that simple goal seemed unattainable. "I hope his book has a happy ending."

Elissia tossed the dagger to him handle first. He managed, barely, to catch it.

"Let's do what we can to make sure it does," she said.

The following day set the ritual Erick followed, with minor variation, the first four days aboard ship. In the morning he studied in his cabin, where curious sailors couldn't glance over his shoulder and question his choice of reading material. In the late afternoon, when the air turned cooler, he practiced knife work with Elissia. First, she had him run ten times around the ship, although by the fifth time it had turned into more of a jog, which eventually devolved into a fast walk. After that, they went through a regimen of calisthenics that soaked Erick's clothing before he even held the dagger.

Practice consisted of throwing and close-in work. Elissia managed to secure a three by three board that she lashed to the foremast. Erick's first throws hit the board but bounced off. Elissia patiently taught him the proper technique for hold and release. "Think of the blade as an extension of your thumb," she said. "Wherever your thumb points, that's where the knife will go."

Erick began to grasp the concept. Soon, the knifepoint stuck in the board as often as it bounced away. When he could stick four of five throws, she backed him up another pace, and they would start over, since any change in distance changed the time of release.

"You have to learn to judge distance," Elissia said. "You'll discover your best range, and you wait for your opponent to get in that measure before you throw. Even if you miss, you may distract them enough to let you get in close with your other knife."

After throwing, she taught him how to handle the knife in close combat, showing him feints, undercuts, overhand slices, and a variety of methods for dealing with a better-armed opponent. "The best is to stop them with some well-placed throws before they can engage. But if they get close enough to swing, you have to get closer, so they can't hit you. At that point, it's about speed. You have to move in, strike, and get out before they have a chance to gut you."

"What if they're wearing heavy armor?" Corby asked as he watched one day.

Elissia grimaced. "A dagger is almost useless until you are good enough to hit the weak points." She pointed at Erick with her dirk. "So in your case, run. You'll certainly be faster than them."

The days passed with Elissia teaching and Erick learning. He improved, pegging the board from ten feet away and increasing his speed with special drills Elissia taught him.

During meals, Erick and Elissia sat together and conversed in quiet tones with their heads bent toward each other. A thrill ran through Erick's body every time Elissia whispered to him, her breath drifting across his ear.

Elissia spoke freely about her days in Draymed and offered as much gossip as Erick could stand about the people in town, most of whom she didn't like, and who didn't like her. But anytime Erick steered the questioning toward events before her arrival on the island, she would shake her head and say, "Some other time." It left Erick frustrated but resolved to wait until she was ready, assuming such a day ever came.

He once considered asking about the mysterious Marcus she'd mentioned but decided against it. She would probably rebuff the question like she had every other one about her past. But Erick's bigger fear was that she would start talking about her true love Marcus, and how she longed to see him again. So Erick left the question unasked and vowed to enjoy the time he had with her. With luck, the unseen but no doubt handsome and witty Marcus had found someone else in her absence.

At first, it worried Erick that they excluded Corby from their conversations, but the good-natured scholar soon lost his shyness and found company among the marine contingent, who gladly talked to him as he scribbled like a demented man on his sheets of parchment. One sailor in particular, a wiry, brown-haired youth with a slight limp, seemed to constantly be in Corby's company when not on duty.

"His name is Murrough," Corby told them at one of the few midday meals the trio spent in each other's company. "He's taught me about the ships and the stars and all sorts of things...things I never even knew about."

With a sly grin, Elissia said, "But you're a scholar. I thought you knew everything."

A blush crept onto Corby's round cheeks. "Not everything. There are some things books don't teach you."

Elissia arched an eyebrow. Corby returned her stare, but soon turned away, his face going more crimson. Elissia grinned and nodded. "I'm glad you're enjoying the voyage."

~

The fourth night aboard ship Erick dreamed of Draymed, and everything changed. He stood on the hill, poised above the sleeping village. Behind him, the manor lay in charred ruins, the dream so vivid he smelled the bitter tang of burnt wood. A cool breeze brought the faint roar of the surf from below, pounding against the rocks as it had for innumerable years. The half-moon hung low, casting minimal light, but Erick's dream-heightened senses allowed him to see details as though the sun hung at its apex.

He spotted a black-haired man moving through the town, his already pale skin robbed of all color by the wan moonlight. A burlap sack rested over his shoulder. He darted toward the town center, moving from shadow to shadow.

Dread overcame Erick. He recognized the man as one of the mercenaries they had encountered on the road to Keystone. One of the mercenaries he had left alive.

The man reached the town well and settled beside it as he placed the sack on the ground. With a glance around, he opened the bag and removed two misshapen lumps. Erick couldn't tell what they had been, but they were long dead. Balled clumps of insects fell from the carcasses as the man lifted them and held them over the well.

No! Erick shouted in his head as the man dropped the infected bodies. They splashed, and the landscape rippled like water across Erick's vision. Black waves followed the ripples and clung to the houses; pestilence dripped from the eaves and seeped into the windows.

The man smiled, tucked the sack into his shirt, and sidled toward the nearest house. He tested the door on the small wooden building. Finding it unlocked, he slipped inside.

Erick tried to leave the hill. He had to warn the town of the danger, but his feet remained rooted. He opened his mouth to shout an alarm, but no sound issued from his lips. His entire being cried in frustration.

The man left the building, a drawn knife in his hand, blood dripping from the jagged blade. Erick shuddered.

Every building in the village turned deep red, the walls glistening with crimson fluid, as if the murder of one family triggered the gory demise of the entire town. The intruder flowed toward the next house. Blood seeped from the structures, pooled at the foundations, mingled with the sticky black pestilence. Erick watched, impotent horror clenching his stomach.

A house burst into flame. Hungry orange fire spouted from the roof, turning the building into a giant torch. Other buildings followed. Soon the entire town blazed like a bonfire meant to warm the gods.

Erick turned from the conflagration. Beatru stood before him, dressed in a nightgown. A thin red line ran around her neck. She spoke, her voice thick. "Avenge us. Destroy the force beckoned by your father. Seek those who remain at *Twr Krinnik,* so you may redeem your father's sin. Beware the Master and watch the shadows. Shun the one who comes forth to tell lies. Beware the–"

She stopped. Her eyes widened. She moved to speak again, but instead of words, blood ran from her mouth and landed at her feet.

His feet finally free, Erick recoiled in horror as Beatru's head fell from her body. It splashed into the puddle of blood with a thick, wet squish. As the gore splattered in warm droplets onto Erick's legs, he screamed.

16

The Covenant is a disgrace, a coward's way out. Why do the Gods not intervene directly? They will leave it to the Necromancers. Countless people will die who did not have to, had the Gods stepped in and not been frightened children. This is why my mistress left Heaven and will no longer counsel her brothers and sisters.

-Gremfel of Vostra's Gap, Primeangel to Alaisanatha

Erick awoke with his hand over his mouth. Blink fell from his ceiling beam perch and landed on the floor with a thump. Erick dropped out of bed onto his hands and knees, the cover tangled around his waist falling with him. He crawled over to the chamber pot and vomited. Blink huddled in the corner, also retching.

A few moments later, he heard footsteps, a knock, and then Elissia's voice drifted through the door. "Erick, what's wrong?"

He tried to speak, but his stomach heaved again, and another spew gushed into the pot. Blink fared no better.

The door opened, and Elissia ran into the room. "Great Caros, what's wrong?" She squinted to focus in the dim light provided by the single porthole and looked from Erick to Blink, covering her nose.

"Bad dream," Blink managed to croak out. He dropped against the wall and dragged himself away from the mess on the floor.

Elissia moved toward Erick, who still held his face over the chamber pot. "Are you okay?"

Erick nodded, afraid to speak for the moment. Blink seemed in better shape, so he sent an answer to his familiar.

Blink translated. "He said to give him a minute; he wants to make sure he's empty." Erick glared at him, and Blink added, "Well, he wasn't that blunt, but that was the gist of it."

Elissia stepped over to the wash table and poured water from the pitcher into the copper basin. She grabbed a cloth, dropped it into the water, wrung it out, and returned to Erick, who had crawled to a sitting position against the wall. Realizing the cover had slipped away, and he sat naked in front of Elissia, he grabbed the sweat-drenched blanket and pulled it over his lower body. "I'm going to start wearing a nightshirt," he growled.

Elissia smiled as she placed the damp cloth against Erick's warm forehead. "I've dreamt some bad dreams before," she said, "but never any that made me physically sick. Does this happen often?"

Erick shook his head. "I've never had one this real before."

"What was it about?" Elissia asked.

Erick started to tell her but shook his head. "Get Corby. Both of you need to hear it. I have to wash out my mouth. I'll meet you back here."

"Why does Corby need to be here?"

"Because he does," Erick snapped. "Please get him."

"Okay," Elissia said, her tone placating. Erick, unable to meet her eyes, stared at the floor until she left the cabin.

After she left, Erick threw on his clothes.

"Do you think it was real?" Blink asked.

"Yes." Erick pointed to the floor where Blink's sick lay in a puddle. "It was a vision from either Caros or Denech. Normal dreams don't do that. Can you clean up for me?"

Blink nodded. Erick left the cabin and walked down the narrow passageway until he reached the galley, which housed large barrels of fresh water. A guard stood at the bulkhead to prevent pilferage of the rations or cargo. He wore a leather vest emblazoned with the twin brown bars and blue wave of the Zakerin navy, a tight-fitting leather skullcap, and a bored expression.

As Erick approached, the man extended his short-hafted spear until he recognized Erick. His bored expression returned. "What do you want?" he asked in a not unfriendly voice.

"I got seasick," Erick told him. "Could I get some water to rinse out my mouth?"

"Landlubbers. Seasick on calm seas," the man said, smiling. "Of course you can. Get some cloves, too. They'll freshen your breath."

"Thank you." Erick stepped past the guard and into the galley. A brief search revealed a tapped keg. He grabbed a large clay mug, filled it with water and rinsed his mouth, spitting several times into a nearby swill bucket. As he gargled, he spied the spice pots on a counter. He found the pot marked "cloves" and dug out one of the tiny brown buds. His mother had also used the plant for sweetening the breath. Erick never cared for the taste, but it would be better than the sour tang of bile. He wished the guilt could be so easily chased away.

To forestall the return to his cabin, he walked onto the deck and leaned on the rail, taking in gasps of fresh air as he listened to the splash of the water against the bow. He looked to the sky and studied the realm of Talan. The thousands of stars, Talan's Diamonds, twinkled fitfully, their light distant and wan next to the brilliant light cast by Talan's Lantern, the yellow moon the scholars used to chronicle the passing of time. The Lantern was half shuttered and closing, just like in his dream. Its aspect denoted the last half of the month, and its low position heralded the beginning of autumn. For the first time in his life, Erick wondered if he would be around to see the Lantern when it again marked this time of year.

They're waiting for you, Blink told him after a few minutes.

Sighing, Erick thought, *I'll be there in a moment.*

He shuffled toward his cabin. If his nocturnal vision was to be believed--and he did believe it--the people of Draymed had been murdered, and the town put to the torch, all by one man. A man he'd allowed to live. Any who survived the initial slaughter would succumb to the poisoned water, a slow and painful death.

When he'd left Draymed, he hadn't cared that he would never see the town again, but to know he had allowed so much destruction, no matter how unintentional, left him hollow. As victims of murder, they were assured a place in the Heaven of Caros. That gave him a measure of comfort. But how would Elissia feel about her aunt's and uncle's deaths, especially knowing he had indirectly caused it? His relationship with her, so tenuous, seemed in danger of being destroyed.

Corby also concerned him. His parents and friends were all gone. He would be devastated. Erick chanced losing both his friends tonight, but he had no choice. If they were to travel with him, he could not have their journey continue with such a secret between them.

He reached the cabin and found Elissia, Corby, and Blink crowded into the tiny space. Geran stood in the corner.

Erick sat on the floor. Corby looked half asleep, but Erick suspected there would be little rest for any of them tonight.

He related the dream, telling them his vision of the town's destruction and the visitation of Aunt Beautru's spirit. He offered no insight into the words spoken by the dead woman since he didn't know their meaning. By the time Erick finished, tears flowed from his friend's eyes.

"Is there any chance it was just a dream?" Corby asked.

Erick shook his head. He and Blink had never shared dreams. That they both experienced this told Erick it had to be more.

You've forgotten something, Blink thought.

No, I haven't, Erick thought back in misery. *I just haven't worked up the courage to say it.*

Do it now, Blink said. *If you wait, it will only get worse.*

Erick wanted to scream at Blink to shut up and leave him alone, but only because the familiar was right.

I know I am, Blink told him. *I don't want to be. Sorry.*

Erick looked at his teary friends and steeled himself. "The man who killed everyone was one of the mercenaries that attacked us on the road."

"But they were all dead," Elissia said.

185

"No," Erick said, dropping his head, unable to meet their tearful eyes. "Blink only put them to sleep. He didn't kill them."

"But you said-" Corby began. "You lied?"

Erick nodded, still unable to look at them, and tears came to his eyes.

"Excuse me," Corby said in a choked voice.

Cushions shuffled. From the corner of his eye, Erick watched the scholar's feet run across the small room. The door opened, and Corby ran out. Elissia followed. As the door slammed shut, Erick closed his eyes, and tears of shame and regret splattered onto the waxed wooden floor, like drops of blood from his soul. He collapsed onto his back. *Great Caros, what have I done?* Anger blended with his shame and Erick wept as he hadn't since his parents' death.

The crying stopped eventually. The tears dried into salty trails that ran down the side of his hairless head. He lay on the floor, staring at nothing, thinking random thoughts about trivial matters, too wrung out to focus on anything significant. Blink sat beside him, offering comfort and silence.

Someone knocked on the door.

"Go away."

"Can I please come in?" Elissia asked, her voice muffled by the thick door.

Erick sat up and brushed the crusted salt from his eyes. "Yes."

The door opened, and Elissia stepped inside. Her almond eyes and small nose bore the redness of grief. She walked over and sat on the floor beside him, resting her head against the bed.

"I'm so sorry," Erick said in a thick voice. "If I had ever thought-"

Elissia put her finger against his lips and shook her head. He sat back. For a long time, they said nothing. Erick wanted to apologize, to explain, but he would wait until Elissia allowed him. Despite the misery of the situation, her presence brought him solace.

Eventually, Elissia spoke. "You know, the whole time I was there, I wanted to be anywhere else. I couldn't wait to get away. The happiest day of my life was when I left with you. For the past few days, I've hardly thought about Draymed. But now that it's gone, I'm going to miss it. I'll even miss my aunt, much as we disagreed." She looked at

Erick's face. "Why is it that we don't think about missing people until there's no possibility of ever seeing them again?"

"But you will see them again," Erick told her. "Years from now, when you go to stay with Caros in his heaven, your aunt and uncle will be there, just as you remember them. And they'll tell you how proud they are that you helped me save the world."

Elissia smiled gently. "Knowing Beatru, she'll tell us both how we could have done things better." The smile disappeared. "She warned me you would bring death to the town."

"But I-" Erick stopped. "I didn't mean to."

"I know you didn't." She sighed and rested her head against his shoulder. He barely breathed, afraid any movement would make her shy away. "It would be a much happier world if we knew the consequences of our actions before we did them."

She pulled away, to Erick's disappointment. "You need to trust us," she said. "You're going to a different world now. I know you can't kill, but now you see it's sometimes necessary. If you can't kill them, I can."

"I don't want you to have to do it either. Or Corby."

"But can you see why we might?"

Erick didn't react for a long time. "Yes, I see."

"If you know they're going to heaven, why do you care if we kill them?"

"Because I don't know they're going to heaven. Especially men like that. Alakaneth judges, and only he knows. I won't take the chance of condemning a soul to Hell." Erick shuddered. "No one should."

"I will," Elissia said. "Better them in Hell than me."

If she knew what I know about Hell, Erick thought, *she might not be so cavalier.* "You won't go to Hell."

Elissia offered one of her crooked smiles. "How do you know? Only Alakaneth judges, remember?"

Erick frowned. He didn't like the thought of Elissia condemned to such an existence. But it did bring him to another question, and he wasn't sure he wanted to know the answer. "How many people have you killed?"

"Those men on the road were the first."

Surprised but reassured, Erick asked, "How could you be so calm about killing?"

"I just told you. I'm not at all calm about dying."

"What about when I first saw you at the manor? You seemed ready to die."

"That was different. My only two friends were dead, Beatru seemed to think everything wrong in the world was my fault, and no one in town other than Corby cared for me. At that point, death seemed almost welcome. But that was before I got to know you."

Erick said nothing, afraid the lump in his throat would choke his words.

"You're going to have to talk to Corby," she said. "He lost more than I did and may not be as willing to forgive you."

"You forgive me?" Erick asked before he could stop himself. Now she would change her mind.

She hesitated a moment before speaking. "Yes. You had no way of knowing any of those men would even go to Draymed, much less destroy-" She stopped and let out a gasp as if she just remembered something.

"What's wrong?" Erick asked.

"Nothing," she said, putting her head on his shoulder again. "I just...what happened to Draymed wasn't your fault."

Erick didn't agree, but the important thing was her forgiveness.

Though loathe to leave, he said, "I should go find Corby."

"Leave it until morning. He'll need some time to work it out for himself. I'll talk to him if you want."

Erick shook his head. "It's my responsibility."

"You have to promise me one more thing," Elissia said. "Never, ever lie again, no matter how painful the truth is. I've heard enough lies to last me forever, and I won't have it from you."

"I promise," Erick said. "I see now what happens when I do."

They didn't say anything more. Comfortable in each other's company, they soon slid to the floor and fell asleep, exhausted by the night's events.

~

The next day, before his studies, Erick sought out Corby, but the young scholar could not be found. Erick spotted Murrough working the ropes and approached.

"Corby's in my bunk," the young sailor said in response to Erick's question. "But you'd best leave him be."

"Does he hate me?"

"Hate?" Murrough let out a harsh laugh. "Corby doesn't have it in him to hate. If I had lost my parents, brother, and a whole town, you can be gods-damned sure I'd be pounding you until some things broke. But Corby's a gentle soul. Cares for you more than you'd ever accept. Deluded himself into thinking it wasn't your fault. Says you're his friend and you had your reasons." The sailor snorted and spat a gob of phlegm at Erick, forcing him to step back to avoid the disgusting missile. "That's what I think of your reasons. Corby will show when he's ready. Now go before I forget my promise and beat you anyway."

Erick backed away, unnerved by the sailor's naked anger. Knees weak, he returned to his cabin and tried to study, to no avail. Suddenly craving physical activity, Erick grabbed the three daggers Elissia had gotten for him. He went on deck, to his scarred practice board, and started throwing. He threw and threw, barely noticing the tears that poured or the sweat that built up on his face. None of the sailors bothered him. He threw, not missing once, until his arm could barely move and fatigue overtook him. He threw until Elissia led him to his cabin and he fell into bed, sleeping the afternoon away in exhausted remorse.

The morning of their seventh day at sea, three days after the dream, Erick stood on deck watching the House of Caros rise over the ocean, its fiery glare reaching across the water. The days since the vision had been difficult. Corby had not shown above deck yet, and Erick worried that their fledgling friendship had disappeared.

Although she claimed no ill feelings about Erick's actions, Elissia seemed changed. She still taught him, and they spoke at meals, but her laughter came less frequently, her glances not as friendly. In some ways, he found it worse than if she had screamed at him, been mad, and then moved on. But he considered himself lucky she even spoke to him.

Erick stared across the water. It was going to be a clear day, much as every day of their voyage had been. One of the sailors on the morning watch noticed stopped for a moment to join Erick in observing the sunrise.

"Always love seein' that," the man said, running his hand through a long brown beard attached to a time and sun-weathered face. "Been a right lucky trip, this one."

"What do you mean?" Erick asked, not taking his eyes off the horizon.

"The dangerous weather don't start for another two months, but it's rare we make all seven days without at least a drop of rain."

"So we'll reach land today?"

"Aye. Sometime before the next bell." He turned his grizzled face to the sky, cloudless and quickly turning from deep violet to blue. "And not a drop of rain," he repeated before wandering off to continue his rounds.

As he stood there watching for the land to make an appearance, soft footsteps approached. He turned to find Corby walking toward him, his clothing rumpled and hair tousled, with no sign of the oil he usually wore in it. Though his face was placid, his eyes seemed glassy and his skin pale and slack, as if he had slept or eaten little in the past days.

He stopped and leaned on the rail next to Erick but had yet to look at him directly. Erick started to speak, but Corby spoke first.

"Murrough told me what he said to you. He shouldn't have threatened you. When I told him that, he got angry with me, so I've lost a friend...a good friend."

"I'm sorry," Erick said.

"We've all lost something," Corby continued, his voice flat, as if Erick hadn't spoken. "I have to carry on my father's search for knowledge. He would want that. Will you help me? Help me learn and remember all we see."

"Of course," Erick said. He swallowed the lump in his throat. "I'm-"

Corby held up a hand, and Erick almost expected Corby to press it against his mouth, silencing him as Elissia would. "Don't apologize. Don't ever offer contrition for sparing someone's life. If you wall off your heart, you're no better than the enemy we're fighting, are you?"

Erick didn't know how to answer. Which was worse, killing one person or inadvertently letting two hundred die because you didn't kill that one? Would Alakaneth consider him a murderer because of his inaction? Should he have risked the battle with *Elonsha* and killed the men? He grew tired of questions for which he had no answers.

"The worst part," Corby said, his voice so lifeless it unnerved Erick, "is that as much as I lost, part of me was happy. There were so many people there that bullied and berated me. People I wished dead. I shouldn't have wished it, but I'm not sorry it happened. I just wish it could have been only them and not the people I loved." He looked at Erick. "Is that a horrible thing?"

Corby's dark thoughts disturbed Erick, as did his lack of remorse. But like his cousin, Corby didn't know the true cost of death. Erick wasn't about to tell him. "I don't know."

"Elissia says it isn't, but she can have an unforgiving nature."

"Is she still mad at me?" Erick asked.

"Not at all. I think secretly, she wanted some people dead too. She can say it's not horrible to feel that way, and we can believe we had nothing to do with it, but wishes have power. They reach Denech's ears and, if they're strong enough, he listens. Maybe your actions were the answer to those wishes, and that thought frightens her. It frightens me too."

Was such a thing possible? Had he been Denech's instrument of fate to make Corby's and Elissia's wishes come true? It seemed illogical, but the logic of gods was incomprehensible to humans. His parents had often told him that. He didn't like the thought of being little more than a pawn to fate, but he could do nothing about it. And if he had no say, did his decision not to kill matter? The bright, beautiful morning suddenly lost some of its luster.

Corby turned and put his hand on Erick's shoulder. "Promise me one thing."

"I won't lie anymore," Erick said.

Corby shook his head. "Thank you, but that's not what I was going to ask. Promise me we'll always be friends, no matter what you learn about me."

"What do you mean? What would I learn about you?"

"Just promise me."

Erick paused a moment, then nodded. "I promise. You will always be my friend."

"Thank you," Corby said. Leaning in, he gave Erick a quick hug, then let go and walked back to the ladder leading below, leaving Erick confused and curious. Other than the nebulous immorality of wishing someone dead and not actually killing them, what dark secret could someone like Corby possibly have?

The cry of "land dead ahead" rang from the crow's nest and chased the dark thoughts from Erick's head. He ran toward the bow, searching for land.

He spotted the coastline, still only a dark clump on the horizon, with a jumbled mixture of fear, excitement, sadness, and uncertainty. He remembered reading of places outside Draymed in his mother's now destroyed library. He had spent countless hours dreaming of traveling to those places, but in the dreams, his parents were alive and with him, not vanished in the uncaring ocean.

Homesickness engulfed him, followed by dismay at all that he and the others had lost. His home and town were gone. As far as he knew, the three people on this ship were the only reminders that a place called Draymed ever existed. The thought crushed his enthusiasm at their imminent arrival in unknown lands.

As the ship drew closer to land, Erick's despondency deepened. It was time to deliberately rid himself of the last remnants of his old home. Although his constant knife training had modestly improved his abilities, his book work had been far more successful. The long unused--and in some cases, never used--Rituals were not forgotten, only buried deep from lack of study. Reading through his father's tomes refreshed them in Erick's mind. He no longer needed the books. He had to get rid of them as he had promised his father's ghost, and he needed to do it soon.

Erick returned to his cabin to find Blink stuffing the last of the tomes into one of the sacks. "I knew you would be coming for these."

Erick nodded. "Are you going to be able to hide out here until nightfall?"

"Yes."

Erick looked at the sacks on the floor.

"You have to do it," Blink told him when he showed no signs of moving.

"I know." Erick walked toward the sacks. He lifted them and lumbered to the door, a bag held low on either side. He awkwardly shuffled down the passageway and up the ladder. He spotted Elissia and Corby on deck, watching the approaching town. He headed in the opposite direction, hoping they didn't see him.

Sailors bustled about in preparation for landfall. They paid him no attention as he reached the railing and dropped both sacks, determined to send them over the side before he changed his mind. Holding the railing, he used his feet to push one and then the other overboard. The full packs hit with a loud splash and sank into the water.

"So long," he said. All he had left from home were his memories, herb box, and the amulet on his neck. All inadequate substitutes, but they would have to do.

He walked across the deck to join the other two. As he came closer, Corby spoke with great animation about the approaching land. It pleased Erick to see some of his friend's old spirit back.

They spotted him, and Elissia said, "Ready for your first visit to the mainland?"

Erick smiled and nodded. Her simple question made him feel worlds better.

The shoreline soon resolved itself into a cluster of buildings. Although Erick hadn't seen much of Keyport, he had sensed its large size. Now, however, his eyes told him that Kalador was *huge*. There were at least forty docks, and ships were towed in and out of the berths while longshoremen hauled cargo back and forth, going from ship to warehouse to ship again. Behind the multitude of warehouses, as far as Erick could see, more buildings sat, some of wood, some of stone, many four and five floors high.

As they drew closer, Erick heard the noises and caught the odors, an odd mixture of fish, bread, and things that had never passed his nose. Dockworkers yelled while ropes creaked under heavy loads lifted from decks. Donkeys brayed as they pulled laden carts. Merchants haggled with captains and brokers. So much clamor and riot almost overwhelmed Erick.

Blink, you have to see this. He sensed his familiar making the connection to see through his eyes and could feel his amazement echoed by the homunculus. Erick's depression faded amidst the excitement of their new destination.

They docked without fanfare, the ship guided in by ropes attached to two rowboats, and Erick mentally summoned Geran to join them. The former soldier still appeared the same, but the sailors gave him a wide berth as he crossed the deck.

"Stay close to us," Elissia warned Erick as he fidgeted while sailors lowered the gangplank to the dock. "It's easy to get lost here, and you have 'newcomer' written all over your face. When I first told you about this place I exaggerated, but not by much. Are you listening?"

"Of course," Erick said. His eyes darted about as he tried to capture everything.

Elissia sighed and grabbed his hand. "Slow down," she said, as he pulled her down the ramp.

It amazed Erick the other two could be so blasé about everything. He would have expected the same reaction of awe from at least Corby, but the scholar only stayed close to Elissia. He studied their surroundings, but nothing showed on his face.

They moved through the docks and past the warehouses and small shanties housing the sailors and dockworkers. They passed one large building where several women and men stood outside and watched the passersby. Erick thought them not much older than himself. The women wore no tops and only the barest amount of material necessary for modesty below, and the men wore loincloths of a snug-fitting fabric that left nothing to imagine. Erick goggled at the bare breasts.

Out of the corner of his eye, he noticed Corby turning the color of a strawberry.

A man dressed in a crimson robe embroidered with outlines of male and female figures stood on a platform above them and shouted to the crowd. "The finest of Amare's disciples here for your pleasure. Take your pick, whatever you desire. Best prices and all blessed by the god of love.

"You there," he said to Erick, "lose your girlfriend for a day and enjoy some fresh cunny. And you, scholar, give your hand a rest and learn new tricks from one of these beautiful ladies." Unaware of Geran's nature, the barker pointed at him and said, "How about you, soldier? Come show these ladies what you can do with your sword."

Erick didn't think it possible, but Corby turned redder. Emotional fire raced through his own body. As he stared at the bare flesh, his penis rose, demanding attention like a needy puppy. The fabric of his undergarment rubbed against the sensitive skin, sending arrows of pleasure through him. Panicked, he shifted the garment, removing the pressure before he had an accident.

Why is that all you think about? Blink asked.

You came from a vat, so I don't think you'd understand.

Elissia avoided the show of flesh but squeezed Erick's hand so hard it was almost painful. "Let's go," she said. "There's nothing to see here."

Erick didn't agree but was thankful when they moved on, leaving the temple behind.

Another two minutes brought them into a less odiferous but no less hectic area. Shops stood everywhere, with tradespeople outside the buildings shouting the virtues of their wares to any who would listen. The scents here were of food and perfume, candles and herbs, exquisite in their variety, but almost sickening in the aroma created by their fusion.

In addition to the aromatic assault, Erick beheld clothing in colors he'd only read about. With the exception of the robes worn by Fathen and his acolytes, the brightest color in Draymed was a light brown. Here, there existed hues and attire Erick could never have imagined, blending in combinations to shame a rainbow. The merchants appeared to be the most brightly dressed, their loud clothes matching their strident voices. Thankful but disappointed he encountered no more displays of naked women, Erick could have stayed watching the nearby activity for hours. When it became evident they were leaving as soon as possible, he asked, "Where are we going?"

Elissia started to answer when a commotion twenty feet away stopped her. From an alleyway came four guards. They wore leather armor, overlaid with the Zakerin army taupe shirts, a silver rose embroidered on the left breast and a sparrow in flight on the right. One of the men wore silver epaulets and a leather helm. The other three wore no helms or markings of rank, but they carried a young man, perhaps Corby's age, his olive skin devoid of even a loincloth. He struggled, but his whipcord-thin frame and sinewy arms were no match for the muscular soldiers. His black hair was clipped to no more than an inch long, and his intense blue eyes gleamed with fear as he looked their way. A disbelieving recognition seemed to cross his angular face. He disappeared, carried into the crowd, which quickly surrounded and followed the escort.

"Come on," Elissia said, running to the alleyway where the quintet had emerged. Another boy, perhaps ten and dressed in a ragged green shirt and faded yellow pants cinched by a dirty rope, stood nearby watching the receding procession. When he saw the quartet approaching, he backed away. Elissia gestured elaborately with her hands, and he stopped, eyes wide.

"What's going on?" she asked.

"Th-the-they're taking Marcus to be hanged," the boy stammered.

Erick's ears perked up. Was this the Marcus that had given Elissia her beautiful daggers? The unknown suitor Erick now knew he would fight if necessary to hold onto Elissia's affection.

"Hanged?" Elissia asked. "For what?"

"Stealing a gem from a noble."

Elissia sighed and shook her head. "Come on; we have to rescue him."

"Rescue him?" Erick asked. "He's a criminal."

"That's true," Elissia said. "But he also happens to be my brother."

Though nowhere near the most powerful of the Necromancer's creatures, taboar, common name ghouls, are (to this humble author) the most frightening. Their speed, savagery, and the tenacity with which they will pursue their quarry can still cause nightmares, even so many years later.
 -Corberin of Draymed, *On the Necromancer's Art.*

Fathen gave the mug of water before him a disdainful sniff. He hadn't realized how much he took the cleanliness of Draymed for granted until he stepped into this tavern, with its smell of stale beer, unwashed sailors, and dockworkers reeking of dead fish. He held his complaints from Andras, whose mood had soured after their late arrival at the docks.

The former priest shared his mentor's ill humor. Fathen's legs had stiffened painfully. Exhaustion from staying up all night tugged at him, and his stomach rumbled. Although a plate of what passed for food sat before him, he vowed to starve before eating anything that originated in *this* tavern.

Andras seemed unconcerned with their environment, forking a mash of meat and potatoes from plate to mouth while he spoke with another man sitting at the table. The man claimed to be captain of a worthy sailing vessel, but Fathen found it unlikely. A Sakenin, he had scraggly black hair, piggish black eyes, and a jagged scar running across his forehead like a stark white ridge against his tawny skin. His ocean blue shirt with bloused sleeves stood open halfway down his chest, and his pants were as much stitched patches as fabric. Three shiny gold hoops hung from each ear. The man appeared disreputable at best.

Of course, Fathen thought as he grudgingly sipped the water to ease his parched throat, *disreputable in this establishment is a step up.*

"Yah," the man said in response to a question from Andras, his voice loud, accent thick, and command of Zatrim tenuous. "Kalador tomorrow is where we sail. You and friend ride two *aesta* each."

"That seems extreme since you are already bound for Kalador," Andras countered. "Two *aesta* for both."

"Nah, nah," the man bellowed, seeming both angered and insulted. "You take up space, eat food. Two each."

"We will bring our food, which in any case will be better than what you offer."

"You still take room on ship, Zakerin gold not spend well in Falan-Dar." A glint appeared in his eye. "You have amber *Drakobi*, maybe? You have that; you pay cheaper."

"I have no amber."

"Then two *aesta* or walk to Kalador!"

Andras leaned in close and lowered his voice, his tone turning menacing. "How about one *Aestes* for both of us and I make sure the Fist leaves your ship intact?"

The captain flinched from Andras, his eyes growing wide. After a panicked moment, he smiled and guffawed. "Ho, you no Fist. Fist dead."

Andras placed his elbow on the table and rolled up the sleeve of his ebon tunic, revealing the underside of his forearm to the captain.

The man flinched as he observed the mark on Andras' forearm. Fathen leaned over and saw a tattoo of an arrow-headed sword; a line ran in a serpentine pattern across the length of the blade, thick in the center and tapering to points at the ends. Centered on the blade, but set underneath, a large ring stood flanked by two smaller ones. It was a fascinating, elaborate tattoo, but Fathen didn't understand why it evoked the fear painted on the Sakenin's face. The man's bronze skin paled as he grabbed his mug of ale. "You ride free," he said and took a deep draught

"No, an *Aestes* for both of us will be fine." Andras gave a cold smile as he rolled his sleeve down. "I wouldn't expect you to sail without a profit."

The captain nodded and stood hastily. "We sail out tide tomorrow. Morning light." He offered a hesitant bow, then turned and walked away, stopping to speak with two other men before they all left the tavern.

Once the sailors were gone, Fathen asked Andras, "What is that tattoo?"

Andras frowned. "Did you study no other faiths beyond your bastard god? It is the symbol of the Fist of the *Inconnu*. The arrow and blade are given to the *Eligoi*, the assassins of the Fist, which is what this meat was before you killed it. Talva received the mark of *Napaei*, a swordsman, and you received the mark of *Ecrin*, a priest.

"Mark?" Fathen asked. "I received no mark."

Andras smiled, a strange expression on his bland face. "Look."

Fathen rolled up his sleeve to reveal his long, thin arm. Where once he had a brand of the sun received upon taking his vows to Caros, he now found emblazoned on his forearm, as if pressed with ebony ink, a tattoo similar to Andras's. The only difference lay in the sword, which had spikes surrounding it, radiating outward, each tipped with a small drop, as if it leaked black blood. Although he had felt nothing, Fathen knew this mark had manifested as soon as he killed the man sitting across from him. Shaken, Fathen rolled his sleeve down.

Andras continued. "The symbol no longer receives the respect it should, but there are some who still recognize it and show the proper obeisance, or at least fear. Soon that number will grow." Andras pointed toward the door where the ship's captain had departed. "Be wary while we sail on that man's vessel. He is not trustworthy."

"All men are untrustworthy," Fathen said. "It is the nature of man. That is why we have the gods to guide us." Andras's smirk made

Fathen flinch. "My god turned away from me first," the ex-cleric muttered.

"Perhaps," Andras said. "So you know the captain cannot be trusted, but would you expect him to try and kill us?"

"He appears dishonorable and greedy. I understand some Sakenin captains deal in slavery, so I would have more fear of that than death. He doesn't look like a murderer."

"Neither do you," Andras said. "He will try and have us killed the first night aboard."

"Won't fear of the Fist keep him at bay?"

"His greed and history will overcome his fear," Andras explained. "We of the Fist are believed mostly extinct, but there are those in your bastard god's temple and the Myrmidons of Sangara who listen for rumor of us to hunt us down. Even without knowing what I truly am, they would pay well for the death of an *Eligoi*. Much more than we are paying for this voyage. The man is also a *Parshera* tribesman."

"What does that matter?"

"The *Parshera* fought against us the first time."

"If you know all this, wouldn't it have been better to pay his price and avoid revealing yourself?"

Andras nodded. "Perhaps. But word must be spread that the Fist is active again, so terror and hopelessness precede my return to power. This Sakenin captain will help spread that word."

Fathen wasn't convinced. Andras must have seen his doubt. "Do not worry. His first attempt won't succeed. I will make sure he has no desire to try a second time."

As Andras finished his breakfast, Fathen's hunger overcame the strength of his earlier vow. He chose the least offensive items available, a slice of dark bread and wedge of white goat cheese, and consumed them with efficiency, if not pleasure.

They retired to their small room and slept through most of the day, exhausted by their rushed journey. Despite the meanness of their lodging, Fathen had never been so happy to lie down in a bed; his pleasure was short-lived. Every overworked leg muscle shrieked in agony as he unfolded on the hard wooden cot. He had to bite his lip to stifle a scream. He tried moving about to find a more comfortable position, but the slightest change caused his muscles to protest even more. He lay still, wondering if sleep would ever come. Eventually, the pain settled to a dull throbbing, and he fell into a deep, dreamless slumber.

~

The next morning found Fathen aboard an ugly but seaworthy carrick called the *Pratanin*. He stood dressed in new clothes: dark blue shirt, soft, blue silk pants that fit tightly into shin-high, leather boots, and a hooded russet cloak. A new sword hung on his side; all acquired when he and Andras woke yesterday afternoon and made preparations for their voyage.

"*Kaloas tas lias!*" the captain yelled from the helm. Even without understanding Sakenin, Fathen found it easy to follow the captain's orders by the crew's actions. In response to the last shout, men at the ship's fore and aft pulled up the mooring lines and tossed them to the dock.

A brisk morning wind blew across the water, chasing away the harbor's brackish odors, as the sun rose and cast a bright coral glow against the wooden warehouses lining the wharves.

Fathen took a deep breath of the cleansing sea breeze, feeling much better after a night's rest despite his aching legs. "Do you know it's been twenty years since I've been on a ship," Fathen said as two rowboats pulled the vessel away from the dock. "Twenty years I've wasted on this pisswater island among mind-numbed sheep." He spat at the water. "I'm glad to be quit of it."

Andras stared across the water. "You're welcome."

"Tell me more about yourself," Fathen told the plain-faced man. The *Inconnu*, I mean, not Andras."

"I shall," Andras promised, drawing his sword. "But first we'll see what you remember of your days with a weapon."

Fathen groaned. "Can't it wait for a day while I get over being sore?"

Andras shook his head. "Your enemies will not wait for your

discomfort to end. You must always be prepared to fight, and I must know how much work needs to be done."

"Very well." Fathen drew his sword and stepped toward the center of the deck. "Teach me."

The training lasted the entire day, with only a brief break to eat from their rations. As Andras predicted in Draymed, Fathen's skills returned despite years of atrophy. The passage of time had made him slower, and he lacked the brute strength of his youth, but he had finesse and a quick mind.

Andras was a demanding trainer, quick with criticism, but equally profuse with praise, and willing to explain anything his pupil did not grasp. As the sun beat down on them and sweat poured from his body, Fathen began to appreciate his new mentor, and he noticed in his teacher's eyes--just behind the disturbing glint they always held--a pleasure in again having a student.

Midway through the day, Fathen rediscovered a feeling he had long forgotten: exhilaration. As Andras demonstrated new techniques and inculcated him in the ways of dealing death, the numbness that had crept into Fathen's spirit left, growing fainter with each passing knot. Although the deaths of Brannon and Bereman still evoked twinges of guilt, he began to accept he had made the right choice in killing Andras to give his new master life. In that act, Fathen's old existence died, and he now walked Krinnik with the eager curiosity of a newborn, ready to experience the life he had missed for twenty years.

Fathen crawled gratefully into the lower bunk that evening, exhausted and sore, but elated. It amazed him how quickly a score of lethargic years could disappear. His life in Draymed belonged to a distant relative he had only heard about. Once Erick was dead, all memories of this phantom cousin would be tossed away, and Fathen could emerge into the world as the *Eloa Ecrin*, high priest of the *Inconnu*. He fell asleep thinking of the power and respect that would soon be his.

He awoke to a scream. His eyes opened and spied a flurry of shadowy movements in the close quarters of the darkened cabin. The cry emanated from a figure standing before him. Fetid breath went across his face in a hot wash. A shape near the screamer moved, and a glint of steel flashed. The scream stopped. As the figure fell to the floor in front of Fathen, a dead hand slapped his leg.

Fathen pushed his way out of bed, desperately reaching for his sword, but found himself forced back, a heavy weight pressed against him. He slammed onto the hard bed, someone on top of him. He flailed and pushed his assailant away.

The weight fell from his chest. Warm wetness coated his torso, but no pain accompanied it.

The cabin grew quiet, the only sounds the muted splash of water against the hull and the creaking of ropes from the sails. A shadow moved in the dim light. Fathen grabbed his sword and tried to fumble it from its sheath.

Sparks flickered in the room as flint struck steel. In the brief glow, Fathen spotted Andras' grim face and relaxed. The lantern wick caught, and light filled the room as Andras placed the glass over the flame.

Fathen checked his blood-soaked shirt, searching for a wound. He found no cut and surmised the blood belonged to the man that had fallen on him and now lay in a lifeless heap.

"I told you he would try to have us killed," Andras admonished. The flickering lamplight cast him as a gore-soaked creature from the lower Hells.

Fathen surveyed the carnage. Five bodies lay in the room, literally stacked on top of each other in the cramped confines of the cabin. Two never made it past the doorway, stabbed through the eye; one lay halfway in, a puncture to his throat ending his days. Holes gaped in the chests of the two at Fathen's feet.

"You killed them all yourself?" Fathen gasped.

"Of course," Andras answered. "They were not used to fighting in the dark. I am. If I wished, I could bring them back from death and have them kill everyone on board the ship."

"Then you should do it, to make them pay for their insolence," Fathen said, a tremor in his voice.

Andras shook his head. "That would leave no one to sail the ship. But I will make the captain aware of his error. Why did you not remain watchful, as I ordered?"

"I apologize," Fathen said, eyes downcast in a sincere display of humiliation. "I should have been more alert, but I was still fatigued by our journey from Draymed."

"That is not an excuse," Andras said, his voice even. "If you are to be high priest, you must survive until I come into my power. To survive, you must be ever alert. I do not command often, but I insist you obey the few I give. Agreed?" The chilling light flashed in Andras's brown eyes.

"Agreed," Fathen said, no longer afraid of those eyes, but respectful of the power behind them. Again looking at the carnage in the cabin, Fathen said, "What do we do now?"

"Now we ensure the captain knows the foolishness of his attempt."

～

Captain Talas-An paced in his cabin, awaiting the return of his men. They were his five toughest. Cold-blooded murderers whom he always used for unpleasant tasks such as this. Killing members of the Fist was dangerous, but they were worth far more as corpses than as slaves. Turning their bodies over to the Paladins of Caros or the Myrmidons of Sangara in Kalador would net him more money than he made in six months of smuggling up the coast to Falan-Dar. It would sit well with his tribal council and the leaders of neighboring Hucara if they learned of his deed.

But as the night wore on, he became uncertain. What was taking so long?

His cabin door flew inward. Talas-An stopped pacing and turned to the open doorway. Jaranas-An, a member of the rigging crew and leader of the ship's thugs, stepped into the room. The captain could tell immediately something was wrong but was unsure what until the thin light streaming into the doorway revealed the crewman no longer had his head.

Talas-An backed into the cabin, eyes bulging in horror. Unable to speak, he watched, terrified, as the abomination threw a canvas sack at his feet. It landed with a dull thump and fell open. Motes of black danced before Talas-An and he trembled as five severed heads rolled from the bag and lay in front of him, staring at him with dead, accusing eyes.

Jaranas-An's body went limp, falling to the deck like a bundle of grain. Blood drizzled from the neck and soaked into the nearby burlap

A voice spoke from the doorway. "Molest us again, and I will watch you burn alive while your ship sinks around you."

The door slammed, leaving the captain in shock, standing amongst the lifeless stares of his five toughest sailors.

～

As Fathen and Andras left their cabin the following morning, the ex-priest noticed the sailors avoided their gaze and came nowhere near. If one accidentally made eye contact, they turned away in haste, but not quickly enough for Fathen to miss the fear in their face. Though he maintained the same stoic manner as Andras, the sailors' terror elated Fathen. This was the sort of righteous dread he could appreciate, the fear of greater than mortal powers he once tried to instill in his congregation, to no avail. Caros--and his priests--no longer commanded respect, but the priests of Eligos, especially the *Eloa Ecrin*, would *demand* it. Once he came into his own, Fathen would never again tolerate the things he accepted in Draymed. Impertinence would be met with severe punishment.

He caught a young sailor staring at him. They locked eyes for a moment before the youth turned and fled across the deck. Fathen smiled.

～

athen's time aboard ship passed quickly. He spent mornings training with his weapon and evenings occupied with learning. Gradually, Fathen discovered the history and ways of his new master. Andras told stories of the arrival of the *Inconnu*, powerful entities from a place entirely unlike Krinnik. As they had with other worlds, the great beings observed first, learning what they could of those they would rule, choosing the few who were worthy enough to be offered places of power in the new world shaped by the *Inconnu*.

Fathen learned of their infinite patience as they drew in more and more followers, playing on the emotions of long-held grudges between nations. The leaders were persuaded, and with the leaders came their subjects and armies.

"Makern we persuaded easily," Andras said as they sat in their cabin. "The Tortured Mountains are full of extractable wealth, and we promised they could have the range."

"But the Tortured Mountains belong to Amelan."

"That mattered little to us. Had Amelan joined us, we would have split the range between the countries.

"We used the territorial disputes between Straphin and Starrasen to gain Straphin's forces. We offered them the means to reclaim all their lands stolen centuries before.

"Most of Falan-Dar came when we convinced the caliph that the fertile lands of Zakerin in the south were more suitable to the great Sakenin tribes than the arid desert where fate chose to place them."

"What do you mean, 'most'?"

"The Caliph is the tribal leader only as far as other nations are concerned; he holds no real power over the tribes. He could only persuade eight of the tribes to join. The others abstained or, like the *Parshera*, fought us.

"We could not persuade the leaders of Zakerin, Amelan, or Starrasen. We promised them power, land, and money, but they refused. When that did not work, we threatened them with war and destruction, but they still would not submit. We gathered some rebels who joined us in hopes of bettering their lot, but despite this, the land would not be ours without a fight, much as we wished it otherwise.

"We planned our offensive carefully; because we had the leaders of three kingdoms, we had three armies under our command. Although it would have been easy, we did not force the armies to fight. Instead, my brothers and I spoke to those whose purpose was to die on the battlefields. I explained to them why they had to fight, and spoke of the rewards for those who did fight, until every man would rather die than *not* fight; thus was the Fist of the *Inconnu* born." Andras glanced out the small porthole in their cabin. "Enough for now; it is time to train."

~

As the days passed, Fathen learned the stories of battles waged in all corners of the world, from the eastern foothills of the Tortured Mountains to the Ruban, the southern swamps of Starrasen. The Fist fought gloriously in these battles, gaining prestige and honor for the *Inconnu*, but the stubbornness of those who could not see the righteousness of Eligos and his brothers were great. The *Inconnu* and the Fist met fierce resistance, but they never faltered, knowing they would prevail.

Over a dinner of dried bread, hard cheese, and their last ration of salted goat, the priest learned how Saburoc, the Master of Plagues and brother to Eligos, discovered the unusual properties of the plants used by certain people to heal the wounded and cure the sick. He showed these to his brothers, and together they devised a way to put the plants to better use.

The first *gateloah* created by Eligos fought alongside Fist members in the battle to take Peretan, a city in northern Amelan. The battle was a rout, the city taken in hours as the defenders fled before the undead that attacked them. Those few who stayed to fight were quickly cut down; their weapons held scant power over the creatures that swarmed around them. Imbued with the power of *Elonsha*, the creatures were nearly impervious to mortal weapons. Blades and axes would not slice through rotted sinew without great strength; stones and maces bounced off dry bones, leaving cracks instead of shatters. Few living things could harm the new creatures of Eligos.

207

Flushed by success, Eligos taught his art to those he found most worthy, and the first Necromancers worked their magic and created legions of creatures to run rampant over the living. Cities fell. The three rebellious kingdoms began to collapse. Victory belonged to the *Inconnu*.

"And then we were betrayed, my brothers killed and myself exiled," Andras concluded bitterly before he fell silent.

Fathen pressed him to explain further, but his mentor would say no more. Fathen realized he could fill in the details with half-remembered stories from his early days in the priesthood. Stories that, at the time, hardly seemed credible.

∿

The third night at sea, Fathen awoke to an eerie thrumming noise, soft but disquieting. He found Andras seated upright in his bed, back rigid, arms at his side stretching toward the floor, and a jagged smile on his face. An aura surrounded him, pulsing from black to deep purple and back. Points of red light shot through the dark nimbus, darting toward Andras from the outer edge. They leapt from their ebony cloud and landed on his skin, burrowing in and disappearing.

Thinking him under attack, Fathen moved to help his mentor, but as soon as he approached the aura, nausea racked through his body. He caught an overwhelming scent of rotted onions. Sweat broke on his forehead, and he doubled over as his stomach clenched, his body rejecting the malignant presence of the throbbing halo.

He retreated, his only thought to be away from this foul thing. The back of his knees hit his bed frame. He fell, landing hard on the thin mattress.

The glow and smell faded rapidly, and with it Fathen's nausea. Once it disappeared, Andras blinked and his eyes glowed pale white with pupils of dull red. Fathen sat on his bed, afraid to move,

Andras smiled. "Do not cower," he said, his voice whispery like dead leaves against a windowpane. "There is reason to be joyous. A Necromancer is dead."

"Erick?"

"No, but one of his kind. Older, but not nearly as powerful, he died in fear with praise to my name on the lips of his killer." Andras brought his hand up and ran fingers across his lips. "The *Elonsha* was so sweet."

"What happened?"

"I absorbed the energy released by the Necromancer's death. When someone is killed in my name, it nourishes me, but only as food nourishes a body. It is fleeting and must be replenished. But when a Necromancer is killed in my name, the nourishment is like sword and armor. It remains and increases my power. As the other Necromancers are destroyed, I will become stronger. When I am strong enough, I will reach into the *Aesir*, the nothingness of creation, and wrench the rest of my being into this world. Then there will be reason for all to tremble."

Fathen shuddered, remembering the unfathomable malice and force emanating from his mentor as the sinister aura surrounded him. For the first time, he truly realized the *Inconnu's* terrifying majesty. Once whole, his master would be unstoppable. It frightened him, and he said a silent prayer of thanks to the chaos that he chose to side with this dark entity.

~

The next morning found Andras in a triumphant mood. "We arrive in Kalador tomorrow, and the boy will soon be in our hands. We shall take the day off from weapons training." Standing at the ship's railing, he turned from the smooth ocean to Fathen. "You show promise as a swordsman. You will be a fine *Ecrin*."

"Thank you," Fathen said, genuinely appreciative. His new teacher showed far more forgiveness and patience than any of the priests he learned under while training in the Temple of Caros.

Andras turned back to the ocean, staring toward Kalador as if willing it to arrive faster. Fathen followed his gaze. "Do you think he's still in the city?"

"Not only do I think he is still in the city, but he's either in an oubliette or chained to a wall waiting for me to slit his throat and take his *Elonsha*."

"How can you be so certain?"

"He is only one child with a few friends. Kalador is crawling with members of the Fist, and we have hired the city's brotherhood of thieves to be on the watch for him. He won't escape."

18

Procurers are nothing but vermin. They are leeches who would suck the life from the city and destroy commerce. If I had my way, we'd burn every warren we found and throw anyone found in black in the deepest dungeon. They want black; we can give them black.

-Narin Tarsk, Kaladorian Merchant

"Your brother?" Erick asked after a moment of stunned silence. "Marcus is your brother?"

"My twin, actually," Elissia answered as she watched the departing crowd.

"Your brother is a Procurer?" Corby asked.

"Is everyone going to state the obvious?" Elissia snapped. "My father is Guild Master of the Procurers; so what?"

A small voice spoke up behind them in a mixture of fear and amazement. "The Banished One."

They turned to the momentarily forgotten boy who stood nearby, wiping his nose with a grubby hand. His glistening eyes grew wider as he stared at Elissia.

"There's no need to announce my presence," Elissia said, but she spoke to the child's back. He slithered into a crevice in the alley wall that Erick would have thought too small for anything larger than a cat. "Shit. This isn't how I wanted things to go." She walked toward the crowd.

Erick followed, dazed. All this time he thought Marcus was a suitor. He would have smiled with giddiness if the circumstances didn't have him so confused.

They soon caught up with the growing crowd; people left their houses, shop owners abandoned their stores, and everyone shouted and laughed as if on their way to a fête.

"Are people always this happy about someone hanging?" Erick asked Corby.

"I don't know, I've never been to one," the scholar answered. "It's a rare punishment, especially for thievery. The usual penalty is either branding or having a hand chopped off. There's also normally a trial, and I would imagine the guilty party is allowed to wear clothes. He must have offended someone really powerful."

"Marcus excels at offending people. But he's the only brother I've got, so I should try and keep him alive."

"Any idea how?" Erick asked.

"Not yet. I'm hoping something comes to mind before they put the rope around his neck."

Several people leapt about joyously, pointing at the naked boy and making rude remarks. There were even children along, some riding on their parent's necks. The whole spectacle made Erick ill.

Blink, can you hear me? Erick asked.

Perfectly.

I don't care who sees you, but I need you to get where I am. We may need a diversion.

On my way.

They walked perhaps a quarter-mile with the growing crowd before they reached a square courtyard surrounded by stone buildings, with a gibbet in the center. The throng spread to form a circle around the scaffold, pushing the wagons of protesting vendors aside. The guards moved toward the gallows, carrying the squirming boy.

Erick had started to grow accustomed to the various smells that ran through the city, but a horribly obnoxious odor assaulted his nose:

copper-tinged blood, mingled with an oppressive undercurrent of decay; it was the smell of death, magnified beyond anything even Erick had ever encountered. "Great Caros, what is that stench?"

"Slaughterhouse," Elissia answered as her eyes searched the common. Two of the guards had stopped at the bottom of the gallows. Two others were carrying Marcus up the stairs to the noose.

"Slaughterhouse? You mean where they kill animals?"

"That's what slaughterhouses usually do."

"Which way and how far?" Erick asked urgently. "I have an idea."

Elissia scrunched her eyes in bewilderment, but she pointed. "Straight down that road about a thousand feet. You can't miss it."

"I don't doubt it. I'll move as quickly as I can, but stall them if you have to."

"Whatever you're doing, good luck," Elissia whispered.

Erick turned and ran down the road. His destination could have been in the middle of a mile-wide labyrinth, and he would have found it by its overbearing reek. In some strange way, it took him home, back to time spent with his father learning the Rituals and skills of his life. The rotting onion smell of *Elonsha* and the coppery tinge of blood were the scents of his childhood. In the midst of this cacophonous city, he had stumbled on to memories of a quieter, better time.

Memories that vanished as soon as he spotted the abattoir.

Shaking off the profound sense of disgusted awe at the acre-sized compound, he pulled off his herb kit and prepared to do what his father had taught him.

E lissia tapped her foot on the ground, anxiety warring with outright terror. She had no idea what Erick planned, but he needed to act now. The guards had already put the rope around her brother's neck; he appeared as frail and terrified as a week-old kitten confronted by a mastiff. The sergeant with the silver epaulets stepped forward, pulled a parchment from his belt, and unrolled it. "Here before you stands Marcus Torin of Kalador, who has been convicted of the crime of theft, in sp-"

"Convicted by who, you lying bastard?" Marcus shrieked, his voice high with fear. "I haven't even seen a magistrate." The crowd cheered at the boy's defiance.

"In specific," the sergeant continued. "The theft of a signet ring from the Geleit D'Arascant, who had taken this lad under his care after being tricked into believing he was an orphan."

"More lies, you dung pile. The Geleit flaunts the law by taking in catamites not sanctioned by Amare's temple. I refused his desires because his wrinkled skin made me ill, so he paid you to drag me out of my bath and bring me here with no evidence. Where's the supposed ring I stole?"

"Yeah, where's the ring?" someone mimicked.

"Probably up his ass," another cried out, and the crowd laughed.

Elissia silently cheered Marcus, hoping he could stall long enough that she wouldn't have to do anything stupid to delay them further. But she knew the guards would only tolerate so much. The fear evident in her brother's eyes told her Marcus knew the same thing. "Hurry up, Erick," she whispered.

"Because of the severity of the crime and the pretenses under which it was conducted-"

"Pretenses? I di-" Marcus started, but at a signal from the sergeant the other guard rapped the boy across the skull, stunning him. The crowd booed; the sergeant was spoiling the show.

"Because of the severity of the crime and the pretenses under which it was conducted, this thief is condemned to hang by the neck until dead and to remain hanging until his body rots, as a warning to all other thieves. The Crown has been far too lenient to certain criminal elements, but no longer. This sentence is passed with the approval of the Jurleit, Bala Ardua of Kalador."

Elissia doubted the sergeant's claim. The law master was likely not even aware of this farce. She sidled her way through the crowd, prepared to scream, yell, or dance like a madwoman until they arrested her in order to give Erick the time he needed.

Someone shrieked as a shadow passed overhead. Elissia followed everyone's gaze skyward. Blink flew over the crowd, swung around, and landed on the gibbet above Marcus. Women and children shrieked, and several men turned pale. People at the fringes ran.

"I am Shatok, demon of the Festering Hells," Blink thundered in the deepest, most terrifying voice he could muster. "This child is my creature. Release him, or I will summon a plague so fier—hey, what the hell are you doing?"

A dark-bearded man in brown robes had flung a clod of dirt at the homunculus and even now reached for a piece of fruit from a nearby cart. "You are no demon," the man yelled as he cocked his arm back. "You are a gargoyle and powerless to do anything but bellow."

The man tossed a large apple, and Blink ducked to avoid being struck in the head. This wasn't the reaction Elissia would have expected, and she could tell it had thrown Blink off too. But it proved Corby's assertion that Blink could pass for one of the northern creatures.

The brown-robed man wore a golden globe and hammer pin on the robe's breast and had a grain sack slung over his shoulder.

Great, Elissia thought. *Must be the earth god's revenge for Erick impersonating an acolyte.* "Priest of Krinnik," she shouted. "You are a fool and will doom us all! Release the boy!"

"You heard her," Marcus screamed. "Release me."

"We will do no such thing," the man screamed back.

Blink spread his wings to their full five-foot span. "Release him no—ouch!"

Several others joined the priest, and a barrage of fruit caught Blink flat-footed, striking him in the wings and chest. He flapped his wings to avoid falling off the scaffold, and then lowered them to his side. "Now that just wasn't friendly," he grumbled, clacking his talons ominously. He brought his barbed tail above his head and bellowed, "You shall rue the day you were ever born." He snapped his fingers.

Nothing happened. People shifted about uneasily, the fruit throwers especially nervous. Even the priest seemed hesitant, doubtless afraid his erudition had failed him.

After several seconds, when lightning failed to strike from the sky, and the ground remained firm without splitting open to reveal flaming pits, the crowd relaxed.

"As I said," the priest shouted to the crowd with a smug smile. "Powerless."

"Thank you, good priest," the sergeant yelled. "Now, enough nonsense. Hang him."

"NO!" Elissia screamed as the guard pulled the lever. The trapdoor sprang open, but miraculously, Marcus didn't fall. Blink had reached down and grabbed the slack end of the rope, preventing the neck-breaking drop. Hanging in mid-air, the choking Marcus struggled while Blink bent down and gnawed at the hemp with his sharp teeth.

"Kill that creature," the sergeant shouted. The two guards moved to grab the crossbows slung across their backs.

Elissia heard it first since she had been waiting for something. A high-pitched noise, with a deep rumbling underneath. Cold, onion-scented wind blew through the courtyard, stirring up dust. People shivered and covered their eyes to guard them against the fine grit that whirled through the air.

The rumbling grew, followed by the sound of hoarse squealing, a shrill bawl that hurt the ears, like a shovel scraped across an iron bar. Several in the crowd yelled and pointed; others soon followed.

A sounder of swine thundered full speed toward the square, appearing through the windblown cloud of dust. At least a hundred squealing and grunting pigs dashed across the cobblestone road and spilled into the common area. Several people dove away from the barreling animals. Most were still enthralled with who the loaded and aiming guards would hit: the gargoyle, or the thief it now tried to fly away with, having bitten through the rope.

Elissia noticed all the pigs had sliced throats, and many had no heads. She needed to make others see. "The demon Shatok has brought creatures back from the dead. Run!"

Her voice carried. Several people followed her pointing finger. As the crowd began to realize the condition of the swine, loud screams of terror challenged the squeals. The panic spread and the gathering scattered, chased by the rampaging porcine zombies. Geran remained immobile as people streamed around him, but the maddened throng almost crushed Corby. After a large man slammed into him and nearly knocked him down, he slipped behind an outcropped stone wall with rugs displayed upon it. Realizing the danger, Elissia joined him.

Carts were smashed, and tables overturned as people cleared the square. Even the stoic guards turned pale as they saw creatures that should have been sausage-in-waiting up on all fours, running freely.

"Hold your stations," the sergeant screamed. The guards on the ground broke and ran for cover.

"I said hold your st-"

The sergeant crumpled as Marcus delivered a double-footed kick to his head.

"Hold that, you bastard," the boy screamed in a raspy voice as Blink flew over the scaffolding and past the surprised guard standing next to his now unconscious commander.

The common soon stood nearly vacant, the crowd having efficiently, if destructively, vanished. The pigs ran about in spastic dashes, ignoring the overturned carts of food that would have stopped them in their living years.

Blink gently sat Marcus on the ground and let go of the rope. He spotted the boisterous priest pressed against a wall and flew toward him. "I'm a homunculus, you stupid man. Familiar to a Necromancer, and these are his pets. Run before I eat you."

Eyes wide with terror, the man fled, his robe flapping behind him. Blink giggled softly and flew back to the group.

Elissia removed the noose from her brother's neck as Erick ran into the courtyard, his breathing heavy, sweat on his forehead. "It worked?"

"Like a charm," Elissia answered in awe. "That was beautiful."

"Undead *pigs*?" Blink asked Erick.

Erick shrugged. "I have to work with what's available."

Marcus rubbed at the raw, red ring around his neck, and spat. His eyes flickered over Erick's shoulders and then back. Before Elissia could turn to see his concern, Marcus slammed his right fist into Erick's jaw. Erick fell to the ground.

The sudden violence so stunned Elissia that she didn't even react when Marcus jumped over, pulled her dagger from her side, and held it toward the advancing Blink. "Marcus, what the hell are you doing?" she asked.

"Something he's about to regret," Blink said, tail poised to strike.

"Looks like Calligan was right," a voice said. Elissia recognized it and her shoulders tensed.

She turned. Six people stood there, including Calligan, the small boy that had first seen her. The others—three boys, two girls—ranging in age from a few years younger than her to several years older. Typical of Procurers, they wore dark clothing, as close to black as they could manage within the law. Each of them wore two daggers on their side. She recognized none of them but Darius, who bore the same curly black hair and rodent eyes he had when she left. A new, scraggly beard patched his tan face, enhancing his weasel features., He wore dark wool gloves with the fingers cut off, and held a bundle of gray clothing. He tossed it to Marcus. "Thought you might want these."

"Thanks," Marcus said as he caught the clothes in one hand.

"Good job," Darius said as he waved a hand toward Erick and Blink. "Only you could go from almost getting strung to finding the choice jewel. Luck of Denech, that one," he told his companions.

"Yeah, I'm just a bundle of fortune," Marcus muttered as he dressed in the overly large clothing.

Erick had sat up and rubbed his jaw. "Guess I should have let you hang."

"Probably would have been the smarter choice," Marcus said.

"Welcome back, Banished One."

"Darius," Elissia said, not bothering to hide the disdain in her voice.

"Nice to see how you've grown. Had your treasure picked yet, or you still keeping it locked tight?"

The others laughed, except Marcus, and heat flared in Elissia's face. Erick stood up with Corby's help and glared at the older boy.

"Glad you came to town." Darius pointed at Erick. "Torin wants to meet your friend."

"But he's not particularly interested in meeting Torin," Elissia kept her tone calm, even though her stomach flopped. Her father's interest in Erick could only mean one thing.

Darius offered a grim smile as his hand went to his side and rested on his dagger hilt. "Then I'm going to have to insist."

Elissia looked at Erick. Something in her eyes must have alarmed him because he turned to his undead soldier. "Geran, *zacare*."

Geran stepped forward, placing himself in front of her, facing Darius, and drew his sword. A ripple of fear swept through the gang. They stepped back, but several pulled their weapons.

"You need to let—" Erick started.

An arm wrapped around Elissia's throat and a knifepoint pressed to her chest.

"Call him off," Marcus said from behind her. Erick's face went pale. Blink hissed in irritation.

"Let her go," Corby shouted, even though he appeared ready to faint.

"What are you doing?" Elissia gasped out through the arm tightened on her throat.

"What I've been ordered to do, sis. Remember taking orders? Something you never managed." Laughter came from the other thieves. Marcus gave Elissia a shake. "Call off your man, or I'll gut her."

"Your own sister?" Corby asked.

"She ceased to be my sister when she was banished."

Elissia almost fell over at Marcus's words, almost pushed herself forward so the dagger would pierce her chest. Out of any pain she would have expected returning home, this hurt the worst. To see her brother again had been her main reason to return, and to have him so casually dismiss her crushed her spirit. Nothing mattered now. The whole trip had been a waste of time.

Scared, resolute faces stared at Erick. Geran could easily kill all the thieves, but Elissia would be dead before anyone could stop Marcus. He had been backed into a corner. "Geran, *alar*."

Geran sheathed his sword and stepped back. The thieves relaxed but didn't put away their weapons.

"Good boy," Marcus said. He stepped away from Elissia, and she almost fell. She stared at the ground, all life missing from her. Her brother's betrayal had hurt her deeply. Erick understood. He imagined it as the same pain when he thought his parents had killed themselves. But at least he had learned he was wrong. Elissia probably wouldn't have that comfort. "You're a bastard."

Marcus jumped in front of Erick, dagger extended. Erick stepped back in surprise. He had never seen anyone move so fast. "I know exactly who my father is and what my place is. The same can't be said for others."

Elissia looked up, seemed about to say something, and then looked back down.

"Easy, Marcus," Darius said with a chuckle as Marcus pushed his way past, slamming his shoulder into Erick's chest. "Search them for weapons. Let's move before the regs get here and things turn ugly."

The thieves moved quickly, forming up around Erick and his friends. They took Corby's staff and blowgun, Elissia's dirks, and Erick's sword and herb box.

Surrounded by seven thieves, the group trotted for perhaps three hundred feet before they turned down an alleyway littered with old smashed and dented wooden crates. Unlike the road, covered in tight, small cobbles, this side lane was uneven and paved with large, rough blocks. Slimy water-filled pockets where stones were absent, and the entire area had an aroma of trash and urine.

One at a time, the thieves crouched and worked their way through a gap between three haphazardly stacked crates.

"Watch your step," Darius said to Elissia. She moved her way through the crates, her face blank. Erick couldn't help but notice the older thief's lustful stare at her. Jealousy flared through Erick. *If we get out of this, I want you to put him down for a day.*

Gladly, Blink thought back. *And that other little shit too.*

Blink went next, folding his wings tight to fit them through the narrow gap, and Erick followed.

A hole in the street lay beyond the crates, which the thieves entered. The murmur of running water drifted up from the opening. Once Marcus and three of the thieves had gone in, Darius pointed to Erick's group and said, "You first, scholar."

Corby gave Elissia a nervous glance. She offered him a weak smile. "It's okay," she said, but she didn't sound convinced.

Corby gave an uncertain nod and started down the hole. Blink went next, again having to fold his wings.

Darius pointed at Erick. "The soldier stays here."

"Why?" Erick asked.

"Azinor's orders. You have my word you'll be safe until you reach the throne room." Darius offered a crooked smile.

Erick had no idea who Azinor was, but he hated the idea of leaving Geran behind. A glance at Elissia's grim face told him she didn't care for it either. "And if I refuse?"

"Wasn't that made obvious earlier?" Darius asked as he rested his hand on his knife.

The thieves behind Elissia had taken up casually aggressive stances. Using Geran, Erick and Elissia could break free, but Corby and Blink were already belowground, effectively hostages. Exactly why Darius had done it, Erick realized. "Geran, *cadais paradial.*"

"I obey," Geran said. Darius took a step back at the groan but returned as the soldier started walking away.

"Where's he going?" Darius asked.

"Away from here," Erick said. "Does it really matter?"

Darius thought about it a moment, then shrugged. "Guess not. Alright, let's get a move on. In you go."

Landing in water deep enough to cover the top of his booted feet, Erick found himself in a coarsely crafted, cylindrical stone tunnel, five feet tall and five across. The smell drifting from the water joined his ever-growing list of aromas that made him wonder why people thought so highly of living in cities. He hadn't been much impressed yet.

Elissia came in next. "Talk to me, Mar. What's going on?" The anguish in her voice made Erick want to scream and punch the thief.

Marcus opened his mouth to speak when Darius dropped into the sewer behind Elissia. Marcus turned away. Elissia's hand went to her eyes and Erick suspected she wiped away tears. Before he could be sure, the sewer cover slammed back into place, throwing them into total darkness.

"Lead the way, Crandon," Darius said.

Erick took Elissia's hand, and the group walked, the silence broken by splashing footfalls and dripping water, the darkness broken by nothing. Erick's shoulders tensed as he stayed low, fearful of cracking his head on the ceiling. The youngest thief and one other had stayed above, putting them at even odds. He wondered if they could make a break for it, maybe free themselves and escape back up to the street.

Elissia must have sensed a shift in his body. She leaned close, and her breath drifted across his ear. "Don't. We wouldn't make it."

He didn't like the resignation in her voice but suspected she was correct.

After several minutes of walking through the cramped tunnels, they stopped. Erick heard shuffling noises and a click. A crack of light appeared and soon became a tunnel of illumination that spilled over the large group. Though not exceptionally bright, it glared at Erick like the blazing noonday sun suddenly popping up in the middle of a moonless night. He squinted at the change.

"Wipe the sludge from your shoes," Darius said. Erick faced the lighted hallway. The other thieves wiped their feet on a large sisal mat just inside the corridor. They left, leaving the group alone with Marcus and Darius. The others wiped their feet. Marcus took the lead and Darius the rear.

Erick expected to encounter more smelly, dank hallways, but instead found that small oil lamps on sconces lit the corridor, giving off a scent of jasmine. The walls, far from being rough-hewn stone, were squared, level, and covered with carved images. Inlaid with gold, silver, and an array of gems, they depicted a variety of events, from great battles to beautiful acts of love.

The group hadn't traveled far when Marcus commanded, "Wait here a second," and slipped into a doorway.

While he was gone, Corby started to dig out his pen and parchment.

"What are you doing?" Erick asked.

"I have to write down descriptions of all these beautiful artworks before I forget what they look like."

Erick didn't know what to think about Corby's attitude. Had he not noticed Elissia's pain? How could he be so callous about it?

"Don't," Erick said. "Now isn't the time." He nodded toward Elissia. Corby followed his gaze, but if he noticed anything unusual in his cousin's behavior, it didn't show on his face. He returned to studying the reliefs, touching them as if making sure they were real.

Marcus emerged a few minutes later, garbed in a dull gray tunic and pants, and a pair of dark brown leather sandals. He had also put on a silver ring with a dagger-shaped piece of jet, just like Elissia's.

"Feel better now?" Darius asked.

"At least I can walk without tripping. Those clothes were way too large."

"I should have left you naked. What happened up there?"

"I got careless, but if you want to see it, I'll show you the Geleit's ring as soon as it comes out." He started walking again, and the others followed.

They moved through a hallway, down a long, steep flight of stairs, and through even more corridors. The artistry of their surroundings continually amazed Erick. Apparently the Procurers wanted to obscure the fact they lived underground by making their dwelling as luxurious and opulent as possible. He couldn't shake the feeling that eyes watched them as they moved deeper into the lair.

We've been watched ever since we walked into this place. Blink thought to him. *You could probably push a stone at random and have a good chance of hitting a secret door.*

Blink's validation unnerved Erick. The deeper they went, the worse their chances of leaving became.

The group descended another flight of stairs that ended in front of a plain steel door. Marcus pushed the door open and walked in. With no real options, the rest followed.

They entered the most extravagant room yet. Round, at least a hundred feet across, its domed ceiling topped at thirty feet. Oil lamps set into the walls ringed the chamber. Their golden glow reflected off the polished white stone of the roof, bathing the entire chamber in rich, soft light. Sturdy tables made of dark, polished woods filled the room, placed in ever-shrinking semi-circles, with dark-stained chairs on the outer side only, so that all who sat faced the center of the room.

In the middle sat a stone slab. A thick, round plate of iron rested on the stone, slightly raised by a hidden pedestal. The plate held a chair made from the same white stone as the ceiling. Its high back faced them so Erick could not tell if anyone sat upon it. He had never seen the rare and expensive marble stone before, but had read descriptions, and knew that had to be the material before him. No other mineral could emit such a pearlescent sheen.

At least seventy-five people turned to them as they entered. Their audience ranged in age from ten to over forty; they sat with the youngest in the outer circles, farthest from the dais, and the older members in closest. Their eyes glittered in the light, and they surveyed the new group without speaking. Erick's heart pounded. Elissia gave him another reassuring squeeze that did nothing to reassure him.

Darius closed the door. It clanged shut with an ominous echo. Erick jumped. *I don't like this,* he thought.

That makes two of us, o creator of mine.

As if the closing door was a signal, the plate on the dais turned with a harsh squeaking sound, spinning the chair around so that it faced the quintet standing at the doorway.

The ugliest man Erick had ever seen sat on the throne. Bushy eyebrows hung over dark eyes that stared from sockets set deep into a pitted and scarred face. His nose was flattened to an almost shapeless blob, and scraggly patches of gray whiskers sprouted from the fleshy, multi-chinned jaw. Wisps of graying black hair that reached down to his shoulders clung to his nearly bald skull. His hefty bulk filled the large chair, almost flowing over the armrests.

"Is that your father?" Erick whispered.

"We favor our mother," she said.

"So, the Banished One has returned," the man on the throne growled, his voice deep and rumbling. "And she seeks to regain my favor by bringing me a gift."

"Gift?" Elissia asked.

"Why yes, the young man standing beside you. We've been looking for him."

"Why?" Elissia's voice faltered, and Erick's heart dropped. He already knew the answer.

A man sitting near the throne stood. Erick started, thinking the pale man who destroyed Draymed had somehow leapt ahead to finish the task, but closer study showed Erick his mistake. Though the man had light skin black hair, there were differences: this man was pale almost to the point of being ghostly, and his hair extended to his mid-back, held in a ponytail by a thick loop of some deep red stone. He wore a short, clipped moustache and goatee, and a gold cap adorned his left canine. Clenching a fold in his loose-fitting robe, the man stared directly at Erick and said. "Necromancer Erick, I am Azinor of Starrasen, *Ecrin* of the Fist of the *Inconnu*. I have paid these people well to capture you and hold you for my Master."

19

Never before had I seen such horror. Thousands of people, once dead, again living. They scaled the walls like ants swarming a lizard, heedless of any injury. Our swords would not pierce, our maces would not crush. Like the lizard that is overtaken by the small creatures it cannot defend against, we were doomed.

-Pannas-Ta, Warlord of the Tascana tribe of Falan-Dar

E rick slammed back into the blank stone wall. The door they entered through had disappeared.

Elissia stepped forward and placed herself between Erick and the others. "You can't have him. I offer him Procurer's Shield."

"But you are no longer a Procurer," her father reminded her. "Shield is not yours to offer."

Moving as quickly as her brother had, Elissia shoved Marcus away and grabbed his dagger from his belt. "I'll kill the first person who comes near him."

"Hold," the man on the throne shouted as the room echoed with sliding chairs and ringing steel. Everyone stopped, weapons in hand. He returned his gaze to Elissia. "There will be no killing in this chamber. We're thieves, not murderers, and there's no profit in wiping each other out."

"So you're going to let us walk out of here?" Elissia asked. "That's the only way this can end peacefully."

The man shook his head, making his jowls shiver. "Still one to overreact, I see. You should know me better than that. Agnon, if you would."

Three sounds, like sharp gusts of wind through a wooden fence. A bee struck his neck. He swatted at it, only to drive a thin iron needle deeper into his flesh. He winced at the stabbing pain.

"You son of a bitch," Elissia said. She held what Erick recognized as a blowgun dart, similar to Corby's except the ball on the end of the needle was black.

She had just started to fall to the ground when his vision went dark.

❧

E lissia came to with a dull throb in her forehead. She rubbed at her eyes, trying to figure out what had happened, and then it all came back. She sat up, expecting to find herself in one of the warren's deep dungeons. Instead, she lay on an overstuffed couch. Light flickered from several lamps, and the scent of lilacs filled the room. They had stuffed her in one of the warren's guestrooms.

"You're awake," Corby said. He laid beside her, head resting on a plump golden cushion, his eyes closed. "They took my hat."

"Where's Erick?"

Corby pointed without opening his eyes. Erick lay on a couch across the room. Blink, also unconscious, had his legs and arms chained against the wall behind Erick.

Elissia wiped at her dry mouth and tasted sour pomegranate. That and the headache told her the soporific her father had used to subdue them. The only thing that surprised her was that his actions had surprised her. "I'm going to go talk to him."

"Who?" Corby asked.

"My father."

Corby opened his eyes and sat up, even though the motion caused him to wince. "Why would you want to do that? He just poisoned you."

"It wasn't poison; it was *paladade*. Strong tranquilizer, but no lasting effects."

"I'll add that information to my book."

"It was a misunderstanding."

"A misunderstanding? Your brother was ready to kill you to get Erick down here. What makes you think Uncle Torin will be any different?"

Elissia winced. "I just have to explain to him what's going on."

"We are talking about the man you want to overthrow and replace, right?"

"What better way to take him down than by getting in his graces?"

Corby sighed. "He won't talk to you."

"You don't know that."

"I do," Corby muttered, but Elissia ignored him. The remark about Marcus hurt, but she couldn't accept anything at face value. Something had been off in her brother. He'd threatened her, but she didn't hear conviction. He wouldn't have killed her. She had to believe that, or she might as well do it for him.

Her whole intention in returning to Kal-Ador had been to take her place at home, beside her brother. She belonged in the city, with the Procurers, not wasting away on an island. Just because she wouldn't be a whore didn't mean she couldn't be a thief. She belonged with Marcus. To accept what had happened was to admit that she had truly lost him, and she couldn't. She still had a chance to make things right. And she needed to do it now, before Erick woke up and she lost her resolve.

Corby let out a sigh. "Do you want me to go with you?"

"No, I'll be fine." She wasn't sure the guards no doubt stationed outside their room would even let her go, much less her and Corby. Blink had woken up and stared at her, curiosity in his eyes, their bright blue so out of place against his grey skin.

If she stayed here, it would break Erick's heart. She cared for Erick a great deal, but not enough. She cared about her twin more. She had been three long years away from Marcus. She needed to be here. Erick had to understand. After all, he now knew what it was like to not have a home.

She wouldn't throw him to the wolves though. She would convince her father to let him go, contract or not. She wouldn't let the Procurers hand Erick over to Azinor. If her father refused, she would—

She had no idea what she would do.

Squaring her shoulders, she said, "I'll be right back."

"Okay," Blink said, and something in his voice almost stopped her. He didn't believe her.

Before her nerve broke, she turned and knocked on the door. Within moments, a man with straight brown hair and a crooked nose opened the door and towered above her. He wore cured leather armor that bore the crooked sword sigil of a Strongarm.

"I need to see my father," Elissia said.

"Our orders are— "

"Stuff your orders, Archel. You've known me my whole life. I'm not going to try and escape." She lowered her voice, hoping Blink wouldn't hear. "Hells, I've been trying for three years to get back."

Archel frowned, seeming to weigh his options. He looked at the other Strongarm.

The other guard, broad-chested and unknown to Elissia, shrugged. "Your dice," he said.

Archel nodded. "Come with me," he told her.

"I know the way."

Archel shook his head. "If you're not with me, then you've escaped."

"Let's go."

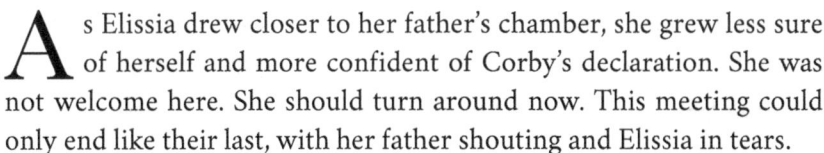

As Elissia drew closer to her father's chamber, she grew less sure of herself and more confident of Corby's declaration. She was not welcome here. She should turn around now. This meeting could only end like their last, with her father shouting and Elissia in tears.

Stop it, she told herself. *You didn't come this far to back down now.*

Most of the warren slept or attended to other duties, so they reached her father's room without encountering anyone else. Large double doors covered in gold that gleamed almost painfully under the light of the nearby sconces marked her father's chamber.

Archel raised a hand to knock and then hesitated. Elissia knew he must be rethinking the wisdom of what he had done.

"You aren't the only one," she murmured as she stepped up beside him and rapped her jet ring against the door, which let out sharp metallic *tings*. "Father, open up."

She paused, waited a moment, and then rapped again.

The door opened as she finished her second round of knocking. Her father, still dressed in the dark clothing he had worn earlier, peered out. When he saw Elissia, his grizzled face dropped into a frown. He glared at Archel, who took a step back under the withering stare.

"Father, I want to talk to you."

"About what?"

"I'm sorry for what happened, but I've learned my lesson. I want to stay here. I want to be a Procurer again. I'll do anything you want." *Well, almost anything*, she thought.

Torin stared down at her, his jowly face set in a grim line. She thought she caught the briefest glimpse of pain behind his eyes, but then it disappeared, and she may have imagined it.

"No," he said and slammed the door in her face.

E rick's eyes fluttered open. The headache caught his attention first, the dryness in his mouth second. He sat up, running his tongue across the roof of his mouth to try and ease the parched feeling and get rid of the sour taste. He was in a large chamber, as lavish as the rest of the thieves' den he had seen. Exquisite woven rugs covered the floor. He rested on a solid, heavily cushioned couch covered in deep hues of blue and gold. Table lamps with scented oils provided light while filling the room with the smell of lilacs.

"As prisons go, it could be worse," Corby said. He sat on a couch on the other side of the room, head resting against a cushion.

Blink, where are you?

"Behind you," Blink said.

Erick turned to his familiar. "Are you okay?"

"Considering what they could have done, fine," Blink said. "Headache, just like you."

"Where's Elissia?"

"On a fool's errand," Corby told him. "Be ready to comfort her when she comes back."

"What do you mean?"

Before Corby could speak, the door opened, and Elissia ran in. A burly man shut the door behind her and threw the lock. Tears ran down Elissia's face; her cheeks burned dark against her olive skin.

She ran over and threw herself onto the couch beside Corby and buried her head in a pillow, muffling the sobs that poured out. Erick pushed aside the hurt by telling himself Elissia had known her cousin far longer than she had known him. Her choice wasn't a rejection so much as a need for the familiar.

"I tried to tell you," Corby said as he rubbed his cousin's back.

"I know," Elissia said, her voice muted by the pillow. "I should have listened to you. I just thought—just--"

"Shhh," Corby said. "I know what you thought, and I told you what would happen. You excel at offering counsel to others, but you're not so adept at accepting it."

Elissia rolled onto to her side as Corby shifted his hand to gently rub her arm. "Is that the scholar's way of saying 'I told you so?'" She offered a weak smile and wiped at her face.

Corby shrugged. "It's my way of saying I would never tell you something to hurt you, only to keep you from being hurt."

Erick couldn't take it any longer. "What happened?"

"I tried to talk to my father," Elissia said.

"Why?"

She paused as if considering her words. "I wanted to explain things to him. About me, about you. He wouldn't even see me."

231

"After how your brother treated us, did you expect any different?" Erick said.

"Yes. Although I guess I shouldn't have. Marcus is another lock to pick."

"Marcus is an asshole," Blink said from behind Erick.

Elissia sat up. Most of her composure had returned. "He can be. But he has his reasons."

Erick didn't know how to react. How could she defend someone who had so callously betrayed her? He tried to imagine what he would do if Blink had done something similar to him, assuming such a thing was even possible.

He realized he would react the same way. For some reason, the thought gave him comfort. "So what happens now?"

"We wait. If they wanted us dead, we'd be dead. My guess is we're waiting for Azinor's master, whoever that is. Then, who knows?"

"Can we escape?" he asked.

Elissia shook her head. "Not without help."

Erick sighed. "If Azinor is who he says he is, then he is going to give me to his head priest. Chances are they'll sacrifice me to Eligos, which will make him stronger and that much harder for the other Necromancers to destroy."

He looked at Blink, and then at Elissia and Corby. "If they come for us, we have to try and run. If I die in the attempt, so be it. Better that than what they have planned. I want all of you to promise that if you have to, and you can, you'll kill me before you let them take me."

"You know I will," Blink said.

Corby nodded, his face grim, and ran a hand across his hair.

Elissia swallowed. "I don't know if I could."

"You have to. Better my soul is released with a chance to go to the Heaven of Caros than consumed and perverted by Eligos."

She blinked her eyes and wiped at them. Then she nodded. "Let's see if we can keep that from happening."

"I'd like that," Erick said, but at the moment he couldn't see how. If they had Geran, maybe.

To take his mind off their situation, and because he didn't know if they would ever have another chance, he asked Elissia, "Remember all those times I asked you about your past, and you said, 'some other time'?"

"Yes," Elissia answered with a resigned voice.

"I think now is about the best time."

Elissia sighed. Corby nodded at her questioning glance, so she walked over, sat beside Erick, and took his hand. "Like every other Procurer's child, I trained from the age of five to do the things thieves do. That was fine; I enjoyed the training and even thrived on it.

"When I turned twelve, I began to develop into a woman. The boys all started noticing me, and my father noticed them. That must have been when the idea started forming in his twisted brain."

"What idea?"

"Shortly after my thirteenth birthday, he sent me to train as an acolyte to Amare. What do you know about Amare?"

Erick shrugged. "Only that he is the god of love and his acolytes promote kindness and love among all people."

Elissia gave a soft chuckle. "That's the romanticized version of it. I suppose it's true to a certain extent, but what acolytes of Amare really do is have sex with worshippers. And a worshiper is anyone who has the money to pay the temple fees."

Erick's face grew warm as he remembered the temple with the half-nude women standing outside. "Is that wrong?"

"Of course it's wrong," Elissia glared at him. "Didn't your parents teach you anything?"

Erick held an angry retort. "They taught me that sex is between two people who care about each other."

Sex should be because you love someone, not because you pay them for it. Do you think it's right?"

Erick feared he might have stepped into a delicate situation from which he would find no easy way out. "I don't know. If Amare has sanctioned it, it can't be completely wrong."

Elissia looked ready to argue, but she stopped, swallowed, and said, "Perhaps, although I think it has more to do with the priests and their greed than it does with the god. But becoming an acolyte should be a choice, shouldn't it?"

"Of course," Erick said. *"The Tome of the Father and Mother* says 'the gods choose the call; the person chooses the answer'"

"I had no choice. My father told me I was going to become an acolyte, or I could find shelter with someone other than the Procurers. So I did what he told me to do."

"Why did your father want you to become an acolyte?"

Elissia gave a grim smile. "He decided I could make more money that way. Some worshippers like to unburden their guilt to Amare's acolytes, confess their crimes or other indiscretions. The Love Temple has a reputation of silence where such things are concerned. Such confessions are worth money. I would hear my companion's secrets and report them to father, who would use the information for blackmail."

"But wouldn't that only work if the person had money?"

Elissia nodded. "That's why father donated to ensure I got the courtesan training. I would attend the wealthiest customers.

"For three months I trained in the ways of sex, or 'Amare's Blessings' as they call it."

Erick shifted uncomfortably as ideas of Elissia training went through his mind. He found the images both erotic and disturbing. Again, he wished he could talk to his parents, who had left him woefully unprepared for the emotions roiling through him.

Some of his feelings must have shown. Elissia said, "Don't worry, it was all instruction and observation. I didn't have to participate until my final initiation. That's when things went wrong."

"What happened?"

"Other initiates took me into the priest's chamber and undressed me. As he walked toward me, naked, I lost my composure. Maybe there's some Zakerin in me somewhere, because I just couldn't let him take me. I want my first time to be with someone I love, not some old, overweight cleric. I told him that. He grew irate and asked me why I had wasted their time if I did not hold true to the belief.

"That's when it all poured out of me. I couldn't help it. I told him about being a Procurer and spilled father's plan to him. 'That's okay, my child,' he said, sitting next to me with his cock still pointing like a weather vane. 'Amare forgives you, and so do I.' Then the bastard tried to force himself on me."

Anger at the unknown cleric flashed through Erick's mind. How dare someone try to take advantage of her. "What did you do?"

"I ran my fingernails across his prick and ran as he fell away bleeding."

Erick gave an empathic shudder at the man's fate even as he thrilled at Elissia's escape.

"I came back home and confessed what happened. I apologized and told father I would do anything to help the Procurers, but I couldn't do that. Instead of forgiving me, he screamed loud enough to stir the whole warren. He called me things I can't even repeat." Elissia's voice choked. Her twisted face relayed the bitter memory of that final conversation. His awkward questions had brought it all back, slicing open an old wound. He put his arm around Elissia's shoulders. She pressed her face against his chest.

"I'm sorry," he said. "I didn't know it would hurt you so much."

"It's okay," Elissia said, her voice muffled against his chest. "It all worked out for the best because I met you."

Erick wondered if it truly was for the best, considering what had happened. "Maybe that's what Caros and Denech intended all along."

"Maybe," Elissia agreed, wiping a tear away. "But I wish they could have picked a less painful way to do it. Anyway, Father held a convocation and banished me in front of the entire Society."

"What about your mother? Didn't she have anything to say about it?"

"Mother?" Elissia laughed bitterly. "No, she didn't even watch me leave. I love her, but she wouldn't raise her voice to a flea on a cat's ass. That's how she ended up saddled with my father."

Erick held her, offering what comfort he could. It struck him that, somewhere between leaving Draymed and arriving in this room, he had fallen in love with Elissia. It wasn't at all like the storybooks. There had been no spark or locking of eyes, no swooning. But there had been hours of delightful conversation, friendly smiles, mutual joy, and shared pain. His mother's torrid romances said nothing about these things, but they seemed to Erick the true actions of love. And

Elissia's resolve to hold to her beliefs at all costs made him care for her even more.

It's about time you admitted it, Blink thought. *I knew it days ago.*

Shut up, Erick thought back.

"His plan wouldn't have worked," Corby said. "Not in the long term. Someone would have gone to the temple and told, and the priests would have deduced who was selling the information."

Elissia shrugged. "I'm sure father had a plan for that eventuality. You get to his position by being a ruthless bastard, not by being stupid."

"So what made you think he would talk to you now?" Erick asked, his voice gentle.

"People change. At least, they're supposed to. Father wasn't why I wanted to come back anyway. It was always about Marcus."

Erick said nothing, not wanting to upset her, but something had happened in the time she had been away to make her lose her brother.

Corby didn't have the same reservations. "People do change, but I don't think your father or Marcus changed for the better."

Elissia tensed, and Erick braced for her angry reply, but noise at the front door caught their attention. Scuffling, some grunts, several thuds, and two heavy thumps as something hit the floor. Elissia jumped up, grabbed the lamp on the nearest table, and reared back, ready to throw. The lock on the door clicked; the door flew open.

Marcus stepped in. He wore a tight-fitting royal blue shirt with a high collar to hide the red ring around his neck, charcoal-colored serge pants, and gray soft leather shoes. He held a cudgel in one hand and a large key ring in the other. Four older boys followed him, faces grim, weapons ready. Erick glimpsed two men lying on the floor.

"Don't stand there gawking," Marcus said. "Let's get the hell out of here while we can."

20

"The smallest pebble can cause the biggest rockslide" is an ancient Makern proverb. So it came to be with us. It started with Erick, a young man on a little-regarded island, but it grew to encompass the entire world.

-Corberin of Draymed, Introduction, *To Twr Krinnik and Back.*

Elissia set the lamp down, and Marcus tossed her the key ring. "Free the creature."

"His name is Blink," Elissia said as she caught the ring.

"I don't care if his name is King of Sewage Row, just get him down so we can get out of here." He walked into the room. The other four thieves dragged the two guards in and shoved them into a corner, then two of them stood in the hallway while the other two stayed in the room.

"What's going on?" Erick asked.

"Isn't it obvious?" Marcus said. "We're getting you out of here."

Erick had no idea what had happened to change Marcus's manner, but he would worry about it later. He noticed a large bruise had formed around the thief's left eye. "What happened to you?"

Marcus shrugged. "I was clumsy, and father didn't approve."

"He hit you?"

"Beats the alternative." Marcus touched his neck gingerly. "But his reaction made this decision easier."

"Was there a point when the decision wasn't easy?" Elissia asked as she freed Blink.

"No," Marcus said. "But offering it to father as a 'fuck you' makes it that much sweeter. You ready?"

"Ready," Elissia said.

Blink stepped away from the wall, leapt into the air, and landed on Marcus, slamming the small boy to the ground. He brought his barbed tail around and poised it above Marcus's face. "Give me a reason I shouldn't pump you full." He glared at the other thieves, who had drawn their knives. "One step closer and I'll stab his eye out."

"What are you doing?" Elissia said. "He's helping us."

"It's his fault we're here in the first place," Erick said. "He could have warned us, helped us get away."

"You're as stupid as the bat here is ugly," Marcus told Erick. "I couldn't warn you, not with Darius and his cronies all over us."

"You threatened to kill Elissia."

"You've never played cards, have you? It's called a bluff."

Elissia ran over and pushed at Blink. "Get off him."

Blink stepped away from Marcus but kept his tail poised.

"A bluff?" Erick asked. "Why?"

"This isn't the time to explain it," Marcus said as he stood up. "Let's wait until—oof."

Elissia had thrown herself around Marcus and hugged him tightly. "You bastard," she said, a catch in her voice. "I could kill you for that, but I knew you wouldn't abandon me."

Marcus returned her hug, tears in his eyes. "I've missed you, Lissi, and I'll explain everything, but right now we have to leave."

As they reluctantly broke the hug and Marcus wiped at his eyes, Erick's estimation of the thief rose.

"How do we know you won't just lead us into the dark and kill us," Blink said.

Marcus cocked his eyebrow, a gesture reminiscent of his sister, and said, "You want to think that one through for a minute?"

"If he wanted us dead, he wouldn't have to take us somewhere," Erick said. "He could have done it while we were unconscious."

Marcus smiled and gave Erick a thumb up. "Maybe you aren't so dumb."

"He's smart enough to keep from getting himself nearly hanged," Blink grumbled, but he lowered his tail.

The boy's smile widened. "Can't argue with that. Hello, cousin, happy to meet you," he said to Corby.

"Would have preferred it to be without the drugging and kidnapping," Corby said.

Marcus winked at him. "Some things can't be helped."

He walked to the door and stopped. "Be as quiet as you can," he told them. "Most of the warren is asleep or away, but your buddy Azinor has things stirred up more than usual. We know the least traveled ways, but if we run into anybody, let us handle it."

"I don't suppose you have our weapons," Elissia said.

"I have someone working on it." Marcus nodded to the other two thieves. The taller one opened the door and stepped aside. "Follow me."

The group followed, Erick behind Marcus and the other two thieves taking up the rear. Being led around by people he didn't know had begun to irritate Erick.

They moved through empty hallways decorated in tapestries and soft rugs and lit at regular intervals by small lanterns. Doors lined the walls on either side. Erick tensed every time he passed one, waiting for someone to jump out and grab him, or for Marcus to turn, say it was all a cruel prank, and shove him into a room outfitted like a true prison cell.

Marcus and the other thieves moved with sure, soft steps and walked on the balls of their feet, slightly crouched with their arms to the side. Erick glanced back and noticed Elissia had adopted the same posture. He tried to copy them but almost fell after five feet.

"Idiot," Marcus whispered after Erick stumbled into him. "It takes years to get it right, so don't even try. If we live through this, get Lissi to teach you."

A few minutes brought them to a dead-end corridor. An ornate mirror, trimmed in gold etched with curlicue patterns, took up the wall. A tapestry hung on either side, depicting violent battles.

"Do all thieves live this well?" Erick asked.

"We live better than many," Marcus admitted. "Because we have to crawl through sewers to get in and out of home, we try to make home as comfortable as possible. Oh, and don't call us thieves. It's insulting."

"It's what you are, isn't it?" Blink asked.

"And you're an unnatural creation formed from jizz and blood, but I bet you don't like to be reminded of that, do you?"

Blink flapped his wings in irritation.

"That's what I thought." Marcus smiled. It seemed to be a common expression on the boy, unlike Elissia, who offered them rarely.

"So why did you bring us to a dead end?" Erick asked.

"This is a thieves' warren," Elissia said. "There's no such thing."

Marcus's reached behind the mirror and gave a tug on something on the wall. With a click, the mirror popped open. A shiver ran through Erick as he recalled the last time he had found a secret room. He hoped his luck ran better with this one.

Marcus opened the mirror and slipped inside. Everyone followed. When the door closed, the hallway went pitch black. "I assume you're a bright eyes now," Marcus said.

"Afraid so," Elissia said. "Didn't have much need for sneaking in the dark this past three years."

"Everyone take hands then," Marcus said.

Great, another unlit corridor, Erick thought as Marcus took his hand and he took Elissia's.

This is too dark even for me, Blink thought. *I don't know how they do it.*

"How did you know about Blink's creation?" Erick asked Marcus.

"I'm a good listener, and sneaky," Marcus said. "Azinor told father quite a bit about you when they thought I wasn't around. None of it flattering. If they weren't waiting for 'The Master' to show up, he would have probably had you killed on the spot."

Erick shivered again and said a small prayer to Denech that his luck had held so far. "Who is the Master?"

He couldn't see Marcus shrug but sensed it in the shift of the boy's grip. "Don't know, but Azinor got all gooey and reverent sounding when he talked about him, so he must be high up in the cult."

Erick had never heard of anyone in the Fist with the title of Master, other than Eligos himself. But Erick had disrupted Eligos when he destroyed the vampire. He couldn't have already found a new host and organized a search for Erick. Could he? "Did-

"Shhh," Marcus said. "Save the chatter. This passage isn't used much, but the walls are thin. We're getting ready to go by rooms where people sleep. Quiet is the key."

They moved on in silence. Erick had no idea how long they walked, consumed instead by a growing dread that Eligos was back on his trail. Azinor's use of the term Master gave him great concern. If Eligos had somehow returned already, how would Erick ever be able to stay ahead?

Don't let it rattle you, Blink told him. *Nothing has changed. You need to get to Broken Mountain, no matter what.*

Yeah, I'm doing a great job of it so far.

The longer they went, the more Erick's nerves frayed. The smooth walls gave way to a rough tunnel, and occasionally Marcus whispered for them to duck to avoid a nasty crack to their skull. Despite the inanity of the idea, Erick couldn't shake the thought they were being led to a trap. The darkness pressed in on him, making it difficult to breathe. Every footfall seemed to whisper doom, and every rustle of clothing sounded like the laughter from his weeks-old dream. Eligos lived and waited for him, possibly at the end of this tunnel. Their escape had been discovered. Darius and Azinor would be waiting as soon as he stepped into the light, ready to—

Stop it, Blink thought. *Everything's okay. The dark is affecting you. We're going to be okay.*

"How much further?" Erick asked, trying to hide his panic.

"Almost there," Marcus said. "See the light."

Erick couldn't at first, but then he caught the faintest glimmer of yellow sunlight, perhaps five hundred feet ahead, shining on to the tunnel floor in a thin square outline. He latched on to it like a parched man seeking water. As they drew closer, his breathing eased, and his fears disappeared in implausibility.

The brightness grew gradually, and Erick made out a wooden ladder that led up to a trapdoor. Light filtered through the dust in the tunnel and Erick smelled the dry scent of burlap.

Marcus motioned to one of the other thieves—the tall, lanky one—and he crawled up the ladder, reminding Erick of a spider. He opened the trapdoor, scanned the room, and then disappeared from view as he went into the barn, closing the door behind him.

"Wh-" Erick started but stopped as Marcus held up a finger, still watching the ceiling.

A minute later the trapdoor opened. The thief looked down and gave a quick, sharp whistle.

"It's safe," Marcus said. "Go on up."

Erick sent Blink up first, then Elissia and Corby, and he followed. He popped up into what appeared to be a warehouse, easily as large as his manor. Burlap bags stacked on wooden pallets filled one side, and wooden crates arranged in large rectangles took up another. Much of the building was empty. Large double doors on rails sat in the middle of two of the walls. Diffused light filtered in from square holes in the roof covered by thin sheets of hide, giving the room a muted orange cast.

The shorter thief came up and closed the door. It all but disappeared into the floor, the gaps in the slats matching precisely with the boards on either side.

"What is this?" Erick asked.

"Escape room, in case the warren is ever raided. Don't think many people know about this one anymore, so I figured it was the safest one to bring you to while we figure out what we're going to do."

"What *we're* going to do?" Blink asked.

Marcus shrugged. "Father's not stupid. It won't take him long to figure out who helped you escape."

"Why did you help us?"

"I think that should be obvious," Marcus told Blink as he stared at Elissia. Erick didn't need more proof of how much the twins cared for each other, but he got it in the adoration on Marcus's face. Elissia walked over and stood beside her brother, her almond eyes alight.

"There's more to it," Elissia said. "I know you acted like an ass because you had to, but your words damn near killed me. Why?"

"It killed up to say them, but I had to prove my loyalty to Darius. I'm already under suspicion, so I've had to tread lightly. Torin has become even more of a tyrant than before. Trying to use you like he did and then banishing you was just the start. He's done far worse things since." He took Elissia's hands. "Our dream to remove him is growing, even beyond our best hopes. But Darius is still loyal, so to make him think I was too, I did what I had to." He looked at Erick and Blink. "Sorry."

"I understand," Erick said. Having listened to Elissia's story, he shuddered to imagine what else the ugly man might be capable of doing.

"Now that you're back, we can make it happen," Marcus said. "Everyone saw how he treated you in the chamber. We can use you as a rallying point and have him out within a month. I can't return to the warren, but there are plenty inside who can help. And I have hiding spots even the Procurers don't know about."

"A month?" Elissia asked. "Father deposed and out of favor?"

Marcus nodded. "You and I in charge. We can make it a better guild, a guild that works together on the wishes of everybody, not the whims of one man."

Erick watched Elissia slipping away from him. She had returned to her brother, and that reunion was probably the only reason she left Draymed with him. The plan they spoke of sounded a long time in the making, ready to come to fruition. She would stay behind and live her dream, leaving Erick to fend for himself. Erick's gut twisted as he realized how he had been used.

"I can't, Mar," Elissia said, pulling her hands from her brother's. "Not yet. Nothing would make me happier than to watch father sent away in shame." She paused a moment, and willfully maintained her composure. "But right now, I have to help Erick do what he has to do. Father will be there when we get back."

"He'll be there. But the situation might not be. Things are on the edge. If we don't strike soon, the chance may disappear."

"Better your chance disappear than everything else," Corby said.

Marcus took a step back from his sister. "What exactly does he have to do that's so Gods-damned important?"

"Eligos of the Inconnu has returned. I have to meet the other Necromancers at Broken Mountain and learn how to destroy him before he raises an army of undead and makes war on the world again."

"Is that all?" Marcus said. He let out a hysterical chuckle. "And I thought our hopes were impossible."

"And I have to go with him," Elissia said. The statement cost her dearly, and Erick's disappointment reversed and redoubled as a fierce love for her.

"Why? Why do you have to go with him?"

"Because if he doesn't make it, then problems with father will be the least of our worries. And because—" she stopped and stared at the floor.

Marcus nodded, his face grim. "I see."

He looked at the other two thieves, then at Elissia, and sighed. "I'm in for the whole run, I guess. After waiting three years, I'm not going to let you out of my sight. I'll go with you and take this idiot to his big mountain." He turned to Erick. "But once you're done saving the world, you have to come back and help save my guild. Agreed?"

Elissia's face lit up so much that Erick didn't let Marcus's insult bother him. "Agreed."

Marcus nodded. "Okay, we wait for night, then gather some supplies, and get out of town."

"We need a better plan," Corby said. "Getting out of town is a start, but what then?"

"Haven't you been listening, cousin?" Marcus said. "We go to Broken Mountain."

"I know that," Corby said. "But so does Azinor. And so will the Procurers Will they pursue us beyond the city walls?" he asked Marcus.

"If they're paid to," Marcus answered. "Hell, father might do it for free out of spite."

"Pursuit greatly reduces our chance of success," Corby said. "We've already had issues. The last thing we need is professional trackers hunting us. So how do we keep that from happening? And no-" Corby continued as Marcus started to speak. "We can't overthrow Uncle Torin first. Something tells me Erick doesn't have that much time."

Uncertain glances passed among the group. Erick wondered if he and Blink should go alone and take their chances, but then an idea came to him. "How long can we safely stay here?" he asked Marcus.

The thief put his hand on his chin and stared at the ceiling. Erick followed his gaze but saw nothing. After a few moments, Marcus pointed to the other two thieves. "Callon and Dere and a few others can run interference, keep people away from here for a while."

"Until three hours after sunrise?"

Marcus looked at the thieves, and the lanky one nodded.

"Okay," Erick said. "I've got an idea, but I'm going to need some herbs and a fresh eyeball."

21

The Wight is another creature in the Necromancer's Art, but unlike most, the souls for these monsters are brought from the middle depths of the Hells. As such, they are difficult to control, unreliable, and unwaveringly evil. The Inconnu used them to great effectiveness, but the Necromancers rarely summoned them during the war.

-Corberin of Draymed, *On the Necromancer's Art*

"The graveyard's on the other side," Marcus told Erick. They stood beside a wall of dingy gray brick, easily twice as high as them and topped with six-inch iron spikes. Patches of moss grew across the stone. The wan light of Talan's nearly shuttered Lantern turned the walls black and leprous, splotches of corruption on a moldy skeleton.

"How do we get in?" Erick asked.

Marcus pointed to two large trees with their trunks rising beside the wall. The lowest branches overhung the rampart.

Erick groaned. "Isn't there a front gate?"

"Sure, and we could walk right through it if you care to explain to the guards why we want to stroll in a graveyard at Melteth's hour, in black."

Erick touched his necklace, a ward against the mention of the evil night god. He smiled at the irony of the act, considering what he planned to do. "Why would anyone have guards for a graveyard?"

Marcus grinned, his teeth shining out against his black clothing and the charcoal smeared across his face. Dressed in a similar fashion, Erick had felt ridiculous until he realized it did make them difficult to see. A good thing, since their wardrobe would have them in the dungeons if they were caught.

"There are jewels and fine clothing in some of the mausoleums," Marcus said. "The Procurers avoid them, but you get the occasional amateur who tries to break in for a quick looting, thinking it's easier to steal from the dead than the living. Like as not, they end up dead themselves."

"Why?"

"Because rich people can afford to have their tombs trapped. Let's move. The guards patrol the outer wall sometimes, and I don't want to get caught up a tree."

Marcus shimmied up the bole and onto the lowest branch. From there, he moved with sure-footed stealth across the limb until he sat above the wall, almost invisible with only his eyes and patches of his face showing dimly in the moonlight.

Erick climbed the tree nowhere near as quickly or quietly. The pack hanging over his shoulder hindered him. He had not climbed in over five years, when he abandoned playing in the palm trees that grew near the manor. But he remembered the basics and soon reached the thief.

Disdain on his face, Marcus whispered, "Any Procurer over the age of seven could have done that in half the time without sounding like a pregnant dog."

"Yeah?" Erick snapped back. "Can any of them bring a hundred dead pigs back to life?"

Marcus's face went blank for a moment, and then he let out a soft chuckle. "We have to drop to the ground. When I get down, lower your pack and then lower yourself and drop." He gave a crooked smiled, teeth glowing. "Try and land like something other than a rock."

Marcus pushed himself off the limb and hit the ground in a crouch with a lack of sound cats would envy.

Erick removed the pack from his shoulder and held it toward the Procurer's outstretched arms. "Be careful with this," he whispered, letting loose the strap. Marcus caught it and stepped to the side, disappearing behind a gravestone.

To Erick, the ground suddenly appeared much further away than it did before he had to leave the safety of the tree. He prepared to jump, remembering from experience that rolling after landing helped avoid a broken leg. Sucking in his breath, he dropped toward the ground.

Almost before he knew it, Erick stood on the ground, having landed and rolled with the ease of an acrobat. A dull stinging went through his ankles at the initial contact, but he seemed otherwise okay.

"Nice," Marcus whispered, coming up behind him. "They only heard that three blocks away instead of the five that heard you climbing."

Erick deflated. "Was it that bad?"

"Pretty bad," Marcus confirmed, handing the pack to Erick. "You should have hung off the branch and dropped. It would have been quieter and safer. But the guards around here are stupid, so we should be okay."

Erick couldn't resist. "Stupid? They caught you."

"That's because I let my feelings get in the way of my common sense." Erick started to speak, but Marcus stopped him. "No, I'm not going to tell you what I did; I don't know you that well. Let's get off the path."

They moved into the shadows behind several large grave markers. Erick set his pack on the ground, opened the leather flap, and reached in to remove a human eyeball wrapped in cloth. Marcus watched as Erick unfolded the cloth to reveal the expertly extracted orb. The two thieves, Callon and Dere, had left the warehouse on Marcus's orders and returned an hour later with the organ in their possession. They assured Erick it had been taken from someone who deserved it. Erick didn't know if he believed them, but he didn't have the luxury of propriety. He could only hope the gods would understand and accept the need.

Pulling a thin silver needle from a holder in the sack, Erick held the index finger of his other hand a few inches over the eye and jabbed the needle into his fingertip. As the blood dripped from his punctured finger and fell onto the dead eye, he recited the Litany of True Vision.

"*Mucalz col cnila phamah, gigipah dorpha dode anoan. Alakanath, amde sibsu, dluga mucalz deteloc pham anoan apila. Krinnik, amde sibsu, dluga mucalz decalz ar anoan uran vaoan. Denech, amde sibsu, drix aldor mucalz od cnila de allor argedca.*"

Erick repeated the incantation twice more, dripping blood until it coated the eye. He sensed Marcus shivering beside him. The *Elonsha* whispered to Erick, as it always did.

Ignore it, Blink thought, his mental voice faint with distance, but with enough power to help Erick in his task.

As he finished the declamation, Erick sensed a shadow behind him, and darkness passed across his eyes. Startled, he turned, expecting a guard. Nothing stood behind him. Goosebumps tickled his body. A tingle crept across his scalp, as if a tiny, clawed spider ran over his head. He shook himself and the sensation disappeared, leaving him unnerved.

Marcus let out a loud gasp as the blood on the eye disappeared, sucked into the orb through the membrane surrounding it. The eye twitched, the optic cord wiggling behind it like a demented tadpole.

"I think I'm going to throw up."

"This is nothing," Erick told him in a distracted voice, still shaken by the odd sensations.

"Not from the eyeball," Marcus said. "I just feel cold and nauseous. And what is that stench?"

"That's from the *Elonsha*." Erick picked up the writhing sphere and placed his still bleeding finger against the tattered string of tissue hanging from the back of the eye. "I should have told you to stand away."

"What is *Elonsha*?"

"The source of the power I use."

"Does it always feel like that?" Marcus asked, shaking.

"Yes, but with Blink's help I'm able to ignore it." *For the most part,* Erick thought. He had never experienced any physical manifestations other than the smell and wasn't sure what had happened.

"What about that stench? It's like-" Marcus stopped, his hands moving as if trying to grab the words he wanted.

"Rotten onions," Erick said. "You get used to that too. We need to find the grave of someone who died around seventeen. Can you subtract numbers?"

Marcus offered a disdainful sneer. "I'm a thief, aren't I?"

"I thought 'thief' was an insult."

"Only when a non-thief says it." Marcus walked off, glancing at the stones as he passed them.

Erick shook his head, baffled by the boy's strange pride. He walked in the opposite direction, reading the dates inscribed on the squat stone markers.

He soon found one, a seventeen-year-old who'd died in 3857, barely over a hundred years ago. Holding the eye in front of himself, he pointed the pupil toward the ground. He cleared his mind and concentrated on the connection created by the power and blood flowing from his finger. With the eye, he looked through the dirt and into the wormhole-riddled, rotting wooden coffin, where he found a skeleton with a few tatters of clothing. *"Zamra oi noromi ast,"* he whispered, and the vision changed. Though still a corpse, the body appeared as it did at death, a black-haired boy with dark eyes and skin.

"Not even close," Erick said to no one, and moved on.

The search took nearly an hour, but--with Marcus's help--Erick found a suitable corpse, taller but close enough for his purposes.

Erick dropped the eye. Deprived of the *Elonsha*-infused contact with Erick's body, the orb shriveled, blood and fluids leaking into the ground until it shrunk to no bigger than a grape. Erick stepped on the dried, withered sphere, and the remaining energy scattered with a powdery crunching sound.

Now comes the hard part, Erick thought. Ideally, they would dig up the body so he could work with direct contact, requiring far less effort and blood. But such an act ran a high risk of attracting attention, so Erick had to do it the hard way. He sat beside the grave and opened his sack. "This will take a while if you want to get some sleep."

"Sleep? This is my daytime. I'll watch." Marcus walked several feet away. "But I'll do it from here."

Erick nodded and returned to his task. He removed his silver measuring funnel, its stand, a triangular cork, and the bottle of regenerative. He set the stand down, placed the funnel upon it, and pushed the cork inside the funnel, tapered side down, until the tip protruded past the funnel's end and sealed the hole. Satisfied, he pulled the top off the bottle.

"What is that?" Marcus asked.

"A special mixture of the herbs you got me," Erick said as he poured the mixture into the funnel. "It will restore motion to the body so it can dig its way out."

"A bunch of crushed plants is all you need to bring someone back from the dead?"

"No, it takes more than that," Erick answered absently, his mind calculating the amount of blood the long-dead body would require. He needed enough to give the creature ample muscle to claw through the rotted coffin and six feet of dirt; he could add skin and details once he had the corpse in reach. Unfortunately, the age of the cadaver meant that even generating that amount of tissue would take a significant amount of energy.

The final calculation came to just under a pint, so Erick rounded off. It paid to err on the side of more, to avoid ending up with an immobile corpse and having to repeat the ritual. He pulled a measuring glass from his pack.

Never having used such a large amount of his blood before, Erick was glad to have Marcus nearby. "I may need your help," he told the young thief. "If I faint, bind my thumb, let me rest for ten minutes and then wake me.

"Bind your thumb? Why would I have to do that?"

Erick pulled a small steel knife from the case and ran it across his thumb, cutting deeply into the flesh.

Marcus hissed as blood squirted from Erick's injured finger and spilled into the glass. They watched as the red liquid ebbed and flowed in time with Erick's rapidly beating heart. The pain, delayed by the suddenness of the trauma, came on full force and Erick gritted his teeth, tears welling.

"Wha-" Marcus started, but stopped as Erick shook his head and returned his attention to the jar, wiping the tears away with his uninjured hand.

After what seemed an eternity, Erick had enough blood. He pulled his thumb away and squeezed at the base to cut off the flow. "Grab that cloth in the bag and wrap this."

"Sure." Marcus wrapped the injured thumb with speed and efficiency.

"Good job," Erick told him, surprised at how well the young thief bound the wound.

"I've had practice," Marcus told him. "I've tended far worse cuts than that one for some of my less lucky companions."

Pushing away a sudden wave of dizziness, Erick picked up the glass and poured the blood into the funnel. "You might want to step back."

As Marcus did so, Erick put his finger into the blood and herb mixture and recited the Invocation of *Duppy* Creation. "*Mucalz col cnila phamah, oln oi allora emetgis. Alakanath, amde sibsu, dluga mucalz deteloc dezacar molap. Krinnik, amde sibsu, dluga mucalz decalz deyolcam molap deolpirt. Talan, amde sibsu, umda domadriax deoln molap gil. Noad ol omaos, umda nonca Duppy, hami mahorela niiso olpirt.*"

Erick repeated the invocation. *Elonsha* built in the funnel, boiling the blood and turning it dark brown. On the last word, he pushed the funnel into the ground, dislodging the cork and allowing the *Elonsha*-charged liquid to flow into the dirt.

As the power continued to swirl around him and into the funnel, Erick sat back, feeling dizzier. He had done the hard part. Now they had only to wait for the body to crawl out of its earthen prison.

Join me.

Erick frowned. Marcus stared back, silent. Erick glanced around, seeking the source of the whispered imprecation.

A chill wind blew through him to his soul, and the disturbing tingle he had experienced earlier ran across his scalp. The voice spoke again, soft but with a menace that made Erick shiver in dread.

Join me or die.

As the last dregs of blood turned a dark black, Erick recognized the voice as the one from his dream after his confrontation with the vampire. The sound of the Master of Shadows.

I am near, and you will be mine. Surrender to me, and you will know power beyond your ken. Resist and suffer despair beyond imagining.

The strength of the voice, the sense that its source stood just beyond his vision, terrified Erick. His skin crawled at the evil resonating through the words. With all the mental force he could muster through his fear, he replied. *My father would not follow you, nor will I. You have already shown me despair I would not have dreamed; there is nothing more you can do to me.*

A tremor of malevolent amusement rattled through the voice as it spoke again. *You know so little, child. When we meet, I will remind you of your words.*

As quickly as it had appeared, the presence vanished, leaving Erick numb and unsettled, as if he awoke to a world of shadow and creatures always on the edge of sight. The blood ran into the ground, soaked up by the thirsty earth.

Are you okay? Blink asked in his faint voice. *I tried to help, but you're too far away. I can come.*

Erick shook his head. *No, stay there. The worst has passed.* He stood. "Now we wait," he told Marcus in a shaky voice. He walked around to dislodge the feelings of dread, but moved slowly to avoid fainting.

"How long?"

"Maybe four hours."

"Four-?" Marcus shrugged his narrow shoulders. "You hungry?"

"Yes," Erick answered, the loss of blood and exertion of the Ritual giving him an appetite even the disconcerting voice couldn't diminish.

"I'll be right back." Marcus ran across the graveyard and scrambled up another tree beside the wall.

Amazed at Marcus's speed and agility, Erick leaned against the grave marker and rested his head on the hard stone. Despite the gnawing worry at the Master's seeming closeness, Erick's unease dissipated, carried away like a dream. Tired and light-headed, he closed his eyes.

He awoke to Marcus shaking him. A bundled cloth sat beside the thief, a dark sausage sticking out of the top.

"How long have you been gone?"

"About fifteen minutes. Sleeping's the best way to get caught, you know."

"Sorry, my thief senses aren't what they should be." He sat up from the stone and arched his back, stretching out knotted muscles.

"Stick around long enough, I'll fix that," Marcus told him.

"No, thank you. I already have your sister teaching me to fight. One new skill is enough for now."

"What were those things you were saying earlier?"

"What things?"

"All those strange words while you had blood draining out of your body."

"It's an old language called *Lonsh*, the language of Necromantic power."

"But *what* were you saying?" Marcus clarified.

"I was calling upon the different gods to provide power to my spell."

"What does 'amde sibsu' mean? You said that a lot."

It surprised Erick that Marcus had picked up words from the Rituals so quickly. "Literally, it means 'called to the covenant,' but in the form I used it, its truer meaning is 'bound by the Covenant.' It reminds the gods of the pact between them and the Necromancers."

"Could they forget?"

Erick smiled. "It's Ritual. It doesn't necessarily make sense."

"What about 'dluga mucalz?' I picked that up, too."

Erick grew alarmed. "Don't repeat the words from the Rituals. They can be dangerous for someone who doesn't wield Necromantic power. They give the *Inconnu* a way into your mind, and that's the last thing you want." Erick shuddered as the memory of the recent mental invasion washed through him again. "If I had known you would pick them out so quickly, I would have made you go away. We should discuss something else."

"Fine, just tell me what those two words mean."

"They mean 'release power.' Now change the subject."

A mischievous grin crossed Marcus's face. "Okay, what about you and my sister? You had her in bed yet?"

Heat radiated from Erick's face as he blushed, shocked as much by the impropriety of the question as its source. "That's not your business," he said, fighting to keep his voice low. "You shouldn't even be asking such a thing."

"So you haven't, huh? I had hoped being on the island would have loosened those rigid morals of hers a bit. She likes you. I bet she'd let you be her first if you asked her."

Flustered almost beyond speech, Erick still managed to blurt out, "Stop it. You're talking about a girl that I... that I care about a great deal." He stopped short of saying he loved her, wanting for some reason to keep the depth of his feelings to himself.

Marcus shrugged. "I care about her, too, but it's time for her to quit being a prude and unlock the treasure chest." Marcus winked, his grease coated eyelid making his eye momentarily disappear. "You might as well be her key."

Erick liked that idea but didn't like discussing it with someone he barely knew. "Don't talk about your sister like that."

Marcus cocked his head to one side. "Why?"

"Because it's not proper."

Marcus smiled. "Right, you grew up a Zakerin, didn't you?" His tone made it sound as if Zakerin were the same as slow-minded. "That explains a lot. Never mind. I wouldn't expect you to understand."

"You're Zakerin too."

"We just happen to live here," Marcus said. "Our mother's Straph, or couldn't you tell that by our skin? And the big city teaches you ways of thinking you wouldn't get out there on your tiny island."

Erick suspected he should be insulted, but he didn't have the energy and just wanted the conversation over. "I'm going to lie down if you don't mind watching."

"Don't you want anything to eat?" Marcus asked, unwrapping the cloth to reveal dark bread, cheese, two apples, and a light-skinned sausage.

"I'm not hungry," Erick said. Marcus had managed to do something even the voice of Eligos couldn't: make his hunger disappear.

"Okay," Marcus said, tearing a chunk from the bread loaf. "When do I wake you up?"

"When you see a hand popping out of the ground," Erick told him, then turned away and curled up on the slightly damp grass. Between thinking about Marcus's comments and hearing his feasting, it took Erick a long time to fall asleep.

~

An urgent shaking woke him. He sat up to find Marcus staring at something, his eyes wide and throat flexing as if he were about to vomit.

Erick rolled over to see the *duppy* halfway out of the ground, spindly muscled arms pushing against the mounds of dirt that lay on either side. Erick sat up, pleased to see the creature's effect on Marcus. It served him right for his remarks about Elissia.

He had to admit the body was in poor shape, covered by only the thinnest strands of dark red and gray muscle fibers clotted with fresh earth, but such things had ceased to bother Erick long ago. He stood up, feeling better physically, if not mentally, after his rest.

Marcus stood behind him. "Now what?" he asked in a strangled voice.

"Now we go back so I can finish."

The creature completed its emergence from the ground and stood unsteadily, awaiting instruction. Though one of the easiest *gateloah* to create, since they were strictly motor function and required no soul, *duppies* had the disadvantage of being able to follow only one order unless controlled like a puppet.

After a moment's consideration, Erick said, "*Duppy*, follow me." The revived corpse lumbered over until it stood five feet from Erick.

"Great Melteth, it stinks," Marcus said in a wavering voice as he backed away.

"Deal with it," Erick snapped. "And you invite trouble by saying the dark god's name, so stop doing it. Let's get out of here."

"Gladly." Marcus headed for the wall. Eyeing the skeletal creature lumbering behind Erick, he added, "But I wouldn't protest too much about dark gods if I were you."

Erick frowned as Marcus led them to a different tree from the one they used to enter. This one seemed more agreeable to being scaled; its thick bole angled toward the wall at a reasonable slope and offered several protrusions and knots for handholds.

Marcus scrambled up the trunk, and Erick followed closely. The *Duppy* had a more difficult time but managed to dig its fingers into the bark and soon joined them on one of the thick limbs extending beyond the graveyard wall.

Marcus jumped and landed with his feline grace. Erick dropped his pack to Marcus and, bolstered by the ease of his previous leap, pushed away from the branch. He landed beside Marcus, crouched his knees, and put out his arms. It hurt, but he succeeded in staying upright and not breaking anything.

"I think I'm getting the hang of this," Erick said, smiling. Marcus didn't answer but stared at the street. Erick followed his gaze.

Darius stood there, casually flipping a dagger end over end. Four other thieves stood with him, dressed in black, their faces grim.

"Well, look what we've trapped," Darius said. "A traitor rat and his mate."

22

Because Eligos was the most powerful, many forget there were three Inconnu. Bolfri the Deceiver and Saburoc the Plague Master aided their brother in causing great misery. Disease and treachery killed as many men as the undead. Perhaps more. Let us thank Caros for his wisdom in seeing two of the three destroyed.

-Baran, Priest of Caros

"Can that thing run?" Marcus asked out of the side of his mouth.

"It will follow me," Erick said. "I don't know how fast."

Blink, we need some help.

On our way, Blink said.

"How did you find us?" Marcus asked.

Darius pointed at the small, blond-haired boy Erick had encountered when they first arrived in town. "Calligan is our best tracker. He has an excellent nose."

"Then he probably needs it cut off," Marcus said.

Darius shook his head. "Not nice. Are you going to give yourself up, or does this have to turn ugly?"

"It's going to turn ugly either way," Marcus said.

Darius stopped flipping the dagger. The other thieves spread themselves out, trying to corner Erick and Marcus against the graveyard wall. "That's true. Torin doesn't want you dead, even though that's the punishment for traitors." He smiled, and Erick had never seen anything so frightening. "But accidents do happen."

"Let us go," Erick said, keeping his voice steady. "Or my creature will kill every one of you."

"Not likely," Darius said. "Azinor has told us all about you. Without a mass of corpses, you're nothing. That thing is repulsive, like you, but it's not dangerous" He held up the dagger, the point in his hand. "I can kill you from here before you can even give it an order."

Having seen proficient Elissia's proficiency while training with her, Erick didn't doubt Darius's skill. "Then go ahead and kill me. I'm not going back with you."

"You don't have a choice about going back," Darius said. "But I don't have to kill you. Remember, we use blowguns."

Two of the thieves raised blowguns to their mouths. Erick prepared to dodge, although he had no idea which way to go. A glint of steel caught his eye, and one of the thieves dropped their blowgun and screamed. A dagger protruded from his forearm. The other thief fell, a victim to Blink's tail.

"Run," Calligan shouted as he fled.

The other two thieves ran with Calligan as Elissia arrived, followed by Corby, Callon, and Dere. They all had weapons drawn. Rage struck Darius' face. He flung his dagger at Marcus, barely missing the boy as he ducked. The blade clattered against the wall.

"You're dead, traitor," He drew his sword and backed away, not running. He pointed the sword at Callon and Dere. "All of you are dead. I don't care how far you go or where you hide, I'll find you."

Shut up, Blink thought, swooping up behind Darius.

Darius must have sensed him. He ducked and swung his blade in an upward arc. Blink rose just in time to avoid being cut in half. The blade sliced a thin line across his stomach. Blink hissed and turned to attack.

Let him go, Erick thought. *You can't win.*

259

Blink backed away, and Darius retreated until he disappeared into the shadows. They heard him turn and run.

"Let's get out of here before the guard shows up," Marcus said.

"Marcus, watch out," Elissia said. Calligan came up behind Marcus. Marcus looked over his shoulder, then turned, glared down at the shorter thief, and smacked him lightly across the head.

"What the hell happened?" Marcus asked.

"Bad timing," Calligan said in his piping voice. "We got here sooner than I thought. You were supposed to be gone already." Calligan lowered his head. "I'm sorry."

Marcus gave the boy a quick hug and tousled his hair. "It's okay. You're still learning. You did well. Now go back and be careful. I'll let you know when to do the next thing."

The boy nodded, smiled, and ran into the dark.

"What are you playing, Marcus?" Elissia asked.

"Not now. Let's get back under hiding."

They moved quickly, although they had to stop a few times to let the duppy catch up. Under Marcus's guidance, they kept to the shadows and avoided the only patrol of two guards they encountered. Soon they were back in the warehouse. Callon and Dere moved to take positions on the roof where they could keep watch. The rest slipped inside and closed the doors.

"Calligan is on our side," Marcus said before Elissia could ask him. "I wanted him to lead Darius close to us so they would know we were still in town."

"Why?"

"He's our inside man. He's young, so no one suspects him. It's believable he could find us. He really does have a nose like a hound. It's almost scary how good he is. So, when he leads them to us in the warehouse, when we tell him to, they'll accept it. And then when he's the one who kills Erick, that will seal everything. We should be able to slip away with no problem."

"Yeah, assuming we survive the attack I'm sure they're going to throw at us now," Elissia said.

Marcus shrugged. "It's not a perfect plan."

"Based on recent events, that's obvious," Corby said.

"But it's the best I've got given the time constraints," Marcus said. "If you can come up with anything better, cousin, feel free."

"I'm not a tactician," Corby said.

"Then you'll have to trust me. It will all work out. Or it won't, and we'll all be dead. Either way, problem solved."

Marcus's speech didn't inspire Erick with a great deal of confidence, but the thief was right. They needed to take the time to set this ruse up, or they would be pursued all the way to Broken Mountain. But the longer they stayed in town, the higher the chance of something going wrong. "I better get to work. I need someplace quiet, hopefully with a table and plenty of water."

Marcus smiled. "I think we can cover that." He grabbed a lantern. They retrieved Erick's sack of herbs and Marcus led them to a spot just off the center of the warehouse. He reached down and lifted another almost invisible trapdoor.

"What's this?" Erick asked.

"It's a miniature warren. A place to hide and stay hidden if we needed to. Provisioned and comfortable. All part of the plan for father's removal." He went down the steps. Erick and the rest followed, the duppy right behind Erick.

"I expected him to be more complete," Elissia said.

"He will be when I'm done. For now, he just needed enough to move."

"He stinks, doesn't he?" Corby said.

"It's not him, it's the *Elonsha* around him," Erick said.

They reached the bottom of the stairs. Marcus lit another lantern, and the group walked down the hall. Though it lacked the opulence and had been shaped from mined earth rather than tiled walls, they truly had created a small version of the thieves' warren. Five of the open rooms held cots, and another hosted racks of weapons. They walked through a large chamber with five round tables, each surrounded by five chairs.

"I'm impressed, Mar," Elissia said.

"You can do a great deal in three years if you put your mind to it. We have five more just like it throughout the city."

Another doorway brought them into the kitchen, which had an

oven, rough cabinets, and a rectangular table made of rough pine planks. "Will that work?"

Erick nodded. "Water?"

"There's a barrel there, and more if you need it."

"Thank you," Erick said. "You know you won't be able to fix food on this table anymore, don't you?"

"That's okay. Not going to be here after tomorrow, am I? I'll tell Callon to have someone replace it. Least of my worries right now."

Erick touched the duppy's forehead. "*Ca mucalz phamah, ar mucalz affad. Ar zoda nonci, noquod gnay, niiso monons de Krinnik.*"

A small sigh escaped the duppy as it collapsed to the floor, all animation gone. The odor of *Elonsha* dissipated, leaving the clean coppery tang of fresh blood. He and Blink placed the creature on the table.

"I'll let you know when I'm done," he told gathered group. "You'll need to leave now."

"Can I help?" Elissia asked as Erick picked up the sack and opened it.

Erick hesitated before answering. "Yes, but only you."

"Good luck," Marcus said. He winked at Elissia and left.

Corby nodded, and Erick noted the disappointment on the scholar's round face.

"I'll pay close attention," Elissia said, "and tell you everything I see."

"And I'll tell you as much about the Ritual as I'm allowed," Erick told him.

Corby smiled. "Thank you." He left.

Erick pulled the thick blue curtain that served as a door. "You sure you want to do this?" he asked Elissia. "You're going to learn why people call me evil."

"Evil? Hardly. You're as kind as they come. Sometimes too kind." Brief darkness came over her eyes. Although she tried to hide it, Erick knew she remembered Draymed.

"But the potential is there," Erick said. "My skills are based on a power that is evil to the extreme. It's only because of the Covenant and our familiars that the remaining Necromancers can avoid succumbing to the power's influence, but it whispers to me every time

I use it, trying to seduce me." His face clouded. "And now that Eligos has returned in some measure, it speaks even louder."

"Then you need me here." She offered a wicked smile. "Since I'm your girlfriend now, I can help reinforce what Blink does."

"Are you my girlfriend?" Erick asked, pleased at the idea, even if uncertain why she chose now to mention it.

"Yes," she told him. "But we'll have to hold off a while before we get married."

She walked to the other side of the table while Erick stood there, stunned. He didn't recall even thinking about marriage, much less mentioning it.

You're doomed, Blink thought.

Shut up, Erick thought back as they both followed Elissia into the room.

23

I regret few things in my life, but the most grievous is that I fell for the lies of the Inconnu and went to war on their behalf. I watched my people slaughter you, and for what? Land we did not need, food you would have freely traded, and the promise of a better lot. I will die with a troubled conscience. Know that I feel every injury I have done to you.

-King Dornas of Makern, upon his execution by the Theocratic Council of Amelan

Erick opened the herb bag and prepared for the arduous task of turning a century-old rotted carcass into a dead version of himself. But first, he had to protect his assistant. He took a gauzy cloth from his kit and dusted it with a lavender-colored powder. He shook it, creating a fine cloud in the air that quickly settled, and offered the kerchief to Elissia. "Wrap this on your nose and mouth."

"What is it?"

"Powder of purple cornflower. It will keep you from catching any diseases the body may have that travel through the air."

Elissia took the cloth. "What about you?"

"I'm immune. It's part of being a Necromancer."

"What about everyone else?" She wrapped the cloth over her mouth and tied it behind her head.

"No one else was close enough for long enough, but you'll be in here for a long time. Just remember, if it bothers you too much, you can leave."

"Okay," Elissia said.

"Here we go."

As Erick started working with the body, straightening the decayed corpse, Elissia's face turned pale, but she swallowed and asked how she could assist. As an extra precaution, he decided not to let her touch the corpse, but he gladly accepted her aid in blending herbs and mixing them with the water that Marcus had provided. She had no knowledge of plants, so Erick often had to stop and explain what he needed, or show her the proper amounts and methods of extraction and mixing. As a result, the preparation took almost seven hours instead of the usual six, but he knew in his heart it was the best time any Necromancer ever had creating a Doppelganger.

The corpse lay before them, bound with strips of cloth coated in a multitude of colored herbs like some madman's painted sculpture, its mouth the only uncovered portion. Erick wiped the sweat from his forehead. "I have to perform the Formation Ritual now, so you might want to leave."

Elissia shook her head. "I didn't get much useful from my aunt, but she stuck by my uncle through anything. 'Stay faithful to those you care about, and the gods will handle the rest,' she told me. I don't know if there's any truth to that, but I admired her loyalty. That's something I've not seen a lot of in my life."

"Okay, you can stay." He poured the vial of blood, gathered earlier from his already injured thumb, into the corpse's mouth. "But you're about to see the true essence of my power, and why people fear us." He looked at Blink. "Ready?"

Blink flipped his barbed tail above his forehead in a strange salute. "Ready."

~

Halfway through the Ritual, Elissia faltered; she dropped to her knees as the power washed over and around them both. Erick almost stopped to help her, but he held steady, continuing the incantation; to stop now would destroy the body, ruining all their work. After a moment she pulled herself off the floor and remained standing, sweat on her olive face, mouth set in a grim line.

I'm coming for you, and you will die to serve me.

The voice in Erick's mind sounded so close he almost stumbled over his words. In the corner, Blink flinched. A dark chill swept through Erick, more potent than the cold breeze of the graveyard, and images of himself dying, his body on a slab, limbs splayed and stomach cut open, flooded his mind.

They're illusions, Blink told him. *They don't mean anything.*

Erick latched on to Blink's voice and continued reciting as his body shivered. Elissia, also trembling, seemed to sense his struggle; she moved toward Erick, but he held up a hand to stop her.

Join me. Pictures of himself on a throne, surrounded by beautiful people, loving servants, and untold riches. *Or die.* His body swung from a noose while carrion birds picked at the loose flesh.

Leave him alone, Blink shouted at the voice. *Ignore them*, he told Erick. *Focus on your work.*

Erick barely managed, with Blink's help, to shut out the voice and visions. He recited the final lines of the Ritual, his limbs shaking to the point of pain.

I will be upon you soon.

Darkness and despair filled his mind but faded as the *Elonsha* not absorbed by the corpse dissipated. Warmth returned to the room; Erick stopped shivering and broke into a deep sweat, thankful the Ritual ended when it did, fearful he could not have endured the assault much longer.

Blink sat on the floor, his head in his hands. *He's getting stronger.*

I know, Erick thought, his mind full of fear.

Elissia's eyes glistened with a mixture of concern and unwelcome awareness. "I think I understand better now. People are wrong, you know. That you can be surrounded by that type of power and not give in only shows how strong you are." She turned to Blink. "Both of you. I just hope it doesn't overwhelm you someday."

Erick nodded, unwilling to give voice to those same thoughts. Eligos was still weak, nowhere near his full strength, and his malevolence already almost crushed Erick. He would be thankful when he reached Twr Krinnik so that others could share the burden.

Elissia walked over and hugged him tightly. As if sensing his thoughts, she said, "I'll always be there to make sure nothing happens to you. If you ever wonder why you shouldn't give in, just look to me."

Her azure eyes swarmed him with dizziness that had nothing to do with the recent work. Those eyes held fierce love, a sense of dedication that kept her by him even when others would have run screaming. At that moment, he loved her as much as he ever had any person. He pulled her mask away and kissed her.

She returned the kiss with fervor, squeezing him tight against her. He could taste the weedy cornflower on her lips. Their tongues met, and bliss ran through Erick's body, heating his face. Tension and love infused their embrace, awkward but sincere, and despite his fatigue, Erick never wanted it to end.

But Elissia drew back all too soon, her eyes glazed, face flush, and breathing heavy.

After a moment, she offered a rare smile. "I'm hungry. How about you?"

Thrown by her shift in mood, he considered it as he stifled a yawn. "Tired more than anything."

"Then we should get you to bed."

Still pressed against her, the idea of them in bed turned his face into a torch.

Elissia must have seen his thoughts written across his burning face. "Not tonight, you'd fall asleep on me. And there's no real privacy here."

"I didn't, I mean, that wasn't. I-"

"Sure it was, but I don't mind," Elissia said. She pressed herself against him, and he almost lost his composure. "It's not like I didn't notice already."

Erick pulled away, fearful of what would happen if he remained close. "I'd best clean myself up," he muttered as he turned to the copper basin, water pitcher, and cake of ambergris soap.

I'm going to bed now, Blink said. *Your emotional swings are wearing me out.*

Imagine what they're doing to me, Erick thought as he picked up the soap.

Blink said his goodnight to Elissia as Erick worked at scrubbing away small flecks of gore on his hands and forearms. Marcus's comments in the graveyard came back to him. If Erick asked, would Elissia let him-

He splashed cold water on his face to chase away the thought. He wouldn't ask her. His mother taught him such things weren't proper. *Of course*, he thought, *they had to be proper at some point, or there would never be any children.* When would it be proper? He had no idea.

As he scrubbed his face Erick realized it was almost as fuzzy as his head; the last time he shaved had been four days ago, while they were onboard the ship. "I should grow a beard," he muttered, thinking about the hassle of scraping sharp metal across his face every few days.

When he finished, Erick studied the motionless duppy, making last assurances he had done everything right. Right now it appeared nothing but human-shaped, but his Necromancer's eye showed him what it would soon become: a duplicate of his every physical feature.

They left the room and headed toward the central chamber. Elissia took Erick's hand. He smiled at her and gave a gentle squeeze. They entered the large common room and found Marcus sitting there, sharpening a dagger and eating pieces of cheese off a plate.

"Where's Corby?" Elissia asked.

"Sleeping," Marcus said. "It's almost bird crow outside. There's some food here if you want it."

Erick nodded, his head drooping.

"I think this one needs to get to bed," Elissia said.

"Have a good time," Marcus said, laughing.

As they left the room, Elissia turned and offered her brother a rude gesture, which made Marcus laugh harder.

Exhaustion tugged at Erick, begging him to give over to sleep. He had performed few complex Rituals, but every one had drained him, and this one had been exceptionally grueling.

They entered the room and found Corby asleep on one cot and Blink curled in a corner, head tucked under his wing. Erick stopped at a cot. Elissia began to undress him. Tired, he didn't protest. She soon had him down to his undergarments and nestled under a thin blanket. She said something to him. Erick caught the word "love" but lost the rest as he drifted into sleep.

~

E lissia ran a hand over Erick's head. The cropped hair tickled her palms. He slept the sleep of the dead. *Or the undead*, Elissia mused. His power frightened her, but she saw the strength in him and the loyalty of Blink. She had told him she would be there, and she meant it. Losing him, or worse, seeing him consumed by whatever strange power he wielded, wasn't anything she wanted to consider.

She stood and roamed back toward the dining area. Despite being up all night, and fatigued from helping Erick, she couldn't sleep yet. Like Marcus, the possibilities had her too keyed up.

"Hi, sis," Marcus said as she entered. "Why so glum?"

"So much going on, and I have no idea how it's going to turn out. That scares me."

"Haven't you learned yet that you can't control anything in life? It's all in the hands of the Gods. All we can do is try and hope they approve and don't interfere too much."

"Well, you know what I think about the Gods. I control my life, not them."

"If that helps." Marcus shook his head. "I've missed you, sis."

Three years of separation welled up in Elissia, almost driving her to tears. "I've missed you, too, Mar," she told him. She leaned over and hugged him fiercely. He returned the embrace in equal measure, and they stayed that way for almost a minute. Finally, Elissia drew back and sat next to him. "I wish things were different. I wish somehow father would have changed."

Marcus offered a bitter smile. "Seasons change, father doesn't. Or if he does, it's for the worst."

"I know," Elissia said. "I tried to talk to him." She coughed to hide the crack in her voice.

Marcus winced. "Should have asked me first. I could have saved you some tears."

"I wouldn't waste tears on that prick."

"Sure you wouldn't," Marcus said.

Elissia smiled. She may have been gone three years, but they were still twins, and Marcus knew her too well. "Do you think we can overthrow him? Do you have that much support?"

He nodded. "We do. Support for father is low. Things have gotten difficult. The Queen and the Merchant's Guilds are at odds, and there's tension building. Between the Royal Sentinels, the City Watch, and guards hired by the merchants, it's hard to pilfer an apple, much less anything worthwhile. Pressure is on father to make it better, but he can't do it."

"And you think you can?"

"I do. With you at my side, I can do even better. That's why I wish it could be now and we didn't have to help your boyfriend."

Elissia started to protest, but Marcus held up a hand. "Peace. I know it has to be done. Doesn't mean I have to like it." He paused a moment. "I don't like you being in harm's way."

Elissia grinned. "He doesn't either, so that's something you have in common."

Marcus offered a broad grin in return. "Why haven't you let him pick your purse yet?"

"How do you know I haven't?"

"He told me. Well, the things he wouldn't say told me. You don't still believe that whole love before lust blasphemy, do you?"

"I do. I don't care what the priests of Amare say, sex without love is emptiness."

"Sex without love is fun. And that's what I say. Besides, it sounds like you love him, so why not lust him?" Marcus raised his eyebrows.

"I might, sometime, but not yet."

"What's stopping you?"

"I don't know," Elissia said, filled with uncertainty that surprised her. "There's something about him that still...scares me." She shifted uncomfortably on the bench.

Marcus shrugged. "Your choice, but I think you're wasting too much energy on emotions. He's handsome, or would be if he'd let his hair grow out."

Glad to steer the conversation away from her confused feelings, Elissia ran a hand over her brother's close-cropped black hair. "You've no room to talk. Besides, his shave was my doing." Marcus gave her a puzzled look, and she added. "It's a long story."

"I'm not tired. And you aren't either, or you wouldn't be out here. So you might as well tell me what strange events brought The Banished One home."

Elissia related her story, starting with the attack of the vampire, and going all the way through their discovery of Marcus, giving him the details she could remember. Marcus remained quiet through the tale, his changing expressions, from mild surprise to outright astonishment, doing the talking for him. By the time Elissia finished, three-quarters of an hour had passed, and her throat rasped with thirst. She poured herself a mug of ale.

"Quite the adventure, Sis."

"There's one part that's not complete. Why were you about to swing?"

Marcus turned red with embarrassment. "I got careless. Have you ever heard of Valadon D'Arascant, the city Geleit?"

"No."

"Not surprised. Since he has a penchant for boys, you would be of no interest to him. I found out about him from some of the harlot masters in the docks, so I walked around outside his home and pulled the old 'poor orphan' routine."

"And he fell for it?" Elissia said.

"I guess so," Marcus told her, scratching his head. "He must have a thing for fuzzy scalps, since that's the only place he likes to see fuzz."

"What about your whiskers and lower hair?"

"That's what razors are for," Marcus answered with a grin. He rubbed at his face. "Whiskers aren't much of a problem yet, and I'm still short enough—everywhere, unfortunately—to pass for a youth. Pitch my voice higher, and the illusion was complete. He took me in and made me his favorite, but I kept him from touching me with teasing and promises."

Elissia arched an eyebrow. "A boy letch takes you into his house, and you keep him from touching you?"

Marcus's face turned grim. "Three others were there, young and frightened, sold by parents eager for his gold. All I had to do was let him watch me pleasure myself. They weren't so lucky. Made me sick."

"Why doesn't he hire Amare initiates?" Elissia asked. "They would be trained and more than willing."

"Says the training stifles their creativity. Personally, I think it stifles *his* creativity. There are some lines even the Amareans won't cross." A moue of disgust twisted Marcus's face, but he pushed it away. "I stayed for two weeks. More than I wanted, but I was seeking something valuable the wretch wouldn't miss for a while. I finally found it: his ring of office. He kept it in a drawer and only used it for finance minister papers. Not worth much itself, but a forger would pay five thousand *aesta* easy. So I took it and tossed it into my mouth with some bread at breakfast.

"That's when I got careless, although stupidly charitable would be a kinder way to put it. I couldn't stand the idea of those other boys being there anymore, so I decided the Society could do with three more recruits. But to get them out, I had to wait for the noon bath."

"You took baths at noon?"

"If that's what you call it," Marcus grimaced. "The ancient pervert would make us undress and frolic in this large pool he had in his house, wrestling and grabbing at each other."

"I would think you would enjoy that."

"I would have if that withered bag of skin hadn't been watching our every move with those dead gray eyes of his. And if the boys had been truly willing and not forced." Marcus took a sip from his mug. "Made me want to vomit. The only blessing was that he drooled over us no more than half an hour. I don't think his heart could take anymore. After that, he'd tell us to dress, and he'd hobble out."

"As soon as he left, I told the boys I wanted them to run away with me that night. I told them about the Procurers and how they wouldn't have to be any man's catamite. They were frightened, but I convinced two of them. The other was so terrified he didn't even want us talking about it. I figured two were better than none. We were about to get dressed when the Count storms back in with two of his armed thugs, screaming that his ring is missing. You can imagine my shock. I had no idea he would be going after it so soon. He yells and starts throwing things, says unless we tell him where it is, he'll beat us. Well, the frightened kid squeaks, pointing at me and telling everything I said about the Procurers. The count's thugs grabbed me while a servant went for the watch. You know the rest."

Elissia stared at her brother, absorbing his story. "I'm proud of you," she said at last. "That was a brave thing."

"Damned foolish is what it was," Marcus argued. "I almost swung for it, the boys are probably worse off, and the Procurers will have to keep low for Melteth knows how long. Plus it could hurt our cause if people think I'm always that incompetent."

"It's not incompetence; it's compassion."

"Name the last time any Procurer considered compassion a desirable trait."

A noise interrupted her reply. She turned to the doorway as Callon ran in, sweating and wide-eyed.

"At least thirty Procurers are approaching, and Torin is with them."

24

With the power of death, I serve your life. My skills and talents I give to you,
to use to your need and purpose, in life, death, and beyond, if it is your will.
-The Vow of the Eligoi

"I t looks just like you," Corby said as he stared at the doppelganger from the kitchen doorway.

Does it? Erick thought as he studied the creature through sleepy eyes. He had barely started to dream when Corby awakened him with the news of the Procurers' arrival.

Everything seemed in place, from the teeth wounds on his throat to the small brown birthmark on his right inner wrist. But was his face really that round? His chest and arms that lacking in muscle? Despite his disappointment in his physique, he took pride in the successful outcome of his first doppelganger, although seeing himself lying dead unnerved him more than he expected.

He approached the creature. A mélange of herbal smells, earthy and almost pleasing except for the rotted onion scent, filled the chamber. The cloths that had bound the body lay in soggy tatters on the floor, shredded by the creation process.

Recalling Corby's eidetic memory, Erick said, "Can you step

outside, please?" He had already said too much in front of Marcus and didn't want Corby repeating any words he heard.

Corby's face showed its usual curiosity, but for once he didn't ask. He nodded and left.

Erick laid his hand on the doppelganger's forehead. *"Noan micalz Elonsha, torzu. Noa cnila phamah, apila. Noa gigipah phamah, gehol."*

The creature stirred. Its eyes flickered open, and Erick found his own blue irises staring at him. *This is too strange,* he thought.

You need to hurry, Blink thought to him. *They're almost here.*

Erick took a thin iron needle he had carried in with him. Positioning it between and just above his eyes, he poked himself. Blood ran down the bridge of his nose. He coated the top half of the needle in blood and poked the creature in the same spot.

He connected with the doppelganger, similar to when he linked with Blink, but different in a fundamental way. A void filled the other end, a lack of any conscious thought. It was Erick's task to fill the creature with movement and emotion. *Smile,* he thought, and the creature smiled. *Way too strange.*

Erick took off his clothes, commanded the creature to dress in them, and then slipped on the clothes Callon had gotten for him: a plain blue tunic, grey trousers, soft leather shoes, and a large grey cloak. He stepped into the hallway where Corby waited for him. At his mental command, the doppelganger followed.

We're on our way, he thought to Blink as he said, "Let's go," to Corby.

Erick connected to the creature's eyes and found himself looking at the back of his own head, in addition to seeing Corby in front of him from two different viewpoints. Disoriented, he pulled himself from the dual vision and shook his head.

They moved up the ladder and into the warehouse. Dere stood at the trapdoor, and as soon as they came out, he closed the door, and it disappeared into the floor. Dere withdrew into the building's depths.

A gasp drew Erick's attention. Elissia and Marcus stared at him. Elissia had wide eyes and her mouth in her shocked O shape. Marcus let out a low whistle.

Marcus let out a low whistle. "That's godsdamned impressive."

"I can't believe that was a hundred-year-old corpse last night," Elissia said.

"It's still a corpse," Erick said. "It's just a corpse that looks and moves like me."

"It should do the trick," Marcus said.

The warehouse's double doors slid open and early morning light streamed in, silhouetting a large group of people.

"You hide," Marcus told Erick. "And send your twin out with us. Let's hope this all works."

Erick slipped himself behind a stack of crates and connected with the doppelganger again. Controlling it like a puppeteer, he followed his friends into the warehouse.

He positioned his double beside Elissia, which put Corby and Blink on his left and Marcus on his right. He counted thirty Procurers. They slipped into the warehouse, and two of them shut the doors. Through the dim light that came in from gaps in the walls and the skylights far above, Erick watched the thieves spread out, with Torin's vast bulk occupying the center. He waddled toward them, and it amazed Erick the large man could move. Azinor walked beside Torin, and Erick had to force himself not to send his twin to throttle the cultist.

Two other people followed the massive guild leader. One was the oldest woman Erick had ever seen. Stunted and gaunt, she had bones that almost showed through her dark, wrinkled skin. She moved with deliberate, measured steps, supported by a thick wooden cane. Her hair had once been black, judging by the few strands that stood bravely amidst the gray mass topping her head and running down her back in a ponytail. Her eyes shone with vigor as they rested in their sunken holes above her protruding cheeks. She wore a shapeless cobalt-colored robe. Sewn on the chest in red thread was the sun symbol of Caros, Krinnik's globe, and the rounded cloud the represented Talan. They were set in a triangle pattern, with Caros above the other two.

A girl followed behind her, carrying a wooden box strapped over her shoulder. Erick guessed her to be somewhere near his age. Though not as tiny as the old woman, she stood at least four inches shorter than Elissia. Her loose-fitting, light blue smock, emblazoned with the triangle emblem, but in yellow thread, hid much, but she seemed sturdy, accustomed to a life of toting and lifting. Her light brown skin reminded Erick of an acorn, and her rust-colored hair appeared uncombed. Erick couldn't see her downcast face.

"Great Caros, she's still alive?" Elissia said.

"Yes, and as much a bitch as ever," Marcus answered.

"Father's expecting trouble."

"Why do you say that?" Erick asked.

Elissia started at the voice coming from Erick, or the creature that masqueraded as Erick. Hearing and seeing him, but knowing it wasn't him, unnerved her almost as much as finding her father outside the warren. "He's brought two healers. That means he's figuring a fight."

"That's close enough, you bastard," Marcus shouted. "I don't want any of you within throwing distance."

Torin stopped and held up his hand. The Procurers froze, all still at least thirty feet away. "I stop in the interest of peace," Torin said in his deep voice. "But what would you do if I decided to continue? You're outnumbered seven to one."

"Am I?" Marcus asked. He whistled. The sound echoed through the warehouse. Other sounds followed. Feet on wood, cloth rustling. Elissia remained facing her father, but she knew that other Procurers, those ready to see her father deposed, gathered behind her, positioning themselves on crates, bags and the catwalk. If this surprised Torin, he didn't show it. He simply watched.

"Procurers," Marcus shouted.

A chorus of cheers went through the warehouse.

When the sound faded, Torin shook his head, his jowls wiggling. "You've made a tactical mistake, boy. You've revealed yourself too soon, although your rebellion wouldn't have succeeded no matter when you tried it."

Elissia forced herself to remain calm and not glance at her brother. Torin knew. How long had he known? How many people standing at her back were actually with her father? She hoped Callon or Dere weren't playing both ends against the middle. They were her brother's lieutenants in this whole insane scheme. If they worked for Torin…

"It'll succeed if I put a knife through your eye." Marcus pulled a dagger and ran forward ten feet. He stopped as three Procurers, including Darius, stepped in front of their leader and drew their weapons.

"See, boy, that's why you could never be in charge. You let your emotions interfere with rational thinking. You have to be dispassionate."

"You're certainly the master of that," Elissia said, unable to keep the bitterness out.

"I've had to be," Torin said. "I don't expect you to understand, and I'm not going to waste time explaining." His gaze took in the other Procurers. "You've all been duped. I know Marcus is a smooth talker and a fine thief. But he's not a leader. Those of you who leave now are still Procurers. We never saw you here."

He returned his attention to Marcus and Elissia. "That goes for you two also, although you are forever banished from the Guild, Marcus."

"No surprise there," Marcus said.

Darius grumbled and shifted his knife in his hand. Torin put a hand on the boy's shoulder, but eyed his son. "For your part in this, boy, you should be put to death. Be thankful there is still some compassion in me. I want no bloodshed; I only want him." He pointed at Erick.

"You can't have him, Father," Elissia said. "Look beyond your greed for once. If Erick dies, the world is that much closer to utter darkness."

"Odd," Torin said. "Azinor tells me the exact opposite. That Erick goes to join his cabal and work toward the world's destruction."

"Azinor lies," Erick said. "His master is the King of Lies and will destroy everything. He would—"

The creature stopped as a crossbow bolt slammed into its eye. Elissia gasped as she watched the thing that looked too much like Erick fall backward, blood spurting from its ruined eye. Dismay echoed from several others in the room.

"I got him," a high-pitched voice said. Calligan came from around a wooden support column, holding a crossbow almost as large as him.

"Stupid boy," Azinor snarled. "I wanted him alive." The man moved over and swung a fist at Calligan, but the boy easily dodged it.

"Attack," Marcus shouted.

With a chorus of screams, the Procurers behind Marcus launched themselves toward those rallied around Torin. The two healers fell back toward the double doors.

Dere landed beside her with a thud, his knife raised, and for the briefest moment, she feared he would bring it down on her skull. But he lowered it and said, "We've got it from here. Get out while you can."

Erick had barely recovered from the shock of watching a bolt slam into his eye before Marcus shouted. He rubbed his eye, chasing away the phantom pain and blinking to make sure he could see. For a few seconds after the bolt had struck, his vision had disappeared. His head hurt, and he suspected it would for a while.

The sounds of chaos filled the warehouse, tempting him to peek over and see what was happening. He resisted. If the wrong person saw him, the whole ruse would be useless. He only hoped they could slip away without being spotted.

The clash of metal and screams of pain echoed. How many people would die to help him escape? He gritted his teeth at the thought of more innocent blood on his behalf. First an entire village of people Elissia knew, and now her brother's friends. Beatru had been right. He brought nothing but death.

Stop it, Blink thought. *It will be far worse if you die before we get to the mountain.*

His friends came around the corner of the crates, and Erick almost shouted. In all the noise, he hadn't heard them approach.

"Come on," Marcus said. "Stay low and keep that cloak on."

Erick stood up and stumbled as the pain in his head doubled. Corby and Elissia grabbed his arms, and they scuttled through the warehouse, sticking to shadows as much as possible, although Erick saw little need. The sounds remained behind them and lessened with distance as they traversed the massive building. He tried to ignore the screaming, pay no attention to the death.

They slipped out a small door and into the morning air. After the burlap and wood smell of the warehouse, Erick relished the cool, crisp air, which smelled of dirt and sawdust.

"Where now?" Elissia asked Marcus.

"The east gate."

"But we have to head west," Erick said.

"You want to walk through the city with what's going on, be my guest. But if you want a chance to survive, we hit the east gate. Your choice."

Erick nodded. He didn't like Marcus's tone, but couldn't fault the logic.

"There's a safe house near there, too," Marcus continued. "Callon laid up some supplies for us."

"Are you sure it's still safe?" Corby asked.

"As safe as anything," Marcus answered.

"See you at the east gate," Erick said to Blink. With a nod, the familiar took off.

They walked down the city street, ignored by the workers heading to their daily labors. Erick wanted to run, to be gone as quickly as possible, but that would attract undue attention.

"Take the cloak off," Marcus said.

"Shouldn't I leave it on so no one recognizes me?"

Marcus shook his head. "A cloak in this weather is suspicious, and we don't want any problems with guards. If Father has any lookouts, they'll recognize Elissia or me before you. We'll have to trust to Denech on this one."

Elissia huffed. "Or just trust that Father wouldn't expect us to run."

"Are the guards that draconian?" Corby asked.

"If draconian means 'pain in the ass' then yes, they are," Marcus answered.

They continued through the city in silence. This early in the morning, with few people going to their labors, it was much quieter and less populated than when Erick had arrived, which wore at his nerves. It would be easier to blend into a crowd, but every eye seemed unfriendly, every shadowy nook a hiding place for a hostile Procurer.

Despite his fears, they reached the safe house, which wasn't a house at all, but a small wooden stable with a second story full of hay.

They slipped inside. There were ten stalls, but only two occupied. One held a brown horse, and the other quartered an odd, four-legged animal tethered to one of the boxes. It had close gray fur, long ears, and a high-pitched, braying whine.

"What is that?" Erick asked Marcus. "It looks like a horse gone wrong."

"That's a pack mule; we'll use it to carry stuff. Don't get near his back legs," Marcus warned. "He'll kick your teeth out if you give him half a chance."

"I'll let you deal with it."

Marcus slipped inside the stall beside the mule and pushed aside a giant pile of hay, revealing several wooden boxes filled with items. He quickly sorted things out. Callan had provided generously. They had two weeks' worth of food, bedding and tents, cooking equipment, a loose-fitting chain shirt, two daggers, and a supply of weapon oil, whetstones, and cleaning supplies. A pouch that clicked with coinage lay in the case; Marcus attached it to his belt.

"This is for you," Marcus said, handing Erick a wooden box with a leather shoulder strap.

When Erick opened the box, he found a vast and varied supply of herbs. A piece of onionskin parchment lay on top. Unfolding it, he saw a message written in a light, flowing script. *I can only assume you use the same things we do, so I hope these are beneficial.* The signature was a single scripted letter: G.

"Who's G?"

Marcus began loading supplies on the mule. "Gabrielle. You saw the two healers?"

"Yes."

"She was the young one."

"How did she know to give this to me?"

"Father may not think I'm a leader, but I'm smarter than he gives me credit for."

"This was never about their rebellion," Corby said. "It was only about getting us out and convincingly faking your death."

Marcus tapped his finger on his nose. "Clever, aren't you?"

"I am a scholar," Corby said.

Erick stared at Marcus. "You let all those people who trusted you die just so we could run?"

"A lot more would die if we didn't get you out," Marcus said. "It's not as dire as that. Dere and the rest disengaged after they knew we were clear. Hopefully, we didn't lose any more than three, and gave just as good or better to Father."

"How can you talk so casually about people you know dying?"

Marcus stopped loading the mule. "What's my option?" He asked Erick. "To moan and wail? There's a risk in any venture. We could have stayed there and let them take you and been safe, or we could get you free and take a chance of people dying. There may be a lot more death before this is over and even after all that, you may not succeed. Welcome to the real world."

"You're right," Erick said, although he didn't like admitting it. "I'm sorry."

"Don't be sorry," Marcus said. "Just make sure you succeed, so none of this was in vain."

Erick nodded. He hoped Caros would accept into his heaven anyone who died defending a Necromancer. He slipped on the padded leather gambeson and a chain shirt, adjusting it for the best fit. He attached the knives to his belt. Laden with the armor and supplies, he sympathized with their beast of burden.

"The gate is three blocks away," Marcus said as he grabbed the reins attached to the mule. He pulled the mule along, while the others followed.

"What about your rebellion?" Erick asked. "Your father knows it's real now. You've failed. And it's my fault."

"You're just determined to flagellate yourself, aren't you? Are all Necromancers like that?"

"I don't know. I've never met any others."

"Father knew about the rebellion anyway, which I suspected. We haven't failed. We've had a setback, but we're better provisioned than he suspects. And we have contacts in the government that he doesn't."

"You mean like the Geleit D'Arascant," Elissia said, smiling. Erick didn't understand the comment, but it made Marcus wince.

"Better than that," Marcus said. "This revolution is just beginning." He jerked a thumb at Erick. "We'll wrap it up handily when you come back with us."

Erick didn't say anything. He didn't know how likely it would be he could return. Even if he did, he didn't have Marcus's confidence the rebellion would still be alive.

They reached the gate and Erick took a last look at the city. It seemed strange to be walking out so casually, as if people weren't fighting, and likely dying, less than half a mile away.

They walked around the outer wall, the way made easy by the cleared and level ground. They encountered few others, mostly merchants with laden wagons that traveled better outside the confining roads. The day already grew warm and humid, the ocean breeze blocked by the intervening city. Sweat formed under Erick's arms and knew it wouldn't be long before beads started popping onto his forehead. The weight of his equipment already wore on him, and they hadn't even started on the road. He shifted the box strap, trying to adjust it so the weight didn't press into his shoulders so much.

"Put that on the mule," Elissia said. "That's what it's for."

The animal had already been laden with supplies. "Doesn't he have enough?"

"He could carry twice what he's got now," Marcus said. "He'd bitch about it, but it wouldn't hurt him."

"Okay," Erick said, pulling the box off his shoulder. They paused and strapped the case to the braying creature before continuing.

As they reached the western gate, Erick spotted a familiar figure standing outside, nervously glancing around as people passed by.

"Here we are, Gabrielle," Marcus called. She turned to them, and the tension eased in her shoulders, but not her face.

"What's she doing here?" Elissia asked.

"She's going with us. We may need a healer before it's over, and I had to get her away from Valarie before the jealous crone squashed her talents."

"I hope she works out better than your last rescue attempt."

They reached her, and she said, "Callon says I'm to go with you."

Marcus cocked his head, and his mouth tightened. "Don't say it like it's a death sentence. I thought you'd be happy to be away from Valarie."

Gabrielle's plain face twisted into an unreadable expression. "I suppose I am. Thank you," she said, although her voice lacked any emotion.

Marcus turned to Erick, his black eyebrows bunched in confusion. "Well, let's go."

Erick studied Gabrielle. The girl appeared miserable, a small backpack and large herb box slung over her broad shoulders. She still wore her shapeless smock with the stitched healer's sigil. "Are you sure you wish to go?"

She glanced between Marcus and Erick with her wide brown eyes. "I do wish to go, and I am grateful. It's just..." She stared at Marcus for a long moment, before returning her gaze to the ground. "Never mind."

Perplexed, but sensing nothing could be resolved here, Erick said, "Then Marcus is right, we should be moving."

Blink flew high above them. *When we're a mile or so away, you can come down,* Erick told the familiar.

"How did you get away from the fight?" Elissia asked.

"I slipped out in the confusion," Gabrielle said. "It was easy, but I shouldn't have gone. There were wounded."

"Valarie can handle the fight," Marcus said. He took Gabrielle's hand. The girl's green eyes lit up. "We need you more than she does."

"Thank you."

Marcus released her hand. Elissia frowned at her brother. "How was the fight going?"

Gabrielle shrugged. "There were people hurt. That's all I know."

"Valarie is going to be livid when she finds you gone, isn't she?"

"Yes."

"Good," Elissia said.

As they left, Erick sent out a thought to Geran but received no reply. They had been out of contact for too long, so Erick had lost his creation. He sighed. It would have made life easier to have the extra weapon.

A mile out, Blink re-joined them. Six travelers and one mule marched their way along Routh Krinnik, the northwestern road that would lead them to Broken Mountain, Erick's destination. His thoughts turned to that distant crag. Once seven miles high, it had been shattered, blown apart by the desperate last battle between the three *Inconnu* and the ten Necromancers, so that now it rose only two miles into the sky, its top a broad plateau, the remains of the devastated peak spread around it like crumbs from a toppled cake.

A troubling memory came to him, hovering at the edge of awareness. Although he had never been to Broken Mountain, he had seen it in a dream; a dream that seemed relevant, but that he could not recall. Putting his hand on his necklace, he prayed, *Caros, Denech, or both, please help me to remember what I have forgotten.* Nothing came to him, and he felt suddenly forsaken, as if it amused the gods to let him figure it out on his own.

He shook off the gloomy thoughts. "We have a long journey, Corby. Tell us the stories you know about Twr Krinnik."

"The Broken Mountain?" Corby asked. "Oh, I know plenty."

Great, Blink thought to Erick as Corby launched into the first of his tales.

25

What is known of the Inconnu *has been gleaned from captured Eligoi or Fist members, and that is precious little. They are not of this world, but whether they are spawned from the Aesir or denizens of the Hells, none can say.*
  -Report from High Commander Bryce Tarn of Kal Adan.

T he *Pratanin* rocked gently in the Bay of Kalador, awaiting permission to dock. A detachment of the Dock Watch, their tan uniforms disheveled, poled out to the ship in a dingy, barely serviceable flatboat. They boarded and began inspecting the vessel for contraband.

While Fathen stood by the wheelhouse to avoid the warm sun, Andras fumed as the guards examined every corner of the vessel. The Watch Commander, bleary-eyed and stinking of drink, pompously badgered a nervous Talas-An to hand over his bills of lading.

After much prodding and poking, they found only bolts of desert cloth and casks of Sakenin sand crab ale, nothing in the least incriminating.

"You may dock and unload," the obviously disappointed commander told the relieved captain.

No sooner were the mooring ropes tossed than Andras moved

amidships in preparation for the lowering of the gangplank. Talas-an stood nearby, returning his papers to their leather satchel. Andras walked toward the captain, and the dark-eyed man flinched when the assassin moved toward him. Fathen followed.

Reaching into the hefty hide pouch hanging on his belt, full of hard currency from the sale of the icons, Andras pulled out a handful of golden coins and offered ten to the captain. Talas-an's beady eyes lit up, but he hesitated.

"Take it," Andras said. "To replace your missing crewmen."

With a toothy grin, the Sakenin extended his hand, watching with delight as the coins clinked into it. "You generous."

"Remember this and tell others you know," Andras said as the last gold piece dropped from his palm. "The Fist is harsh, but the *Inconnu* do forgive. To those who are friends, the rewards can be great. The Sakenin tribes of Falan-Dar were friends to the Fist once; the Fist wishes them to be again."

The captain bowed his head and clenched his fist around the money. "The *Parshera* were not friends to *Inconnu*, but Talas-An will be friend."

"Then spread the word. Friends of the *Inconnu* will prosper. Those who oppose us will be crushed." Andras turned and walked away, leaving Talas-an making profuse promises of loyalty to his back.

"Ten *aesta*?" Fathen asked as two large sailors lowered the gangplank. "That's almost as much as he'll make this whole trip."

"Yes."

"But why? It seems like a waste for someone who tried to kill us."

"You heard what I told him?"

"Yes, but how do you know he'll obey?"

"The tribesmen of Falan-Dar respect power and their traders respect money. I have shown him both. He will obey because I paid him and because he fears me. Did you note the other sailors watching? At the least, his crew will spread the word of my generosity. Until I return to my full power, the Fist needs allies. When I am again whole, those allies will help us gain armies."

The sailors left, their job finished, and the two men started down the gangplank toward the docks. Andras said, "We must seek out a Procurer to learn news of the Necromancer."

They moved across the docks, and Fathen forgot his questions as he soaked in the mostly forgotten sights, sounds, and smells of a large city. The odors this close to the docks and fish warehouses seemed a delectable perfume after the boring purity of soil and plants that had been his home for twenty years. He knew he would soon tire of the stench, but for now, it provided an exhilarating reminder of real life.

"There," Andras said, nodding toward a brown-haired boy no older than ten who lounged on bundles of thick hemp rope, his feet dangling over the sides. He had a slothful manner, but his alert eyes belied his lazy posture.

As the two men approached, the boy sat up straighter and stared at them with his round face and dark brown eyes. His hands rested on the hemp, ready to spring him away.

"I would speak to your master," Andras said.

"Orphan," the boy said, his voice reedy and quiet. "Don't have a master."

"What's your name, boy?"

"Jyme."

"I am Andras of the Fist."

"Fist?" Jyme pondered a moment. "Many say Fist, none show Fist."

Andras studied the crowd a moment. Fathen followed his gaze and saw nothing but people going about their business. Andras turned to the boy and casually rolled up his sleeve.

Jyme leaned in close to examine the tattoo. He spat on his hand and gave a brusque rub across the ink. "Seem real. Why see?"

"I think you know."

"You want boy that bring back dead?"

"Exactly."

"Could be problem,"

"Why is that?"

Jyme shrugged. "Have to ask master." He leapt off the ropes, landed on the dock, and walked away, not even bothering to see if they followed.

As they moved through the crowded streets, the boy kept a

watchful eye in all directions. Seeing a quartet of Royal guards in their brown hauberks, carrying shields with the silver rose painted upon them, he slithered behind a vendor's stall, and Fathen momentarily lost sight of him. Once the guards passed, the boy reappeared and waited for the two men to catch up.

"Royal Sentinels in the docks?" Fathen asked Jyme. "What's happened?"

"Queen harassing Procurers. Boy steal Geleit's ring. Geleit is friend of Alekita."

"What is a Geleit?" Andras asked.

"A Finance Master," Fathen said. "He controls the treasury and taxes." Fathen asked the boy, "Is he the Prime?"

The boy shook his head. "Nah, is only Geleit for Serberc."

"He's only in charge of the southern region of the kingdom, not all of it," Fathen told Andras.

"Still a powerful man," Andras observed. "What is this Geleit's name?"

The young thief held out his hand. When no offering seemed forthcoming from either man, he dropped his hand and shrugged. "Boy has to eat."

Fathen reached out and grabbed him by his shoulder. "Look here, you lit–"

The thief whipped out a black blade and laid it against the priest's fingers. Fathen turned pale as the iron rested against his knuckles.

"Good way to lose finger, heh?" Jyme said with a wicked grin. "You lucky you *Inconnu*." The boy lifted the knife and replaced it on his belt. "Take hand away now."

His face red and shaking, Fathen pulled his hand away and rubbed at the small indention that ran across his knuckles.

Andras reached into his pouch and removed a *teres*. "You are a brave lad," he told the small thief as he handed over the copper coin, which disappeared into Jyme's shirt. "The name?"

"Count Valadon D'Arascant. He steal untrained boys." The thief spat on the ground.

"We must remember that name," Andras whispered to Fathen. "A finance minister would be most useful."

289

"I will remember this boy's impudence," Fathen whispered back.

"Let it pass. It is the nature of the thief; he means nothing personal."

Fathen kept his thoughts to himself.

"Inside here," Jyme said, slipping into *The Pig's Knuckle.*

The boy made for the dim back of the building, and Andras followed. He ignored the sailors and dockworkers gathered in the dark corners and drinking from spotted mugs. Smoke floated through the room, carrying the pungent scent of *gilko* leaf.

"Are all dockside taverns filthy?" Fathen asked.

"Almost without exception," Andras answered. "Your fastidiousness grows tiresome."

"I did not grow up in squalor."

"Nor did I," Andras said, an edge in his voice. "But you will learn to accept your circumstances without complaint, or you may seek another master."

"My apologies. As always, I will try to do better."

"See to it."

Jyme opened a door and walked down a set of creaky wooden steps that ended at another closed door. He stopped and faced the men as he grabbed two black strips of cloth from a stack laying in a niche. "Now blindfolds."

"Blindfolds?" Fathen asked. "Why?"

"Procurer home secret. Needs to stay secret."

"I don't want to wear a blindfold," Fathen protested.

The boy shrugged. "Then stay here."

"Put on the blindfold," Andras said. "I don't care for it either, but it's standard practice and arguing is useless."

"Let's knock this snipe out of the way and go in without him," Fathen said.

The child seemed unconcerned by the threat. "Good luck finding path."

"Did you learn nothing outside?" Andras asked. "We are on the Procurer's land now. Hurting this child would get us both killed. I am not yet powerful enough to fight an entire legion of thieves. Are you?"

Fathen shook his head.

"Then wear the blindfold."

Fathen glared at the boy but took the proffered cloth. "How do we know you won't get us inside and have your friends ambush us?"

The thief gave him a gap-toothed grin. "Give my word you safe."

Fathen stared at the boy's smirk and wanted nothing so much as to slap the insolence off the child's face. But he considered Andras' words and knew he would have to wait. The boy could afford to be disrespectful, but Fathen would remember. He put the cloth over his eyes and tied it at the back. He could only assume Andras did the same when the boy said, "Take hands."

Fathen reached out until he found Andras's sizeable calloused hand and gripped it. The door before them opened and they began moving.

They walked for at least five minutes, and Fathen quickly lost any sense of direction. If the boy were to let them go now and disappear, they would wander for hours before finding a way to the surface; the thought made for an anxious journey.

After roughly another five minutes, the little voice said, "Stop and take off." Fathen gladly halted his movement, released Andras' hand and removed the blindfold.

For a moment he thought he still wore the black cloth. Darkness engulfed him, leaving him unable to see the others in front of him, even though he could hear breathing. He wondered how their small guide had managed to lead them here.

"About to get bright," the boy said. A crack appeared in the wall before them as he pushed open a door Fathen hadn't even seen. The dim torchlight gave adequate illumination for their momentarily light sensitive eyes. Their guide walked in, and they followed him down the hallway about fifty feet before he stopped at another door and pushed it open. He stepped aside and indicated the two men should proceed.

They walked into the main chamber to find the Guild Master--one of the largest and ugliest men Fathen could ever remember seeing--sitting on his throne in the center. He had a sling on his arm and a cut on his forehead. Four other thieves stood at the base of the throne, two of them also with evidence of minor injuries. Their youth astounded Fathen, the oldest no more than seventeen and the youngest ten at most.

The big man spoke in a jovial voice. "Welcome to the home of the Procurers. I am Guildmaster Torin. Come in and share a glass of wine."

"We need no wine," Andras said as he strode across the room toward the dais, ignoring the others in the room. Fathen followed close behind.

"Very well," Torin answered, pouring himself a dark red liquid from a silver pitcher. "You'll forgive me for indulging. It's been an interesting morning. I take it you're Azinor's master."

"I am. Where is my priest?"

"Coming along momentarily. There have been complications and your man was injured."

"What about the Necromancer?"

Torin took a slow drink of his wine, and Fathen suspected the man stalled. As Torin lowered the cup, a side door opened. A man, almost Fathen's height, with ghostly pale skin, thin facial hair, and a ponytail gathered with a ruby collar, walked up to Andras, knelt, and bowed his head.

"My lord, I have failed you. The Necromancer is dead."

Andras's eyes widened in shock but soon turned to amusement, not the reaction Fathen expected. "Rise and explain."

The man stood, glanced at Fathen, and then turned to Andras. "We had the Necromancer captured, but the guild master's incompetence allowed him to be freed."

Torin shifted his bulk in the seat. "You'd best watch your tongue in my warren."

Andras stared at Torin. "I am paying for your services, so my man will speak as freely as he desires. Especially where it concerns the Necromancer. Continue," he told Azinor.

"This man's son was spearheading a rebellion against him. He freed the Necromancer and his companions and fled. Those still loyal tracked them to a warehouse, and we confronted them. The rebellion was broken, but the Necromancer was killed in the first shot."

Again an amused expression on Andras's plain face that Azinor either didn't notice or refused to acknowledge. It confused Fathen. His master should be furious at losing Erick.

Andras turned to Torin. "And where is this brave hero who brought down the Necromancer. I would meet this person."

Torin's thick eyelids drew tight, rife with suspicion. "I thought you wanted the boy alive."

"I preferred him alive, but dead is acceptable. Now, let me meet the man or woman responsible."

Torin didn't relax immediately, but eventually, his eyes opened, and he said, "Calligan, step forward."

The smallest and youngest of the four thieves in front of Torin stepped forward. Fathen almost laughed. The boy appeared harmless as a two-week-old puppy. Then he remembered a knife blade against his fingers and the laughter froze.

Andras walked toward the child. The other thieves tensed, but Andras ignored them. He put a hand under the small lad's chin. "And how did you take down the Necromancer? A knife in the back?"

"Crossbow." Calligan lifted his head in pride. "Right in the eye."

Andras smiled and patted the boy's cheek with his free hand. "Were you aware that he was supposed to be taken alive?"

"Yes."

"But you killed him anyway. Why?"

Calligan's brows bunched in confusion. He tried to pull away, but Andras took a firm grip on the boy's chin.

"Why?" he asked in a harsher voice.

"Unhand him," Torin said.

"When he answers the question," Andras said. "Why did you kill him?"

Calligan shook his head. Andras pulled a knife from his belt and pressed it against the boy's throat. The boy cried out. The other three thieves drew blades and advanced toward Andras. He glared at them.

"Take another step, and I'll slit his throat, then resurrect him and have him kill every one of you." Red light flickered in his pupils, and his voice took on the whispery quality that raised the hairs on Fathen's neck. It worked on the thieves as well. They stepped back.

One dropped his knife, his hands shaking. Torin had not moved. Calligan wailed and shook.

"Answer the truth, or I'll kill you," Andras told the terrified thief. "Why did you shoot the Necromancer?"

"Marcus told me too," the boy said, his words so caught up in his crying that Fathen barely understood them.

"Marcus?" Torin said, leaning forward in his chair.

"Who's Marcus?" Fathen asked.

"The man's son," Azinor said. "The leader of the rebellion."

"It seems there are still snakes in your nest," Andras said. He shoved Calligan to the floor where the boy lay in a heap and sobbed.

"Get him out of here," Torin said. "Take care of him."

"Wait," Andras said. He turned to Fathen and held out the dagger. "Kill him."

"What?"

"This child is a traitor to his people, and he has displeased the Fist. As *Eloa Ecrin* it will often fall to you to mete out punishment. Kill him."

"No," Calligan screamed, his wet eyes wide. He tried to stand, but two of the others grabbed him and held him tight.

"I'd rather not have the blood on my floor," Torin said.

"You'll be compensated for the clean-up," Andras snapped. He walked toward Fathen, dagger still extended. "Kill him."

Fathen took the knife and moved toward Calligan.

"Please, no, I'm sorry. I didn't mean it. I was forced. They made me do it." Tears ran down Calligan's face, and he fell into inarticulate babbling.

The child seemed so small and pitiful, not at all like the swaggering imp that had led them to this hole. This boy had done nothing to him. He had killed Erick, but Andras, for all his talk, didn't seem as upset as he should be.

You are already damned, a voice said. *Why hesitate?*

Why indeed? Fathen put the knife against the boy's throat.

"Great Caros," Calligan blubbered through his tears, "please accept me into your heaven, though I have done wrong. Absolve my transgressions and bathe me in your light, as you bathe your child Krinnik. Remove the...remove..."

Fathen leaned in and whispered into Calligan's ear. "Remove the darkness on my soul as you remove the darkness of night's embrace." Pain spiked him as he recited the words; he rocked back, momentarily blinded.

When he could see again, he found Calligan staring at him, his face wet but calm. "Remove the darkness on my soul as you remove the darkness of night's embrace," he repeated, voice firm.

Eyes looked with Fathen, he continued. "Make my soul pure again, as I was when first parted from the bosom of your wife, Calea. Take me, broken as I am, and make me whole."

Fathen's hand shook, the dagger suddenly hot as a spike fresh from the forge. He dropped the blade and turned to Andras. "I'm sorry, master. He is a child of Caros. Forgive me, but I was too long in the Sun God's embrace to readily murder one of his disciples."

Fathen bowed his head. He sensed his end. Eligos would reject him as unworthy, and he would share the traitor's fate.

"Look at me," Andras said. Fathen did as commanded. His master's face was grim, but not as angered as Fathen expected. "We will discuss this later." He picked up the blade and walked toward the boy.

"Thank you," Calligan said. Fathen turned to see the boy's bright eyes and sad smile.

Andras ran the knife across the child's throat.

Fathen closed his eyes, unable to look at the boy's beatific face, but he could hear the gurgling, the gasps of interrupted air, the dull kick of feet against stone. After far too long, the noises stopped, but Fathen didn't open his eyes until he heard them dragging the dead child away. Blood pooled on the floor and trailed in two small lines toward the room's entrance. Fathen caught a glimpse as the two thieves carried the limp body through a door. It had to be his imagination, but Fathen thought Calligan still smiled.

Fathen knew he would see the boy's face and hear his death long after today. But the thief's actions had brought about his fate. He deserved his punishment.

Fathen hoped he could eventually make himself believe that.

295

"This has not been my best day," Torin said. The large man rested his jowls on his meaty fist. "I've lost my son, several highly-trained thieves, and a promising healer has disappeared, probably run off with the rebels who escaped." He paused and started as if just realizing Andras and Fathen were still present. "It appears I owe you a debt for revealing I still have work to do."

Torin laughed, an odd but pleasant sound. "I'll hand it to the boy; he had his hooks deeper than I suspected. Shame he wasn't on my side." His smile turned to a pained grimace. "I will return your deposit."

"Keep it, to clean your floor," Andras said. "And I may still need your services. I suggest you have your house in order when I return, or I won't be so lenient."

The large man appeared ready to take insult, then reconsidered. He nodded. "I will. Things may get ugly for a while, but Darius here is a solid man. He'll help me rout out the rats."

"Azinor," Andras said. "You did well, considering the circumstances. Stay and help the Guildmaster with his task."

"That's not necessary."

"I insist." Andras's eyes flashed. "I want to make sure my investment is protected."

"As you say," Torin said, but he clearly wasn't happy.

"You can return us to the surface now."

"Jyme," Torin yelled, and their escort stuck his head into the door. "Take these two back to the top."

"The same place where you took us in," Andras added.

～

Jyme, his subdued manner evidence he had witnessed his comrade's fate, returned them to the stairway leading to the dingy tavern. At the boy's request, they removed the blindfolds and returned them. With nothing more than a dark glance at both of them, he disappeared back through the doorway to his lair.

They trudged up the stairs, Fathen's footsteps heavy as he followed Andras. They reached the top and pushed the doorway open. A few patrons looked their way but returned to their affairs with only a cursory glance.

"Why so morose?" Andras asked.

"I have displeased you. I am worthless."

"You have displeased me, but it was not entirely unexpected. You are worthless, but so is a lump of iron until it is forged into a useful tool. I will forge you, or break you in the process."

"Thank you, master. I will prove myself worthy."

"Yes, you will," Andras said, and Fathen shivered at the malice in the words. The phantom touch of a knife whispered across his throat, and he flinched.

They left the tavern and returned to the bright day. Down in the dimness of the thieves' warren, Fathen had forgotten it was still morning. "What do we do now?"

"What we were doing when we came here. Searching for Erick."

"But he's dead."

"Follow me." Andras moved toward a crowded market across the street; the stale, smoky air of the tavern gave way to the smell of salt water and fish. Vendors hawked seafood and vegetables, while peddlers walked among the crowd holding boxes filled with trinkets and sweets.

Andras found a corner in the midst of the thriving, cacophonous bazaar. "We can speak here without the chance of being overheard. The Necromancer is not dead."

Unsure how much he should hope, Fathen said, "How do you know?"

Andras frowned, and his eyes narrowed, giving his plain face a much more sinister countenance. "Am I not Eligos? Do you not think I would know when a Necromancer has died? You would also know. Remember what happened aboard ship?"

"Yes," Fathen said with a shudder as he recalled the nauseating cloud of churning crimson and ebony that had surrounded Andras. "Nothing like that has happened since."

"And therefore, no other Deathmage has been killed, least of all this boy."

"So why did you let Torin believe he had failed?"

"He has failed. Erick is not dead, but he has escaped, making our task more difficult and wasting time. Such incompetence is not acceptable, but for now, I must let it go. I am too weak to punish him properly, by destroying his whole organization. They may yet prove useful." Andras smiled. "It's almost always better to keep the snake close and use its venom against others than it is to cut off the head."

"So Erick is free and heading for Broken Mountain," Fathen said. "He will be taking the Routh Krinnik, so he should be easy to track down and kill."

Andras offered Fathen a tight, less than friendly smile. "How much do you hate the Necromancer?"

Fathen didn't bother to hide his indignation. "I'm surprised you would even ask. I hate him enough that I have destroyed any chance at salvation."

"Do you hate him enough to protect him and see him safely to Twr Krinnik?"

"I don't understand."

"I thought to kill the boy and take his *Elonsha*, but he has survived this far, so I will let him reach the mountain and sacrifice him there. With his power, I will shatter open the doors sealed against me. I will take the *Elonsha* of the souls buried there and build my new fortress upon the home of my exile. From Twr Krinnik I shall rain terror and dismay upon all who will not bend to my will. From the crushed remnants of that pathetic rock, I shall raise forth a world for my people, and will turn those who oppose us into our slaves and fodder."

Caught in his vision, Andras's voice had steadily become thick and scratchy, like a pen stroked across parchment, and risen so that he almost shouted. People stared at them with puzzled and alarmed expressions; the noise level subsided as vendors and patrons turned to find the source of such dire ranting.

Andras returned the stares of the crowd. His eyes flared, the pupils swirling black with flittering red points. He stood straight, seeming to grow in height, as he spoke in a trembling, whispery voice. "Enjoy your pitiful existence while you can. Soon you will all bow to the whim of Eligos."

He stormed through the crowd. People screamed and scattered to avoid his touch as he waved his arms. Caught off guard, Fathen scrambled to keep up with him.

After several blocks, Andras slowed down and Fathen walked beside him. He had again become nothing more than Andras, a man dressed in deep blue traveling clothes with a forgettable face, lank hair, and muddy brown eyes.

"You will reunite with the boy," Andras said, as if their conversation continued uninterrupted. "Tell him you are the only survivor from his destroyed town. Travel with him and ensure that he is safe until he reaches Broken Mountain."

"He will make it there without me," Fathen said. "Why do I need to join him?"

"Consider it a test of your loyalty."

Fathen stopped in the middle of the street. "I should think my loyalty would not be in question."

Andras turned to face him, surprise on his ordinarily unreadable features. "Everyone's loyalty is in question. Are you so absent that you have forgotten what happened but five minutes ago? Your bastard god has influence over you still, much as you wish it otherwise. He tries to reclaim you even in my midst, so while you are away from me, his call will be stronger. If you are true to me, you will resist him. When you reach Twr Krinnik with the others, I will know if you are his or mine. Can you kill the Necromancer?"

"You know I can."

"I *thought* you could. What I have witnessed gives me doubts."

Fathen waved his hand as if chasing away a fly. "A lapse. The boy's piety caught me unawares, and I confess that Car—the bastard god called to me, and I answered. But my hatred for Erick and his family outweighs such considerations. I will not fail you."

An amused expression crossed the assassin's face. He pulled one of his sealed daggers he had retrieved from the guardhouse in Draymed and held it toward his apprentice. "If you are still truly mine when you arrive at Twr Krinnik, you will know when to use this. Speak praise to my name and bury this in the Necromancer's back."

Fathen's eyes flickered with excited delight as he took the proffered blade.

"That's correct," Andras told him. "Your reward for bringing Erick safely to the mountain will be the chance to sacrifice him and make me whole again. Then you shall have power you never dreamed of."

Fathen grinned as he slipped the blade into his boot and pulled his pants leg over it. "He will get there alive; this I promise."

"We shall see."

"What will you be doing?" Fathen asked

"I shall ride ahead and prepare a welcome party for his companions." Andras smiled once more, a malice-filled grimace. "We shall let him see their terror before he dies."

26

Blackness covered the land, a plague of death and undeath. The cities burned,
the people starved, and all was dark. But then, the light of Caros scorched the
miasma and cleared the heart. The Necromancers found the true path. Gods
and man together subsumed the evil, and the world was again made whole.

-Introduction to "A Time of Dark War" by scholar Treyan Nob of
Amelan

As soon as they walked away from the walls of Kalador,
Elissia noticed a change in her brother. His breathing deepened, and his pace slowed. At a gentle prod from Blink, he
quickened his stride. She assumed the stress of leaving his rebellious
cohorts behind affected Marcus deeply. Guilt at their sacrifice plagued
her, but she assuaged it by knowing the importance of Erick's cause.

As they continued to travel, Marcus grew more agitated; his head
darted from side to side as he surveyed the fields of corn and wheat.
He slowed again. When Blink tapped him on the shoulder, he turned
on the homunculus and snarled.

"What's wrong with you?" Elissia asked.

"Nothing," he snapped. "Just getting my bearings." He sped up, placing himself close to Gabrielle, who gave him a desultory glance before returning her attention to the road and Corby's current story.

He seemed fine, keeping pace and focusing on the path, until the fields ended, revealing wide-open grasslands dotted by farmhouses and grazing animals to his left, and a large expanse of forested highlands to his right.

He stopped in his tracks and Erick, who followed behind, ran into him.

"What are-" Erick stopped. Marcus's head swiveled in spastic motions, his eyes wide, breath coming in harsh gasps, hands and body shaking.

"Hold on," Erick yelled to those in front. "What's the matter?" he asked Marcus as the others returned.

"I can't go," Marcus answered in a small, quivering voice. "It's too big."

"What's too big?" Corby asked.

The thief flailed his hands about at the open space as his olive face drained of color. "This! There's too much."

Erick didn't know what to do, and neither did the others, based on their perplexed expressions.

Gabrielle emerged from her solemn state and gently took his hand. "Is this the first time you've left Kalador?"

"Of course," Marcus answered. "I've never had any reason to leave before." He pulled away from the girl and crouched on the ground. "I'm going back."

"You can't, idiot," Elissia said.

"Watch me."

"Go back to what?" Elissia asked. "A shattered rebellion and life on the streets? Father would have you hunted down and brought back in chains, if he didn't outright have you killed."

Gabrielle set her box on the ground and opened it. She reached into the bottom and pulled out a bottle and a small measuring cup.

"I'll take my chances," Marcus said. He dropped to his hands and knees. "Anything is better than this."

"You can't crawl back to town," Corby said.

"Yes, I can."

Gabrielle poured a measure of foul-smelling green liquid into the cup and stepped in front of Marcus. "Drink this," she said, holding out the cup. "It will help you to keep going."

"I doubt it," Marcus muttered, starting to crawl around her.

"If you go back, then I go back, too, and you know what that means."

Marcus stopped moving and faced Gabrielle. "You'd have to return to Valarie."

Gabrielle nodded. "And she'd revoke my apprenticeship and strip me of my prestige as Healer."

"You'd sacrifice your prestige for me?"

Gabrielle nodded again. "Callon said you wanted me to come along and help, so let me help *you*."

Marcus turned over and sat on the ground, staring at Gabrielle and nothing else. "Okay," he said, "help me."

Gabrielle handed him the cup. She watched as Marcus downed the liquid, grimacing as he drank, then took the cup from him. She smiled as Marcus stood up.

"Interesting," Elissia whispered to Erick. "I think Gabrielle loves my brother."

"How can you tell?" Erick whispered back.

"I can tell. That explains her reluctance about joining us."

"What do you mean?"

Elissia opened her mouth to explain when Marcus stumbled and almost fell. Gabrielle caught him before he hit the ground and Corby moved in to help her.

"Is he okay?" Erick asked.

"I'm fine," Marcus said, his voice slurred and blue eyes glassy. "Let's go."

Gabrielle lowered her eyes in apology. "I may have overestimated his weight and given him too much. The worst of it should wear off soon. Will you help him while I put my items back?"

"What did you give him?" Erick asked, taking her place in keeping Marcus upright.

"Tincture of Valerian root. It will settle his nerves and make him not mind the open spaces so much."

"Looks like it's working," Elissia said, staring at her slack-jawed brother.

"Yes, it's very potent," Gabrielle agreed.

Once the healer finished packing, they continued down the road. As Gabrielle promised, Marcus followed without hesitation, supported by Erick and Corby, utterly heedless of the open land. He giggled at odd times.

"What's wrong with him?" Elissia asked Gabrielle.

"I forget the name for it," Gabrielle said. "But some people have a great fear of open areas."

"Agoraphobia," Corby said.

"Yes, that's it. I guess Marcus has it because he's always lived inside the city wall, where everything is close together. He should adjust once he's been outside for a time."

"I hope so," Erick said, hefting the lithe thief as he stumbled and laughed at his clumsiness. "He's not much use to us like this. It doesn't seem to bother you. Have you been out before?"

"No," Gabrielle answered, her head down. "But I've wanted to leave for so long that this is more like a dream come true than something to fear." She glanced at Marcus and returned to her downward gaze. "Well, almost."

The girl's behavior perplexed Erick, especially when he considered Elissia's comments. If she loved Marcus, why did she seem so dispirited around him? The only reason Erick could imagine was that Marcus didn't return the feeling, but it seemed Gabrielle would have known this for some time and accepted it.

Marcus gradually regained his motive powers. After an hour, he could walk without support. His eyes were still glassy, and his angular face held an odd, open-mouthed expression as if he knew he should be scared but couldn't figure out why.

As they traveled, Corby continued his stream of talk. The sound of his chattering voice filled the ears of his companions as he regaled them with tales, some songs, and tidbits of trivia about their surrounding environment. He spoke quicker than usual, as if trying to make up for the time lost with the Procurers.

During one anecdote, Marcus suddenly blurted out, "Don't you ever shut up?"

Corby's face turned dark, his mouth forming a hurt pout.

"Ignore him, it's the Valerian speaking," Gabrielle said. She stepped beside Marcus and gently took his hand. "Let him talk. It's comforting."

"Then go ahead," Marcus said, taking his hand from Gabrielle's. "But walk here next to me. If I'm going to have to listen to you, I might as well watch your mouth move."

Corby's face scrunched in confusion, but he soon stepped beside Marcus and smiled.

"Now, where was I?" the scholar said to Marcus, who studied the other boy's face as if were the most fascinating landscape on Krinnik. "Oh, yes, the Death of Great Narsan-Ya on the sands of Falan-Dar. So, Narsan-Ya stood with his sword ready..."

The hurt standing out as clearly as her blemishes, Gabrielle walked faster until she ended up beside Blink and the nameless mule. She rested her hand on the animal's flank, her head hanging down.

Elissia sighed. "I'm going to have to talk to her," she murmured. "She'll be useless to us doing nothing but moping. If I had known she'd be like this, I wouldn't have let her come."

"What's going on?" Erick whispered. "You say she loves him. Doesn't he love her?"

"No, he doesn't love her."

"Why not?" Erick asked.

"You tell me," Elissia said, pointing toward Marcus. Erick found Marcus staring enraptured at Corby, who continued his tale. The thief's eyes had grown clearer and his footing steadier; he smiled as he watched the scholar. Erick noticed a great resemblance between Elissia and her brother in that crooked grin.

He turned back at Elissia to find her staring at him. She expected him to comprehend something about Marcus, but it eluded him. "I don't understand."

Elissia frowned. "Don't you see the way he's looking at Corby?"

"Yes."

"Well?" Elissia asked.

Erick studied Marcus again. After a few moments, he said, "I'm sorry, but all I see is someone relying on a friend to help them through something difficult."

Elissia clenched her fists and muttered, "Sometimes your naivety is irritating." In a louder but still conspiratorial voice, she said, "Marcus doesn't love Gabrielle because he is interested in Corby."

"But Corby is a boy."

Elissia's eyes widened, and her stare made Erick feel dense as a clump of mortar. He wanted to understand, but try as he might, he–

It struck him like a bolt. "Your brother only cares for other boys," Erick whispered in a shocked voice.

"Finally," Elissia said, throwing up her hands and letting out a pent-up sigh of frustration.

"Why didn't you just tell me?"

"Well, I thought it would be more fun letting you guess, but I forgot about your damned sheltered life."

"It won't do him any good," Erick said. "Corby isn't like that."

Elissia's mouth opened in disbelief. "You really are that blind, aren't you?"

Erick suddenly remembered the looks Corby had given him as they traveled, shy glances when he thought Erick wasn't watching. He recalled Murrough, the fiercely protective sailor, and Corby's request that Erick always be his friend, no matter what. Was that Corby's secret? Did he think of Erick the way Erick thought of Elissia? "They can't do that. It's wrong."

"Wrong? According to who?"

"It's not natural," Erick said, keeping his voice low. "The goal of a man is to marry and produce children, so that the populace may flourish and fill Krinnik. Any other proposition goes against the order of nature."

Elissia's, almond eyes went wide. "Who fed that load of warmed-over cow's dung?"

"My mother," Erick said, his voice taking on a bitter edge. "The same person who taught me all the things you find so nice about me."

"She did a fine job," Elissia said, raising her hands in a placating gesture. "But I think she was misguided about this. Did she worship Calea?"

"Yes." Elissia's conciliatory attitude did nothing to soothe Erick. "Calea and Caros, both of whom see the love of other men as a sin. It is written in the *Tome of the Father and Mother*."

"Were you born at night?" Elissia asked.

The unexpected question threw Erick. "What?"

"Were you born at night, yes or no?"

"Yes, but wh–"

"So was I, and do you know what my Aunt Beatru told me every chance she got? She said I was wicked and would come to an evil end, because all children born at night belonged to Melteth, and he would someday come to claim them as his own. To Beatru's mind, all people born at night were destined for wickedness. Do you know where she got that?"

Erick nodded. "It's also written in the *Tome of the Father and Mother*."

"Yes, it is," Elissia said. "Do you believe I'm wicked, or that you're wicked?"

Avoiding her gaze, Erick shook his head.

"So why are you so quick to believe one thing and not another, both from the same book? You know priests wrote the *Tome*, supposedly on the words given directly by the gods, but how do you know they didn't throw their own beliefs in there?"

"Because they wouldn't dare change the words of the gods," he said, startled.

Elissia snorted. "That's right, and Fathen never distorted the truth about you or your family. The priests of Caros see Marcus's love as a lack of moral strength. Priestesses of Calea find it a sin because it doesn't produce children. But what makes them right any more than the followers of Amare, who say that any form of love—or sex for that matter—is a blessing?" Elissia's tone turned derisive. "And I should think you'd be the last one to criticize anything that 'goes against nature,' Necromancer." She quickened her pace, leaving Erick alone.

As Elissia walked away, Erick's eyes fell on Marcus and Corby. The thief watched while the scholar rambled away with the tale of Narsan-

Ya, the mighty Warrior of the Sands, and his sacrifice to defeat the monstrous Koba-Fe, the Giant Desert Lizard who had destroyed several of his tribe's villages.

Above their obvious physical similarities, Erick realized now why Marcus looked so much like his sister. The stare he offered Corby was the same Elissia often gave to Erick: a gaze of admiration. Try as he might, Erick couldn't understand the possibility of such a thing. When he considered Corby, he thought of him as a friend, someone he would sacrifice much to protect or defend, but there existed none of the emotions he experienced when he thought of Elissia. Corby didn't make his brain tingle or his hands shake when he stood near. Erick had no desire to do with Corby the things he someday hoped to do with Elissia and knew of no way such actions could physically occur anyway.

No matter how he mulled it over and tried to understand it, the concept seemed unnatural, despite Elissia's assertions. His mother had been correct about so many things; he had to believe she was right about this.

But Elissia has a point, Blink offered. *What you do is unnatural. When it comes down to it, I'm unnatural. Just because it's unnatural doesn't make it wrong.*

Maybe, Erick said. *But if it's not wrong, why do the gods condemn it?*

Blink shrugged. *Apparently, not all gods do, but you'll have to ask a priest about that. You could try to ask Caros, but I doubt he would answer.*

Erick sighed, again wishing he were back home in Draymed, lonely but unaware of the bewildering complexities of the world.

Elissia walked ten feet ahead, still behind Corby and Marcus. Erick made a quick jog to walk beside her. She glanced at him, and then returned her gaze forward without any acknowledgement.

As he watched her, the sun gleaming in her black hair and casting a glow upon her face, beautiful despite her anger, the fierce joy of loving her shook him to his core. In that moment he knew he would do anything for her. Could Marcus feel the same depth of love for another boy? Was it wrong if he did?

It had to be wrong. The lessons of his childhood told him so, but

Elissia's idea that everything about his *existence* was wrong rankled him.

"Please don't be mad at me." He kept his voice low to avoid disturbing Corby, who had begun singing a Zakerin farming song in his bright tenor voice. "I'm trying to understand, but I can't, not yet. All I know is that I love you, and that's the only thing that matters to me. That and getting to Twr Krinnik."

Elissia said nothing for a moment, but when she looked at him, her stony face melted. "I shouldn't have expected you to understand right away. To be true, it bothers me some, but only because they're cousins. It's not my place to interfere." She paused, then said, "But give some thought that their love is as acceptable as any."

"I will. I mean, I'll try, but if I do, it means..." He stopped, unable to even talk about betraying his mother's beliefs. "Does Corby...love me?

"Only as a friend," Elissia said. "But he considers you his best friend and would do anything for you."

"And I'd do anything for him." He glanced at the slump-shouldered Gabrielle. "Why did Marcus want her to come along if he doesn't love her?"

"Because he doesn't want to see her life wasted away with Valarie. Beneath his sarcasm and rudeness is a gentle person who cares about people a great deal, even though he would deny it."

Corby still held Marcus, in rapt attention. He almost asked if she thought Corby had feelings toward Marcus but decided he wasn't yet ready to know. He had no idea how such knowledge would affect their friendship. He still couldn't determine his feelings about Marcus.

The dead are so much easier to deal with than the living, Erick thought.

That's because you can tell the dead what to do, Blink thought back.

Erick smiled. He had resolved nothing in his mind, but he decided to leave it behind for now. Instead, he gripped Elissia's hand tight. "I'm so glad you're with me."

"I'm glad I'm with you too."

Marcus looked back at them. "Are you two going to mutter goo-goo at each other this whole trek of are you going to listen to Corby's entertainment?"

They smiled, and Elissia said, "I see you're feeling better."

They walked in silence, listening as Corby launched into a war song about a battle between the Horsemen of Hucara and the *Pandara* tribes of Falan-Dar. Erick tried to let his mind wander on less weighty thoughts and focused on the relative peace of merely walking after such a hectic past few days.

As he walked, it startled Erick to remember that only a week had passed since his home burned down. If someone in Draymed had told him he would one day be walking up the Routh Krinnik with daggers on his belt, a hot, chaffing chain coat around his chest, and a girl he loved at his side, he would have laughed at the absurdity.

Now the absurdity had become a reality, and concern and self-doubt filled him. Would he be up to the task? There would be five other Necromancers to help, but would he be able to pull his weight? When the time came to face Eligos, would he be brave, or would he run screaming at the first glimpse of the Master?

These thoughts overtook other concerns, dominating his mind even as he took pleasure in the open road and the soothing sound of Corby's voice. He waved to the occasional caravan that passed by, escorted by guards who cast a wary and astonished eye at the young group of travelers. Farmhands harvesting the fields also greeted them, but the messengers, wearing the maroon cloak of the Royal Post, ignored them as they galloped by on their saddlebag laden horses. Whenever Blink saw wagons or people approaching, he drew his cloak tight and lifted the hood. If anyone wondered why he was so covered on such a warm day, they didn't ask.

An hour before sunset, Erick spotted the dark shapes of buildings.

"That's the village of Firstlast," Corby said. "They named it that because it's the first or last waypoint on the Routh Krinnik, depending on your direction."

"We should stay here," Elissia said. "It's almost dark, and Devin's Rest is ten miles away."

"Does it have an inn?" Erick asked.

"It does," Corby said. "And the food is good."

"I don't care if the food tastes like dog dung," Marcus said. The valerian had worn off, returning him to normal, his eyes clear and step firm. Using Corby's presence as an anchor, he had managed to disregard the environment, but his hands exhibited a nervous jitter, and his mouth occasionally twitched. "Let's just get there so I can get some walls around me."

"Do we have enough money?" Erick asked.

"We do," Marcus said with a smile. "Father didn't have all the vault keys hidden as well as he thought. We won't lack for comfort."

Erick returned the smile. He still wasn't sure about Marcus's strange love, but he couldn't help but like the boisterous thief.

A few minutes later, the sound of clattering hooves drew their gazes back down the road. Two men on dark brown horses thundered toward them, kicking up dust tinted orange by the low sun. They wore rust-colored cloaks instead of the Royal Post maroon, but moved as quickly and heedlessly. Their tunics and pants were so dark blue they came dangerously close to black; they had hoods drawn, hiding their faces. The travelers stepped off the road, and the riders galloped by without slowing, their passing rustling the roadside grass.

"Hope they get there in time," Elissia said, waving her hand to chase away the dust.

The horsemen stormed through the village and were long gone as the others reached the first buildings.

The town of Firstlast consisted of ten structures that served as businesses, with perhaps twice that number of houses surrounding the main village. They quickly spotted the inn since, even at this early hour, it was the only building doing business.

"And I thought Draymed shut their doors early," Elissia said as they walked toward the inn's open door, over which hung a sign declaring it as *The Firstlast Inn.*

"What an original name," Marcus said.

"Typical Zakerin practicality," Elissia said.

"I imagine I won't be welcome, so I'll be on the roof," Blink said, and flew off.

"I need to figure out a way to let him be around people," Erick muttered.

They entered a warm, homey common room. Candles and lanterns cast yellow light throughout. The unlit fireplace had wood stacked, awaiting a spark. At least thirty people gathered at the square oak tables, talking, eating, and laughing. Most appeared to be caravan drivers and escorts, and all seemed to be enjoying the food and drink. The scents of roasting meat and well-brewed beer filled the room.

Once inside, Marcus visibly relaxed, the tension leaving his body. "This is more like it," he said, patting his hand against the solid wooden wall beside him.

"Don't get used to it," Elissia told him. "We have to leave tomorrow morning."

Marcus's expression soured. "I'll deal with that when I have to. For now, let's eat and drink."

"Welcome to *The Firstlast Inn*," a brassy voice called from across the room. A woman headed their way. Short, busty, and with bright red hair, her ruddy face and cheery smile exuded charm and friendliness. "I'm Gert, the owner. Have a seat where you can find one, and I'll serve you directly."

"Thank you, ma'am," Erick said.

Gert laughed heartily. "Ma'am? Gert will do. Ma'am makes me sound like I own a brothel."

"What," a man seated nearby said. "This isn't a brothel? I'm leaving." His friends laughed raucously while Gert slapped him lightly across his back and went to attend to other customers.

Despite the crowd, they found an open table capable of holding their company. Almost before they had sat, Gert stood at their sides. "The menu tonight is stewed mutton with roast vegetables from Renner's farm down the road, and a cheese wedge with bread, for a *teres*. For an extra half-*aestes*, you can have some dried *lamparis*, brought in from Starrasen just this week. Of course, it's not as good as fresh, but the fresh would spoil before it got here, I'm afraid. How many plates?"

"Five, please," Erick said. The others nodded in agreement.

"Very well. Drinks?"

"Ale, please," Erick said. His parents had often had the drink but never let him try it. Erick thought it was time for a taste.

"How old are you, honey?" Gert asked him.

"I have reached my majority."

"That may be, but The Queen's decree says no strong drink until majority plus one. Silly rule, but I'm not the Queen." She thought for a moment. "When's your birthday?"

Erick did a quick mental calculation. "Just under two months."

"Close enough," Gert said, smiling. "Consider it an early birthday present from the *Firstlast*, dear. Just don't tell Her Majesty."

Erick smiled. "We'll also need rooms for the night."

"Of course," Gert said, laughing. "Didn't expect that you'd be leaving before the morning, but we can settle all that after you've eaten. Now, what does everyone else want to drink?"

"What sort of milk do you have?" Marcus asked.

"Goat and cow," Gert answered.

"Perfect," Marcus said, smiling. "I'd like both mixed in a cup and add a spoon of honey."

Gert cocked an eye at his request but nodded.

"That sounds appealing," Corby said. "I'll have one of those, too."

"I'd like a cup of bitter black tea if you have it," Gabrielle said.

"Chilled mulled cider," Elissia said.

"And, ah," Gert shuffled in discomfort. "Don't take offense, but considering your age, I need to know, ah…"

"I've got it," Marcus said as he laid a small pile of coins on the table.

"Very good then," Gert said and left to fill their orders.

You sure I can't come in? Blink asked.

Sorry. I don't think it would be safe. There're too many people here. Maybe later, when we go to bed.

Would they buy that I'm a gargoyle?

I don't want to chance it, Erick said.

Fine. I'll sit out here on the roof and sulk.

You can watch through my eyes if you want.

Sure, that would be fun. I'm going to find something to eat.

Okay. Erick shuddered. Most of the time, Blink ate the same foods as him, but the homunculus wasn't above hunting down a field mouse or rabbit and eating it alive. Erick once accidentally connected and caught Blink in the middle of such a meal. From that day forward, he made the familiar warn him, so it never happened again.

Their drinks and dinner soon arrived. A large, fair-skinned man with straw-colored hair and a round belly took a seat on the small stage at the back of the inn, lyre and flute in hand. He wore a blue doublet edged with silver taffeta, a pair of blue breeches made of velvet with yellow piping, and periwinkle shoes with a pearl sewn into the center of each.

"See that," Elissia said to Corby. "Good bards make good money."

"Certainly more than scholars," Corby said, picking up a fork.

As the group dug into their food--except Gabrielle, who picked at hers and ate only a small portion--the singer began a lay, his voice clear and melodious, his pudgy fingers dancing with surprising delicacy over the strings of his lyre.

Hungrier than he realized before the savory food arrived, Erick ate with gusto. The taste of mutton was a new flavor experience for him. Although not as agreeable as the beef his mother made, it still made a passable meat. The ale, a thick, nutty-flavored drink, was another enjoyable taste. As he drank it, Erick's head tingled. He found it pleasurable, and decided another would make him feel even better.

"Gert, may I have more ale?" he asked, holding the pewter tankard out to her.

Gert shook her head, her fiery curls bouncing around her face. "I pushed Denech's favor with one, two would be asking for trouble," she said. "Besides, it looks as if one has done you fine."

Erick moped until a thick-armed man in brown leather armor placed a mug in front of him, gave him a wink and smile, and walked away.

"Thank you," Erick said to the man's back. Taking up the mug, he drained half the contents in one draw. As the drink worked through him, he grew giddy with unbridled happiness, a feeling he never thought to again experience. He took Elissia's hand, and she smiled at him. The bard's song had transformed into a jaunty flute piece that had much of the inn clapping their hands in rhythm.

"Would you like to dance?" Erick asked Elissia, the words coming out slowly.

"Do you know *how* to dance?"

"My mother taught me."

"I'd be honored." She stood, bowed, and giggled.

Erick drained the last of the ale, muffled a belch, and stood. He wobbled a moment as his head gave a small spin, then he walked with Elissia to a clear space in front of the singer.

At first, their movements were stiff and uncertain, but they found the rhythm and moved with more assurance; while not graceful, the exuberance of youth infused their dance, and they soon had the crowd cheering.

The bard ended his song with a rousing finish as the two young dancers went into a spin around each other, moving to the rapid flute trills. As he played out the final flourish, Erick and Elissia collapsed against each other, giggling with the giddiness of children. The audience let loose with uproarious clapping and cheering as they recovered and bowed along with the flutist; copper coins flew through the air.

"Thank you, gentles all," the bard said, waving to the assembly. He traded the flute for his lyre as he regarded the two heavily breathing adolescents. "And now, to give my impromptu assistants a break, I will play the *Air of Seasons Changing.*" He strummed the lyre softly, and Elissia moved in close and wrapped Erick's arms around her waist. She put her arms around his neck. They moved in a slow circle as the tune played, sweet and gentle.

"I love you," Elissia said, resting her head on his chest.

"I love you, too," Erick said as he clasped her tightly, surprised at how natural the words sounded.

As they danced, Erick two distinct sensations besieged Erick, one in his head and the other much lower. His head buzzed with a strange murmur, like a bee on a summer day. The effect of the drinks still lay upon him, but the nattering drone in his brain threatened to chase away the euphoria.

Go away, he thought, trying to push the whine from his head. To his surprise, it left.

He knew the other feeling would not be so easily dispersed. The ales, close contact, and his own body conspired to put him in a state of lust so intense it almost blinded him. His passion nearly crushed him, and the longer they danced, the more vehement it became. He knew Elissia must be aware of his arousal, but she did nothing to dissuade him. Indeed, she pressed herself closer, nearly overloading him with pleasure. Through the fog of desire, every thought in his head told him to stop, while every nerve in his body demanded he stay close.

Too soon and not soon enough, the song ended, and they reluctantly parted. Erick glanced down. Embarrassment cut through the haze of alcohol; his pants were much tighter than he realized.

Before anyone else could notice his unease, Blink flew through the open door, startling everyone in the room. Cries of fear and bewilderment rattled among the patrons and a few brave souls leapt up and drew weapons.

Flying directly up to Erick, Blink landed on the stage next to him and yelled through clenched teeth. "Am I getting through to you now?"

"Yes," Erick said, puzzled.

"Then if you can get past enjoying your drunken stupor and your pointing dagger, you might want to join me outside. Fathen is on the road, and he's been badly beaten."

27

---

*After the Inconnu War, the Makerns took to removing the heads of their dead
and burying them in a separate grave, while placing the body in great stone
coffins. The Zakerins burned their loved ones and scattered the ashes while
saying prayers to Caros. The Starrans tied rocks to bodies and threw them in
the swamps, the Amels removed all the internal organs, and the tribes of
Falan-Dar left their dead in the desert to feed the creatures there and thus
return to the sand. All sound methods that all ultimately proved useless.*

-Corberin of Draymed, *The Second Inconnu War*

They found the priest stumbling down the road five hundred
feet from the inn, his long black hair tangled and matted
with blood, his left eye swollen shut, his right arm dangling
at his side.

Erick's first reaction upon seeing the savaged cleric was joy at the
justice in the world; if anyone deserved such a fate, it was this
pompous jackass. When they got closer, and he saw the extent of the
damage, his thoughts changed to guilt. Fathen would never be a
friend, but he was most likely the only other survivor from Draymed.
That gave them some strange, tenuous connection. At the least, the

priest could confirm Erick's dream and tell them if any others escaped.

Maybe he started the fire, Blink thought.

I'll deal with you later. Erick thought back and cut himself off, leaving Blink flapping in place with a dumbfounded expression.

"What happened?" Corby asked, doing his best to help the tall priest walk.

"Bandits," Fathen said. Blood spotted his yellow robe in dark clusters and ran from his split lip as he let out a series of weak coughs. "I need water."

"Get him inside, please," Gabrielle said. "I can't examine his injuries in the dark."

The group shuffled toward the inn, Fathen aided by Corby and Gabrielle while the others led, unable to help due to the cleric's injured arm. Blink knocked at his thoughts, but Erick refused to open himself.

"Where's Marcus?" Erick asked.

"When we came out to get your friend, he stayed inside," Gabrielle said morosely.

"He's probably using the confusion to pick some pockets," Elissia told them. "And Fathen isn't a friend."

~

F*ar from it,* Fathen thought as they walked toward the tavern, every step racking him with pain. After he and Andras had ridden past Erick's company, they stopped on the other side of the village, out of view, waiting to see if the travelers would halt for the night.

Once sufficient time had passed, Andras told Fathen, "Change into your old clothing." Fathen did as instructed, donning the yellow robe he wore the night he liberated Eligos.

With no warning, Andras punched him in the face.

Fathen reeled from the pain. Before he could recover, Andras fell upon him, punching furiously and knocking him to the ground. Fathen attempted to protect himself, bringing his arms up to shield his face, but Andras gave him a savage kick. His arm snapped and turned into fire.

Terror raced through the priest, fear that Andras had changed his mind and would kill him for his lapse at the thieves' warren. He tried to yell for his mentor to stop, but nothing would come from his mouth, which warmed from the blood filling it.

As Fathen went limp, resigning himself to death, Andras stopped. He leaned down and spoke. "This is a test of your faith. A group of bandits ambushed you and left you for dead. Get up and walk to the tavern. Make the deathmage and his companions pity you. Win their trust. You are not as close to death as you feel; if you die before you reach the tavern, then you did not have strong faith. Keep your thoughts on revenge and the power that will be yours when the Necromancer is dead. That will give you strength."

Fathen opened his sticky eyes and saw the smiling, dead face of Calligan, which soon faded into Andras riding off, trailing Fathen's horse behind him.

Burning with pain, Fathen willed himself to live. He rolled onto his knees, using his uninjured arm for support. He almost fainted as his broken arm swung lifelessly, the bone grinding under the skin. He stood and swayed, dizzy. He focused on the chance to kill Erick and the vertigo passed. As he lumbered toward town, the pain grew almost intolerable. Faith in his newfound master began to desert him, his anger unable to sustain his suffering body.

Then Blink found him.

As they drew closer to the tavern and his mind's eye played out Erick's demise in front of Broken Mountain, Fathen smiled inwardly despite the agony that racked his body. Watching Elissia and Erick walk ahead of him, he thought, *your friend is one thing I am not.*

Inside the inn, questions raced through Erick's mind. He had tried asking them as soon as Fathen had been seated in a tavern chair, but Gabrielle had ordered him--in a surprisingly authoritative voice--

to step away wait until she had a chance to examine the man's wounds and tend to the worst.

The others stood nearby, and Erick paced while the healer went to work. Erick's head ached; the tingle brought by the ale had left. He wanted to drink another to get that carefree feeling back, but his thoughts needed to be clear, although he didn't know how lucid they would be with the throbbing that invaded his temples.

He turned to retrace his path when he found Blink standing in his way, staring up at him.

"What did I do to make you so angry?"

Trying to ignore the buzz of conversation that sprang up around them, Erick said, "We'll talk about it later." He tried to step around, but Blink intercepted him.

"No, let's talk about it now, while we have time."

For only the second time ever, Erick found himself infuriated with the homunculus, angered to the point of wanting to strike. He clenched his fists.

Blink took a step back. "The only thing hitting me is going to do is make us both sore."

Erick blinked and shook his still pounding head. What had he been thinking? Being upset with Blink was one thing. But to be willing to hit him? Recent events had begun to affect him, and he could almost hear the whispery snigger of Eligos in his mind.

The anger receded, but Erick was not prepared to let his familiar off easy. Opening his mind, Erick thought, *look around, and you can see why I'm pissed off.*

Blink scanned the common room. Vaguely aware of the previous festivities by glimpsing them through Erick's alcohol haze, Blink realized the mood in the room had turned bitter. The patrons gathered far away from the group, eyeing them and murmuring. A small cadre of armed men stood in one corner, muttering to each other. Even the previously gregarious Gert only grunted noncommittally at Fathen's weakly mumbled thank you as she handed him a steamed cider, brought at Gabrielle's request.

How is this my fault? Blink asked.

You flew into the room and scared the holy Hells out of them.

320

Then if it's anybody's fault, it's yours! I tried to call you to come outside, but you told me to go away. I guess you were having too much fun drinking and rubbing your little dagger against Elissia.

Erick prepared to fire back an angry retort until he remembered the insistent buzzing in his head while he danced. It had been Blink trying to get his attention, muddled by the effects of the ale.

The sun suddenly rises, Blink thought. *I'm sorry if I ruined the party, but it was the only thing I could think to do.*

On the verge of offering a chagrined apology, Erick stopped when Elissia sidled next to him.

"This looks familiar," she said, glancing at the muttering ruffians. "Those four are going to give us trouble."

"How long before we can go to our rooms?" Erick asked Gabrielle.

"I can have his arm healed in twenty minutes, and we can move then, but I wouldn't advise it until I've healed his head wound," Gabrielle answered as she rubbed a dark green cream gently on the priest's arm. Erick caught the fresh smell of comfrey root and lavender.

"The sooner, the better," Elissia told her. "This might turn ugly soon."

Gabrielle nodded, held her hands over Fathen's arm, and began speaking a Healing Litany, her voice low.

The healer's skill amazed Erick. Being a Necromancer required him to study healing, even though he could never put the theories into practice. Mending a broken arm in twenty minutes showed a major degree of power, talent, and herbal knowledge. "We'll leave as soon as possible," he told Elissia. "Where in the Festering Hells is Marcus?"

As if summoned, the thief entered from the kitchen area, swinging open the wooden door and walking into the room with a smile on his face. It quickly disappeared.

Rushing to stand by his sister, he asked, "What's going on?"

"You'd know if you hadn't disappeared," she hissed at him. "What were you doing?"

"I found some extra money tucked away in the pantry that wanted to be in my pockets."

Gert, who had been in whispered conversation with some of the patrons, hesitantly lumbered toward the group, her face a mask of stern sorrow.

"Here it comes," Elissia said.

"I'm sorry," the innkeeper told them in genuine sympathy. "But I'm going to have to ask you to leave."

"Why?" Erick asked, even though he already knew the answer. "We have money."

"Gert don't take money from those that consort with demons," one of the armed men grumbled.

The innkeeper glanced back at him. "I'll take care of this, Wilser." She returned her gaze to Erick. "You seem a friendly enough group, but your creature there has people worried."

"Blink? He's not a demon. He's a—"

"He's a fiend from the Festering Hells, bent on destroying us," Wilser growled, hand drifting toward his sword.

For a moment, it was as if he had never left Draymed. Were people everywhere so ignorant and frightened?

"Friends, please," Corby said, stepping out from the group, to Erick's surprise. "I am Corberin, son of Corin, famed scholar of Keystone Island, and I assure you we are simple travelers who stopped for a night of rest before moving on to our destination. None of us deals with demons. This creature is a garg-"

"He is a servant of Caros," Fathen interrupted through clenched teeth.

He forced himself to sit up straighter despite Gabrielle's fretful attempts to keep him reclined. "Let me speak, girl," he said, a touch of the arrogance Erick despised returning. "I'll live long enough for you to heal me."

Gabrielle stepped back, and Fathen spoke to the patrons. "This creature is a servant of Caros, sent to protect this boy, who is doing the work of the Sun God and was driven from Keystone Island because of his servitude to the holiest of the Ten Gods. I am Fathen, a priest of Caros. I came to aid this boy in his great deeds when bandits waylaid me. I would be dead were it not for the benevolence of Caros, who sent his servant to chase these bandits away. The ruffians gazed upon this holy creature flying at them from the dark and fled, fearing death because of their wicked ways."

Blink blinked in disbelief and Erick looked down at him, a question on his face.

For a priest, he can tell some whoppers, Blink thought. *I never even saw bandits, much less sent them fleeing.*

"And so, my children, you would be doing a great service and receive the favor of Caros if you allowed us to stay at your most humble inn." Finished, Fathen collapsed back in the chair; Gabrielle immediately returned to tending him.

Fathen's passion and conviction, even in his injured state, impressed Erick. If the priest spoke with such fervor in the thrice-weekly services he held in Draymed, it made sense that the town thought so highly of him. Erick regretted never seeing one of his sermons, but then recalled why he couldn't, and the feeling passed.

Gert returned to the patrons, and they spoke among themselves. Erick began to hope they might be able to stay. There would be enough camping on his journey, and he didn't want to start it tonight.

Though voices were kept low, the discussion grew heated. The group waited silently. Erick tried to catch any snatch of conversation that would help them get a sense of how things lay.

Only Gabrielle remained oblivious to their fate, working to heal the injured cleric. The debate among the inn's residents lasted long enough that Fathen's arm finished healing. "Your arm will be stiff for several days, but you can use it," she told Fathen in a low voice as she worked on the large gash in his skull.

Finally, when both Erick and Blink had chewed their thumb down to the quick, Gert turned and walked toward them; her face told all.

"I hope it's warm out tonight," Elissia said.

"I'm sorry," Gert said. "You may be as your friend says you are, but my guests are still nervous, and most have said if you stay, they'll leave and never come back. I can't afford to lose the business."

"What about the stable?" Elissia asked.

"We don't want you or your demon anywhere near us, bitch," Wilser said.

Gert wheeled on the mercenary. "Wilser, shut your mouth, or you and your rabble can leave. I'll take the likes of these over your foul-mouthed lot any day."

Wilser prepared to retort, but a hand from one of the other men stopped him. "As you say," he said in a low voice. "My apologies."

Gert turned back to Erick.

"Thank you," Erick said. "You've been much kinder than many I've known." He resisted glancing back at Fathen. "We'll leave as soon as the priest can travel."

"We can leave now," Fathen growled. He pushed Gabrielle aside and stood. "I'll not stay another second among heretics and doubters. "If ill befalls us this night," he told Wilser and his cronies, "Caros will see that you all burn in the Festering Hells."

"Don't worry," Wilser's voice followed them as they left the tavern. "If anything attacks, your protector can save you."

The laughter of the tavern's guests cut off abruptly as Gert closed the door behind them.

28

Vidali is mad, as are all his followers. They are murderers and thieves and stealers of children, who they inculcate into the mysteries of their debauched rituals. We can only be thankful that the god gives little thought to his followers. Was The Insane One ever to turn his eye to Krinnik, we would have a ravaging upon the land that would make the Inconnu appear as children.

-Agnaes Palea, Supreme Monial of the Church of Calea.

The slamming door took with it Fathen's last vestiges of faith to Caros. The sun god's name no longer provoked the proper respect, only mirth, and Fathen knew how weak Caros had become. Over twenty years wasted on a deity who no longer had the strength to control his followers. Fathen's devotion now rested not with some nebulous, unseen entity of questionable influence, but with Eligos, a being he could see and whose prowess he had witnessed. Eligos would show these wretches the meaning of fear, and Fathen vowed to return to this tavern and watch as the Master made them cower in terror.

Such thoughts made his pain bearable as the group moved away from the tiny village of Firstlast and sought a place near the road to set up camp.

～

Disappointment and doubt warred within Erick. Despite Elissia's harsh assessment of the outside world, Erick had hoped things would be better once they left Keystone Island. But they stood over fifteen leagues, and an ocean away from his home and people were no different; in some ways, they were worse.

Fathen's arrival fueled his uncertainty. Erick's vision aboard ship showed no survivors, but the priest had somehow escaped the massacre and ensuing inferno. Perhaps others had also fled before the town's destruction. Erick wanted desperately to ask Fathen but forced himself to wait until they settled for the night and could all hear the tale.

They stopped about a mile outside the village. Gabrielle continued mending Fathen. Only Corby had done any extensive traveling, so he took the lead in setting up the camp. Under his direction, the others chopped and flattened the thin, high bluestem grass that grew beside the road until they created a sizable area, and then pitched tents. The mule released a bray of contentment as they removed the weight of supplies from its back.

Despite the warm air, clouds covered the sky, threatening rain, so Corby, with Blink's assistance, scrounged up deadwood from a nearby copse of birch trees and started a fire with the chopped grass. "A fire adds cheer," he said. "And I think we could all use some right now."

As the fire blossomed, chasing away the night, Erick sat across from Fathen and asked, "How did you survive Draymed's destruction?"

～

Fathen stared at the child. How had the boy learned about the town's demise? Had someone managed to warn him? Did Erick know of his involvement with Andras?

He knows nothing, a voice whispered in his head, startling him. *Lie.*

"Draymed has been destroyed? How do you know this?" Fathen asked.

"A dream revealed it to me," Erick said. "A vision from Denech."

Of course, the voice whispered again. *Another of your bastard gods meddling. Here is a chance to show me your skills. Convince the boy of your ignorance.*

Fathen bridled at Eligos' choice of words as five curious faces stared at him over the flickering firelight. He licked his lips. "Draymed was well when I left it two days after your departure. What happened?"

"Why did you leave?"

"The prisoner confessed much after you were gone. It required extensive interrogation, but Brannon and I pulled information from him, and the things he said frightened me. You were correct, Erick. The *Inconnu* have returned, or, at least, the Master of Shadows has." Fathen made the gesture of warding evil. It amused him to see Corby and the healer follow suit.

"The prisoner revealed people were searching for you, aiming to end your life. He spoke at length about the dark days that would follow when all the Necromancers were dead, and Eligos had again taken his rightful place as the Dark Emperor of Krinnik."

A fitting title, the voice said in his head. *I shall use it.*

Pleased, Fathen continued. "He felt convinced you would be killed almost as soon as you set foot in Kalador.

"After hearing these words, I prayed to Caros until dawn, asking for his wisdom and guidance in this dark time. He spoke to me." Fathen stared toward the sky and allowed his eyes to take on the glassy, far-away glaze of a man remembering a divine visitation. "He said I must find the Necromancer and aid him. He said, 'The child Erick is a Necromancer of power beyond all others. If he dies, all hope is lost. You must protect him and guide him safely to Twr Krinnik. All the forces of Eligos are arrayed against him. He will need every ally.'"

Fathen's eyes returned to the present--a place his mind had never left--and he said to Erick., "The past is gone, and my personal feelings about you, right or wrong, are irrelevant. There is more at stake here than the desires of one simple priest. The god to whom I have dedicated my life told me to protect you and guide you, and that I will do. The haughty priest you knew in Draymed is gone, burned away by the holy light and unflagging wisdom of Caros. I am your servant, if you will have me." The knot in his stomach and burning in his throat almost choked Fathen, but he kept the serene, penitent expression on his face, consoled by thoughts of the ultimate revenge that would come from his actions this night.

〜

E rick stared at the priest, flummoxed. He wanted to believe the priest's offer of aid, but he couldn't completely accept the sudden conversion. Fathen seemed almost *too* humble, *too* willing to help after so many years of contempt. Perhaps Caros had changed the priest's heart, but Erick wasn't convinced. *Blink, what do you think?*

He seems sincere, Blink thought, *but who knows? Something beat the hells out of him, that's certain.*

"What did you do with the prisoner after you interrogated him?"

"He was left in the guardhouse. I delivered a message to the authorities in Keyport, and they assured me guards would be sent to escort him to Keystone's prison. But perhaps he was killed. Please tell me about Draymed. What happened?"

"What truly happened, I can't tell you," Erick said. "I can only tell you my vision." Erick related his dream to the priest, offering every detail he could remember. In the course of the tale, Gabrielle finished tending Fathen's wounds and stood listening, eyes widening in growing horror as the story unfolded.

The others also listened, and Erick wondered what went through their minds on this second telling. Were they reassessing Erick's guilt, reconsidering the extent of his crime? Would Elissia and Corby's forgiveness be taken back?

〜

328

When Erick finished, Fathen remained silent, digesting the story. To his surprise, a glimmer of remorse lodged into his heart, a sliver of regret at the town's death. Until now, he never actually thought Na-Talva could accomplish the task Eligos set for him. How could one man obliterate a town of two hundred? Had he appealed to Keven, Fathen's favorite acolyte, to help? Or did he now lay dead like the other acolytes, always so eager to do his bidding and follow the words of Caros?

The faces of those acolytes came to him, along with many others. The widow Onora, who always had a favorable word on his visits, and sometimes more if she felt especially lonely. Elissia's aunt Beatru, who respected him as a faithful and wise man of the cloth. All gone, murdered and reduced to ashes. Calligan's face appeared again, this time burning and blistering.

Leave me be, Fathen thought. All the sacrifices wouldn't matter when Erick lay dead, and Eligos came to power, taking Fathen as his trusted advisor and priest. He had told Erick the truth. The past was gone. The old Fathen of Draymed *had* been burned away, not by the holy light of Caros, but the dark truth of Eligos. "I don't know what to say, except that I will pray for their souls."

Silence reigned among the group, leaving the night to the crackling fire and the chirruping insects. Gabrielle moved away from Fathen and sat beside Elissia.

Finally, Marcus spoke. "What about the bandits. Think we'll see them?"

"There were five of them, and they came from the direction of the mountains," Fathen told him. "I guess they marked me as an easy target, a man alone with only a sword, so they jumped me in the dark, beat me, then took everything but my clothes."

Corby suddenly jumped up. "Excuse me," he said, and ran down the road, disappearing into the darkness.

"Corby!" Elissia yelled, but he didn't turn back.

"What's going on?" Marcus asked, watching with a bewildered expression as Corby fled.

"He's upset," Erick said.

"Obviously. About what?"

"Me, most likely." Erick stared into the darkness. "I'd better go talk to him." He stood and walked down the road, his back to the group.

Fathen watched Erick leave, pleased at his skill in making the hated boy accept him. Elissia frowned at him. He smiled, but she turned and walked into her tent. His smile faltered. She wasn't convinced. He would have to watch her, since she would certainly be watching him.

∽

"I'm here," Corby said from behind Erick. The thin clouds obscured the light of Talan's Lantern, transforming the landscape into a dim void.

Startled, Erick turned. The scholar sat with his back to the road, staring at the tall grass. Erick walked over and sat beside him, while Corby wiped at his eyes.

Neither spoke for a long time, Erick unsure what he could offer other than useless apologies.

Finally, Corby cleared his throat and said, "The people in Draymed died because of me and a boy named Quinn, not you."

Erick stared at Corby, stunned beyond speech. How in the name of Caros had the scholar come to that conclusion?

Corby continued in a toneless voice, his eyes dry. "The man who destroyed everyone was a demon sent to punish our families for our sin. But demons can't be controlled and once they start killing, they can't stop, so the whole town died."

Erick started to speak, but the words poured from Corby. "I thought by leaving and getting away from Quinn I could spare them and stop, but then I boarded ship and found Murrough, and I couldn't control myself, and the demon punished my family anyway. It had to be a demon. Why would a man you let live go out of his way to destroy an entire town? It's divine retribution. It's-"

The scholar seemed close to hysteria. His voice had risen, his tone growing more frantic. Erick reached over and grabbed Corby's arms.

"Stop it," he said, shaking him. "You're not making sense. The man was a hired killer who destroyed Draymed because it was my home. He wasn't a demon."

"But he was. A demon sent to punish us."

"For what?"

"For what Quinn and I did."

"What did you do?" Erick asked, holding back the urge to scream at his friend.

"We loved each other," Corby said. He dropped his face into his hands and tears poured. "Caros help us, but we loved each other. Quinn's mother caught us. She wouldn't let us get dressed, but made us sit in the shed until Quinn's father returned from the blacksmith shop. They never yelled, but they told us we could not do such a terrible thing again. If we did, a demon would come to murder them and my parents and devour their souls. They told us in great detail how they would be murdered. I never thought I would see Quinn cry, but when his parents finished, we were curled into corners sobbing like babies. Like I am now." Corby wiped at his tear-covered face in disgust.

"They left us alone in the barn, and we dressed, promising never to do such things again. Quinn's parents said no more about it, to us or anyone else. I guess they thought their talk worked. And it did for two weeks, but then we were together again, even though it terrified us. I prayed to Caros every night to protect my family, telling him that if a demon had to kill anyone, let it kill me. We were terrified, but we couldn't stop."

Corby paused and forced himself to regain his composure. He dried his eyes. "When you said you were leaving Draymed, I saw my chance. I came with you because you are my friend, but also because I thought I could stop my sins and protect my family. I didn't even say goodbye to Quinn because I knew he would try to stop me. On the ship I made you promise to like me no matter what, but I won't hold you to it. If you want me to leave, I will."

Corby put his head down on his knees. Erick sat beside him, uncertain what to say. Emotions whirled through his mind, foremost amazement that Corby had somehow come to blame himself for Draymed's destruction.

331

"The man was no demon," Erick said again. "Draymed died because of me, because I lied and because my father summoned Eligos. I have to atone for those sins, which I hope to do by destroying the Master of Shadows."

"But I've sinned," Corby said, his voice cracking again. "I've sinned, and I'm going to burn in the Festering Hells, and Quinn is too."

Erick thought back to Elissia's words. "I think Quinn's parents were wrong. The gods and demons don't care who we love; only other people care about that. Quinn's parents were afraid, and they wanted you to be afraid."

"Do you think it's wrong?"

"I don't think it's a sin, not anymore."

"But do you think it's *wrong*?" Corby asked.

"What does it matter?"

"Because you're my friend and I want you to think well of me."

Another long silence followed, then Erick said. "I know it's wrong for me, but I can't say what's right for other people. Only Alakanath judges."

"Are we still friends?"

"Yes," Erick answered. "We will always be friends. You were willing to die for me. What sort of person would I be if I turned away from you now?"

"Thank you." Corby reached out and hugged Erick. He drew back when Erick tensed. "I'm sorry."

"It's okay." Erick put his hand on Corby's shoulders. "You just surprised me." Erick smiled, and Corby smiled back.

Erick, where are you?

Erick looked toward the still glowing fire. *About three hundred feet from camp. Why?*

You need to get back here. Marcus says unfriendly people are heading our way.

Be right there. "We need to go," he told Corby, standing up. "Blink said there might be trouble."

Corby stood up beside him. "Please don't say anything to anybody else. I'll tell them eventually, but I still have some thinking to do."

"I won't break a silence," Erick said.

They arrived to find the others gathered to one side of the fire. Despite the urgency in Blink's thoughts, everyone seemed surprisingly calm. Only Gabrielle appeared nervous, but Erick suspected that might be her normal condition.

As they arrived, Marcus said, "I did a quick scout and found twelve sword arms heading this way bent on nastiness. They're trying to be quiet, but they suck at it."

"Twelve? From the town?" Erick asked

"Doubt it. They're coming from the wrong way."

"More Fist members, then," Erick said. "I hope to Caros they're not all *Eligoi*. Blink, take off and spot them for me." As Blink took to the air, Erick asked Elissia, "What do we do?"

Before she could speak, Gabrielle said, "Can't you make some creatures to chase them away?" Her voice trembled.

Erick shook his head. "I need a dead body for that."

Blink located the approaching men and sent the information to Erick. He judged their attackers to be still over a thousand feet out, crawling slowly through the tall grass to avoid detection, unaware they had already been discovered.

"Almost two to one odds," Elissia said. "And none of us with real combat experience." She shook her head. "This isn't good."

"We need a more defensible position," Corby said, trying to scan the nearby mountains through the darkness.

"Guess we should have thought of that before we set up camp," Marcus said.

Corby nodded. "I wish the clouds would break and give us some light."

"If wishes were coins, thieves could retire," Marcus muttered.

"What would you do if you had a dead body?" Fathen asked.

"I could reanimate it, and it could fight for us."

A few of the men glanced up, perhaps hearing the flutter of Blink's wings, but they could not see him against the night sky. *Try and be quieter*, he thought as his hand went to his knife.

I'll try, Blink thought, his mental voice tense, *but I have to flap occasionally.*

333

"We can get you a body," Elissia said. "You up for it?" she asked Marcus.

"I guess," Marcus said. His hands twitched as his eyes darted over the grass. "I wish there were some alleys out here, though."

"If wishes were coins," Elissia reminded him. "Come on, it'll be just like old times," she boasted with all the air of a grizzled veteran, instead of a young girl.

"What are you doing?" Erick said. The idea of Elissia leaving his direct sight frightened him more than the imminent attack.

"Don't worry," she said, giving him a light kiss on the cheek as she drew one of her daggers. "You trained to save the world; this is what I trained to do."

Corby touched Marcus's arm. "Be careful."

Marcus smiled at the scholar. "Never anything but," he said, giving the other boy a wink.

The two thieves ran into the darkness, making no sound as they disappeared into the field.

As the others waited in anxious expectation, Erick focused his entire attention on observing through Blink's eyes. He watched, body filled with tension, as Marcus and Elissia spread out with speed and stealth, moving like a well-coordinated pair of hunting animals. Even using Blink's exceptional vision, Erick had trouble seeing his companions when they crouched low and slowly advanced on the unsuspecting attackers.

In a flash, it was over. Marcus dashed in from one side, then dashed away with Elissia following; the man stopped moving. Erick shuddered at the brutal efficiency of it. "They got one," he told the others.

Glad they're on our side, Blink thought.

The twins paused, making sure their victim didn't move. They moved back in, Elissia at the man's head and Marcus at his feet. Erick noticed they had picked one of the smaller fighters, but even so, they had trouble lifting the man. Erick couldn't imagine how they were going to get him back without alerting the other attackers.

In the distance, an animal Erick didn't recognize let out a series of short barks.

"I should go help them," Erick said.

"Don't," Corby said. "They know what they're doing, and you'll only make noise and alert the rest."

Erick nodded. He desperately wanted to go, certain they wouldn't make it back, but the wisdom in Corby's words kept him anchored. He busied himself by opening his case and getting the few ingredients ready he would need to reanimate the newly-dead attacker.

By the time he had everything ready, Marcus and Elissa were still a hundred feet out with their burden, but had managed to remain silent and not alert their opponents, who were still five hundred feet away and approaching slowly.

The plan might actually work.

Marcus suddenly let out a high-pitched keen of fear. He dropped his half of the body, which tore it from Elissia's hand. Pulling his knife, Marcus swung viciously at something on the ground.

Like voles popping out of hiding, the men stood up, shadows in the dim light. "Attack!" one of them shouted.

29

Although the fall of Broken Mountain revealed great veins of gold and precious gems, it was hundreds of years before the Camp (as the miners call it) came to exist. Before that, people avoided the mountain and the Ruins around it, complaining of nausea if they approached too close. It seemed that animals also remained away for a long time.

-Corberin of Draymed, *The History of Prospector's Camp*

The cloud cover broke, and the moon shone down upon the road, brightening the area. "Got my wish," Corby said as he readied his staff. Fathen drew his sword.

Erick pulled his knife, grabbed his ingredients, and ran toward where Marcus flailed at the ground. Elissia turned to face the attackers.

"Marcus, it's dead," Elissia screamed. "Let's go."

Marcus quit swinging at the ground, his breath coming in harsh gasps. As Erick drew near, he saw a sinuous black tube on the ground. A snake.

"How long will it take you?" Elissia asked.

"Not long," Erick said as he knelt by the dead man.

"There he is," someone yelled. Several men stared toward Erick. They charged.

"Come on, Mar," Elissia said. She and Marcus ran to meet the crowd.

Blink, help them! Erick thought, his mouth suddenly dry.

Okay.

Trying his best to ignore the noises of battle around him, and refusing to wonder how his friends fared, Erick spread dried burdock leaves over the two knife wounds, then a handful of motherwort stem went into the man's mouth. He sliced his thumb over the dead man's mouth. The blood soaked into the motherwort.

Erick prepared to recite the incantation when movement caught his eye. A man advanced with his sword held low. Erick grabbed at his knife, knowing it would be useless.

Corby and Fathen blindsided the fighter, slamming into him with their shoulders. He fell to the ground but retained his weapon. They pressed their advantage, swinging wildly as the man rolled on the ground, blocking and dodging their blows.

Erick's ignored the parchment feeling in his mouth. He had to get the *quana* up and fighting. "*Mucalz col cnila phamah allar soygha. Alakanath, amde sibsu, dluga mucalz deteloc pham allar soygha. Krinnik, amde sibsu, dluga mucalz decalz ar anoan allar soygha. Denech, amde sibsu, drix aldor mucalz od cnila de allar soygha.*"

The whispery breath of *Elonsha* tickled his mind with its allure. Fear for himself and his friends drained it of much of its power, but he thanked Caros the voice didn't speak to him. Fighting it would waste precious time.

He recited the litany a second time, expecting at any moment to get a sword in his back.

A silver nimbus surrounded the body. The man's eyes opened. Erick pushed his will, subjugating the man before he was aware he had returned from the dead.

"What do you wish?" the warrior asked, voice rough but intelligible.

"Protect me," Erick screamed as another attacker approached. Still engaged with their opponent, Corby and Fathen were unaware of the danger to Erick. The swordsman would be on him in five strides.

The dead man jumped up and grabbed the sword from its scabbard. He faced the attacker. Newly dead, he still moved as quickly as when he had been alive.

The attacker stopped, confusion on his pockmarked face as his friend confronted him. "What are you doing, Nels? Help me capture the brat."

Nels hesitated, and Erick again asserted his will, pushing his wishes over the dead man's. Nels swung his sword and caught his former friend a brutal slash across the face. Blood welled. The man screamed as a portion of his large nose fell away. He raised his hands to his ruined face and Nels drove the sword into his chest, straight through the leather armor. The screams stopped, and the man fell.

The dim light made it impossible for Erick to tell how his friends fared. He risked a glance through Blink's eyes and found the homunculus hovering over Marcus, who stood with his back against someone, two men facing him and another on the ground, blood running from his crotch. The men seemed reluctant to advance, but Erick knew such hesitance wouldn't last forever. *Blink, where are you?*

To your left.

Erick spotted Blink in the air, fifty feet away. He glanced to Fathen and Corby. They had finally beaten down their man, although Corby had a small gash across his cheek.

"Protect Gabrielle," he shouted to them, hoping she was still behind him and unharmed. He looked at Nels. "Follow me," he told Nels as he ran toward Blink. The *quana* kept up with him. As Erick drew close, four men surrounded Marcus and Elissia, and two lay dead on the ground. "Attack the men with swords," Erick ordered.

The first man went down with a sword in his back. The other three looked in shock at their former comrade attacking them. The next man closest to Nels took a swing and caught him in the side. The blade sank into the leather armor but went no further. The *Elonsha* stopped the metal before it could slice the flesh. The man's last expression was one of surprise as Nels rammed the sword into his throat. He gurgled and dropped as blood sprayed from the wound.

That was enough for one of the attackers. He turned and ran.

"I've got him," Elissia said. Drawing a second dagger, she ran toward the retreating man. She leapt, slammed both knives into his unprotected neck, and went to the ground with him as he dropped. Rolling forward, she pulled the knives with her. Gouts of blood flew into the air.

The remaining attacker turned pale as he realized he stood alone.

"Surrender," Erick said.

Nodding, the man lowered his sword and dropped it.

Erick took a few steps toward the man. "Tell me-"

The man's face changed. A crazed gleam came to his brown eyes. His thick moustache twitched. "The Fist never surrenders."

Before Erick could react, the man punched him in the face.

It was the first time in Erick's life he had ever been seriously hit. The pain stunned him. Stars flashed in his eyes. He tasted copper in his mouth as the blow knocked him to the ground. Through blurred vision, he watched the fighter drop toward him, elbows extended.

The elbows landed on his chest, followed by the man's full weight. A cracking sound turned his breast into a lance of fire. Breathing became difficult. Hands around his throat squeezed, and dots appeared in front of his eyes.

Through the mist of pain, Erick heard a violent tearing sound. Warm liquid sprayed on to his face and chest. He forced his eyes to focus. His attacker no longer had a head. Nels had cut it off. The pressure on his throat lessened, and the body slid to one side, taking the weight from his chest.

He tried to sit up, but something popped in his sternum. He screamed and fell back, losing all strength.

Elissia, Marcus, and Blink looked down at him. Nels stood motionless, bloody sword in hand.

"They're all dead," Elissia said as she knelt beside him. Corby, Fathen, and Gabrielle drew within Erick's sight.

"Except for three of them," Blink said. "I got them with my tail."

"Kill them," Erick said.

Gabrielle gasped.

"Are you sure?" Elissia asked.

Erick nodded. "I won't make the same mistake I made last time."

Marcus pointed at the headless corpse. "Probably should have done that to him, instead of accepting his surrender."

"Yeah, good idea," Erick rasped, wanting to laugh with joy that they had survived. He tried to suck in a deep breath; the intense pain immediately rendered him unconscious.

～

E rick came from the darkness into a world of fire. Flames danced around him in a circle. They soared above him and trapped him in the center. Heat poured off the flickering blaze. Sweat ran from every pore of his body. He peered toward the inferno, trying to find a means of escape, but none presented itself.

The fire edged closer, the circle tightening, and his skin burned and smoked, bringing with it deep pain. Cracks appeared in the flesh of his arms. He screamed in agony as blood bubbled from his blistered limbs. The flames moved even closer until he became part of the blaze, his body and hair burning and writhing as he continued to screech, pleading for the torture to end.

It stopped, and blissful obscurity engulfed him again.

When he awoke, he found Blink sitting by his head, Elissia kneeling on one side holding his hand, worry on her face, and Gabrielle on the other, frowning as she applied a pungent smelling paste to his chest.

"This is becoming a familiar sight," he said weakly, coughing. Noticing Gabrielle's frown, he asked, "What's wrong?"

"Don't talk," she said quietly. "Nothing's wrong; it's just not healing as quickly as it should."

"It's because I'm a Necromancer. The *Elonsha* resists the healing. And also makes it painful."

"I understand," Gabrielle said. "But that doesn't explain--"

She stopped as shadows fell over her. Fathen came into Erick's line of sight, followed closely by Corby and Marcus. The priest towered over all of them, a grim expression on his craggy face. "How is our young Necromancer?"

"He'll heal," Gabrielle answered, her voice barely audible. "He had a broken rib, some torn muscles, a large bruise on his chest, a broken nose, and a small scalp laceration. He'll be able to move without too much trouble by morning."

The alacrity of Gabrielle's curative magic amazed Erick again. Judging by his recent pain, he expected to be incapacitated at least a week. But as he did a mental check of his injuries, he found only some stiffness, and his nose throbbed like a toothache. He started to reach for his face, but Gabrielle stopped him.

"Don't. I haven't healed that yet."

"Gabrielle is a miracle worker," Elissia said, causing the healer to blush.

Fathen spoke up. "Can we talk while you work?"

"If you must," Gabrielle said as she threaded a shiny curved needle.

"Where is Nels?" Erick asked.

"The fighter you animated?" Corby asked. "He collapsed as soon as you passed out."

"Good," Erick said. Had he somehow remained animated without Erick's will guiding him, he would have turned on the others. He noticed Elissia, sitting beside him, frowning. "What's wrong?"

She shook her head. "Later."

Fathen lowered himself with care until he sat on the ground with his long legs crossed.

"Thank you," Erick said to the priest.

"For what?"

"You and Corby saved my life."

"We're all in this together," Fathen said. "What happened?" he asked Marcus

"I hate being outside," Marcus answered, abashment in his voice.

"Yes, but why did you scream?"

Marcus muttered at the ground.

"He walked over a snake," Elissia answered for him.

"A *large* snake," Marcus said.

"What kind?" Erick asked. He had seen it but hadn't recognized the breed.

"A giant striper," Elissia said.

341

"Completely harmless," Corby added.

"Nothing that large is *completely* harmless," Marcus said. "It could have swallowed me whole."

"Four-footer at best." Corby smiled and gave Marcus a gentle poke in the arm. Marcus grimaced back at him.

"Giant striper," Erick said. "Do they taste anything like ratter?"

"Very much like ratter," Gabrielle said. "If you want, I can cook it for dinner tomorrow."

"That would be wonderful," Erick said, his mouth already watering.

"You better start learning to cook, sis," Marcus said, earning a glare from Elissia.

With a shy smile at Erick's compliment, Gabrielle said, "Close your eyes."

~

As Erick closed his eyes, Fathen took a moment to study the boy. How simple it would be to kill him now, as he lay on the ground in complete trust of the goodwill of those around him. Fathen hoped Erick accepted his sincerity since he had saved the boy's life, a stroke of luck for which he offered profound thanks to Eligos. Something in the boy's pure gratitude struck Fathen, much the same way Calligan's thankfulness had. But the thief had died, and Erick had lived. Fathen wished it had been the other way around, so the dead boy would leave him alone.

Fathen glanced at Elissia but found her attention focused on Erick. She would never accept him, but that didn't matter. He only had to convince Erick. "Corby and I have been talking. We both feel it would be best for us if we took a different route to Twr Krinnik."

Erick gasped as Gabrielle pushed the sewing needle into his scalp and began stitching up his gash. "Different route? I thought this road was the only way from Kalador."

"It's the easiest," Fathen said. "But it's the route the Fist will expect you to take, so that means they may have more ambushes planned along the way in case this one failed. At the least, every village or town we come to will most likely have an *Inconnu* looking for you."

Fathen suspected there was no truth to what he said. Andras wanted the boy alive at Twr Krinnik, so he would stop any further attacks. This ambush had either gone too far to stop or had been a test of Fathen's resolve to help Erick. It disturbed Fathen his master didn't trust him, but it was perhaps not entirely unwarranted. He vowed to do what he needed to gain Eligos's graces.

"If they had other warriors, they would have sent them," Marcus said. "If this is the best they've got, we're good."

"Perhaps," Fathen said. He found the boy's bravado amusing, but he also knew too well that these men *did* represent the best available. On-board ship, the sad state into which the Fist had fallen enraged Eligos, and he declared that once he came to power, such ineptitude would be removed through pain and blood. "But there may still be spies and assassins, some quiet enough to sneak into camp. All the *Inconnu* want is to kill Erick. They don't need a frontal attack for that."

Marcus looked at his sister. "So that whole ruse we concocted in town with Erick's double was just a waste of time and resources. These bastards are still after him."

"Hopefully not as many," Elissia said. "At the least, we don't have to worry about the Procurers trying to find us."

"How do we avoid them?" Erick asked.

"We go up through The Ruins and come back down when we reach Prospector's Camp," Fathen said

"The Ruins?" Elissia burst out. "Are you insane?"

Erick opened his eyes to find Elissia staring at Fathen as if he had declared they should walk into a burning building. Disbelief warred with fear on her face. He reached out and took her hand. Her palm felt warm.

"What's wrong with the Ruins?" he asked.

"They're cursed. If we go up there, we'll never come out."

He closed his eyes again. "They aren't cursed."

"Then what would you call it?" Elissia asked. "Every hillock has a ghost behind it, and undead roam the valleys. People who have survived time in the mountains have gone insane or become undead themselves."

"Fairy tales," Fathen spat. "Told to scare children and old women."

"Like the *Inconnu*?" Elissia shot back. "You thought they were a fairy tale, too."

"They're not cursed," Erick repeated. "There is residual *Elonsha* left from the battle between Eligos and The Ten, and there are *gateloah* to be found in the mountains, but there's hardly a ghost behind every hillock, and any undead that do exist are most likely aimless and not much of a threat to anyone who's the least bit alert."

"That's easy for you to say," Elissia said, but the conviction in her voice had started to waver.

"How do you know that?" Marcus asked. "This is the first time you've even been off your tiny island."

Erick smiled, his eyes still closed. "And this is the first time you've been outside your city," he reminded Marcus. "I'm a Necromancer. If it involves the *Inconnu* or *gateloah*, I know about it."

"What about the insane people?" Elissia asked.

"Did you ever actually meet, or even see, one of them?"

"No."

"My father always said, 'the older the story, the bigger the lie.' *Perhaps* one person lost their sense after being in the Ruins, but anything could have caused that. Someone put the two facts together and created the idea that the mountains were cursed."

"Maybe," Elissia said.

Erick squeezed her hand gently. "You should know all too well the difference between the story and the reality."

Elissia squeezed back. "When you put it that way, I guess it makes sense."

As he lay with his eyes closed, Erick debated between the assumed relative safety of the mountains and the delay such a detour would cause. Some inner sense told him delay could prove disastrous, but Fathen's assessment of the *Inconnu* threat seemed accurate. Hadn't the danger already been shown to him several times over? Having to fight

Fist members every step of the way could prove as much a delay as the mountains, and more dangerous. Fathen's mention of assassins struck close. He had survived the *Eligoi* attack through blessings of Denech, a fickle god, and he did not wish to press his favor. "Okay, we'll go into the Ruins."

"Your decision," Corby said. "But there are practical matters you might want to consider."

"Such as?"

"Going through the mountains will add at least a week to our journey, so we'll have to ration our provisions. We can hunt, but that will delay us more, and I don't know that any of us are any good at it. There will probably be wild animals we'll have to fight or avoid. I'm the only one familiar with mountain travel, and that was a jaunt in the Spires with my father when I was ten."

Erick felt a slight tug, and then the snip of thread being cut. "You can open your eyes if you want," Gabrielle said. He did so and found his company gathered around, awaiting his decision.

"Can I sit up?"

"No, you need to stay here until the morning, then you should be healed enough to move. There's going to be some pain, but if it becomes too much, I can give you some bogbean leaves or valerian."

"Okay. Anything else?" he asked Corby.

"This time of year it will get cold, but not enough to be dangerous."

"I've read the Ruins are fairly jagged. Do we have the equipment to traverse them?"

Corby's brows bunched in thought. "From what I remember of my studies, we should be able to find paths and manage with a minimum of climbing. As long as we have rope, we should be okay."

"We're going through the mountains, aren't we?" Marcus said, his voice bitter with resignation.

"Yes," Erick answered. "I hate losing the time, but if we get attacked again, I don't think we'll survive. I almost got killed. What if the next attack has more people?"

"Yeah, but what if the *Inconnu* are in the Ruins, too?" Marcus asked him.

"The odds are slim they'll send people up there," Fathen said before

Erick could speak. "Even if they are there, we have a better chance of hiding in the mountains than in open farmland."

"Or getting ambushed," Marcus muttered.

"I should think you would be pleased," Fathen said. "Less open space."

Marcus muttered again, but Erick couldn't hear what he said.

Fathen smiled, a disconcerting expression on his craggy face. "If that's settled, we should plan on rising early in the morning," he said. "I'm going to retire."

"I'll take watch," Blink said.

Saying their evening greetings, everyone moved toward their tents except Blink, who positioned himself outside the circle of the dying fire, and Elissia, who retrieved a blanket and laid it over Erick before lying next to him and gently placing her arm on his chest. He winced as the weight settled close to his recently healed rib, but he said nothing. The warmth of her closeness outweighed the discomfort. Exhausted from the fight and injuries, he drifted toward sleep.

"Are you still okay?" Elissia asked. Something in her voice told Erick she was asking about more than his physical condition.

"What do you mean?"

"You killed those men."

"I didn't kill them. Nels did."

"But he was under your control. You brought him back, and then he killed. Isn't that the same as you killing?"

Erick frowned. He hadn't thought about that, but he didn't feel different. No overwhelming urge to kill again, no taint of *Elonsha* tugging at his soul. "I don't think it is. The *gateloah* are like my children. You aren't responsible if your child kills someone."

"I am if I tell them to do it."

Erick didn't speak for a long time, considering the implications. More things his father never got around to explaining. He realized exactly how deficient his father's instruction had been and a burst of anger hit him. "I honestly don't know. All I know is the Covenant forbids me from killing with my own hands. I can't make *gateloah* out of anyone my *gateloah* kill, but I can use them to kill if I have to. Maybe intent comes into it. I was defending myself. *Elonsha* is an evil force. If I had used Nels to murder innocent people, it would have a foothold. But my cause was just, so it had no way to hook into my soul."

"Sounds like a bunch of religious horse shit," Elissia murmured, drifting off to sleep.

"No, it's all too real," Erick said. Her questions had him wondering. The next time the *Elonsha* whispered to him, would he be less resistant to it? Was killing with a *quana* under his direct control the same as doing it with his own hands? Hopefully, the other Necromancers at Broken Mountain could ease his mind. He let the worries go. He had done it, and fretting about it now would get him nowhere.

Are you sure we want to go through the mountains? Blink asked before Erick dozed off. Maybe *he's changed, but Fathen suggesting it makes it instantly not a good idea to me.*

I think it's a better idea than even he realizes.

What do you mean?

There's gateloah *in the Ruins, which means I'll be able to get us reinforcements, in case we need them, without using a whole lot of blood or herbs.*

Great idea.

Erick thought nothing else, already asleep.

347

30

They stood on the walls, five hundred souls against a sea of undead. The woman and children had fled, and these brave men stayed to buy them time to escape. At twilight the ravenous horde attacked, and by dawn not one person stood in Carlair. But we who lived because they died will always remember their sacrifice.

-Malas Prith, survivor of the sack of Carlair

When Corby told Erick going through the Ruins would add a week to their journey, he thought the scholar too pessimistic. After the first day's trek into the mountains, he began to believe the estimate was overly *optimistic*.

"I've never been so sore in my entire life," he told Elissia as the group set up camp for the night.

The day started with his still healing ribs aching, a dull throb made worse by his forced sleep on the hard ground. As they traversed the undulating slopes of the mountains, his legs began to sting, followed soon by stiffness in his back. Three hours into their travel he had discovered soreness in muscles he never knew existed.

They stopped to rest often, everyone rubbing their legs or feet as they drank from water skins and nibbled on bits of cheese or dried meat, conversation kept to a minimum. Although everyone needed these respites, it cut deeply into their progress. As they stopped for the evening, Corby informed them he calculated they had traveled under three leagues, less than half the distance they would have achieved on the road.

"It should become easier," Corby said as he hammered a tent peg into the side of a hill, moving as slow as the rest of them. He placed the guide rope on the peg while Blink held the tent pole. "Tomorrow we'll need to move slower because of the pain. The next day will be better. We'll move faster as we get used to it. Barring accident, we'll get to Twr Krinnik in twenty days."

Marcus fell back against his bed pack with a groan. "Twenty days? Let them attack and kill us now."

"Sort of defeats the idea of going through all this pain, doesn't it?" Elissia asked.

"But if they kill me now, I won't have to go through any more pain."

"That's enough talk about killing," Fathen said, his voice harsh. He pinned Marcus with his eyes. "Trust me, my young friend, you know nothing about pain. Ask any here who lived in Draymed." Turning away, he walked into his tent and let the flap close behind him, leaving the rest to stare at each other in bewilderment.

"Certainly knows how to shut down a good bitch, doesn't he?" Marcus said.

From where she laid out kindling for a cooking fire, Gabrielle said, "Erick, can you help me a moment?"

Erick walked over and knelt beside the healer, groaning at the stiffness in his legs. "What do you need me to do?"

Gabrielle glanced at Fathen's tent with fear in her doe eyes and then returned her attention to the kindling. "I'm afraid this may be blasphemy, but I don't like your priest."

"If that were blasphemy," Erick said, sitting to take the pressure off his knees. "Caros would have struck me dead a long time ago."

Her eyes widened. "You don't like him either?"

Erick shook his head. "Haven't ever since I've known him, which has been almost all my life." He paused a moment, thinking. "Known probably isn't the right word. I've been aware of him. He seems to have changed since he left Draymed, and for the better."

Gabrielle took out her flint and steel. "He's mean."

Erick smiled slightly. "I don't think he'll ever change enough to get over that, but you never saw him when he was *really* mean."

The girl shivered as she struck a spark to the kindling. "I'd hate to have known him then."

That surprised Erick. "From what Elissia has said, I should think Fathen's temper would be mild compared to Valarie's."

"Valarie was nothing," Gabrielle said, tending the small flame that had started in the chips of wood. "I learned to ignore her because I knew she had to die someday and I would take her place."

Erick said nothing, shocked at the girl's bluntness. Gabrielle looked up from where she knelt and frowned. "Was that an evil thing to say?"

"Not at all," Erick said. "It just surprised me that you would be so pragmatic." At her furrowed brow, he added. "It's a compliment. But if you were content in Kalador, why did you come along with us?"

Satisfied with the fire's progress, she sat back. "I wasn't content, but I knew my life's journey. I can always return to Kalador, but I want to see places other than my home."

"Besides," she continued, a sad smile on her plain face. "I still have hope Marcus will love me."

Erick shifted on the hard rock, uncertain what to say.

"I know all about him," Gabrielle said. "Everyone in the warren knew, but that doesn't mean I don't have a chance. Maybe now that he's away from Kalador, I can show him how much he means to me."

Erick glanced at Marcus, who lay against his pack. Corby sat beside him; the two engaged in quiet conversation. Erick suspected Gabrielle's hopes were doomed. He stared at the crackling fire. "I didn't actually help. Did you call me over just to talk to me about Fathen?"

"Is he a Necromancer?"

Erick laughed out loud, causing the others to look at them. He waved briefly and then turned back to Gabrielle. "Not at all. Why do you ask?"

"Because you two heal the same way."

"What do you mean?"

"He heals slowly like you do. Not as slow, but slower than he should. Aren't Necromancers the only ones who don't respond correctly to herbs?"

"Necromancers and ser—" He stopped, not wanting to utter the impossible. Fathen might be pompous, arrogant, and utterly without regard for others, but he would never become a servant of the Master of Shadows.

Why not? Blink thought. *Isn't that the exact type of person Eligos would want?*

Erick saw a yellow glow flicker inside the priest's tent, evidence of a lighted candle. Was the man who lit that candle someone the *Inconnu* would seek for a convert?

I won't believe it. Erick thought back. *Our dislike of him makes us think the worst, but he served Caros far too long to fall from grace so easily. I don't trust him, but I won't accuse him of being* Inconnu. *Why would a servant of Eligos save my life?*

I'm going to watch him, because if he isn't Inconnu, *why doesn't he heal?*

I don't know. Erick broke contact to find Gabrielle staring at him, concern plain on her face.

"Are you okay?" she asked. "Does your head hurt?"

"My whole body hurts, but I'm fine. I was talking to Blink, which distracts me sometimes."

"Talk—? Oh, I understand. 'The Necromancers were able to propagate their foulness through the use of bonded imp-like servants called familiars. This unholy bond allowed servant and master to communicate through spiritual mental projection.'" She smiled at him.

"We just call it telepathy," Erick told her. "But Master Herbalist Howrena's writing always was flowery, if you'll pardon the pun."

"You've read her work?"

"All seven books. She may not write well, and I don't like her bias, but she is informative. Is it possible some people naturally don't heal well?"

"I guess it's not unheard of," Gabrielle said. "It may be nothing, but I thought you might want to know."

351

Marcus spoke up from where he still lay against his pack. "So is there going to be dinner soon, or are you two going to whisper at each other all night?"

"I'm working on it now," Gabrielle said over her shoulder, her tone light with love.

"Thank you for letting me know," Erick said as Gabrielle grabbed the striper snake and a sharp knife. "I'll keep it in mind." He stood to leave.

"Erick," Gabrielle said as she sunk the knife into the snake's throat. "Tell Marcus I'm a better cook than anybody he'll ever meet."

Erick stared at the girl a moment, then nodded his head in bewilderment and walked toward the group.

Dinner that night consisted of giant striper snake with fresh corn purchased in Kalador; they all ate ravenously despite their aches. Fathen rejoined them to eat, apologizing to Marcus for his outburst.

As they ate, Erick studied the priest for signs of change. He didn't know what he expected to see. Outwardly the man appeared no different; same waist-length black hair, now greasy and shorn of its ornamental braiding. Same angular face and deep-set eyes, covered with healing bruises. His blood marked yellow robe had collected dust. Erick noticed he no longer wore his chain and bracelets, but the bandits had most likely stolen those.

Fathen's personality had changed, seemingly for the better, but Erick still sensed a note of pretense, like the priest exerted a conscious effort to keep his true essence hidden. It slipped earlier when he berated Marcus, but the mask had been firmly put back in place.

But was the mask real, or created by Erick's own desire for it to be there because he could not accept the priest as anything but his nemesis?

A headache threatened, so he left off pondering and decided to continue with the course of action he had determined earlier in the day. It would provide them with extra safety in either case.

But not tonight, he thought. *I'm too tired.*

∾

As Corby predicted, they were all so sore and stiff the next morning they could barely move. They traveled slowly that day, making even less distance than the day previous. Several times, Erick almost stopped the march so they could rest for the day, but he wanted to arrive at Twr Krinnik as soon as possible, and every mile closed the distance.

The third day proved better. Their muscles were growing accustomed to the strain, and they began to travel at a reasonable pace, the only delays caused by the nameless mule, which often had to be coaxed to travel the occasionally treacherous terrain.

Marcus took well to the mountains, his phobia disappearing in the close paths and tight crevices that surrounded the group. He even volunteered to scout ahead with Blink, seeming to enjoy crawling over the rocks and gullies, spotting the most accessible course for the rest to follow through the jagged crevices.

The days passed. Despite Elissia's concern, they encountered no undead or ghosts. No wild animals attacked them, although Erick did spot a mountain lion in the distance one day, its blond coat and brown mane glistening in the sun. Corby's book knowledge of mountains combined with Blink and Marcus's scouting abilities allowed them to find enough small game and fresh water to supplement their rations. The weather remained mild. The nights grew brisk, but a cloak and campfire were enough to stave off the chill. Rainfall struck on the fifth day, making for uncomfortable, dangerous travel, but it was thankfully brief, and the worse that happened was a scraped arm when Corby slipped on a wet rock.

They divided the nights into three watches. Erick stood guard with Elissia. She was the only one he could trust to say nothing to the others about his nightly sojourns into the hillsides, since he wanted to keep it from Fathen. She asked once why he disappeared and he only offered that he worked to ensure their protection. She accepted it without further questions.

353

Blink, who needed less sleep, took the first watch, but also stayed awake with Elissia to make sure no one woke early and questioned Erick's whereabouts. Such concerns proved to be misplaced. Everyone was so tired at the end of the day that sleep came quickly and remained until forced to leave.

As they drew closer to their destination, Erick's morale soared higher than it had for weeks. He was exhausted, sore, hungry, his face itched from sunburn, various bug bites covered his body, and a scraggly beard had begun to appear on his face, but he knew the end was near. Once he reached Twr Krinnik, the numerous questions burning through his mind would be answered. They kept a steady pace, everyone cooperated, and even Fathen appeared content, offering scant complaint.

Only Gabrielle concerned him. As they traveled, she grew more withdrawn, saying few words during the day and offering nothing more as they sat for their evening ration of provisions. She sat beside Marcus and would laugh if he made a joke or stare at him like a puppy if he spoke, but to anyone else, she remained cold.

Except for Corby. For him she reserved a whole range of frowns and glares, offering one whenever she felt it appropriate, which seemed often. Corby sensed it and did his best to avoid her, but his desire to be near Marcus made things difficult. Erick's brief encounter with the jealous Keven gave him great empathy for the young scholar.

"This needs to get resolved one way or the other," Elissia whispered to him one night at dinner. He studied the trio: Gabrielle glared at Corby, Marcus smiled at him, and the scholar did his best to ignore one while conversing with the other. "She lays in our tent muttering and crying, cursing Corby. Things could get ugly."

"What should we do?" Erick asked.

"I'm going to talk to Marcus and get him to do something about it," Elissia told him. "He's the only one she'll listen to anyway."

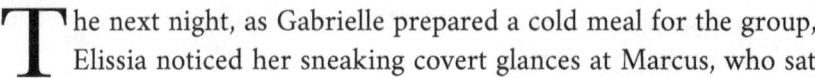

The next night, as Gabrielle prepared a cold meal for the group, Elissia noticed her sneaking covert glances at Marcus, who sat away from the camp, nestled in a niche created by two rocks, sharpening his favorite dagger.

"She doesn't like me much, does she?" Corby said, walking up next to her and Erick.

"She's jealous," Elissia said.

"Jealous? Why?"

Elissia glared at him. "For a scholar, you're awfully stupid sometimes." She stood up and walked toward Marcus, almost feeling Corby's dumbfounded stare on the back of her head.

She plopped down in front of her brother, who stopped working on the blade.

"Are you going to talk to Gabrielle or just let her continue suffering?"

"What are you talking about?"

"Don't play the idiot with me, Mar. She's in love with you for some idiotic reason, and it's causing her to hate Corby. I don't know about you, but I'm not comfortable with our healer having divided loyalties. You need to talk to her."

"What am I supposed to say?"

"I don't know," Elissia said. "Tell her how you feel. Make her understand."

Marcus sighed. "I suppose you want me to do it now, don't you?"

"The sooner, the better."

He stood and walked over to Gabrielle while Elissia rejoined Erick and Corby.

"What are they doing?" Corby asked as Marcus and Gabrielle began to walk away.

"They're going to get things straightened out," Elissia told him. "You're in love with my brother, aren't you?"

Blushing, Corby nodded. "Caros forgive me, but I am."

"Caros doesn't give a damn," Elissia told him. "But Gabrielle does. She loves Marcus, too, even though she knows better. Marcus has to convince her to find a more suitable target."

Marcus and Gabrielle disappeared around the corner of a rock outcropping.

"You do remember he's your cousin, right?" Elissia said.

"That doesn't matter. Since we can't procreate, there's no chance of a deformed offspring."

"So if being cousins doesn't bother you, why does it matter you're both boys?"

Eyes on the ground, Corby said, "Because it's wrong in the eyes of the gods."

Elissia stared at her cousin, astounded he still thought that way, after all the time she spent trying to convince him otherwise. If he stuck to such thoughts, he would never be truly happy, and his self-pity tired her.

"I'm only going to say this once," Elissia said. "The gods have better things to do than worry about who you give your love—or anything else—to. They might be concerned about Erick since he has a special relationship with them, but if you think they give more than a passing thought about the rest of us, you have an inflated sense of your importance. If they have a problem with you and Marcus, then they can go fuck themselves." She turned and walked away, ignoring the shock on Corby's and Erick's face. The gods had shown her nothing special. She had no reason to give them any power over her, especially when it came to people she cared about. She could only hope Corby would consider her words and take them to heart.

Fathen stared at her, a frown on his craggy face. "You have something to say?"

"I don't approve of your language, but I think you're correct. The gods don't care about us. They've left us to fend for ourselves. Man and child alike, we are alone." He walked into his tent, leaving Elissia as stunned as if he had turned into a bird and flown away.

Marcus and Gabrielle remained gone for almost an hour. Occasionally, a voice rose in anger, but the echoing rocks made the speech unintelligible. Erick chewed at his thumbnail and Corby paced. Elissia sat nearby, flipping a dagger and contemplating Fathen's surprising comment.

Eventually, Marcus came around the rock and motioned for Corby to join him. With a nervous glance at Erick and Elissia, Corby walked across the rocks and followed Marcus until they again became hidden from view.

"Ouch," Erick said as he drew blood from his thumbnail. "Blink, fly over there so I can hear what's going on."

"Don't even think about it," Elissia said, grabbing the homunculus by the tail. "It's not our business. They'll get it fixed, or they'll kill each other."

"Did you mean what you said about the gods?" Erick asked.

"I did," Elissia said. "Is that going to be a problem?"

"You know they exist, right?"

"I never said they didn't; I just said they don't care. Or if they do, they care about the wrong things."

"Maybe, but I don't think being disrespectful to them helps."

Elissia nodded. "Probably not, and I'm sorry. I was trying to shock Corby out of his asinine way of thinking. Do you think it worked?"

"The shock part certainly did."

Elissia smiled. "You're easily shocked. I suspect the gods have tougher skin. And if not, then they'll probably strike me down sometime soon."

"Don't say that," Erick said. "Not even joking." He hugged her. "I just found you. I don't want to lose you."

Elissia hugged him back. She glanced at Fathen's tent, closed and quiet. Something about his attitude disturbed her. She could speak her mind, but for a priest so entrenched in his faith to agree struck her as beyond odd. He would bear close watching. "I'm not going anywhere," she told Erick. "Gods or not, I'll always be here for you."

By the time the others reappeared, Erick had chewed both thumbs to the quick and his stomach wound in knots. He had no idea why it concerned him so much until he realized that, despite their differences and the brief time he had known them, he already accepted Marcus and Gabrielle as companions, and it upset him to consider them disliking each other.

They came around the corner. Marcus and Corby were smiling and, although Gabrielle's face held no grin, her steps seemed lighter and she wasn't glaring at Corby as if she wanted to strangle him. As she returned to finish her interrupted food preparations, Marcus and Corby joined Erick and Elissia.

"What happened?" Erick asked.

"We took care of it," Marcus said. "Gabrielle's fine, we're fine, and things are great. Now if we had a town and four walls around us, things would be outstanding."

"That's it," Elissia said. "You took care of it? Nothing else?"

"That's all that matters, isn't it?"

"I guess," Elissia said, shrugging.

Erick wanted to know more but knew better than to ask. He studied Gabrielle as she fixed their meal. Perhaps things had been resolved, but he couldn't help but wonder if such matters could be so easily fixed.

Two days later, almost two weeks out of Firstlast, Erick had another dream. It appeared to him faint and scattered: a beautiful auburn-haired woman studied herself in a mirror. Her lips moved as she uttered words he could not hear. She turned to something behind her, but the mirror image, instead of turning away, stared over the woman's shoulder. This was no looking glass but two women, identical down to the clothing and jewelry they wore. Someone out of Erick's vision spoke to them, and they answered. The image grew dark, then light, and then dark again before returning once more to light; still, the women spoke to their unseen visitor. As they talked, they changed. Subtly at first, their clothing transformed to a darker color, their hair grew more unkempt. Then almost at once, they converted completely, their dresses stained to mottled black, hair matted and greasy, faces still beautiful but eyes cruel, dancing with red and black light in gray pupils.

Metamorphosis complete, they searched the room, as if seeking for something they had lost. Their gaze roamed for several minutes, becoming more frantic as they hunted in vain, until suddenly both their heads snapped up and they scowled at Erick.

He started awake with a small gasp as drops of rain hit the outside of his tent. His necklace pulsed with warmth, but it faded quickly, and he thought it might be a residual feeling from the dream. *Did you see that?* He asked Blink, who sat outside on watch.

Yes, but I have no idea what it was.

Marcus flipped open the tent flaps; Erick jumped, startling the boy. Corby rolled over and muttered, but remained asleep. "Oh, you're awake. Time for your watch. Elissia's already up."

Erick left his bedroll confused and uneasy. The vision of Draymed, horrific as it had been, at least made sense. This dream seemed far too cryptic. Erick fretted at its meaning, and what the consequences might be if he couldn't decipher it.

He discussed it with Blink as they sat beside Elissia, huddled in cloaks and hats against the steadily falling water, but the homunculus had no enlightened wisdom. Erick stayed in camp. The chill rain and a sense of dread made him want to remain close to Elissia.

As the rain tapered away the next morning, leaving them with overcast skies, a renewed sense of urgency infused Erick. Something about the vision told him time had become precious. He ached to reach Twr Krinnik, to be among others like him and learn what he needed to know. They pushed on, stopping less frequently; Erick's anxiousness affected them all.

The next day they caught their first glimpses of Broken Mountain, peeking through the Ruins when they crested a high point in their path. Erick didn't find it nearly as impressive as he expected until Corby reminded him they were still at least six days away from the base.

Slowly the mountain drew closer, and Erick discovered the understatement of calling it; it was *huge*, even though the top had been destroyed in the battle with Eligos over a millennium ago. Erick couldn't even begin to imagine the mountain's massive size when it had been intact.

They all shared his awe at the immense base, which extended farther than they could see. Soon, the mountain dominated their view, blocking out the horizon.

"How large is that gods-damned thing?" Marcus asked.

"Don't blaspheme," Fathen said.

"The base is almost fifty leagues from east to west and thirty-five north to south," Corby said. "It extended five miles into the sky before the war between the *Inconnu* and the Necromancers, now it stands just over a mile."

Marcus whistled. "You could make a hell of a warren out of that," he said.

"I think they have," Corby said. "Except they call it a mine."

As they drew closer, they began to spot birds floating above the top of the base, spying down on the small figures that moved through the fragmented boulders and granite spires that made up the mountain's crown.

"Prospectors," Corby told them. "Seeking precious metals, rocks and the few herbs that grow there."

Erick found it hard to believe they were people. They moved across the vastness of the Twr, tiny as insects. It struck him that never in all his reading had he come close to imagining something this colossal. To read about Broken Mountain's was one thing, but to see it in its glory truly astonished him; it made it worth all the pain he had suffered getting here.

Midway through the twenty-second day after leaving Firstlast, they came to the end of the Ruins. As they walked down the gentle slope of the last foothill, Twr Krinnik filled their world, the top barely visible from where they stood. A mile ahead they spotted buildings, specks almost invisible against the base of the mammoth mountain. The road lay on their left.

"There it is ahead of us," Corby said. "Broken Mountain and Prospector's Camp."

Erick stared, dumbfounded. Instead of the cluster of weatherworn tents and wooden lean-tos he expected, there stood a town that, even from this distance, showed signs of a sizable and prosperous population. Numerous structures, most at least two floors high, ran along rows of level streets. Buildings and boulevards both were made from dull orange rock, but at least half the structures had mosaics of colored stones decorating the front and sides in simple geometric patterns. Several had the red hammer and globe symbol of Krinnik, and one the golden sunburst of Caros. Though no threat to Kalador, the town spanned easily three times the size of Draymed. None of his reading had even mentioned its existence.

"How long has that been there?" Erick asked

"Not certain," Corby answered. "At least two hundred years."

"Who cares?" Marcus said. "Let's get down there."

"Hold on," Erick said. "I'm not sure we should."

Marcus stared at Erick as if horns had sprouted from his head. "What in the Festering Hells are you talking about? We've been outside of a decent city for almost a month. Of course we should go in."

"Inconnu are searching everywhere, and they know where I'm heading, which means they're probably scouring the town for us."

"No," Marcus disagreed. "They're scouring the town for *you*, not us."

"I wouldn't be so sure," Corby said. "They may know each of us by now."

"How?" Marcus asked. "Nobody who's encountered us and attacked has escaped alive."

"What about anybody we didn't see?" Corby asked. "What about the people who witnessed the fiasco in Kalador? What about Firstlast? You're the cautious one, aren't you?"

"Cautious doesn't mean paranoid. So far all I've seen are some half-assed attempts to kill us by a bunch of amateurs. Whoever these people are, I don't think they're organized."

"Their attempt on me in Draymed wasn't half-assed," Erick told him.

"You're still alive, so it couldn't have been too well thought out."

"Children," Fathen said, stepping between them and raising his voice. "You could argue all day and be no closer to an agreement. As much as I disapprove of his profession and his language," he gave Marcus a reproachful stare, "I agree with the thief."

"My name is Marcus. And I'm a Procurer."

"Why?" Erick asked Fathen.

361

"You've reached the mountain. What are you supposed to do now?"

"Meet the other Necromancers."

"Where?" Fathen asked.

Erick blinked, startled by the question. "Somewhere inside the mountain."

"It's a large mountain."

Erick stared at Twr Krinnik. He had no idea. He had spent so much energy reaching the destination he never gave thought to his course of action once he arrived. He had unknowingly assumed answers would be provided. Stupid, since no one had presented any easy answers before.

"So," Fathen continued, "at the least, we need to go into town for provisions while you figure out what to do. The *Inconnu* may be here, but it's possible our delay has confused them and made them lax about hunting us."

"It's also possible the *Inconnu* aren't even searching for us anymore," Elissia offered. "Any *Inconnu* who showed up in Kalador would get to see a dead body that resembles Erick."

"I guess they forgot to pass that on to the people who attacked us outside Firstlast," Corby said.

"They were probably set in advance in case Erick bypassed Kalador," Elissia said. "They didn't act like professional soldiers. I don't know what to expect here, but we need supplies."

"We can split up," Marcus said. "I and two others can go into town, and the rest of you can go up the mountain. We'll meet you there in a couple of days."

"No," Erick countered. "We're going to stick together. Either way we go, it's better if we travel as a group." He ran his hand over his head; the inch-long stubble that had grown in the past month tickled his palm. *What do you think?*

How should I know? Blink answered. *I'm just a familiar. I vote for going straight to the mountain and hoping there's something to show us the way, but that's because I know if you go to town I'll be left out here twiddling my talons.*

Erick considered while the others waited for his answer. It baffled him that they turned to him for decisions. He certainly never thought of himself as a leader, and the circumstances that put him in charge of other lives mystified him. Certainly Corby or--Gods forbid--even Fathen had more wisdom for such things.

At last, the need for provisions decided him. Without guidance, they could trek across the mountain for months before he found what he sought. Erick pushed back his anxiety, trusting that Caros or Denech would show him the way before it came to aimless wandering. Elissia may not have faith in the Gods, but he did. Regardless, they needed supplies, and Erick found himself also desperately wanting to get clean. *Sorry Blink,* he thought. "We'll go into town, but we need to be cautious."

"I guess I'll sit here and twiddle my talons, then," Blink said.

They walked toward the town, descending from the mountains. Erick could only imagine what the townspeople would think when his company, dirty, bedraggled, and foul-smelling, arrived. He had a rat's nest of fine brown fuzz on his cheeks and chin, and brush bristles on his scalp. Fathen had almost three weeks growth of unkempt beard, greasy hair, and a bedraggled robe, once yellow, that had turned almost brown, the blood stains closer to black. Corby's scholarly haircut had lost all definition, the crown matted and the hair beneath having grown out. Marcus was still free of facial hair, but grime coated his clothes and face; grease and dirt glazed his black hair, now not as short as when Erick had met him.

Even Elissia, whom Erick thought could never be less than attractive, was covered with dirt and sweat, her clothes torn and travel-worn.

Gabrielle, surprisingly, appeared the least rumpled of all. The blemishes had disappeared from her clean face, and her skin had grown darker in the constant sun. Her eyes shone, and her gray robe, although dirty, showed little sign of actual wear. He wondered how she managed it, and decided to ask her when they were all sitting in a tavern room. The thought of a tavern made him realize he would really like a mug or two of ale.

As they drew closer, he noticed a lack of life on the streets. Earlier, Erick had seen people from a distance, but now the area appeared deserted. Buildings were closed, shutters were drawn, and the inhabitants had gone missing. A butter churn sat outside one building and a child's rocking horse, turned on its side, outside another. A lone dog came upon them and ran, whining with its tail between its legs

"Something's wrong," Marcus muttered, his eyes darting toward every corner. Elissia also scanned the area.

"Everyone must be working inside," Gabrielle said.

They were a hundred feet into the town proper, with still no signs of life, when Marcus said, "I think we should leave now."

"What are you talking about?" Erick asked. "You were the one who wanted to come in the first place."

"And now I want to leave."

"It's a good idea," Elissia said. "Something's amiss. This feels like an am-"

A whistle blew from inside a building. From both sides of the street there came the clatter of wood as shutters and doors swung open. Townsmen poured out from the buildings, brandishing swords and pickaxes. In the windows above, soldiers wearing the taupe and gray tunic of the Zakerin army leaned out and pointed crossbows down on the party. Within seconds, the tiny group found themselves surrounded by a mob of armed citizens and warriors.

The companions pressed tight together and drew their weapons. Erick did his best to stand in front of Elissia, knowing it would do precious little good if they were rushed. But the crowd simply surrounded them and kept their distance.

What should I do? Blink asked.

Stay put for now, Erick told him. *Hopefully, they don't know about you.*

"What is the meaning of this?" Fathen thundered, his voice booming over Erick's head. "Who dares to assault a priest of Caros and his companions?"

A section of the crowd parted as a squad of soldiers with pikes stepped forward. An exceptionally stocky man with close-cropped brown hair and a weather-worn face walked ahead of the squad. The gold epaulets and silver triple rose pin on his tunic marked him as a captain. He scanned the group, and his dark eyes settled on Erick. "Which of you is Erick Darvaul of Draymed?"

Stunned the man would know both his appearance and his full name, Erick said, "I am."

The officer favored him with a frown of disgust. "I am Captain Cerin of her Majesty's Army. You have been charged with the crime of Necromancy. Therefore, I am placing you and your companions under arrest. You will accompany me to the prison, where you will remain until tomorrow morning, when you will be put to death."

31

I will honor Krinnik, for he provides the home that grows me
I will honor Talan, for he provides the tears that nourish me
I will honor Caros, for he provides the light that strengthens me
I will honor, and they will provide, and I shall heal in their name.
-Healer's Oath

Fear struck Erick at the captain's proclamation, but it flared into anger. He had stepped back into Draymed, and nothing had changed. The faces and names were different, but the hatred and fear emanating from the people surrounding him wasn't.

He had not traveled this far through fire, blood, and pain, only to be thwarted by a throng of ignorant townspeople unaware he had come to save their miserable lives. Necromancy was not a crime, and these people were going to learn that. His hands tensed.

Elissia reached out and grabbed his hand. "This is not Draymed. They're afraid, but if you say the wrong thing, they'll kill you."

They're going to kill us anyway, he thought, but Elissia's touch and voice curbed his fury. They might be able to figure a way out, given time. They needed to speak to someone who would listen to their story, someone they could make see reason.

If it came to the worst, Erick had a way to escape. He relaxed his posture. "May we know our accuser?" he asked the captain.

"The others are not accused," Captain Cerin told him. "Only you and your winged demon, whom I expect to show up here within one minute or I will kill you. The rest are free to leave tomorrow after your execution. As for your accuser, you will find out soon enough."

"If you kill him, you might as well kill me," Elissia snarled. "Because I'll put a knife in your ugly face the minute you let me go."

Captain Cerin smiled at her. "Very well. I'll mention it to the Magistrate, and we'll make sure you hang, too."

"Those bastards in Firstlast must have ratsnaked us," Marcus said as a squad of guards formed around them.

"No talking," the Captain said. "Stay quiet and place your weapons and equipment on the ground. And your creature has thirty seconds."

What now? Blink asked.

Come in, Erick thought back. As the group relinquished their weapons, Erick considered Marcus's comment. The people in the village had shown fear when they saw him and Blink. But were they frightened enough to send someone over forty leagues to warn these people?

The thought lead him to another question. The inhabitants of Firstlast thought of him as one who dealt with demons, but they had no inkling of his true nature. Yet the captain immediately named him a Necromancer. Had the villagers figured out later and sent a messenger? Something didn't figure right.

They didn't know where we were going.

Erick started at Blink's thought. *What?*

The people in Firstlast. We never told them where we were going, so they would have no way to know where to send someone. Even if we were followed, which we weren't, they would have lost us once we went into the Ruins.

You're right, Erick thought back. *Then how do they know about us?*

The only person I can figure was the man who destroyed Draymed, but he would have had to fly to beat us here.

Could that even be possible? Had the man destroyed Draymed and then returned across the ocean and voyaged so far, all on the chance

Erick would reach the mountain? It didn't fit for a simple mercenary, or even for a Fist member, who would know others would take over should he fail. Erick knew he had missed something vital.

People looked up as Blink landed among the group. A few gasps and mutters broke out among the civilians, but a sharp glance from the weathered captain silenced them.

"I'm glad you decided to save your master," Cerin said. "A hanging is so much cleaner than a stabbing. Let's go."

A man took the mule's reins from Corby and led it away. At a command from Captain Cerin, the contingent of guards and captives moved down the street, followed by those who didn't stay behind to scavenge the forfeited equipment.

"My herb box," Gabrielle wailed, tears forming in her eyes.

"Quiet!" Cerin said, leading the way.

As they walked, windows and doors opened, revealing the curious faces of those who had stayed inside during the capture. Children stared and giggled, while the women and elderly pointed and gawked.

"Why don't all of you kiss my naked ass," Marcus screamed at a gaggle of onlookers.

"I said quiet!" Cerin shouted. He turned and rapped Marcus across the side of the head with his fist.

Marcus stumbled forward, crying at the sharp pain, but Corby caught him before he hit the ground.

"I should let you fall," Corby said, a catch in his voice. "Stay quiet, and maybe we can get out of this alive."

"Oh, we'll get out, don't worry." He gave Corby a quick kiss on the cheek.

Corby blushed, and then stepped away from the grinning Marcus.

Erick studied the town. It was clean and well cared for, the cobbled streets and orange stone buildings free of dirt and debris. The townspeople dressed in typical Zakerin fashion: brown, practical clothing, not fancy, but unsoiled and in good repair. Erick found Prospector's Camp not at all what he expected. It seemed a shame such high dwellings held such low minds, but it gave him hope they could talk their way out of their predicament. Certainly, a town could not be kept in such a fine manner without competent leadership.

They passed through the town square. A gallows—freshly built judging by the glistening wood, still leaking sap—sat in the center. A stocky man in gray clothing, a leather breastplate, and a dark grey hood worked on tying the rope into a noose. The group passed by in silence.

They stopped at a squat, square building with a thick wooden door and no windows, crafted of the same orange stone as the rest of the structures. A simple wooden sign proclaimed it as the jail. Two guards stood outside the door. They nodded at Cerin as he opened the door and had his men usher the group inside.

The anteroom they entered held a desk, behind which sat a thin, balding man with a grayish-brown beard. He wore a deep purple cloak and had a gold ring with a garnet stone on his pinkie.

The man looked up from the papers he studied and waited until they all stood inside. Captain Cerin stepped forward, pushing his way through the now crowded room.

"Your honor," Cerin said with a sharp salute. "I have here the Necromancer and his companions for incarceration."

"So I gathered, Captain," the magistrate said in a voice surprisingly deep for such a slight man. He regarded Erick with thoughtful brown eyes. "So you are the criminal. Your *Inconnu* friend has told us all about you. He said you were young, but I somehow expected you to at least *look* older. Nonetheless, villainy comes in all ages, and a child can be as predisposed to wickedness as a man of years." He addressed Cerin. "You may proceed, Captain."

Erick decided to take a chance. The magistrate had authority, and Erick sensed intelligence and warmth in his eyes. He might also find reason and compassion. "Sir..."

Cerin cuffed him across the back of the head. "No speaking to the magistrate."

"Captain, please," the magistrate said in a mildly reproving tone. "The child is dying tomorrow; I think we can forgo rudeness." He looked at Erick and Erick looked back, trying to keep the renewed hope from showing on his face. "You may speak. Address me as 'your honor.'"

"Your honor, I'm afraid the *Inconnu* has lied to you."

"Lied? You are not a Necromancer?"

"Yes, I am a Necromancer, but I've come here to help save the world from the Master of Shadows."

The Magistrate stared at him for a moment, and then broke into a deep, booming laugh; a hearty chuckle that the Captain and guards soon echoed.

Corby spoke, his tight voice cutting through the humor like a knife. "Why do you laugh, your honor? Erick speaks the truth."

"Perhaps he does, but what makes you think the world wants to be saved? The Captain and I don't want to be saved. We eagerly await the arrival of Eligos."

Hope left Erick. "What has he promised you? "Power? Wealth? Nobility?"

"More than you could imagine."

"The *Inconnu* speak only lies," Fathen said. "You will regret your decision."

He gave Fathen a wry smile. "I might not be the only one, hmmm? Put them away, Captain."

"Yes, your honor."

One of the guards pushed open an inner door and led the group into a dimly lighted room divided into two cells, separated by a wide hallway. Large and bare, each cell held nothing but two rough wooden bunks and a chamber pot. The beds had no mattresses or pillows, only thin woolen sheets.

Cerin divided them between the cells: Marcus, Corby, and Erick went into one, while Elissia, Fathen, Gabrielle, and Blink were herded into the other. As Blink walked by a blond-haired soldier, the man shoved him against the cell bars.

"By the Ten, you are an ugly beast," the soldier told him, and the others chuckled.

"Perhaps," Blink said as he turned around and faced his tormentor. "But at least I'm not laying on the floor unconscious with a bloody nose."

Blink lashed out with his tail and struck the man behind the knee. The force of the blow buckled the soldier's legs, pitching him forward as the venom rendered him senseless. He hit the floor gracelessly, and his head landed on the hard wood with a dull thump.

The other soldiers looked aghast at their stricken comrade, frozen at the unexpected sight of blood pooling on the floor. One of the warriors brandished his sword and advanced on Blink. The homunculus reared up to his full height, wings flared and talons bared.

"Come on then, I'm going to die anyway!" he snarled, tail poised above his head.

Despite being almost two feet taller and a hundred pounds heavier than the familiar, the soldier hesitated.

Get in the cell, Erick thought quickly.

But–

GET IN THE CELL NOW!

Blink flinched and backed into the cell, folding his wings to fit through the doorway. The guard shuffled forward and closed the door, while the captain walked over and locked it.

"If you weren't already going to die tomorrow, I'd let him kill you," the captain said, pointing to the unconscious soldier.

"If I weren't going to die tomorrow, he wouldn't be sprawled on the floor."

"Move out, men."

After the squad left the room, dragging their immobile companion with them, Erick stared across the room at Blink. *What in the name of the Ten were you thinking?*

I was thinking that I don't want to go out without a fight. I thought my master would support me.

Ten armed soldiers against eight unarmed people isn't a fight; it's a massacre.

So what do we do, wait until tomorrow and then go quietly up and let them hang us?

No, if it comes down to it, we fight. Until then, we use the time to figure a way out.

How?

I don't know yet, but there's always the gateloah. A vision popped into Erick's head, a fragment of memory from his first dream in Draymed.

A man in black surrounded by undead attacked Erick, who countered with his own force, while beside them loomed the mountain, a ponderous judge gauging the fight to determine the meddle of the combatants. He shared the vision with Blink. *See, if the dream is right, we'll escape.*

So we can die screaming at the claws of a thousand gateloah. *Great!*

"Is anyone hurt?" Gabrielle asked after the last soldier left and the door shut behind them. No one had injuries to report.

"That's good," Gabrielle told them, her voice quivering. "Because they destroyed my herb box." She collapsed on a bed, put her head in her hands, and broke into loud sobs. Elissia moved over to comfort her, hugging her while whispering into her ear.

"So what do we do now?" Erick asked Marcus.

"How should I know?" Marcus asked back.

"Don't you have experience with this sort of thing?"

"That's a hurtful assumption." Marcus glanced at the door the soldiers had just exited. It was solid, unbroken by a window. He scanned the floor and ceiling, and then looked back at Erick. "But it's obvious these people have never had real criminals here." He removed his boot.

"What are you doing?"

Marcus turned over his boot, dumped a square strap of leather into his hand, and folded it open. Several pieces of oddly shaped metal lay in the center. "They never check the shoes," he said, smiling.

"What is that?" Erick asked.

"Lockpicks. The prime tool of every good thief." Marcus moved to the lock, selected a tool, and inserted it into the keyhole. A second later a soft click announced his success. "Nothing to it."

In the other cell, Elissia comforted Gabrielle, whose sobs had quieted to sniffles. Marcus shifted from foot to foot until his sister glanced up. He held up the pick, a question on his face. She spoke softly to Gabrielle, and the young girl nodded. Standing, she walked to the bars and waited.

"You still remember how to use one of these?" Marcus asked as he threw the sliver of metal across the corridor.

Elissia caught the pick. "I could open this lock with my fingernails if I didn't bite them."

"So we get the locks picked," Fathen said. "Then what? We still have to fight our way out and get away from town. Perhaps we would be better served trying to deal again with the Magistrate."

"We'll get no help there," Erick told him. "The *Inconnu* have already corrupted the officials in this town with promises. Our only chance is to escape."

"Or die trying," Blink added.

I think we all could have done without that, Erick told him.

"All we have to do is wait until night," Marcus told them. "When they come in to feed us, we take out the guard, then move and take out whoever's left. Places like this won't have more than two or three watching. We take their weapons, then sneak away to the mountain under the darkness."

"What if they don't feed us?"

"Then we'll have to do something to make them come in here. Or, if it comes down to it, we rush them and run like the Hells."

"Here," Elissia said. She tossed the pick back to Marcus. "Now comes the hard part. Waiting."

Marcus walked over to a lower bunk and lay down. "Might as well sleep while we can." Corby crawled next to him on the same bed and put his arm around Marcus's waist. Wondering how Gabrielle would react, Erick found that she had also laid down on one of the hard cots, ignoring the others. It seemed stupid to worry about her emotions at a time like this, but he couldn't help himself. He turned to Fathen. "Any thoughts?"

Fathen cramped his tall body into the other lower bunk, the wooden bed creaking as he settled. "Pray. And try to rest." He lay on his back, but Erick noticed he didn't close his eyes.

Too keyed up to even think about sleeping, Erick paced, rolling numerous questions over in his head, coming no closer to solving any of the mysteries.

"Erick, please sit down," Elissia said, sitting against the back wall. "You're making me tired."

"I'm sorry," he told her, and sat on the floor. An overwhelming urge to be beside her and hold her close struck him. It seemed all too possible they would die tonight, and he would have no last chance to tell her how much he truly loved her. A chill ran over him as he pictured her on the ground dead, a vision that held the power of premonition.

The unlocked cell doors tempted him. He wanted nothing more than to walk over to her, but he couldn't. If a guard walked in, he would notice something had changed, ruining any chance of surprise they had. "Elissia, will you let Blink put his arm around you so I can hold you?"

Her face bunched in puzzlement for a moment, then cleared with understanding. "Of course," she said.

Blink, will you?

Certainly. Blink ambled over and sat beside Elissia. As he placed his arm across her shoulders, Erick released his thought entirely into Blink's body. He could feel the soft warmth of Elissia's skin. He curled in on himself as Blink hugged her fiercely and she squeezed back, both caught in the uncertain knowledge that this might be their last embrace.

As they held each other, Erick relaxed; the questions were pushed aside and the worries sublimated into a temporary peace of mind. Comforted, he slept.

❧

Fathen didn't sleep. He had closed his eyes, but when he did, the face of the young thief from Kalador, his throat slit, floated before him.

"I'm only the beginning," Calligan said. Blood spilled from his wound every time he opened his mouth. Fathen opened his eyes and stared at the bunk above him. The afterimage took a long time to fade into bare pine.

He closed his eyes again. This time Beatru haunted him, naked, her skin black and charred, the side of her face sliced open.

"You are filled with lies," she said, voice raspy from her inflamed throat. "There is still hope for you."

He opened his eyes again and clenched his teeth, willing the phantoms to leave him alone.

He tried once more. Another specter visited him. Four of his acolytes stood there, skin red and blistered, robes burnt, silver necklaces and bracelets melted and seared into their skin. Only Keven was absent.

"This is not what you want," they said in chorus, four voices as one. "You can flee and be forgiven. Do not do what you are commanded. Let us be the last."

"Leave me be," Fathen growled as he opened his eyes. He looked to the others, but they did not turn his way. He returned his stare to the bunk. Wooden, it would burn quickly, just like Draymed had burned. Drops of dried sap, red like the blood from Calligan's throat, dotted the plank. These visions were tricks, pleas sent by Caros to win him back. He would not heed them.

But he would cry. And he would not close his eyes again.

A loud noise from somewhere outside woke Erick. His head snapped up. Corby and Marcus listened, their faces alert.

"What is it?" he asked as he stood.

"Don't know," Marcus answered. In the other cell, only Gabrielle still slept. The others stood and listened, Fathen's eyes red and swollen.

For a moment no sound came to their straining ears, then a loud crash of crumbling stone reverberated through the building, followed by several eerie growls and loud screeches.

Gabrielle bolted up, almost hitting her head on the top bed, fear in her wide eyes. "What is that?"

"*Gateloah*," Erick said. "And they're attacking." As if to prove the truth of his words, a loud scream sounded outside the building. Something thick sliced through the air and the shouting stopped. There was a pause, followed by a wet ripping sound.

"That's not cloth, is it?" Corby asked, his face pale.

"No," Erick answered.

"How can there be undead?" Marcus asked.

Erick didn't get a chance to answer, distracted by a commotion in the anteroom. They all listened to the muffled sounds as the outer door slammed open, followed by a hasty discussion, none of which came through clear except the words, "Kill them all."

"Okay, get ready for anything," Marcus said.

The inner door slammed open and three soldiers, faces pale but resolved, walked in with unloaded crossbows.

Blink, go!

The homunculus launched into the air almost before Erick had the thought out. He slammed into the cell door, and it flew open, startling the soldiers. One of them dropped his bow. Elissia followed Blink. Marcus rushed through the other door. Blink barbed a guard in the stomach with his tail, while raking across the lightly armored chest with his talons. Blood flowed; the man dropped.

Marcus slipped behind the second guard and buried his foot into the back of the soldier's knee. The man collapsed as his knees buckled. As the fighter fell, Marcus reached toward the fighter's belt, retrieved the dagger hanging there, and stabbed the man with his own knife.

Dropping in front of the last guard, Elissia reached under his leather and grabbed his testicles. The guard screamed piteously. As his knees buckled, Elissia stepped back and kicked him in the face. His head snapped back, and he collapsed to the floor.

It was over so quickly that Erick had just reached into his pocket and removed an herb when the trio turned to him.

"What's that?" Marcus asked as Erick walked out and knelt down to one of the fallen soldiers.

"Something I hoped I wouldn't have to use anytime soon," Erick answered, listening with apprehension at the ever-growing noise outside. He didn't know what they would face out there, but if his vision were any indication, it was going to be unimaginably more difficult than fighting a single vampire. He could only hope he had made sufficient preparations.

Hands shaking, he took one of the soldier's daggers and cut himself deeply across the palm. He put the herb in his palm and squeezed his hand into a fist, wincing at the pain. "*Mucalz col cnila phamah, zodireda oi* Feverfew. *Alakanath, amde sibsu, dluga mucalz deteloc pham nocig hami apila. Krinnik, amde sibsu, dluga mucalz decalz pham zacar. Sangara, amde sibsu, dluga mucalz decnila qaas bagie."*

Marcus grabbed Corby and Elissia and backed away quickly as Erick began the incantation a second time.

"What is that?" Corby asked, shivering.

"Nothing good," Marcus told him.

YOU WILL SOON BE MINE! The voice screamed in Erick's head, almost knocking him over. His mind reeled as blackness covered his vision.

You'll not have him! Blink appeared in Erick's mind, a nimbus of gold around him, wings spread and tail flared. The darkness withdrew.

There is no hurry, the voice whispered, and Erick's mind cleared. He spoke the incantation a third time, his voice shaky, and then opened his blood-coated fist. The herb, once a bright green six-pronged leaf, was now rusty brown and smashed into the center of his hand. Lifting his palm, he removed the leaf with his tongue and pulled it into his mouth.

Ignoring the disgust on his friend's faces, Erick stood up, the *Elonsha* running through him as blood dripped from his hand. This close to the mountain, the power felt different, more vibrant and energetic, but it also carried a deeper undercurrent of malice.

Surrender, the voice whispered, fighting to break past Blink and Erick's resistance. *You face your master. Surrender now and die without pain.*

"Let's go," Erick said through clenched teeth, moving toward the open door as he fought to ignore the insistent whispering.

I demand your capitulation. Give in now or suffer as your father did.

I reject you! Erick screamed back. *Your pathetic book of power couldn't corrupt me, neither will you. We shall destroy you utterly this time.*

We? The voice sounded amused. *Very well then, come forth and fight me, little Deathmage.*

Screams of panic blended with wails and growls crashed in on him, overlaid by the roaring of fire. Though trembling inside, Erick walked forward with a show of confidence. His friends had carried him this far; now it fell to him to see them through the darkness.

As Erick walked away, Fathen grabbed a sword, while Marcus snatched two daggers and tossed one to Elissia. Corby picked up a crossbow and a handful of bolts and remained at the rear with Gabrielle.

They stepped out of the jail and into a nightmare. Fires burned in the few wooden areas of the stone buildings. The orange light, reflected by the night sky, cast a hellish glow on the carnage. People fled, pursued by an array of undead: ghouls, zombies, and skeletons. Bodies lay in the streets, fed upon by the ravenous ghouls and packs of undead wolves. The stench of blood mingled with decayed flesh to create a perfume of damnation. Gabrielle fell to the ground and threw up while Corby knelt beside her.

Four guards ran past them and attacked a ghoul, body thin and desiccated, as it feasted. Their swords swung down almost as one. The impact knocked the creature flat, but the blades did no damage. The creature sprang up with a hiss and slashed out with dagger-sharp fingernails. Two men fell, blood spraying from severed arteries.

"Run," Erick screamed at the two unharmed soldiers, but they either didn't hear him or were resolute in their duty. They attacked again, but the ghoul, with the quickness of its kind, sidestepped both weapons and leapt at the closest guard. The monster landed on him like a frog, clawed feet digging into legs and hands latching onto shoulders. The guard stumbled backward.

Ripping away the man's half helm, the ghoul spread its large mouth and buried triangular teeth into the guard's skull. The crunch sounded like the cracking of a hundred eggshells. The guard gave a brief scream and dropped as the ghoul yanked back, taking half the skull and brain into its maw. The other guard fled, but a wolf, its fur missing and skin black with rot, hamstrung him. As the man landed on his face, three more lupine undead pounced and tore the chainmail easily as parchment, ripping away chunks of flesh and dropping them to the ground.

The presence of so many *gateloah* overwhelmed Erick. An attack of this size required time and preparation. Who could have done it?

"What now?" Elissia asked in a strained voice as Corby helped the sickened Gabrielle to her feet.

"Toward the mountain," Erick said, talking with difficulty around the herb still in his mouth. Power thrummed through him, ready to find release, and his body tingled with the dark energy. He glanced at the mountain, and it seemed alight with vibrant purple-black and red light, *Elonsha* crackling from the roots of the world. "Stay close to me. Warn me if a creature comes near."

"I can't do it," Gabrielle said. Her face grew paler as she watched a small child, screaming for her mother, set upon and mauled by a zombie.

Corby took her hand. "Close your eyes, I'll guide you."

"We'll guide you," Marcus said, stepping up and taking her other hand.

They headed for the mountain. Thankful the whispering voice left him alone, Erick set a quick pace, doing his best to watch for imminent attack while also trying to ignore the death around him. Despite the accusations and his imprisonment, these people didn't deserve this, and Erick had to fight every inclination to help them. To do so would be suicide; his preparations and powers paled compared to the hordes that ran through the town. *Elonsha* danced in the air, making him dizzy. It called to him, its seduction present even without the whispering voice. Blink had problems walking, drunk on the energy that sizzled over the town.

A nearby woman screamed as razor sharp ghoul talons dug into her chest.

Fathen shouted to Erick. "We need to help these people fight."

"We can't," Erick said, his voice breaking.

"Why not?"

"Because I'm not powerful enough," he answered, close to tears. "Our only hope to survive is the mountain."

It horrified Erick that some part of him, a primal being deep within his soul, relished the carnage. The blood and *Elonsha* stirred his darkest longings, arousing him like a wicked woman's touch.

This last leg of his arduous journey impressed on Erick as the longest of his life. The screams of the dying and groans of the dead surrounded them. Guilt at his inability to save the town warred with the strange bloodlust that ravaged him. He ran from the thing he had been taught from the beginning to fight, even as he longed to join in the destruction. He wept as he walked.

Stay with me, Blink said in his mind. *We'll make it through. You don't want to kill.*

But I do, Erick thought as he watched three zombies attack a man in a baker's apron and break him like a wishbone.

Look to your left.

Brave Elissia, her dirt-smeared face grim, stood near, a dagger in her hand. Fear clouded her olive round eyes, but below that he saw more. She would die for him because she loved him.

That's what you're fighting for, Blink told him. *All the rest is a distraction.*

Erick's mind cleared, and he ignored the carnage, his focus on nothing but attaining the mountain entrance.

Their path took them into the town square, which sat oddly untouched by the destruction, although the smell of burning wood and despoiled flesh still whirled on the wind. Merchant stalls stood unmolested, their fruits and trinkets spared. Three puppies huddled under a wooden cart, whimpering but healthy.

The gallows stood in the square's center. *The gallows they were going to use for me,* Erick thought.

Beneath the platform lay several bodies. On the gallows, one hand through the noose, stood a man dressed in a black, hooded outfit: The man from Erick's dream.

Seeing their arrival, the man threw back the hood. "So you finally made it, little Deathmage."

Erick looked at the man poised above them, the face so plain that it took Erick a few seconds to recognize him. It was the assassin; the man Erick had refused to kill in Draymed. But the man had become more than that.

Filled with the power of *Elonsha* and the vibrant dark spirit of Eligos, the man glared down at Erick with soulless black eyes. As brilliant points of red shot through the pupils, he said, "You've all arrived just in time to die."

32

I am often praised for the role I had in the events that came to pass. To that I say, save your praise for those who deserve it, those who are no longer with us. I only did what had to be done, and was "lucky" enough to be there to witness the bravery and sacrifice of others.

-Excerpt from lecture by Corberin of Draymed, given at the University of Straph

A s the others stared in mute shock at Andras, Fathen knew he would never have a better chance to kill Erick. But he hesitated as he witnessed the destruction around him. A woman in flames rolled in the street, and that woman was Beatru. A child screamed as a skeletal creature grabbed him, and that child was Calligan. The town burned, as Draymed had burned.

A bright light flashed in his head, a warmth that offered salvation and a chance for redemption. *It is not too late for you, my child,* the light told him.

But it is, a darker voice said. *This one is mine now. Leave him.*

You must decide, the gentle voice told Fathen. *To me, you are a revered follower. To the* Inconnu *you are but another pawn, a means to assert his*

will. But know I have never left you. Defend the Necromancer and claim your place in my Heaven.

"I don't believe you." Fathen pulled the knife from its covering; the wax seal broke with no noise. He glanced at the blade, glistening black and red with corruption. The blade pulsed, power coursing through it. Moving forward, he put the knife to his side, his hand trembling.

~

E rick recovered from his shock. "You! You did all this?"

"Yes. I've not been idle your father released me. I am filled with the *Elonsha* of your brethren, and soon yours will join it. The place of my defeat will become my fortress. From here I shall destroy this world and remake it for my people."

People? Erick had never heard of the *Inconnu* as a people. "Go while you can," Erick said with a bravery he didn't feel. "I will not allow your foulness to spread through this place. I will stop you."

"No," Eligos said. His eyes glittered and dark energy radiated from his being. "You will be *dead*."

~

F athen raised the dagger. Erick's back was to him; all eyes were on Andras. All he had to do was strike Erick and scream the praise of Eligos.

"Don't," Calligan said, standing at Erick's back. He spread his ghostly arms to encompass the burning town. "Let this be the last sacrifice. Caros loves you; he forgives you. He is a god of strength, and you are his priest. Show your strength." Yellow light radiated from Calligan until it consumed him and washed over Fathen.

Remorse, sharp as a razor, gutted Fathen and he closed his eyes. Faces of the dead flashed across his lids, the most piteous the young soldier he had killed all those years ago. He could do it no more. The light of Caros, so long missing, returned to Fathen's soul. Eligos offered power, but the burning town and a child's slit throat showed

Fathen the price of that prestige. It was more than he wanted to pay. His hatred for Erick still burned, but killing him would only give Eligos leave to turn every town into Draymed, every child into a murdered soul. Fathen would not give his life for the Necromancer, but neither would he take Erick's life for the benefit of the *Inconnu*. It had always been their fight. He would slip away and let them fight it.

He opened his eyes, and Elissia stood before him, hatred in her blue eyes. "I knew you were false," she snarled. "You should have stayed a priest; you make a lousy assassin."

Fathen looked at the knife, still raised. "No," he said. "I'm not—"

Pain flared in his right arm, his tattoo burning as if hot cinders pressed into his flesh. *You are my chattel, priest. Do as you are commanded.*

Malevolent energy surged through Fathen, the pain blinding as it infused his limbs. He tried to resist, but he was a scarecrow in a tornado. He lunged forward.

Elissia sidestepped, lifted her foot, and kicked, landing a solid blow to the side of Fathen's kneecap. The bone snapped with a loud crack and Fathen dropped to his knees. He felt no pain, only a burning urge to do his master's bidding.

Elissia's foot smashed against Fathen's face, breaking his nose. Eligos roared in anger through his puppet and lashed out with the knife. Elissia backed away, but the blade sliced through her pants and nicked her. She punched Fathen in the eye, and the tall man fell back.

You will pay for your treachery, just as the Necromancers did, Eligos whispered in Fathen's mind. The dark energy fled Fathen's body, leaving him stunned with the pain of Elissia's assault.

～

Erick watched as Fathen fell to Elissia's punch, uncertain what had provoked the attack. Elissia looked at Erick and smiled. Her grin changed to a grimace. She wobbled. Her face turned pale, and sweat burst onto her forehead.

"Something's wrong," she said, and collapsed.

Erick saw the knife in Fathen's outstretched hand--its blade turning crystalline as the poison dried--and the splotch of blood on Elissia's pants.

"No!" Fury boiled up as the depth of his mistake in Draymed came crashing in on him. With crystal clarity, his mind played out the events that transpired to culminate in this place and time. The *Inconnu* had done what Erick hoped wasn't possible; Fathen had become a thrall to Eligos.

And it all started because Erick had been too kind-hearted to allow a man to die.

As the wrath built in him at Fathen's betrayal, such reluctance disappeared. He flung his injured hand out, sending splatters of blood toward the treasonous cleric.

"Rise!" Erick yelled as the droplets struck the ground around the prone Fathen. He flicked his hand again, sending out more blood. "Rise!"

Fathen watched with dazed, wide eyes. Each droplet soaked into the ground and the dirt exploded as a creature, human in shape but desiccated and long beyond living, forced its way from the earth.

"No, you don't understand," Fathen said as he tried to crawl away.

"I understand too well," Erick said in a choked voice. "*Qaas*,"

The *vohquana* moved in on Fathen.

"Eligos, help me!" the priest shouted, swinging the tiny dagger wildly as the ten creatures advanced on him. The blade struck one of the zombies and bounced harmlessly off the magically imbued flesh, skittering from Fathen's hand. As the first creature grabbed his arm, Fathen screamed. The creature bit and tore, severing Fathen's hand in a spray of blood. Another dug its fingers into the helpless man's stomach, pulling flesh and muscle aside to reach the tender organs inside. "Caros, save me. I'm sor-" Fathen's cries stopped, replaced by the noise of ten zombies rending and chewing.

Erick turned to face Andras. "Your turn," he said, sending more blood to the ground.

"You won't find me so easy," the man on the gallows said, waving his hand in a circle before him. The bodies beneath the gallows sprang to life, rising and shuffling toward Erick, even as his *vohquana* broke from the ground to defend him. Erick continued to toss drops of his blood to the ground; everywhere his vital essence touched, a *gateloah* broke forth, called by the power coursing through Erick.

The others watched in horrified awe as battle between Erick and Andras raged, Erick summoning more creatures as Andras drew the beings around him into the combat. Neither sorcerer spoke, their concentration focused on each other and their enchanted warriors. Erick had only zombies, but Andras had ghouls, wights, and death hounds. Snarls, growls, and moans filled the air, clashing with the thud of desiccated flesh striking brittle bone. Creatures on both sides fell with torn limbs or severed heads.

"Can't we do anything?" Gabrielle sobbed as tears streamed down her tan face.

Corby loaded the crossbow with shaking hands and tried to aim at the man standing on the gallows. He breathed deep, steadying the bow.

A black fog drifted across the man, and he changed, shifting into a pale-skinned, slavering creature with deep black-red eyes full of evil and bony fingers that formed the symbols of ultimate malevolence. It seemed to Corby as it the essence of Death had obtained quivering life. Too terrified to even scream, he let the crossbow fall from his numbed hands.

"Where's Marcus?" Gabrielle asked in a trembling voice. When Corby didn't answer, she turned to him. "Corby, whe-" the question died as she looked at the pale, slack-jawed scholar. "Corby?"

The zombies over Fathen stood and stumbled away from the decimated corpse, recognizable only by his shredded robe, once yellow, now soaked with blood. They moved to Erick's side and defended him against a group of skeletons barely covered in thin sheets of graying flesh.

Erick stepped back as Andras called more *gateloah* to his cause.

Shaking his hand weakly, he dripped blood onto the ground, but only one more creature appeared. He shook his hand again, and nothing happened. Erick's heart sank. All the *gateloah* he had managed to gather on their trek through the Ruins were here, and they were not nearly enough.

The creatures of Andras outnumbered his two to one, and the *Inconnu* continued to call forth more. All Erick had were the cobbled, ancient remains of people left roaming the Ruins, some warriors, but most farmers and miners. They were the only thing available to him with his limited herbs, blood and time. The power of Eligos had summoned a war horde.

Erick's forces had destroyed many of the enemy. Their dismantled corpses littered the ground, but nearly the same number of Erick's lie motionless, and he could ill afford the losses.

The battle raged on three sides. Erick backed up, ready to tell the others to break and run through their remaining avenue of retreat. When Gabrielle screamed, Erick found another force advancing toward them, closing the gap and surrounding the party.

Erick had never--even at the death of his parents--known such utter despair. They would all soon fall under the weight of the *Inconnu's* assault. Death did not bother him as much as the knowledge that he had failed. The other Necromancers would have to do their best without him. He had made it to the base of Twr Krinnik only to be denied by treachery conceived from his compassion. Perhaps he deserved it, but the others didn't.

He wrapped his hands around the talisman on his neck, closed his eyes, and offered a prayer to the Eight Good Gods. "I am your servant, as I have always been. If death must come, let it come quickly for all of us, and let us not return as servants to Eligos." Warmth radiated from the medallion, and a tingle flashed through Erick's body.

A strangled cry of pain cut the air nearby, a sound of agony and frustration.

Erick opened his eyes. To his astonishment, the attacking *gateloah* slowed, the fury of their assault lessening. Erick's forces continued to cut them down.

The death hounds launched themselves at the nearest creature, ally or foe, and the ghouls left off their attacks and began feasting on nearby bodies, paying no attention as Erick's creatures walked up and wrenched their heads off.

On the gallows, Marcus stood on one side and Andras on the other. The assassin reached for his back, out of which protruded two knives. Blood ran from the wounds, and Andras's legs collapsed from under him. As he landed on the wooden planks, he glared at Marcus with fearsome hatred. "You haven't won," he gurgled.

His face a grim, emotionless mask, Marcus pulled a third dagger. The emerald on the handle flashed with green fire as Marcus rammed the silvered blade into the man's chest and drove it up to the hilt. "Yes, we have." He spat in Andras' face.

Blood bubbled from the assassin's mouth as he let loose a gurgling laugh. He pointed a finger at Marcus. "You are marked."

A sizzling beam of chilling black shadow flew from Andras' finger and struck Marcus in the forehead. Screaming, Marcus reached for his head and stumbled backward. He tumbled off the edge of the gallows and slammed into the ground ten feet below.

The scream snapped Corby from his daze. "Marcus," he shouted as he and Gabrielle ran toward the prone thief.

On the scaffold, Andras let out a last wheezing gasp and died. Erick watched as a shadow, blacker than night and shot through with scintillating points of red light, left the assassin's body and flew away. Corby stumbled, his face blanching as the nauseating chill of the creature's passage swept by.

You have not won, a voice whispered to Erick as the ebon void fled into the night. *I am more powerful than death, and you will bemoan the day you defied me.*

Elissia! Erick ran to the stricken girl and dropped to his knees in front of her supine form. The cut on her leg was so tiny, but the skin around it had turned dark green and puffy. She had been so brave protecting him, and it had earned her this.

Tears welled in his eyes. He put his arms around her and lifted her head to his chest, rocking her gently. Eligos' words were right; they hadn't won at all.

A hitch of breath, so soft he wondered if he imagined it, renewed his hope. He put his ear against her mouth. The faint tickle of her breath played over his ear, a slap at death's face.

"She's still alive," he told Corby and Gabrielle, who had helped the stunned Marcus into a sitting position. "We have to go to the mountain."

"What?" Marcus said, rubbing at a dark scar on his forehead.

"The mountain," Erick said, knowing beyond doubt that they needed to go there to save her. *Elonsha* still crackled about it, visible only to him. The energy of death, but Erick knew, without knowing how, that it would bring Elissia back. "We have to go into the mountain."

"If we move her, she may die," Gabrielle said.

"If we don't, she *will* die. The mountain can save her."

"I'll help you," Marcus said, his gait unsteady as he stood and walked to Erick.

"I should apply a tourniquet to slow the poison," Gabrielle said. Erick pulled off his shirt, exposing his chain coat, and handed it to her. Grabbing the knife from Elissia's belt, Gabrielle quickly cut a long strip from the garment.

"Do you know where to go?" Marcus asked as he dropped beside his sister, Corby standing behind him.

"We'll find a way," Erick assured him. A circle with three dots over it in a curve had been seared into the flesh of Marcus's forehead, the skin red and angry. Erick shivered. The *Inconnu* had branded the young thief with a *morazol*, a death mark.

Gabrielle wrapped the bandage around Elissia's leg, just above the wound. She pulled the cloth tight, and Erick winced as pale green ooze splashed from the cut. The healer sliced into the puffy skin around the wound and squeezed, forcing more of the sickly liquid onto the dirt.

Turning away, Erick concentrated and sent his thought out to his *gateloah*, calling them back from their hunting. Of those he initially summoned, less than a tenth returned to his call. Only fourteen *vohquana* to protect them, but it would be enough. With the driving force behind the attacking creatures gone, they wandered aimlessly.

"Ready," Gabrielle said, tying a knot in the strip of cloth.

Erick took Elissia's arms, and Marcus grabbed her legs. They lifted her and moved toward the mountain

Corby led the way and Blink flew ahead to warn of trouble. They moved quickly through the rest of the town, avoiding the worst fires and the largest gatherings of undead. The battle for Prospector's Camp was all but over, the citizens either dead or escaped, the few wooden buildings left to the conflagration that ravaged them. Once or twice a cry for help shrilled from an upper window, but Erick ignored it. He took pity on them before, but his mood changed with Elissia's fall. The town had wanted him dead, and he happily returned the favor.

Within ten minutes the mountain loomed above them, the road turning into a path that wound up the side into an opening thirty feet above.

At Erick's nod, Corby continued, and the rest followed. Erick's arms ached, and his legs burned, but he didn't care. He would carry Elissia up the side of the mountain if he had to. The determined set to Marcus's back told Erick her brother had the same determination.

They reached the entrance. A door of dark wood, seven feet high and five wide, barred their way. Corby turned to Erick.

Erick studied the door. Set in the center, burned into the wood, was the pattern of Denech: eight interlocking circles pierced by an arrow. "Take my necklace and hold it to the door."

The scholar slipped the amulet off Erick's neck and pressed the symbol against the wood, aligning it to match the seared pattern.

The talisman flared, flickered for a brief span, and then pulsed with a dim glow. The door swung open, and Erick's mind cleared. It revealed the path they needed to take as plainly as if he navigated his manor. "Put the amulet back on my neck and follow me."

They went into the mountain, though the mineshafts and further, deep into long-abandoned caves. An hour passed and still they moved, deeper and deeper until they trod in caverns unseen by humans for over a millennium. Erick's arms and legs went beyond pain into numbness, but still they continued. Although Gabrielle and Corby occasionally stumbled in the darkness, Erick, Blink, and Marcus never faltered.

Time soon lost meaning, and Corby and Gabrielle began to flag, fatigue overtaking them. Neither complained, and instead renewed their efforts, driven by Erick's determination and their desire to save Elissia.

At last, when it seemed to Erick they had traveled through the mountain and would soon come out the other side, they entered a large cavern, the biggest they had seen so far. As soon as Erick crossed the threshold, the amulet flared again, and the cavern sparked to life, the glow starting low and growing until every wall in the hollow became suffused with rich amber light.

Much like the mountain that held it, the cavern was huge, five hundred feet across and equally as high. As illumination filled the room, they saw ten figures standing in the center, looking toward them.

"Welcome, Erick Necromancer," they said; the voices echoed through the cave until ten became a hundred.

"Who are you?" Erick asked, his voice reverberating across the chamber.

"We are your past," they answered. "Come closer and bring your companions with you."

They marched across the floor. Six men and four women stood before them. Different ages and races, they each appeared solid, but an ethereal white glow surrounded them. As he neared, the power emanating from them flushed through him, *Elonsha* strangely untainted by the evil of Eligos.

"Evil surrounds us and permeates the mountain," one of the women told him. "It is only in this holy chamber, where Eligos was banished, that his diablerie holds no sway."

The cavern struck Erick with awe. The final struggle with the Master of Shadows took place here. A millennium ago, these walls echoed with the sounds of battle as the ten fought the three, the fury of their conflict reducing the summit of the world to a fraction of its glory. Erick could almost envision it. He turned back at the people before him. "You are the Ten."

"We are."

The ten original Necromancers! The immensity of it all overwhelmed Erick. He swayed on his feet as fatigue and shock took hold.

"You may put your mate down," a man told him. "She is safe here."

They carefully lowered Elissia to the ground, and Erick shook his arms, wincing at the dull throb that reverberated through his leaden limbs. "Which of you is my grandfather or mother?"

A man walked over and stopped in front of him. He stood two inches taller than Erick, about forty years of age, with periwinkle eyes and tightly curled brown hair. Erick looked at his past, but also stared into a mirror twenty-five years in the future. "Grandfather?"

"Yes, with a substantial number of greats- in front."

"Elissia is dying. Can you heal her?"

The man looked at Elissia's body. "Heal her? No. We were Necromancers. Healing is not our calling. But the corruption in her body is of Eligos. This we can remove, and she will recover, but the poison will still be within, dormant until some unknown agent brings it to life. This we cannot remove."

"But if you remove the corruption, she will live?"

"Yes, but for how long we cannot say. And the poison may do terrible things to her. Perhaps she would be better as she is until you can find a cure."

It tore Erick's heart to see Elissia's pale face and still body, as if death had already taken her. It wouldn't stand. "Please bring her back."

"Move away."

Erick stepped back, and the Necromancers surrounded Elissia. They held their hands over her and chanted in the dread language of *Lonsh*, but their words spoke not of rescinding death, but of restoring life. They used words unknown to Erick and beseeched the Gods to bring their power to bear on destroying the corruption within Elissia. The words of Eligos, infused with the holy energy of the Covenant, turned against his foulness.

A blinding white light suddenly arced from the ceiling and slammed into Elissia. Her body convulsed as the light speared her, but Erick no fear followed it, only a sense of cleansing. His aches and worries dissolved away in that pure luminance and he emerged almost newborn.

The light faded and Elissia's eyes fluttered open. "Well, this is different," she said. "I'm usually the one looking down on you."

Erick choked back a sob as he dropped to his knees beside Elissia. His relief at her recovery was so intense as to be painful.

Marcus ran to her. "You're okay, sis. I thought we had lost you."

Erick looked at his ancestor. "Thank you."

The older man bowed his head. "We have done what we could. Had she died, she would have returned as a servant to Eligos. That will not happen now, but until the poison is purged from her system, she is still in mortal danger."

"What will trigger the poison?" Erick asked.

"Such answers are beyond our ken. You must ask your healer."

Erick turned to Gabrielle. The plain girl shrugged. "Without knowing what species of poison it is, I can't tell."

"How can you tell what the poison is?"

"If we had the knife that cut her, I could find out."

"You mean this knife," Corby said, holding the black dagger gingerly by the hilt. "I grabbed it so I could study it if we survived."

"Oh, you beautiful person." Marcus leapt up and gave Corby a fierce hug. Corby returned the embrace with one arm, holding the knife as far away as possible.

"That is all well," one of the female Necromancers, a stern-faced woman with piercing eyes even in ghost form, said. "But there are more important matters to discuss. Eligos has already grown in power, and it is only because he underestimated the resolve of your companions that you are still alive. You have done well and destroyed his *talba*. This has set him back and given you valuable time, but he will soon have another vessel for his spirit and will not be so overconfident the next time. There are things you must know to stop him."

"Should we not wait for the others?" Erick asked.

At the mention of the others, the Ten lowered their heads and the room suddenly dimmed.

"What's wrong?" Erick asked, although the words spoken by

Andras suddenly became clear. *I am filled with the* Elonsha *of your brethren.*

His ancestor looked at him sadly. "That is why Eligos has become so strong. There are no others. Three are dead, and two have betrayed the Covenant and turned to serve Eligos. You are the only Necromancer left, Erick Darvaul."

END OF BOOK ONE

ACKNOWLEDGMENTS

Like the Academy Awards speeches, I'll try to keep it brief. Thanks to the Brinkers Writers Group, who helped me shape this story. Thanks to my cats, who kept me company and "helped" with the writing. And especially thanks to Tony, who has been there through it all and cheered me the whole way.

ABOUT THE AUTHOR

Paul Barrett has lived a varied life full of excitement and adventure. Not really, but it sounds good as an opening line.

Paul's multiple careers have included: rock and roll roadie, children's theater stage manager, television camera operator, mortgage banker, and support specialist for Microsoft Excel.

This eclectic mix allowed him to go into his true love: motion picture production. He has produced two motion pictures and two documentaries: His film *Night Feeders* released on DVD in 2007, and *Cold Storage* was released by Lionsgate in May 2010.

Amidst all this, Paul has worked on his writing, starting with his first short story, about Ziggy Stardust and the Spiders from Mars, at age 8. Paul has written and produced numerous commercial and industrial video scripts in his tenure with his former creative agency, Indievision.

Paul lives in North Carolina with three cats and his film director/graphic designer husband.

CPSIA information can be obtained
at www.ICGtesting.com
Printed in the USA
BVHW081001160921
616888BV00012B/316/J

9 781946 926920